ous

gue of Publications of Societies Other Periodical Works in the of the Smithsonian Institution, 1858

original.

23 | ISBN: 978-3-38230-775-2

n imprint of Outlook Verlagsgesellschaft mbH.

utlook Verlag GmbH, Zeilweg 44, 60439 Frankfurt, Deutschland
gt (Authorized to represent): E. Roepke, Zeilweg 44, 60439 Frankfurt, Deutschland
on Demand GmbH, In de Tarpen 42, 22848 Norderstedt, Deutschland

Anonym

Catalogue of Publica
and of Other Period
Library of the Smiths
July 1,

Anatip

Anonym

Catalo
and of
Library
July 1,

Reprint of th

1st Edition 2

Anatiposi Verlag i

Verlag (Publisher)
Vertretungsberec
Druck (Print): Boo

SMITHSONIAN MISCELLANEOUS COLLECTIONS.

CATALOGUE

OF

PUBLICATIONS OF SOCIETIES

AND OF

OTHER PERIODICAL WORKS

IN THE LIBRARY OF

THE SMITHSONIAN INSTITUTION,

JULY 1, 1858.

FOREIGN WORKS.

WASHINGTON:
SMITHSONIAN INSTITUTION.
1859.

PUBLICATIONS

OF

LEARNED SOCIETIES, PERIODICALS, AND ENCYCLOPÆDIC WORKS IN THE LIBRARY OF THE SMITHSONIAN INSTITUTION, JULY 1, 1858.

SCANDINAVIA.

Skandinaviske Naturforskeres Forsamling.*

Förhandlingar vid det af Skandinaviska Naturforskare och Läkare haallna Möde i Götheborg. Aar 1839. *Götheborg*, 1840. 8vo.

Andet Möde, 1840. *Kjöbenhavn*, 1841.
Fjerde Möde, 1844. " 1847.
Femte Möde, 1847. " 1849.
Sjette Möde, 1851. " 1855.
Syvende Möde, 1856. " 1857.

Om Sundhedsvæsenet ombord paa danske Krigsskibe. Et Foredrag ved de Skandinaviske Naturforskeres Sammenkomst i Stockholm i Juli 1851, af Dr. F. B. MANSA. *Kjöbenhavn.* 8vo.

Nordisk Universitets Tidskrift.

Nordisk Universitets Tidskrift. I, III, IV; II; III, I, II, III. *Christiania* (and alternately in *Lund*, *Upsala*, and *Copenhagen*), 1855–57. 8vo.

---

* The works mentioned in this list are generally donations from the society or party under the heading of which they are recorded.

NOTICE.

The following catalogue includes all the regular serial publications of foreign learned societies, state governments, universities, public libraries, and private parties, in possession of the Smithsonian Institution, July 1, 1858. The new publications which have been received while the List was passing through the press, are added in a Supplement.

The Institution, being particularly desirous of completing its collection of works such as are recorded in the catalogue, would respectfully request of its correspondents that deficient series, volumes, or parts of volumes, be supplied, and that any works of the same kind which are not found in the catalogue be added, whether published by the donors or duplicates at their disposal.

JOSEPH HENRY,
Secretary S. I.

WASHINGTON, August, 1859.

STOCKHOLM.

Kongliga Svenska Vetenskaps Akademien.—*Cont'd.*

Zweifaches Universal Register über die ersten XXV Bände von den Abhandlungen aus der Naturlehre, &c. *Leipzig*, 1771. 8vo.

CRONSTRAND (S. A.). Aarsberättelse i Astronomien. Den 31 Mars 1836. *Stockholm*, 1836. 8vo.

PASCH (G. E.). Aarsberättelse om Technologiens Framsteg. Afgifven den 31 Mars 1837. *Stockholm*, 1837. 8vo.
" 1838. " 1839.
" 1844. " 1849.
" 1845. " 1851.
" 1846. " 1849.
" 1847. " 1851.
" 1848 och 1849. " 1852.

BERZELIUS (Jac.). Jahres-Bericht über die Fortschritte der physischen Wissenschaften. I—XXIII, 1822—43. *Tübingen*, 1822—43. 8vo.

Vollständiges Sach- und Namen-Register zu dem ersten bis siebenzehnten Jahrgang vom Jahres-Bericht. *Tübingen*, 1839. 8vo.

BERZELIUS (Jac.). Aarsberättelse om Framstegen i Fysik och Kemi.
Afgifven den 31 Mars 1837. *Stockholm*, 1837. 8vo.
" 1838. " 1838.
" 1839. " 1840.

BERZELIUS (Jac.). Aarsberättelse om Framstegen i Kemi och Mineralogi.
Afgifven den 31 Mars 1842. *Stockholm*, 1842. 8vo.
" 1846. " 1846.
" 1847. " 1848.

SVANBERG (L. F.). Aarsberättelse om Framstegen i Kemi, under aar 1847. *Stockholm*, 1849. 8vo.
" 1848. " 1850. "
" 1849. " 1851. "

EDLUNG (E.). Berättelse om Framstegen i Fysik, under aar 1849. *Stockholm*, 1851. 8vo.
" 1850. " 1852.
" 1851. " 1854.

SWEDEN.

LUND.

Kongliga Universitetet.

Physiographiska Sällskapets Tidskrift. I. *Lund*, 1837—1838. 8vo.

STOCKHOLM.

Kongliga Svenska Vetenskaps Akademien.

Kongl. Svenska Vetenskaps Academiens Handlingar. I—XL, 1739—1779. *Stockholm*. 8vo.

Kongl. Vetenskaps Academiens Nya Handlingar. I—XXXIII, 1780—1812. Register: 1739—1812. *Stockholm*, 1755—1821. 8vo.

Kongl. Vetenskaps Academiens Handlingar. För Aar 1813—1854. *Stockholm*, 1813—1856. 43 vols. 8vo.

Plancher till Kongl. Vetenskaps Academiens Handlingar. 1846. 4to.

Kongliga Svenska Vetenskaps Akademiens Handlingar. Ny Följd I, I, 1855. *Stockholm*, 1857. 4to.

Öfversigt af Kongl. Vetenskaps Academiens-Förhandlingar.

Aarg. I,	1844.	*Stockholm*,	1845.	8vo.
II,	1845.	"	1846.	
III,	1846.	"	1847.	
IV,	1847.	"	1848.	
V,	1848.	"	1849.	
VI,	1849.	"	1850.	
VII,	1850.	"	1851.	
VIII,	1851.	"	1852.	
IX,	1852.	"	1853.	
X,	1853.	"	1854.	
XI,	1854.	"	1855.	
XII,	1855.	"	1856.	
XIII,	1856.	"	1857.	

Der Königl. Schwedischen Akademie der Wissenschaften Abhandlungen, aus der Naturlehre, Haushaltungskunst und Mechanik. I—XLI, 1739—1779. *Hamburg* and *Leipzig*, 1749—1783. 8vo.

STOCKHOLM.

Kongliga Svenska Vetenskaps Akademien.—*Cont'd.*

WIKSTRÖM (Joh. Em.). Aarsberättelse om Botaniska Arbeten och Upptäckter för

Aar 1836.	*Stockholm*, 1838.	8vo.
" 1837.	" 1839.	
" 1839–42.	" 1844.	
" 1843–44, I & II.	" 1849.	
" 1845–48, I & II.	" 1850 & 1855.	
" 1849.	" 1852.	
" 1850.	" 1854.	
" 1852.	" 1857.	

Bihang till de Botaniska Aars-Berättelserna för aaren 1843 och 1844. *Stockholm*, 1849.

Register öfver de till Kongl. Vetenskaps-Akademien af *Joh. Em. Wikstrom* afgifna Aars-Berättelser i Botanik, för aaren 1820 till och med 1838. Paa *Kongl. Vetenskaps-Akademiens* Föranstaltande upprättade af N. J. ANDERSON. *Stockholm*, 1852. 8vo.

WIKSTRÖM (Joh. Em.). Jahresbericht der Königl. Schwedischen Akademie der Wissenschaften über die Fortschritte der Botanik in den Jahren 1839—1842. Der Akademie übergeben am 31 Marz 1840, 1841, 1842, 1843. *Regensburg*, 1846–47. 8vo.

ANDERSON (N. J.). Berättelse om Botaniska Arbeten och Upptäckter under aaren 1853 och 1854. *Stockholm*, 1856. 8vo.

FRIES (B. Fr.). Aarsberättelser om nyare Zoologiska Arbeten och Upptäckter. Afgifne den 31 Mars 1835 och 1836. *Stockholm*, 1837. 8vo.

SUNDEVALL (C. J.). Aarsberättelser om nyare Zoologiska Arbeten och Upptäckter, till Kongl. Vetensk. Akad. afgifne för aaren 1837—1840. *Stockholm*, 1841. 8vo.

SUNDEVALL (C. J.). Arsberättelse om Framstegen i Vertebrerade Djurens Natural Historia

under aaren 1840—1842.	*Stockholm*, 1844.	8vo.
" 1843 och 1844.	" 1847.	

SUNDEVALL (Carl J.). Berättelse om Framstegen i Vertebrerade Djurens Natural Historia och Ethnografien under aaren 1845—1850. *Stockholm*, 1853. 8vo.

STOCKHOLM.

Kongliga Svenska Vetenskaps Akademien.—*Cont'd.*

LOVEN (S.). Aarsberättelse om Framstegen i Crustaceernas och de lägre Skelettlösa Djurens Natural Historia under aaren 1840—1842. *Stockholm*, 1844. 8vo.
" 1843—1844. " 1848. "

LOVEN (S.). Berättelse om Framstegen i Molluskernas, Crustaceernas, och de lägre Skelettlösa Djurens Natural Historia under aaren 1845—1849. *Stockholm*, 1852. 8vo.

BOHEMAN (C. H.). Aarsberättelse om Framstegen i Insekternas, Myriapodernas och Arachnidernas Natural Historia för 1840 och 1842. *Stockholm*, 1843. 8vo.
1843 " 1844. " 1845.
1845 " 1846. " 1847.
1847 " 1848. " 1851.
1849 " 1850. " 1852.
1851 " 1852. " 1854.
1853 " 1854. " 1857.

Kongl. Vitterhets Historie och Antiquitets Akademien.

Kongl. Vitterhets Historie och Antiquitets Akademiens Handlingar. I—XX. *Stockholm*, 1789—1852. 8vo.

Handlingar rörande Skandinaviens Historia. I—X. *Stockholm*, 1816—1822. 8vo.

Nya Handlingar rörande Skandinaviens Historia. I—IV (XI—XIV). *Stockholm*, 1824—1828. 8vo.

Handlingar rörande Sveriges äldre, nyare och nyaste Historia, samt Historiska Personer. Utgifna af *ett Sällskap.* I—IX. *Stockholm*, 1830—1833. 8vo.

Samlingar utgifna af *Svenska Fornskrift-Sällskapet.* I, I, II, III (1844–5); II, I, II, III (1845), IV (1849); III, I (1846), II (1853), III (1847); IV, I, II (1847), III (1849), IV (1851), V (1852); V, I, II (1850); VI, I (1848), II (1851); VII, I, II (1853). *Stockholm.* 8vo.

Svenska Akademien.

Svenska Akademiens Handlingar, ifraan aar 1786, I—V; ifraan aar 1796, I—XVI, XVIII—XX. *Stockholm*, 1801—1843. 8vo.

STOCKHOLM.

Miscellanea.

Iduna. En Skrift för den Nordiska Fornaalderns Aalskare. I—X. *Stockholm*, 1811—1824. 12mo.

UPSALA.

Kongliga Vetenskaps Societeten.

Nova Acta Regiae Societatis Scientiarum Upsaliensis. II—V, VII—XIV. *Upsaliae*, 1775—1792, 1815—1850. Seriei Tertiae I, II, I, 1855, 1856. 4to.

Svea. Tidskrift för Vetenskap och Konst. I—XIV. *Upsala*, 1818—1831. 8vo.

Skandia. Tidskrift för Vetenskap och Konst. Utgifven af *Svenska Litteratur-Föreningen*. I—X. *Upsala*, 1833—1837. 8vo.

DelaGardiska Archivet, eller Handlingar ur Grefl. DelaGardiska Bibliotheket pa Löberöd. I—X. Utgifven af P. WIESELGREN. *Stockholm & Lund*, 1831—1838. 8vo.

NORWAY.

BERGEN.

Bergen's Museum.

Urda, et Norsk Antiquarisk-historisk Tidsskrift, udgivet af *Directionen for det Bergenske Museum*. I, 1837; II, 1842. *Bergen*. 4to.

CHRISTIANIA.

Det Kongelige Norske Frederiks Universitet.

Det Kongelige Norske Frederiks Universitets Aarsberetning 1847; 1849—1855. *Christiania*. 8vo.

Akademiske Love for de Studerende ved det Kongelige Frederiks Universitet. *Christiania*, 1850. 8vo.

Norske Universitet og Skole Annaler VI; VII, I, 1851—53. *Christiania*. 8vo.

CHRISTIANIA.

Physiographiske Forening.

Nyt Magazin for Naturvidenskaberne. Udgives af den *Physiographiske Forening i Christiania* ved CHR. LANGBERG. IV, II, III, IV; V; VI; VII; VIII; IX. *Christiania*, 1843—1857. 8vo.

TRONDHJEM (DRONTHEIM).

Kongelige Norske Videnskabernes Selskab.

Det Trondhjemske Selskabs Skrifter [Title changed at Vol. IV to Det Kongelige Norske Videnskabers Selskabs Skrifter] I—V. *Kiöbenhavn*, 1761—74. 8vo.

Nye Samling af det Kongelige Norske Videnskabers Selskabs Skrifter I, 1784; II, 1788. *Kiöbenhavn.* 4to.

Nyeste Samling af det Kongelige Norske Videnskabers-Selskabs Skrifter I. *Kjöbenhavn*, 1798. 8vo.

Det Kongelige Norske Videnskabersselskabs Skrifter i det 19de Aarhundrede. I, 1817; II, 1824—1827; III, 1829—1843; IV, I, 1844. *Trondhjem.* 4to.

DENMARK.

KJÖBENHAVN (COPENHAGEN).

Danske Landmands-Forsamling.

Beretning om den fjerde danske Landmands-Forsamling, afholdt i Kjöbenhavn fra den 5te–9de October 1852. Ved C. F. LINDE. *Kjöbenhavn*, 1854. 8vo.

Femte, i Flensborg, 1854. *Kjöbenhavn*, 1855.

Sjette, i Aalborg, 1856. *Kjöbenhavn*, 1857.

Kongelige Danske Selskab for Fædrelandets Historie og Sprog.

Danske Magazin, indeholdende allehaande Smaa-Stykker og Anmerkninger til Historiens og Sprogets Oplysning. I—VI. Udgivet af det *Kongelige Danske Selskab til den Nordiske Histories og Sprogs Forbedring. Kjöbenhavn*, 1745—1752. 4to.

KJÖBENHAVN.

Kongelige Danske Selskab for Fædrelandets Historie og Sprog.—*Continued.*

Nye Danske Magazin, &c. &c. Udgivet af det *Kongelige Danske Selskab til den Nordiske Histories og Sprogs Forbedring.* I—IV. *Kjöbenhavn,* 1794—1827. 4to.

Det Kongelige Danske Selskab for Fædrelandets Historie og Sprog, i dets förste Aarhundrede. Ved E. C. Werlauff. *Kjöbenhavn,* 1847. 8vo.

Tillæg til Skriftet: Det Kongelige Danske Selskab for Fædrelandets Historie og Sprog, i dets förste Aarhundrede. Ved E. C. Werlauff, med J. Langebeks Portrait. *Kjöbenhavn,* 1847. 8vo.

Det Kongelige Danske Videnskabernes Selskab.

Det Kongelige Danske Videnskabernes-Selskabs Skrivter for Aarene 1800—1812. I—VI. *Kjöbenhavn,* 1801—1818. 4to.

Det Kongelige Danske Videnskabernes Selskabs Philosophiske og Historiske Afhandlinger. I—VII. *Kjöbenhavn,* 1823—1845. 4to.

Det Kongelige Danske Videnskabernes Selskabs Naturvidenskabelige og Mathematiske Afhandlinger. I—XII. *Kjöbenhavn,* 1824—1846. 4to.

Det Kongelige Danske Videnskabernes Selskabs Skrifter. Femte Række. Historiske og Philosophiske Afdeling. I; II, I, *Kjöbenhavn,* 1852—1856. 4to.

Det Kongelige Danske Videnskabernes Selskabs Skrifter. Femte Række. Naturvidenskabelige og Mathematiske Afdeling. I—IV, I. *Kjöbenhavn,* 1849—1856. 4to.

Det Kongelige Danske Videnskabernes Selskabs Historie i dets förste Aarhundrede. 1742—1842. Af C. Molbech. *Kjöbenhavn,* 1843. 8vo.

Oversigt over det Kgl. Danske Videnskabernes Selskabs Forhandlinger og dets Medlemmers Arbeider i Aarene 1842—1856. Af Selskabets Secretair H. C. Oersted, 1842—1850; G. Forchhammer, 1851—1856. *Kjöbenhavn.* 8vo.

Collectanea Meteorologica sub auspiciis *Societatis Scientiarum Danicae* edita. Fasc. IV. *Hauniae,* 1856. 4to.

KJÖBENHAVN.

Det Kongelige Danske Videnskabernes Selskab.—*Continued.*

Regesta Diplomatica Historiae Danicae, cura *Societatis Regiae Scientiarum Danicae.* II, II. Ab anno 1559 ad annum 1588. *Kjöbenhavn,* 1856. 4to.

Naturhistoriske Forening.

Videnskabelige Meddelelser fra den Naturhistoriske Forening i Kjöbenhavn, for Aarene 1849—1856. Udgivne af *Selskabets Bestyrelse. Kjöbenhavn,* 1851—1857. 8vo.

Kongelige Nordiske Oldskrift-Selskab.

Antiquariske Annaler. Udgivne ved den Kongelige Commission i Kiöbenhavn for Oldsagers Opbevaring. I—IV, 1812—1827. *Kjöbenhavn.* 8vo.

Annaler for Nordisk Oldkyndighed. Udgivne af det *Kongelige Nordiske Oldskrift-Selskab.* 1836—1854. *Kjöbenhavn.* 8vo.

Mémoires de la Société royale des Antiquaires du Nord. 1836—1839, 1840—1844, 1845—1849. *Copenhagen.* 8vo.

Tidsskrift for Nordisk Oldkyndighed, udgivet af det *Nordiske Oldskrift-Selskab.* I, II. *Kjöbenhavn,* 1826, 1829. 8vo.

Nordisk Tidsskrift for Oldkyndighed. Udgivet af det *Kongelige Nordiske Oldskrift-Selskab.* I—III, 1832—1836. *Kjöbenhavn.* 8vo.

Antiquarisk Tidsskrift. Udgivet af det *Kongelige Nordiske Oldskrift-Selskab.* 1843—1845; 1846—1848; 1849—1851 (1852—54). *Kjöbenhavn,* 1845, 1847, 1852, & 1854. 8vo.

Die königliche Gesellschaft für Nordische Alterthumskunde zu Kopenhagen. Jahresversammlungen in den Jahren 1848—1852. 8vo. pp. 4.

Royal Society of Northern Antiquaries at Copenhagen. General anniversary meeting 15 Feb. 1851. 8vo. pp. 8.

Société Royale des Antiquaires du Nord. [Tracts.] 1845—1854. 8vo.

Société Royale des Antiquaires du Nord. Rapport des Séances Annuelles de 1848—51. 8vo. pp. 16.

KJÖBENHAVN.

Kongelige Nordiske Oldskrift-Selskab.—*Continued.*

Société Royale des Antiquaires du Nord à Copenhague. Extrait des Statuts Constitutifs. 8vo. pp. 4.

Société Royale des Antiquaires du Nord. [Mélanges.] 8vo.

Report addressed by the Royal Society of Northern Antiquaries to its British and American Members. *Copenhagen*, 1836. 8vo.

Leitfaden zur Nordischen Alterthumskunde. Herausgegeben von der *Königlichen Gesellschaft für Nordische Alterthumskunde. Kopenhagen*, 1837. 8vo.

Antiquitates Americanæ, sive Scriptores Septentrionales Rerum Ante-Columbianarum in America. Samling af de i Nordens Oldskrifter indeholdte Efterretninger om de gamle Nordboers Opdagelsesreiser til America fra det 10de til det 14de Aarhundrede. Edidit *Societas Regia Antiquariorum Septentrionalium. Hafniae*, 1837. 4to.

Americas Opdagelse i det Tiende Aarhundrede, efter de Nordiske Oldskrifter, ved C. C. Rafn. *Kjöbenhavn*, 1841. 8vo.

Mémoire sur la Découverte de l'Amérique au Dixième Siècle, par Charles Christian Rafn. *Copenhague*, 1843. 8vo.

The Discovery of America by the Northmen and Connection of the Northmen with the East, by Charles C. Rafn. 8vo. pp. 4.

Same in French and German.

Americas Arctiske Landes gamle Geographie, efter de Nordiske Oldskrifter, ved Charles Christian Rafn. *Kjöbenhavn*, 1845. 8vo.

Cabinet d'Antiquités Américaines. 8vo. pp. 8.

Guide to Northern Archæology, by the *Royal Society of Northern Antiquaries* of Copenhagen. Edited for the use of English readers, by the Right Honorable the Earl of Ellesmere. *London*, 1848. (2 copies.)

Royal Society of Northern Antiquaries of Copenhagen. British and Irish Section. [Programme.] 8vo.

Remarks on a Danish Runic Stone from the Eleventh Century, found in the central part of London. By Charles Christian Rafn. *Copenhagen*, 1854. 8vo

KJÖBENHAVN.

Kongelige Nordiske Oldskrift-Selskab.—*Continued.*

Aperçu du Fonds permanent de la Société Royale des Antiquaires du Nord, avec la Liste de ses Membres Fondateurs. 1840, 1850, 1852. 8vo.

Selskabet for en forbedret Retskrivnings Udbredelse.

Nordisk Ugeskrift, udgivet af *Selskabet for en forbedret Retskrivnings Udbredelse.* 1837—1838. *Köbenhavn.* 8vo.

Skandinaviske Litteratur Selskab.

Det Skandinaviske Litteratur Selskabs Skrifter. I—XXIII. *Kjöbenhavn,* 1805—1832. 12mo.

Skandinavisk Museum, ved *et Selskab.* 1798, I, II; 1800; 1802; 1803, I, II. *Kiöbenhavn.* 12mo.

Veterinair-Selskab.

Veterinair-Selskabets Skrifter. I—III. *Kjöbenhavn,* 1808—1818. 8vo.

Miscellanea.

Skírnir, ný tídhindi hins Islenzka Bókmentafélags. I—XII. Argáng 1827—1838. *Kaupmannahöfn,* 1827—1838. 8vo.

Rit thess Islenzka Lærdóms-lista Félags. I—XIV. 1780—1793. *Kaupmannahöfn,* 1781—1796. 12mo.

Nye Samling af Danske Norske og Islandske Jubel-Lærere, &c. I, 1779; II, I, 1781; II, 1783; III, 1786. *Kjöbenhavn.* 4to.

Den Nordiske Kirke-Tidende. Udgiven af J. C. Lindberg. Aarg. I—VI. 1833—1838. *Kjöbenhavn.* 4to.

Brage og Idun, et Nordisk Fjærdingaarsskrift. Udgivet, med Bistand af *Danske, Svenske og Normænd,* af Frederik Barfod. I—V, I, 1839—1842. *Kjöbenhavn.* 8vo.

Tidsskrift for Landœkonomie. Udgivet af J. C. Hald. I—VII. *Kjöbenhavn,* 1831—1839. 8vo.

Bidrag til Kundskab om de danske Provindsers nærværende Tilstand i œkonomisk Henseende. I—IX. *Kjöbenhavn,* 1826—1837. 8vo.

(*Part VII is wanting.*)

KJÖBENHAVN.

Miscellanea.—*Continued.*

Medicinisches Schriftsteller-Lexicon der jetzt lebenden Aerzte, Wundärzte, Geburtshelfer, Apotheker, und Naturforscher aller gebildeten Völker. Von ADOLF CARL PETER CALLISEN. I—XXXIII. *Copenhagen*, 1830—1845. 8vo.

Perseus, Journal for den Speculative Idee. Udgiven af JOHAN LUDVIG HEIBERG. I, II, 1837, 1838. *Kjöbenhavn.* 8vo.

Naturhistorisk Tidsskrift, udgivet af HENRIK KROYER. I, II. *Kjöbenhavn*, 1837.

RUSSIA.

DORPAT.

Gelehrte Estnische Gesellschaft zu Dorpat.

Verhandlungen der Gelehrten Estnischen Gesellschaft zu Dorpat. I, 1842-46; II, 1847-52; III, I, 1854; IV, I, 1857. *Dorpat* und *Leipzig*. 8vo.

Kaiserliche Universitats-Sternwarte.

Beobachtungen der Kaiserlichen Universitäts-Sternwarte zu Dorpat, von Dr. J. H. MÆDLER. XII, XIII, XIV, 1856. *Dorpat*, 1850. 4to.

HELSINGFORS.

Societas Scientiarum Fennica.

Acta Societatis Scientiarum Fennicae. I, 1842; II, I, II, 1847; III, 1852; IV; V, I, 1856. *Helsingforsiae.* 4to.

Notiser ur Sällskapets pro Fauna and Flora Fennica Förhandlingar. Bihang till *Acta Societatis Scientiarum Fennicae.* I, II. *Helsingfors*, 1848, 1852. 4to.

Observationes Astronomicae in specula Universitatis Litterariae Fennicae factae. I—III, 1824-28. *Helsingforsiae.* Fol.

Sveriges Rikes Stadslag. Ofevrsättning paa Finska spraaket af LJUNGO THOMAE, paa *Finska Vetenskaps-Societetens*

HELSINGFORS.

Societas Scientiarum Fennica.—*Continued.*

bekostnad utgifven af *Wilh. Gabr. Lagus. Helsingfors,* 1852. 4to.

Sveriges Rikes Landslag, Stadfästad af Konung Christopher aar 1442. Öfversättning paa Finska spraaket af Ljungo Thomae; paa *Finska Vetenskaps-Societetens* bekostnad utgifven af *Wilh. Gabr. Lagus. Helsingfors,* 1852. 4to.

Observatoire Magnetique et Meteorologique.

Observations faites à l'Observatoire Magnétique et Météorologique de Helsingfors, sous la direction de Jean Jacques Nervander. Première Section.—Observations Magnétiques. I—IV. Deuxième Section.—Observations Météorologiques. I—IV. *Helsingfors,* 1850. 4to.

KAZAN (KASAN).

Imper. Kazanskii Universitet (*Imper. Univ. of Kasan*).

Utshenyja Zapiski, izdavaemyja *Imperat. Kazanskim Universitetom* (Scientific Memoirs), 1853. Parts I—IV. *Kazan,* 1853–54. 8vo.

MITAU (MITTAU).

Kurlændische Gesellschaft fur Literatur und Kunst.

Jahresverhandlungen der Kurländischen Gesellschaft für Literatur und Kunst. I. *Mitau,* 1819. 4to.

Sendungen der Kurländischen Gesellschaft für Literatur und Kunst. II, 1845; III. *Mitau,* 1847. 4to.

Arbeiten der Kurländischen Gesellschaft für Literatur und Kunst. I—X. *Mitau,* 1847—1851. 8vo.

MOSKVA (MOSCOW).

Societe Imperiale des Naturalistes de Moscou.

Nouveaux Mémoires de la Société Impériale des Naturalistes de Moscou. Tomes IX & X, formant les Tomes XVe et XVIe de la collection. *Moscou,* 1851, 1855. 4to.

Bulletin de la Société Impériale des Naturalistes de Moscou. I—XXX, I, 1829—1857. *Moscou.* 8vo.
(*Wanting XXI.*)

ODESSA.

Obshtshestvo Seljskago Khozjaistva Juzhnoi Rossii (*Society of Rural Economy of Southern Russia*).

Ottshet i Rjetshi, tshitannye v tshrezvytshaïnom Sobranii Obshtshestva Seljskago Khozjaistva Juzhnoï Rossii (Report and Speeches delivered at an extraordinary meeting of the Society of Rural Economy of Southern Russia, on the completion of the 10th year of its existence, December 20th, 1838). *Odessa*, 1837. 8vo. pp. IV, 46, and VII.

Ottshet o Djestvijakh Imper. Obshtshestva Seljskago Khozjaistva Juzhnoï Rossii (Report of the Operations of the Society of Rural Economy of Southern Russia). By J. Palimpsestoff, Secretary of the Society. *Odessa*, 1855. 8vo.

Demolle (J.). Rutshnaja Kniga Ovtsevodov (Manual of Sheep-Breeding), 2d edit. *Odessa*, 1842. 8vo. pp. 53.

Ottshet Komiteta dlja Pooshtshrenija Shelkovodstva na Odesskoï gorodskoï Zemlje za 1847i god (Report of the Committee for the Encouragement of Silk-Culture on the Soil of Odessa for the year 1847). *Odessa*, 1848. 8vo. pp. 20.

Katalog Rasteniam i Sjemenam prodajushtshimsja v Imper. nikitskom Sadje, na juzhnom beregu Kryma (Catalogue of Plants and Seeds sold in the Imperial Nikitski Garden, on the Southern Shore of the Crimea). *Odessa*, 1848. 8vo. pp. 60.

Skaljkovski (A.). Opyt Statistitsheskago Opisanija Novorossiïskago Kraja (Attempt at a Statistical Description of Southern Russia). Part I.—Geography, Ethnography, and Census. Part II.—Economical Statistics. *Odessa*, 1850 & 1853. 8vo.

Odesskoe Obshtshestvo Istorii i Drevnostei (*Historical and Antiquarian Society of Odessa*).

Dshik (A.). Vosporskoe Tsarstvo s ego paleographitsheskimi i nadgrobnymi Pamjatnikami, raspisnymi Vazami, Planami, Kartami i Vidami (The Kingdom of Bosporus, with its Palæographic and Sepulchral Monuments). Parts I—III. *Odessa*, 1848–49. 4to.

RIGA.

Naturforschender Verein.

Correspondenzblatt des Naturforschenden Vereins zu Riga. Redigirt von Dr. C. J. G. Müller. Jahr I—IX, 1845—1856. *Riga*, 1846—1857. 8vo.

Arbeiten des Naturforschenden Vereins zu Riga. Redigirt von Dr. Müller und Dr. Sodoffsky. I. *Rudolstadt*, 1848. 8vo.

ST. PETERSBURG.

Gidrographitsheskii Departament Morskago Ministerstva (*Hydrographical Department of the Ministry of Marine*).

Zapiski Gidrographitsheskago Depo (Memoirs of the Hydrographical Depot). Parts I—V. *St. Petersburg*, 1835—1837. 4to.

Zapiski Gidrographitsheskago Departamenta Morskago Ministerstva (Memoirs of the Hydrographical Department of the Ministry of Marine). Parts I—IX, 1842—52. *St. Petersburg*. 8vo.

Gidrographitsheskoe Opisanie Sjevernago Berega Rossii (Hydrographical Description of the Northern Coast of Russia). By Lieut. Capt. M. Reineke. Part I.—White Sea. Part II.—Lapland Coast. *St. Petersburg*, 1850 & 1843. 4to.

Opisanie Majakov, Bashen i drugikh Predosteregateljnykh dlja Moreplavateleĭ Znakov Rossiĭskoĭ Imperii (Description of the Lighthouses, Towers, and other Beacons for Mariners of the Russian Empire). *St. Petersburg*, 1853. 4to.

Imperat. Akademija Nauk (*Imp. Academy of Sciences*).

Commentarii Academiae Scientiarum Imperialis Petropolitanae. I—XIV. 1726—1746. *Petropoli*, 1728—1751. 4to.

Novi Commentarii Academiae Scientiarum Imperialis Pe-

ST. PETERSBURG.

Imperat. Akademija Nauk.—*Continued.*

tropolitanae. I—XX, 1747—1775. *Petropoli*, 1750—1776. 4to.

Acta Academiae Scientiarum Imperialis Petropolitanae. Pro annis 1777—1782. *Petropoli*, 1778—1786. 4to.

Nova Acta Academiae Scientiarum Imperialis Petropolitanae. I—XIII, 1783—1796. *Petropoli*, 1787—1802. 4to.

Mémoires présentés à l'Académie Impériale des Sciences de St. Pétersbourg par divers savans et lus dans ses séances. I, 1831; II, 1835; III, 1837; IV, I—V, 1837-43; V, 1846; VI, I, II, III, V, VI, 1846-51; VII, 1854. *St. Pétersbourg.* 4to.

(*Vol. IV, livr.* 6, *and Vol. VI, livr.* 4, *wanting.*)

Mémoires de l'Académie Impériale des Sciences de St. Pétersbourg. VIe série.—Sciences politiques, Histoire, Philologie. I, 1832; V, 1845; VI, 1844; VII, I—V, 1843-47; VIII, 1855. *St. Pétersbourg.* 4to.

(*Vols. II, III, IV, and VII, livr.* 6, *wanting.*)

Idem. VIe série.—Sciences mathématiques, physiques, et naturelles. Première partie.—Sciences mathématiques et physiques. I, III—VI; II, 1841; III, 1844; IV, 1850; V, 1853; VI, 1857. *St. Pétersbourg.* 4to.

(*Vol. I, livr.* 1 *and* 2, *and titles to Vol. IV, wanting.*)

Idem. VIe série.—Sciences mathématiques, physiques, et naturelles. Seconde partie.—Sciences naturelles. I, 1835; II, I, II, IV, V, VI, 1836-38; III, I, II, III, V, VI, 1839-40; IV, 1845; V, 1849; VI, 1849; VII, 1855. *St. Pétersbourg.* 4to.

(*Vol. II, livr.* 3, *and Vol. III, livr.* 4, *wanting.*)

Bulletin Scientifique publié par l'Académie Impériale des Sciences de Saint-Pétersbourg. I—V, 1836—1839. *Saint-Pétersbourg* et *Leipzig.* 4to.

Bulletin de la classe Physico-mathématique de l'Académie Impériale des Sciences de St. Pétersbourg. I, 1843; II, 1844; III, 1845; IV, 1845; V, 1847; VI, 1848; VII, 1849; IX, 1851; X, 1852; XII, 1854; XIII, 1855;

ST. PETERSBURG.

Imperat. Akademija Nauk.—*Continued.*

XIV, 1856; XV, 1857. *St. Pétersbourg* et *Leipzig.* 4to.
(*Vols. VIII and XI wanting.*)

Bulletin de la classe Historico-philologique de l'Académie Impériale des Sciences de St. Pétersbourg. I, 1844; II, 1845; III, 1847; IV, 1848; V, 1848; VI, 1849; VII, 1850; VIII, 1851; IX, 1852; X, 1853; XI, 1854; XII, 1855; XIII, 1856. *St. Pétersbourg* et *Leipzig.* 4to.
(*Wanting, Title to Vol. III.*)

Compte Rendu de l'Académie Impériale des Sciences de St. Pétersbourg, 1852–55. *St. Pétersbourg,* 1853–56. 8vo.

Observations Météorologiques, faites à l'Académie Impériale des Sciences de St. Pétersbourg, de 1822 à 1835, et calculées par M. A. T. KUPFFER. (Lu le 16 Septembre, 1836.) *St. Pétersbourg.* 4to. [Mém. VI sér.—Sc. math., phys. et nat. Tome IV, 1re partie.]

Résumé des Observations Météorologiques faites dans l'étendue de l'empire de Russie et déposées aux archives météorologiques de l'Académie des Sciences. Publiées, sous les auspices et aux frais de *l'Académie des Sciences,* par A. T. KUPFFER. 1er Cahier. *St. Pétersbourg,* 1846. 4to.

Mélanges Biologiques tirés du Bulletin Physico-mathématique de l'Académie Impériale des Sciences de St. Pétersbourg. I (1849–53), 1853; II, I.—V, 1854–57. *St. Pétersbourg.* 8vo.

Recueil de Mémoires présentés à l'Académie des Sciences par les Astronomes de Poulkova ou offerts à l'Observatoire Central par d'autres Astronomes du Pays. I. *St. Pétersbourg,* 1853. 4to.

Beiträge zur Kenntniss des Russischen Reiches und der angränzenden Länder Asiens. Auf Kosten der *Kaiserl. Akademie der Wissenschaften* herausgegeben von K. E. v. BAER und Dr. v. HELMERSEN. I—XIX. *St. Petersburg,* 1839–54. 8vo.
(*XVI wanting.*)

ST. PETERSBURG.

Imper. Russkoe Geographitsheskoe Obshtshestvo (*Imperial Russian Geographical Society*).

Etnographitsheskiĭ Sbornik, izdavaemyĭ *Imp. Russ. Geographitsheskim Obshtshestvom* (Ethnographical Magazine). Vols. I, II. *St. Petersburg*, 1843–44. 8vo.

Zapiski Russkago Geographitsheskago Obshtshestva (Memoirs of the Russian Geographical Society). Vols. I—XI. *St. Petersburg*, 1849–56. 8vo.

Comptes Rendus de la Société Impériale Russe de Géographie pour les années 1853, 1854, 1855, 1856 (in Russian). *St. Petersburg*, 1855–57. 8vo.

Sostav Imperatorskago Russkago Geographitsheskago Obshtshestva (List of Members of the Imper. Russ. Geographical Society), April, 1856. *St. Petersburg*, 1856. 8vo. pp. 60.

Vjestnik Imperatorskago Russkago Geographitsheskago Obshtshestva za 1856 god (Messenger of the Imper. Russian Geographical Society for the year 1856). Vols. I—VI. *St. Petersburg*, 1856–57. 8vo.

Seljskaja Ljetopis, sostavlennaja iz Nabljudeniĭ, mogushtshikh sluzhitj k Opredjeleniju Klimata Rossii (Rural Year-Book, consisting of Observations that may serve to determine the Climate of Russia, for the year 1851). Year I. *St. Petersburg*, 1854. fol.

Sbornik Statistitsheskikh Svjedjenii o Rossii, izdavaemyĭ Statistitsheskim Otdjeleniem *Imperatorskago Russkago Geographitsheskago Obshtshestva* (Magazine of Statistical Details concerning Russia), Vols. I, II. *St. Petersburg*, 1851—1854. 8vo.

Imperat. Volnoe Ekonomitsheskoe Obshtshestvo (*Imperial Free Economical Society*).

Trudy Imperatorskago Volnago Ekonomitsheskago Obshtshestva (Transactions of the Imper. Free Economical Society). Years 1842–54, 1856. *St. Petersburg*, 1842–56. 37 vols. 8vo.

Khozjaistvennaja Gazeta: Ekonomitsheskija Zapiski (Economical Gazette). Years I, III, 1854, 1856. *St. Petersburg*, 1854, 1857. fol.

ST. PETERSBURG.

Imperat. Volnoe Ekonomitsheskoe Obshtshestvo.—*Continued.*

Mittheilungen der kaiserlichen freien ökonomischen Gesellschaft zu St. Petersburg. Jahrg. 1844–56. *Leipzig.* 8vo.

Khozjaistvennyja i Tekhnitsheskija Rukovodstva, izdavaemyja ot *Imper. Volnago Ekonomitsheskago Obshtshestva* (Economical and Technical Manuals, published by the Free Economical Society):—

Obshtsheponjatnaja Mekhanika primjenennaja k Seljskomu Khozjaistvu, Promyshlenosti i Domovodstvu (Practical Mechanics applied to Rural Economy, Commerce, and Domestic Economy). By N. Pisarevski. Parts I, II. *St. Petersburg*, 1854. 8vo.

Kurs Tekhnitsheskoï Khimii (Course of Technical Chemistry). By A. Khodneff. Part I.—Inorganic. Part II.—Organic. *St. Petersburg*, 1855–56. 8vo.

Auswahl öconomischer Abhandlungen welche die freye öconomische Gesellschaft in St. Petersburg in teutscher Sprache erhalten hat. I—IV. *St. Petersburg*, 1790–93. 8vo.

Preisschriften und Abhandlungen der kayserlichen freyen ökonomischen Gesellschaft zu St. Petersburg. I. *St. Petersburg*, 1795. 8vo.

Kais. Russ. Mineralogische Gesellschaft.

Schriften der in St. Petersburg gestifteten Russisch-Kaiserlichen Gesellschaft für die gesammte Mineralogie. I, i, ii. *St. Petersburg*, 1842. 8vo.

Verhandlungen der Kaiserlich-Russischen Mineralogischen Gesellschaft zu St. Petersburg. Jahrg. 1842—1851, 1854—1856. *St. Petersburg.* 8vo.

L'Etat Major du Corps des Ingenieurs des Mines de Russie.

Annuaire du Journal des Mines de Russie. Introduction et Travaux Statistiques. Années 1835—1842. *St. Pétersbourg*, 1840—1845. 8vo.

Annuaire Météorologique et Magnétique du corps des Ingénieurs des Mines, ou Recueil d'Observations Météorolo-

ST. PETERSBURG.

L'Etat Major du Corps des Ingenieurs, etc.—*Cont'd.*

giques et Magnétiques faites dans l'étendue de l'Empire de Russie, &c. Année 1845. *St. Pétersbourg*, 1848. 8vo.

Observatoire Physique Central de Russie.

Annales de l'Observatoire Physique Central de Russie. Année 1847–54. *St. Pétersbourg*, 1850–56. 4to.

Compte Rendu annuel adressé à Mr. le Comte Wrontchenko, ministre des finances, par le directeur de l'Observatoire Physique Central, A. T. Kupffer. Année 1850—1855. *St. Pétersbourg*, 1851–56. 4to.

Observations Météorologiques faites à Nijné-Taguilsk (Monts-Ourals), gouvernement de Perm. Années 1848—1851. *Paris*, 1850, 1852. 8vo.

(1850 *and* 1851 *from Prince Demidoff.*)

Correspondance Météorologique, publication trimestrielle de l'Administration des Mines de Russie, rédigée par A. T. Kupffer. Année 1850—1854. *St. Pétersbourg*, 1851—1856. 4to.

Idem. Publication annuelle. Année 1855. *St. Pétersbourg*, 1857. 4to.

Miscellanea.

Neue nordische Beyträge zur physikalischen und geographischen Erd- und Völkerbeschreibung, Naturgeschichte und Œkonomie. I, III, IV. *St. Petersburg* und *Leipzig*, 1781–83. 8vo.

Morskoï Sbornik, izdavaemyĭ ot *Morskago Utshenago Komiteta* (Nautical Magazine). I—XXXI, I. *St. Petersburg*, 1848–57. 8vo.

HOLLAND.

AMSTERDAM.

Bataafsch Maatschappij van Taal- en Dichtkunde.

Werken der Bataafsche Maatschappij van Taal- en Dichtkunde. I—V. *Amsterdam*, 1804–09. 8vo.

AMSTERDAM.

Koninklijke Akademie van Wetenschappen (*Konink.-Nederl. Instituut.*)

Verhandelingen der Koninklijke Akademie van Wetenschappen. I—III. Met Plaaten. *Amsterdam*, 1854—1856. 4to.

Verslagen en Mededeelingen der Koninklijke Akademie van Wetenschappen. Jaarg. I—III. *Amsterdam*, 1853—1855. 8vo.

Idem. Afdeeling Letterkunde. I, II. *Amsterdam*, 1856, 1857. 8vo.

Idem. Afdeeling Natuurkunde. IV—VI. *Amsterdam*, 1855–57. 8vo.

Koninklijk Besluit tot Forming der Akademie van Wetenschappen. Organisk Reglement der Akademie. Memorie van Toelichting, ingediend door de Staats-Commissie. Personelle staat der Akademie op 28 April 1855. Lijst der Binnen- en Buitenlandsche Akademien waarmede de Akademie in Verbinding is. *Amsterdam*, 1855. 4to.

Eerste Onderzoekingen met den Mikrometer van Airy, volbragt op het Observatorium der Hoogeschool te Leiden. Door F. Kaiser. *Amsterdam*, 1857. 4to.

Octaviae Querela. Carmen cuius auctori Johanni Van Leeuwen, e vico Zegwaart, certaminis poetici praemium secundum e legato *Jacobi Henrici Hoeufft* adiudicatum est in consessu publico Academiae Regiae Scientiarum die IX m. Martii anni 1857. *Amsteludami*, 1857. 8vo.

Koninklijk-Nederlandsche Instituut.

Verhandelingen der Eerste Klasse van het Hollandsch Instituut van Wetenschappen, Letterkunde en Schoone Kunsten, te Amsterdam. I—III, VI, VII, I. *Amsterdam*, 1812–23. 4to.

Nieuwe Verhandelingen der Eerste Klasse van het Koninklijk-Nederlandsche Instituut van Wetenschappen, Letterkunde en Schoone Kunsten, te Amsterdam. VII—X, XII, I, II; XIII, I, II, III. *Amsterdam*, 1837—1847. 4to.

AMSTERDAM.

Koninklijk-Nederlandsche Instituut.—*Continued.*

Verhandelingen der Eerste Klasse van het Koninklijk-Nederlandsche Instituut van Wetenschappen, Letterkunde en Schoone Kunsten, te Amsterdam. Derde Reeks. I—V. *Amsterdam*, 1848—1852. 4vo.

Verhandelingen der Tweede Klasse van het Koninklijk-Nederlandsche Instituut van Wetenschappen, Letterkunde en Schoone Kunsten. VI, I, II; VII; VIII. *Amsterdam*, 1836—1843. 4to.

Tijdschrift voor de Wis- en Natuurkundige Wetenschappen. Uitgegeven door de Eerste Klasse van het Koninklijk-Nederlandsche Instituut van Wetenschappen, Letterkunde en Schoone Kunsten. I—V. *Amsterdam*, 1848—1852. 8vo.

Verslag van de Openbare Vergadering der Tweede Klasse van het Koninklijk-Nederlandsche Instituut van Wetenschappen, Letterkunde en Schoone Kunsten. *Amsterdam*, 1826. 4to.

Commentationes Latinae Tertiae Classis Instituti Regii Belgici. VI. *Amstelod.*, 1836. 4to.

Gedenkschriften, in de Hedendaagsche Taalen, van de Derde Classe van het Koninklijk-Nederlandsche Instituut van Wetenschappen, Letterkunde en Schoone Kunsten. V. *Amsterdam*, 1836. 4to.

Jaarboek van het Koninklijk-Nederlandsche Instituut van Wetenschappen, Letterkunde en Schoone Kunsten, voor 1850 & 1851. *Amsterdam*, 1850, 1852. 8vo.

Koninklijk Zoologisch Genootschap "Natura Artis Magistra."

Jaarboekje van het Koninklijk Zoologisch Genootschap Natura Artis Magistra voor het Jaren 1852—1857. *Amsterdam.* 16mo.

Bijdragen tot de Dierkunde. Uitgegeven door het *Koninklijk Zoologisch Genootschap Natura Artis Magistra.* Zesde Aflevering. *Amsterdam*, 1854. fol.

AMSTERDAM.

Genootschap ter Spreuke Voerende: "Een onvermoeide arbeid komt alles te boven."

Nieuwe Wis- en Natuurkundige Verhandelingen van het Genootschap te Amsterdam ter Spreuke Voerende: Een onvermoeide arbeid komt alles te boven. Verhandeling over eene Merkwaardige Dynamische Eigenschap van eene bijzondere soort van Driehoekige Piramiden, door G. F. W. BAEHR. II, II. *Amsterdam*, 1851. 8vo.

Miscellanea.

Uitgezogte Verhandelingen uit de Nieuwste Werken van de Societeiten der Wetenschappen in Europa en van andere geleerde Mannen. Met naauwkeurige Afbeeldingen. I—X. *Amsterdam*, 1756—1765. 8vo.

Tijdschrift voor Natuurlijke Geschiedenis en Physiologie. Uitgegeven door VAN DER HOEVEN, M. D. Prof. te Leiden, en W. H. DE VRIESE, M. D. Prof. te Amsterdam. I—XII. *Amsterdam*, 1834—1845. 8vo.

GRONINGEN.

Academia Groningana.

Annales Academiae Groninganae. 1815—1837. *Groningae*, 1817—1839. 22 vols. 4to.

HAARLEM.

Bataafsche Maatschappij der Wetenschappen.

Natuurkundige Verhandelingen van de Bataafsche Maatschappij der Wetenschappen te Haarlem. I—V. *Amsterdam*, 1799—1810. 8vo.

Hollandsche Maatschappij der Wetenschappen.

Verhandelingen, uitgegeven door de *Hollandsche Maatschappij der Wetenschappen te Haarlem.* I—XXX. *Haarlem* en *Amsterdam*, 1754–93. 8vo.

(*Wanting XIV*, II.)

Register. I—XII. *Haarlem*, 1772. Idem. XIII—XXVIII. *Haarlem* en *Amsterdam*, 1793. 8vo.

HAARLEM.

Hollandsche Maatschappij der Wetenschappen.— *Continued.*

Natuurkundige Verhandelingen van de Hollandsche Maatschappij der Wetenschappen te Haarlem. Tweede Verzameling. V, II; VII. *Leiden*, 1849, 1851. VIII—XI, I; XIII. *Haarlem*, 1853–54. 1857. 4to.

Historische en Letterkundige Verhandelingen van de Hollandsche Maatschappij der Wetenschappen te Haarlem. I. *Haarlem*, 1851. 4to.

Extrait du Programme de la Société Hollandaise des Sciences à Harlem pour l'année 1850, pp. 7; 1851, pp. 6; 1854, pp. 6. 4to.

Verhandelingen, uitgegeven door de Commissie belast met het vervaardigen eener Geologische Beschrijving en Kaart van Nederland. I, II. *Haarlem*, 1853, 1854. 4to.

LA HAYE (THE HAGUE).

Koninklijk Instituut van Ingenieurs.

Verhandelingen van het Koninklijk Instituut van Ingenieurs. 1852–53, 1853–54, 1854–55. *Gravenhage*, 1853–55. fol.

Uittreksels uit Vreemde Tijdschriften voor de Leden van het Koninklijk Instituut van Ingenieurs. 1852–53, 1853–54, 1854–55, I, III. *Gravenhage*, 1853–55. fol.

Koninklijk Instituut van Ingenieurs. Algemeen Verslag van de Werkzaamheden en Notulen der Vergaderingen. 1852–53, 1853–54. *Gravenhage*, 1853, 1854. 8vo.

Notulen der Vergadering van het Koninklijk Instituut van Ingenieurs. 12de September, and 14de November, 1854. 8vo.

Societe Entomologique des Pays-Bas.

Mémoires d'Entomologie publiés par la Société Entomologique des Pays-Bas, sous la direction de MM. J. VAN DER HOEVEN, M. C. VERLOREN, et S. C. SNELLEN VAN VOLLENHOVEN. Livr. I—III. *La Haye*, 1857. 8vo.

LA HAYE.

Societas Hagana pro Vindicanda Religione Christiana.

Het Genootschap tot Verdediging van de Christelijke Godsdienst geschiedkundig geschetst. Feestrede ter viering van het vijftigjarig bestaan des Genootschaps, uitgesproken in's Hage, den 23 October 1855. Met Aanteekeningen en Bijlagen, door HERM. JOH. ROYAARDS. *Gravenhage*, 1836. 8vo.

LEYDEN.

Academia Lugduno-Batava.

Annales Academiæ Lugduno-Batavæ. 1816—1837. *Lugduni Batavorum*, 1817—1838. 4to.

Annales Academici, 1837–38, 1838–39, 1839–40. *Hagae Comitis*, 1840–42. 3 vols. 4to. Idem. 1840–49, 1849–50, 1850–51, 1852–53. *Lugduni Batavorum*, 1851–56. 4 vols. 8vo.

Vereeniging voor de Flora van Nederland.

Nederlandsch Kruidkundig Archief, onder redactie van F. DOZY. Vierde Deel, 1ste Stuk. *Leiden*, 1856. 8vo.

MIDDELBURG.

Zeeuwsch Genootschap der Wetenschappen.

Nieuwe Verhandelingen van het Zeeuwsch Genootschap der Wetenschappen. I—V. *Middelburg*, 1807—1835. 8vo.

Nieuwe Werken van het Zeeuwsch Genootschap der Wetenschappen. I, II. *Middelburg*, 1839, 1845. 8vo.

Verhandeling van Mr. A. F. SIFFLE, over den Oorsprong en de Grenzen van het Wettig Gezag in den Staat. *Middelburg*, 1852. 8vo.

Archief vrogere en latere Mededeelingen, voornamelijk in betrekking tot Zeeland. I, II. *Middelburg*, 1856. 8vo.

ROTTERDAM.

Bataafsch Genootschap der Proefondervindelijke Wijsbegeerte te Rotterdam.

Verhandelingen van het Bataafsch Genootschap der Proefondervindelijke Wijsbegeerte te Rotterdam. I—XII. *Rotterdam*, 1774—1798. 4to.

Nieuwe Verhandelingen van het Bataafsch Genootschap der Proefondervindelijke Wijsbegeerte te Rotterdam. I, 1800; IV, 1806; V—XI, 1810—1851; XII, I, 1851. *Amsterdam*. 4to.

(*Wanting, Vols. II and III, and continuation from the 2d part of Vol. XII inclusive.*)

Programma van het Bataafsch Genootschap der Proefondervindelijke Wijsbegeerte, gesticht door Steven Hoogendijk te Rotterdam. *Rotterdam*, 1850. 4to.

UTRECHT.

Academia Rheno-Trajectina.

Annales Academiæ Rheno-Trajectinæ, 1815—1837. *Trajecti ad Rhenum*, 1817—1837. 8vo.

Historisch Genootschap.

Berigten van het Historisch Genootschap te Utrecht. I—V. *Utrecht*, 1846—1856. 8vo.

Kronijk van het Historisch Gezelschap te Utrecht. Jaarg. II—V, 1846—1849. Kronijk van het Historisch Genootschap gevestigd te Utrecht. Tweede serie. Jaarg. VI—X, 1850—1854. Derde serie. XI, I, 1855. *Utrecht*. 8vo.

Register op de Kronijk van het Historisch Genootschap gevestigd te Utrecht. Jaargangen 1846—1854. *Utrecht*, 1857. 8vo.

Codex diplomaticus Neerlandicus. Verzameling van Oorkonde, betrekkelijk de Vaderlandsche Geschiedenis. Uitgegeven door het *Historisch Gezelschap gevestigd te Utrecht*. I. In twee Afdeelingen. *Utrecht*, 1848. 4to.

Idem. Tweede serie. III, I, 1855; II, 1856. *Utrecht*. 8vo.

UTRECHT.

Koninklijk Nederlandsch Meteorologisch Instituut.

Meteorologische Waarnemingen in Nederland en Afwijkingen van Temperatuur en Barometerstand op andere Plaatsen in Europa. 1852, 1853, 1854. *Utrecht*, 1852, 1854, 1855. Oblong 4to.

Meteorologische Waarnemingen in Nederland en zijne Bezittingen, en Afwijkingen van Temperatuur en Barometerstand op vele Plaatsen in Europa. 1855 & 1856. *Utrecht*, 1855, 1857. Oblong 4to.

Provinciaal Utrechtsch Genootschap van Kunsten en Wetenschappen.

Verhandelingen van het Provinciaal Utrechtsch Genootschap van Kunsten en Wetenschappen. I—IX. 1781—1801. *Utrecht.* 8vo.

Nieuwe Verhandelingen van het Provinciaal Utrechtsch Genootschap van Kunsten en Wetenschappen. I—XV. 1822—1845. *Utrecht.* 8vo.

Aanteekeningen van het verhandelde in de Sectie-Vergaderingen van het Provinciaal Utrechtsch Genootschap van Kunsten en Wetenschappen, ter gelegenheid van de algemeene Vergadering gehouden in het Jaren 1845—1855. *Utrecht*, 1846—1854. 8vo.

Verslag van het verhandelde in de Algemeene Vergadering van het Provinciaal Utrechtsch Genootschap van Kunsten en Wetenschappen, voor het jaar 1850. 8vo.

Verhandeling over de Verdiensten van Gijsbert Karel van Hogendorp als Staatshuishoudkundige ten aanzien van Nederland, door Mr. O. Van Rees. *Utrecht*, 1854. 8vo.

Uitkomsten der Meteorologische Waarnemingen gedaan te Utrecht in de Jaren 1839-43. Medegedeeld door R. Van Rees. *Utrecht*, 1844. 8vo.

Uitkomsten der Meteorologische Waarnemingen gedaan te Breda van 1839-46, door en onder de leiding van Dr. W. Wenckebach. Medegedeeld door zijnen opvolger, Dr. C. H. D. Buijs Ballot. *Utrecht*, 1848. 8vo.

UTRECHT.

Provinciaal Utrechtsch Genootschap, etc.—*Cont'd.*

Uitkomsten der Meteorologische Waarnemingen gedaan in 1849 en 1850 te Utrecht, en op eenige andere Plaatsen in Nederland. Met ondersteuning van het *Provinciaal Utrechtsch Genootschap van Kunsten en Wetenschappen. Utrecht*, 1851. 4to.

Windwaarnemingen in Nederland gedurende de jaren 1849 en 1850, bijeenverzameld door Dr. F. W. C. Krecke. Behoorende bij de Uitkomsten der Meteorologische Waarnemingen gedaan in 1849 en 1850 te Utrecht en op eenige andere Plaatsen in Nederland. Uitgegeven, met ondersteuning van het *Provinciaal Utrechtsch Genootschap van Kunsten en Wetenschappen*, door Dr. C. H. D. Buys Ballot. *Utrecht.* Oblong.

ZWOLLE.

Overijsselsche Vereeniging tot Ontwikkeling van Provinciale Welvaart.

Handelingen der Overijselsche Vereeniging tot Ontwikkeling van Provinciale Welvaart. *Zwolle*, 1841. 8vo.

Algemeen Verslag uitgebragt door de directie der Overijsselsche Vereeniging tot Ontwikkeling van Provinciale Welvaart, op de Algemeene Vergadering, 1845, 1847. *Zwolle*, 1845, 1848. 8vo.

Algemeen Jaarlijksch Verslag van de directie der Overijsselsche Vereeniging, &c. 1847; 1850; Jan. 6 and Nov. 24, 1854; 1856. *Zwolle*, 1847–56. 8vo.

Mededeeling over het Statistiek Bureau der Overijsselsche Vereeniging, &c. *Zwolle*, 1848. 8vo.

Bijdrage over de Hulpbronnen voor Nationale Welvaart in den Molukschen Archipel. Uitgesproken in de Overijsselsche Vereeniging ter Bevordering van Provinciale Welvaart, 17 Mars 1848. Gevolgd door eene Bijdrage tot de Statistieke Kennis van de Z. W. en Z. O. Eilanden, door den Heer G. De Seriere. *Zwolle*, 1848. 8vo.

Landhuishoudelijke Luchtkasteelen in Nederland. Voorlezing in de Overijsselsche Vereeniging tot Ontwikkeling

ZWOLLE.

Overijsselsche Vereeniging, etc.—*Continued.*

van Provinciale Welvaart, door Dr. W. C. H. Staring. *Zwolle*, 1849. 8vo.

Onze Banken van Leening. Verhandeling uitgesproken in de Overijsselsche Vereeniging, etc., op den 8 December 1848, door Mr. J. Kalff. *Zwolle*, 1849. 8vo.

Bronnen van Volkswelvaart. Voorlezing, gehouden in de Vergadering der Overijsselche Vereeniging tot Ontwikkeling van Provinciale Welvaart op den 14 December 1849, door J. Zeehuisen, lid der Staten van Overijssel. Met het Portret van den Heer Mr. Willem Jan Baron van Dedem tot de Rollecate. *Zwolle*, 1850. 8vo.

Lijst der Voorwerpen in het Museum van Oudheden en Zeldzaamheden der Overijsselsche Vereeniging tot Ontwikkeling van Provinciale Welvaart te Zwolle. *Zwolle*, 1852. 8vo.

Tijdschrift voor Staathuishoudkunde en Statistiek, door Mr. B. W. A. E. Sloet tot Oldhuis. I—XI. *Zwolle*, 1841 -55. 8vo.

GERMANY.

Norddeutscher Apotheker-Verein.

Vereins-Zeitung, redigirt vom Directorio des Vereins.
(From Arch. d. Pharm. CX Bds 1 Hft. pp. 81—112. 8vo.
" " CXXVI " 2 " 209—224.
" " CXXVII " 1 " 73—120.
" " CXXXI " 1 " 73—104.
" " CXXXVIII " 1 " 81—112.
" " CXLII " 1 " 81—128.
" " CXLIII " 1 " 81—112.)

Biographisches Denkmal für Heinr. Wilh. Ferd. Wackenroder. (From Arch. d. Pharm. Bd. CXXXV. Heft 1, pp. 13.) 8vo.

Literatur and Kritik. (From Arch. d. Pharm., pp. 207—216 & 328—336.) 8vo.

Verein der Suddeutschen Forstwirthe.

Die XII. Versammlung Süddeutscher Forstwirthe an Pfingsten 1855 in Stuttgart. *Stuttgart.* 8vo. pp. 51. [Program.]

Idem. (Abgedruckt aus den neuen Jahrbüchern der Forstkunde.) *Frankfurt am Main*, 1855. 8vo. pp. 144 & 136.

Idem. Schluss der Berichte über die Excursionen. (Aus den neuen Jahrbüchern der Forstkunde.) 8vo. pp. 86.

Idem. Nach ihrem Schlusse geschildert von Forstrath Dr. v. GWINNER. *Stuttgart*, 1855. 8vo. pp. 35.

Notizen für die 12. Versammlung süddeutscher Forstwirthe, zur Excursion in das Revier Engelberg, am Pfingstmontag den 28 Mai 1855. Von Revierförster ZAISER zu Hohengehren. *Reutlingen.* 8vo. pp. 16.

Versammlung deutscher Land- und Forstwirthe.

Amtlicher Bericht über die XI. Versammlung deutscher Land- und Forstwirthe zu Kiel, im September 1847. Redigirt von W. HIRSCHFELD und H. CARSTENS. *Altona*, 1848. 8vo.

Idem. XVI. Versammlung in Nürnberg 1853. *München*, 1854.

Idem. XVIII. Versammlung in Prag 1856. *Prag*, 1857.

Tageblatt für die XIX. Versammlung deutscher Land- und Forstwirthe in Coburg. I—V, 1857. *Coburg.* 8vo.

Tägliches Verzeichness der eingeschriebenen Mitglieder der XIX. Versammlung deutscher Land- und Forstwirthe in Coburg. I—IX, 1857. *Coburg.* 8vo.

Statistische Mittheilungen über das Herzogthum Sachsen-Coburg, mit besonderer Rücksicht auf Land- und Forst-Wirthschaft. Für die XIX. Versammlung deutscher Land- und Forstwirthe zusammengestellt im Sommer 1857, von HERMAN ROSE. *Coburg.* 8vo.

Hippologischer Vortrag zur Beantwortung der nach dem Programm der XIX. Versammlung deutscher Land- und Forstwirthe gestellten Frage II. der Plenarsitzung. Coburg, den 31 August 1857. *Coburg.* 8vo. pp. 20.

Versammlung deutscher Naturforscher und Aerzte.

Amtlicher Bericht über die [siebente] Versammlung deutscher Naturforscher und Aerzte zu Berlin in September, 1828. *Berlin*, 1829. 4to.

8te, in Heidelberg, 1829. *Heidelberg*, 1829.

9te, in Hamburg, 1830. *Hamburg*, 1831.

10te, in Wien, 1832. *Wien*, 1832.

11te, zu Breslau, 1833. *Breslau*, 1834.

12te, zu Stuttgart, 1834. *Stuttgart*, 1835.

14te, zu Jena, 1836. *Weimar*, 1837.

15te, in Prag, 1837. *Prag*, 1838.

16te, in Freiburg, 1838. *Freiburg*, 1839. 8vo.

18te, zu Erlangen, 1840. *Erlangen*, 1841.

19te, zu Braunschweig, 1841. *Braunschweig*, 1842.

20te, zu Mainz, 1842. *Mainz*, 1843.

21te, in Gratz, 1843. *Gratz*, 1844.

22te, in Bremen, 1844. *Bremen*, 1845.

24te, in Kiel, 1846. *Kiel*, 1847.

29te, in Wiesbaden, 1852. *Wiesbaden*, 1853.

(*Purchased.*)

Die Versammlung der deutschen Naturforscher und Aerzte in Berlin i. J. 1828, kritisch beleuchtet. *Leipzig*, 1828. 16mo.

Die achtzehnte Versammlung deutscher Naturforscher und Aerzte, von Carl Rösch. *Stuttgart*, 1841. 8vo.

Die 24. Versammlung deutscher Naturforscher und Aerzte. Ein Beitrag zur Characteristik naturwissenschaftlicher Zustände der Gegenwart, von C. Tr. Sachse. *Dresden*, 1846. 8vo. pp. 44.

Die XXVI. Versammlung deutscher Naturforscher und Aerzte im Allgemein geschildert von Prof. Dr. Fürnrohr. 8vo.

Die Verhandlungen der Section für Psychiatre und Anthropologie während der 29sten Versammlung deutscher Naturforscher und Aerzte zu Wiesbaden 1852, redigirt von Dr. A. Erlenmeyer. 8vo.

Tageblatt der 32. Versammlung Deutscher Naturforscher und Aerzte in Wien im Jahre 1856. No. I—VIII. 4to.

ALTENBURG (Saxony).

Naturforschende Gesellschaft des Osterlandes.

Statuten der Naturforschenden Gesellschaft des Osterlandes zu Altenburg. *Altenburg*, 1846. 8vo.

Tafellieder zum Stiftungsfeste der Naturforschenden Gesellschaft des Osterlandes. *Altenburg.* 8vo.

Festlied gesungen am Stiftungsfeste der Naturforschenden Gesellschaft des Osterlandes den 7 Juli 1852. 8vo.

Pomologische Gesellschaft.

Mittheilungen aus dem Osterlande. Gemeinschaftlich herausgegeben von dem *Kunst- und Handwerks-Vereine* der *Naturforschenden* und der *Pomologischen Gesellschaft zu Altenburg.* I—XIII, I, II. *Altenburg*, 1837—1856. 8vo.

Mittheilungen der Pomologischen Gesellschaft zu Altenburg über die Feier ihres 50jährigen Bestehens und Wirkens. *Altenburg*, 1854. 8vo.

Miscellanea.

Universal-Lexicon der Gegenwart und Vergangenheit, oder neuestes encyclopädisches Wörterbuch der Wissenschaften, Künste und Gewerbe, bearbeitet von mehr als 300 Gelehrten. Herausgegeben von H. A. Pierer. Dritte Auflage. (Vierte Ausgabe.) I—XVII. *Altenburg*, 1849–52. 8vo.

Supplemente zu Pierer's Universal-Lexicon. I—III. *Altenburg*, 1851–53. 8vo.

Atlas der Abbildungen. Gratiszugabe zur zweiten Auflage von Pierer's Universal-Lexikon. (Auf 68 Tafeln an 4000 Gegenstände.) Fünftes Heft, Zweite Abtheilung, Acht Tafeln. *Altenburg.* Oblong fol.

BENDORF.

Deutsche Gesellschaft fur Psychiatrie und gerichtliche Psychologie.

Correspondenz-Blatt der deutschen Gesellschaft für Psychiatrie und gerichtliche Psychologie, herausgegeben von deren Vorstand. Redigirt van Dr. A. A. Erlenmeyer. Dritter Jahrgang, 1856. *Neuwied.* 4to.

BERLIN.

Deutsche Geologische Gesellschaft.

Zeitschrift der Deutschen geologischen Gesellschaft. I—IV; V, I, II, III; VIII, IV; IX, I, II. *Berlin*, 1849—1857. 8vo.

Gesellschaft fur Erdkunde.

Statuten der, am 20ten April 1828, in Berlin gestifteten Gesellschaft für Erdkunde. *Berlin*. 4to.

Monatsberichte über die Verhandlungen der Gesellschaft für Erdkunde zu Berlin. Redigirt von J. LEHMANN und WILH. MAHLMANN. Jahrg. I—IV, 1839-43. *Berlin*. 8vo.

Idem. Neue Folge. I—X, 1844—1853.

Zeitschrift für allgemeine Erdkunde. Mit Unterstützung der Gesellschaft für Erdkunde zu Berlin, und unter besonderer Mitwirkung von *H. W. Dove*, *C. G. Ehrenberg*, *H. Kiepert*, und *C. Ritter* in Berlin; *K. Andree*, in Bremen; *A. Petermann*, in London; und *J. C. Wappaus*, in Göttingen; herausgegeben von Dr. J. E. GUMPRECHT. I—VI. *Berlin*, 1853—1856.

Idem. Neue Folge. I—III, 1856-57. 8vo.

Erste jährliche Uebersicht der Thätigkeit der Gesellschaft für Erdkunde in Berlin nach dem ersten Lustrum des Vereines für das Jahr 1833 (4 Mai) bis 1834, von dem zeitigen Director C. RITTER vorgetragen am 3 Mai. 4to.

Zweite, in Berlin, 1834-35.
Dritte, " " 1835-36.
Vierte, " " 1836-37.
Fünfte, " " 1837-38.

Geographische Gesellschaft.

[Letter from the Society to Alexander von Humboldt.] Berlin, 14 September, 1849. *Berlin*. 4to. pp. 4.

[Reply of Alexander von Humboldt to the Society.] Potsdam, 20 October, 1849. *Berlin*. 4to. pp. 4.

Zur Erinnerung an die Feier des fünf und zwanzigjährigen Stiftungsfestes der Geographischen Gesellschaft in Berlin am 24 April 1853. *Berlin*, 1853. 8vo.

BERLIN.

Gesellschaft naturforschender Freunde.

Schriften der Berlinischen Gesellschaft naturforschender Freunde. I—IX. *Berlin*, 1780–89. 8vo.

Der Gesellschaft naturforschender Freunde zu Berlin Neue Schriften. I—IV. *Berlin*, 1795—1803. 4to.

Der Gesellschaft naturforschender Freunde zu Berlin Magazin fur die neuesten Entdeckungen in der gesammten Naturkunde. I—VIII, 1807—1818. *Berlin*. 4to.

(*Purchased.*)

Gesellschaft zur Befœrderung des Flachs- und Hanfbaues in Preussen.

Mittheilungen der Gesellschaft zur Beförderung des Flachs- und Hanfbaues in Preussen. I—VII. *Berlin*, 1851—1857. 8vo.

(*From the Polytechnische Gesellschaft in Berlin.*)

Kœnigliches Landes-Œconomie-Collegium.

Annalen der Landwirthschaft in den Königlich Preussischen Staaten. Herausgegeben vom *Präsidium des Königl. Landes-Œconomie-Collegiums*, und redigirt von dem General-Secretair desselben, Dr. ALEXANDER VON LENGERKE. Jahrg. X, 1852; XI & Suppl. 1853; XII, 1854; XIII, 1855; XIV, I, 1856; XV, I, V, VI, 1857. (Bde. XIX—XXVII, XXXVIII, 1, XXIX, 1, 5, 6.) *Berlin*. 8vo.

Denkschriften zu den Berathungsgegenständen:

I. Die Verwendung des etatsmässigen Landeskultur-Fonds. *Berlin*, 1850. 8vo.

II. Die Gründung landwirthschaftlicher Meliorations-Fonds. *Berlin*, 1850. 8vo.

III. Entwurf eines Planes zur Herstellung einer landwirthschaftlichen Statistik sämmtlicher Vereins-Bezirke. *Berlin*, 1850. 8vo.

IV. Der landwirthschaftliche Unterricht in den Volkschulen. *Berlin*, 1850. 8vo.

V. Landwirthschaftliches Versuchswesen. Einrichtung eines Versuchsfeldes. *Berlin*, 1850. 8vo.

BERLIN.

Kœnigl. Landes-Œconomie-Collegium.—*Continued.*

VI. Das landwirthschaftliche Prämienwesen. *Berlin*, 1850. 8vo.

VII. Das ländliche Gesinde-Wesen. *Berlin*, 1850. 8vo.

IX. Die Ueben- und Füll-Arbeiten der kleineren Landbewohner. *Berlin*, 1850. 8vo.

X. Die Vermehrung der Lohnarbeit auf dem Lande. *Berlin*, 1850. 8vo.

XI. Die Benutzung der Kreisblätter für Belehrung des Landvolks. *Berlin*, 1850.

XIII. Die Runkelrübenzucker-Fabrikation als landwirthschaftliches Nebengewerbe. *Berlin*, 1850. 8vo.

XIV. Die Samen-Varietäten und der Wechsel des Saatgetreides. *Berlin*, 1850. 8vo.

XV. Ueber die Veranstaltung allgemeiner Ausstellungen der Erzeugnisse des Land- und Gartenbaues. *Berlin*, 1850. 8vo.

Denkschriften zu den Berathungsgegenständen XVI bis LI, für die landwirthschaftliche Versammlung in Mai 1850. *Berlin*, 1850. 8vo.

Kœniglich Preussische Akademie der Wissenschaften zu Berlin.

Abhandlungen der Königlichen Akademie der Wissenschaften zu Berlin. Aus den Jahren 1822—1856. *Berlin*, 1825—1857. 4to.

Bericht über die zur Bekanntmachung geeigneten Verhandlungen der Königl. Preuss. Akademie der Wissenschaften zu Berlin. Aus den Jahren 1848—1856, 1857, I—VIII. *Berlin*. 8vo.

Astronomisches Jahrbuch für das Jahr 1803. Nebst einer Sammlung der neuesten in die astronomischen Wissenschaften einschlagenden Abhandlungen, Beobachtungen und Nachrichten. Mit Genehmhaltung der *Königl. Akademie der Wissenschaften* berechnet und herausgegeben von J. E. Bode. *Berlin*, 1800. 8vo.

BERLIN.

Kœniglich Preussische Akademie der Wissenschaften zu Berlin.—*Continued.*

Idem für das Jahr 1819. *Berlin*, 1816.
" " 1820. " 1817.
" " 1821. " 1818.
" " 1822. " 1819.
" " 1823. " 1820.
" " 1824. " 1821.
" " 1825. " 1822.
" " 1826. " 1823.
" " 1827. " 1824.
" " 1828. " 1825.
" " 1829. " 1826.
" " 1855. " 1852.
" " 1856. " 1853.
" " 1860. " 1857.

Physikalische Gesellschaft.

Die Fortschritte der Physik. Dargestellt von der *Physikalischen Gesellschaft zu Berlin.* Jahrg. I, III—X. *Berlin*, 1847, 1850–57. 8vo.

(*Jahrg. II, wanting.*)

Polytechnische Gesellschaft.

Bericht über die Verhältnisse und die Wirksamkeit der Polytechnischen Gesellschaft zu Berlin. Hefte I—VII, Jahre I—XII (1839—1851). Als Manuscript gedruckt zur Kenntnissnahme für sämmtliche einheimische und auswärtige Mitglieder der Gesellschaft. *Berlin*, 1845—1851. 4to.

Sach- und Namenregister zu den ersten sieben Jahrgängen der Berichte über die Verhältnisse und die Wirksamkeit der Polytechnischen Gesellschaft zu Berlin. Als Manuscript gedruckt zur Kenntnissnahme für sämmtliche einheimische und auswärtige Mitglieder der Gesellschaft. *Berlin*, 1848. 4to.

Verhandlungen der Polytechnischen Gesellschaft. Jahrg. XIII—XVI (1851—1855). 4to. Jahrg. XVII, XVIII (1855—1857). 8vo. Als Manuscript für die Mitglieder der Gesellschaft gedruckt. *Berlin*, 1852—1857.

BERLIN.

Polytechnische Gesellschaft.—*Continued.*

Alphabetisches Sachregister der wichstigsten technischen Journale für den Zeitraum von 1 Januar 1847 bis 30 Juni 1853; 1 Jan. 1855 bis 31 Dec. 1856. Bearbeitet von Dr. PHILIPP. Für die Mitglieder der Polytechnischen Gesellschaft. *Berlin,* 1847—1853, 1855–57. 16mo.

Verzeichniss der Mitglieder der Polytechnischen Gesellschaft in Berlin. *Berlin,* 1853. 16mo. 1855. 8vo.

Verzeichniss der Bücher und Zeitschriften in der Bibliothek der Polytechnischen Gesellschaft in Berlin. Geschlossen im April 1853. *Berlin,* 1853. 8vo.

Statuten der Polytechnischen Gesellschaft zu Berlin. *Berlin,* 1853. 8vo. pp. 16.

Vorträge gehalten in der Polytechnischen Gesellschaft zu Berlin im Winter 1854—1855. Stenographirt von Dr. G. MICHAELIS. *Berlin,* 1855. 8vo.

Stenographischer Verein.

Anleitung zur deutscher Stenographie oder Kurzschrift, herausgegeben von dem *Stenographischen Verein zu Berlin.* Siebente, verbesserte Auflage. *Berlin,* 1853. 16mo.

(*From the Polytechnische Gesellschaft in Berlin.*)

Verein fur Deutsche Statistik.

Zeitschrift des Vereins für Deutsche Statistik. Unter Beyrath mehrerer Mitarbeiter herausgegeben von Dr. Freiherrn VON REDEN in Berlin. Jahrg. I, II, 1847, 1848. *Berlin.* 4to.

(*Wanting I,* IV—VII.)

Verein zur Befœrderung des Gartenbaues in den kœniglich preussischen Staaten.

Verhandlungen des Vereins zur Beförderung des Gartenbaues in den königlich preussischen Staaten. Bde II—XXI, 1826–53. *Berlin.* 4to.

Idem. Neue Reihe. Jahrg. I, 1853; III, Juli—Dec. 1855; IV, 1856–57. *Berlin.* 8vo.

Sach- und Namen-Register zu den Verhandlungen des

BERLIN.

Verein zur Befœrderung, etc.—*Continued.*

Vereins zur Beförderung des Gartenbaues in den königlich preussischen Staaten. Erster Band, zu der ersten bis einschliesslich ein und zwanzigsten Lieferung der Verhandlungen. *Berlin,* 1836. 4to.

Verzeichniss von den Büchern, Zeitschriften und Broschüren der Bibliothek des Vereines zur Beförderung des Gartenbaues in den königlich preussischen Staaten zu Berlin, nach dem Inhalte geordnet und mit einem Register der Verfasser versehen von dem. General-Sekretaire. Vierte Auflage. *Berlin,* 1852. 4to. pp. 46.

Verein zur Befœrderung des Gewerbfleisses in Preussen.

Verhandlungen des Vereins zur Beförderung des Gewerbfleisses in Preussen. Vier und dreissigster Jahrgang. Dazu ein Sach- und Namen-Register für die Jahrgänge 1851-55. *Berlin,* 1855. 4to.

Miscellanea.

Archiv für Naturgeschichte. Gegründet von A. F. A. WIEGMANN. Fortgestzt von W. F. ERICHSON, in Verbinding mit Prof. Dr. *Grisebach* in Göttingen, Prof. Dr. *Leuckart* in Giessen, &c. Jahrg. I—XXII, XXIII, I—III, 1835—1857. *Berlin.* 8vo.

Archiv für Mineralogie, Geognosie, Bergbau und Hüttenkunde. Herausgegeben von Dr. C. J. B. KARSTEN, I—X, 1829—1837; und Dr. H. v. DECHEN, XI—XXVI, 1838—1855. *Berlin.* 8vo.

Archiv für Anatomie, Physiologie, und wissenschaftliche Medicin. In Verbindung mit mehreren Gelehrten herausgegeben von Dr. JOHANNES MULLER. Jahrg. 1835—1857, I, II, III. *Berlin.* 8vo.

(*Purchased.*) (*Wanting,* 1852, *Hefts* IV—VI.)

Archiv für pathologische Anatomie und Physiologie und für klinische Medicin. Herausgegeben von R. VIRCHOW. IX, X, 1856. Neue Folge, I, II, 1857. *Berlin.* 8vo.

BERLIN.

Miscellanea.—*Continued.*

Archiv für wissenschaftliche Kunde von Russland. Herausgegeben von A. Erman. I—XVI, i, ii. *Berlin*, 1848–57. 8vo.

Eldenaer Archiv für landwirthschaftliche Erfahrungen und Versuche. Herausgegeben von D. Rhode, C. Trommer und F. Jüllke in Eldena. Jahrg. 1854, i; 1855, i—iii. *Berlin*, 1854, '55. 8vo.

Physikalische Belustigungen. I—III. *Berlin*, 1751–53. 8vo.

Landwirthschaftliche Zeitung für Nord- und Mitteldeutschland. Herausgegeben von Dr. C. Schneitler. Mit Holzschnitten. 1855; Jan.—Apr., 1856, 1857. *Berlin.* 4to.

Magazin für die Literatur des Auslandes. Erster Band. Februar bis Juni 1832, and 3 Januar bis 30 Marz 1854. *Berlin.* fol.

Repertorium der Physik. Enthaltend eine vollständige Zusammenstellung der neuern Fortschritte dieser Wissenschaft. Unter Mitwirkung der Herren *Lejeune-Dirichlet*, *Jacobi*, *Neumann*, *Riess*, *Strehlke*, herausgegeben von Heinrich Wilhelm Dove und Ludwig Moser. I—VIII. *Berlin*, 1837–49. 8vo.

BLANKENBERG.

Naturwissenschaftlicher Verein des Harzes.

Bericht des Naturwissenschaftlichen Vereins des Harzes für die Jahre 1840–41. 4to.

Idem für die Jahre 1842–3 und 1843–4.
" " 1844–5.
" " 1845–6.
" " 1846–7.
" " 1847–8.
" " 1848 und 1849.
" " 1851.
" " 1852.
" " 1853 und 1854.

BONN.

Naturhistorischer Verein der preussischen Rheinlande und Westphalens.

Verhandlungen des Naturhistorischen Vereins der preussischen Rheinlande und Westphalens. Jahrg. I—XIII, 1844—1856. *Bonn.* 8vo.
(Jahrg. VI, wanting.)

Correspondenzblatt des Naturhistorischen Vereins der preussischen Rheinlande und Westphalens. 1851, I—V; 1852, I—IV; 1853, I—III; 1854, I—III. *Bonn.* 8vo.

Kœnigl. Rheinische Friedrich-Wilhelms Universitæt.

Astronomische Beobachtungen auf der Sternwarte der Königlichen Rheinischen Friedrich-Wilhelms Universität zu Bonn, angestellt und herausgegeben von Dr. Friedrich Wilhelm August Argelander. Zweiter Band. Zonenbeobachtungen am Südhimmel. *Bonn,* 1852. 4to.
(From the Author.)

Verein von Alterthumsfreunden im Rheinlande.

Jahrbücher des Vereins von Alterthumsfreunden im Rheinlande. I, II. *Bonn,* 1842 & 1843. 8vo.
Idem XIII. *Bonn,* 1848.
" XVII. " 1851.
" XVIII. " 1852.
" XIX. " 1853.
" XX. " 1853.
" XXII. " 1855.
" XXV. " 1857.

Das Coelner Mosaik. Programm zu Winckelmanns Geburtstage, am 9 December 1845. *Bonn,* 1846. 8vo.

Apollon, der Heilspender: übersilberte Erzstatuette des Museums der Gesellschaft für nützliche Forschungen zu Trier. Fest-Programm zu Winckelmann's Geburtstage, am 9 December 1847, von Dr. Laurenz Lersch. *Bonn,* 1848. 4to.

Die Kapitole. Einladungs-Programm zu der am Geburtstage Winckelmann's stattfindenden Generalversammlung

BONN.

Verein von Alterthumsfreunden im Rheinlande.— *Continued.*

des Vereins von Alterthumsfreunden im Rheinlande; herausgegeben vom *Vorstande des Vereins. Bonn*, 1849. 4to.

Die römische Villa bei Weingarten. Einladungs-Programm zu der am Geburtstage Winckelmann's, den 9 December 1851, stattfindenden Generalversammlung des Vereins von Alterthumsfreunden im Rheinlande. *Bonn*, 1851. 4to.

Das Judenbad zu Andernach. Einladungs-Programm zu der am Geburtstage Winckelmann's, den 9 December 1853, stattfindenden Generalversammlung des Vereines, etc. *Bonn*, 1853. 4to.

Zur Geschichte der Thebaischen Legion. Fest-Programm zu Winckelmann's Geburtstage am 9 December 1855. *Bonn*, 1855. 4to.

Die Trojaner am Rheine. Fest-Programm zu Winckelmann's Geburtstage am 9 December 1856. *Bonn*, 1856. 4to.

BRAUNSCHWEIG.

Miscellanea.

Magazin für Insektenkunde. Herausgegeben von Karl Illiger. Sechster Band. *Braunschweig*, 1807. 8vo.

Encyclopädie der gesammten theoretischen Naturwissenschaften in ihrer Anwendung auf die Landwirthschaft; umfassend Physik, unorganische Chemie, organische Chemie, Meteorologie, Mineralogie, Geognosie, Bodenkunde, Dungelehre, Pflanzenphysiologie, Thierphysiologie und Theorie des rationellen Ackerbaues. Von Dr. M. J. Schleiden und Dr. E. E. Schmid. In drei Bänden. I —III. *Braunschweig*, 1850. 8vo.

BRESLAU.

Kaiserliche Leopoldinisch-Carolinische Akademie der Naturforscher.

Miscellanea Curiosa Medico-physica Academiæ Naturæ Curiosorum, sive Ephemeridum Medico-physicarum Ger-

BRESLAU.

Kaiserliche Leopoldinisch-Carolinische Akademie der Naturforscher.—*Continued.*

manicarum Curiosarum annus primus, anni scilicet MDCLXXmi.; continens celeberrimorum medicorum in et extra Germaniam Observationes Medicas et Physicas, vel Anatomicas, vel Botanicas, vel Pathologicas, vel Chirurgicas, vel Therapeuticas, vel Chymicas. Prefixa Epistola invitatoria ad celeberrimos medicos Europæ. Idem, Ann. II—X.—Decuriæ II, Ann. I—X.—Decuriæ III, Ann. I—X. *Lipsiæ, &c.* 1670—1706. 4to.

(*From the Royal Library, at the Hague.*)

Academiæ Cæsareo-Leopoldinæ Naturæ Curiosorum Ephemerides, sive Observationum Medico-physicarum a celeberrimis viris tum Medicis tum aliis Eruditis in Germania et extra eam communicatarum Centuriæ I—X. Cum appendice et privilegio Sacr. Cæs. Majestatis. *Francofurti et Lipsiæ, Noribergæ, Augustæ Vindelicorum,* 1712—1722. 4to.

(*From the Royal Library, at the Hague.*)

Nova Acta (s. Novorum Actorum) Physico-medica Academiæ Cæsareæ Leopoldino-Carolinæ Naturæ Curiosorum. IX, 1818; X, I, 1820; XI, 1823; XII, 1824–5; XIII, 1826–7; XIV, 1828–9; Suppl. 1829; XV, 1831; XVI, 1832–3; XVII, 1835–6; Suppl. 1836; XVIII, 1836–8; Suppl. I, II, 1841; XIX, 1839–42; Suppl. I, II, 1843; XX, 1843–4; XXI, 1845; Suppl. 1846; XXII, 1847–50; Suppl. 1852; XXIII, 1851–2; Suppl. 1856; XXIV, I, 1854; Suppl. 1854; XXV, 1855–6. *Bonnæ* et *Vratislaviæ.* 4to.

Vorwort zum vierundzwanzigsten Bande der Verhandlungen der Kais. Leopoldinisch-Carolinischen Akademie der Naturforscher. Zur Geschichte der Säcularfeier der K. L. C. Akad., etc., am 21 September 1852. *Breslau,* 1853. 4to.

Nova Acta Academiæ Caes. Leopold.-Carolinæ Naturæ Curiosorum. Vorwort zur zweiten Abtheilung des XXIV Bandes, 1854. *Breslau.* 4to.

Bonplandia. Zeitschrift für gesammte Botanik. Officielles

BRESLAU.

Kaiserliche Leopoldinisch-Carolinische Akademie der Naturforscher.—*Continued.*

Organ der K. Leopold-Carol. Akademie der Naturforscher. Jahr I, VII; II, IV, V; III, I—XVIII; IV, IV, 1853–56. *Hannover.* royal 8vo.

Fest-Rede bei der Jubelfeier der Kaiserl. Leopoldinisch-Carolinischen Akademie der Naturforscher. Gehalten den 21 September 1852 in der zweiten öffentlichen Sitzung der Versammlung der Naturforscher und Aerzte Deutschlands zu Wiesbaden vom dem Adjuncten der Akademie Dr. GEORGE VON JÄGER. *Breslau,* 1853. 4to. pp. 46.

Preisfrage der k. k. Leopoldin-Carolinischen Academie der Naturforscher. Ausgesetzt von dem Fürsten ANATOL DEMIDOFF, Mitglied der Academie (Beinamen *Franklin*), zur Feier des allerhöchsten Geburtsfestes ihrer Majestät der Kaiserin ALEXANDRA VON RUSSLAND am 17 Juni n. St. 1854. *Breslau.* 4to.

Idem 17 Juni n. St. 1855; and 13 Juli 1856.

Concours de l'Académie Impériale Leopoldo-Caroline des Naturalistes de Breslau, proposé par le Prince ANATOLE DE DEMIDOFF membre de l'Académie, sous le surnom de *Franklin,* à l'occasion de la Fête auguste de sa Majesté l'Impératrice ALEXANDRA DE RUSSIE le 17 Juin (n. St.) 1854. *Breslau,* 1853. 4to.

Idem 13 Juillet (n. s.) 1856 and 13 Juillet (n. s.) 1858. *Florence,* 1855, 1857. 4to.

Sternwarte.

Uranus, oder tägliche für Jedermann fassliche Uebersicht aller Himmelserscheinungen im Jahre 1846. *Glogau,* 1845. 8vo.

Idem, 1847. *Glogau,* 1846. 8vo.

Idem, 1848. " 1847. "

Resultate der von der Section für die Sudetenkunde im Jahre 1843, veranlasste meteorologischen Beobachtungen zu hypsometrischen und klimatologischen Zwecken.

Idem, 1845.

BRESLAU.

Sternwarte.—*Continued.*

Bericht über die Verhandlungen der Meteorologischen Section im Jahre 1852. *Galle.* 4to.

On the Use of a new Micrometer, &c. BOGUSLAWSKI. 4to.

Schlesische Gesellschaft fur vaterlændische Kultur.

Uebersicht der Arbeiten und Veränderungen der Schlesischen Gesellschaft für vaterländische Kultur. Jahre 1824—1849. Zur Kenntnissnahme für sämmtliche einheimische und auswärtige wirkliche Herrn Mitglieder der genannten Gesellschaft. *Breslau*, 1825—1850. 4to.

Achtundzwanzigster—Vierunddreissigster Jahresbericht der Schlesischen Gesellschaft für vaterländische Kultur. Enthält: Arbeiten und Veränderungen der Gesellschaft in den Jahren 1850—1856. *Breslau.* 4to.

Denkschrift zur Feier ihres 50-jährigen Bestehens, herausgegeben von der *Schlesischen Gesellschaft für vaterländische Kultur. Breslau*, 1853. 4to.

Auszug aus der Uebersicht der Arbeiten und Veränderungen der Schlesischen Gesellschaft für vaterländische Kultur in den Jahren 1840—1848. *Breslau.* [11 pamphlets.] (*From the Observatory, Breslau.*)

Bericht über die Thätigkeit der allgemeinen naturwissenschaftlichen Section der Schlesischen Gesellschaft für vaterländische Cultur im Jahre 1851, von H. R. GOPPERT. *Breslau.* 4to.

BUDA.

A' Magyar Tudos Tarsasag (*The Hungarian Scientific Association*).

A' Magyar Tudós Társaság Evkönyvei (Year-books of the Hungarian Scientific Association). Kötet I—VII. *Pesten & Budán*, 1833-46. 4to.

Régi Magyar Nyelvemlékek (Monuments of the old Hungarian Language). Kiadta *a' Magyar Tudós Társaság.* Döbrentei Gabor. Kötet I—III. *Budán*, 1838-42. 4to.

CASSEL.

Miscellanea.

Journal für Ornithologie. Ein Centralorgan für die gesammte Ornithologie. Herausgegeben von Dr. JEAN CABANIS. Jahrg. I—V, 1853–57. *Cassel.* 8vo. (*Purchased.*)

Malakozoologische Blätter. Als Fortsetzung der Zeitschrift für Malakozoologie herausgegeben von Dr. KARL THEODOR MENKE und Dr. LOUIS PFEIFFER. Bde I—III. *Cassel,* 1854—1856. 8vo. (*Wanting Title-page and Table of Contents to Vol. III.*)

CRACAU (CRACOW).

Sternwarte.

Allgemeine Übersicht der an der K. K. Krakauer Sternwarte vom Jahre 1826 bis 1852 gemachten meteorologischen Beobachtungen, zusammengestellt von Dr. MAX WEISSE. *Krakau,* 1853. Fol.

Resultate der an der Cracauer Sternwarte gemachten meteorologischen und astronomischen Beobachtungen. *Cracau,* 1839. 4to.

DANZIG.

Naturforschende Gesellschaft.

Neueste Schriften der Naturforschenden Gesellschaft in Danzig. I, 1820—1825; II, II, 1827; III, IV, 1831; III, II, 1839; IV, 1842; IV, 1843—1851; V, 1853—1856. *Danzig* and *Halle.* 4to. (*II,* I; *III,* I, III, *wanting.*)

Versuche und Abhandlungen der Naturforschenden Gesellschaft in Danzig. I, II. *Danzig,* 1747, 1754. 4to.

DARMSTADT.

Mittelrheinischer Geologischer Verein.

Die Entstehung und seitherige Wirksamkeit des Mittelrheinischen geologischen Vereins. 8vo.

Statuten des Mittelrheinischen geologischen Vereins. 8vo. pp. 4.

DARMSTADT.

Mittelrheinischer Geologischer Verein.—*Continued.*

Reports of Meetings of April 18 and Sept. 5, 1852; April 3, 1853; April 30, 1854; April 15 and Sept. 23, 1855; April 6, 1856. 8vo.

Geologische Specialkarte des Grossherzogthums Hessen und der angrenzenden Landesgebiete im Maasstabe von 1 : 50000. Herausgegeben vom *Mittelrheinischen Geologischen Verein.* Section Friedberg der Karte des Grossh. Hess. General-Quartiermeister-Stabs, geologisch bearbeitet von R. Ludwig. *Darmstadt,* 1855. 8vo. with fol. map.

Idem. Section Giessen, von Ernst Dieffenbach. *Darmstadt.* 8vo. with fol. map.

Idem. Section Büdingen, von R. Ludwig. *Darmstadt,* 1857. 8vo. with fol. map.

Naturhistorischer Verein fur das Grossherzogthum Hessen.

Verhandlungen des Naturhistorischen Vereins für das Grossherzogthum Hessen und Umgebung. Erstes Heft. *Darmstadt,* 1847. 8vo.

Verein fur Erdkunde und verwandte Wissenschaften.

Beiträge zur Landes-, Volks- und Staatskunde des Grossherzogthums Hessen. Herausgegeben vom *Vereine für Erdkunde und verwandte Wissenschaften zu Darmstadt.* Hefte I, II. *Darmstadt,* 1850, 1853. 8vo.

Notizblatt des Vereins für Erdkunde und verwandte Wissenschaften zu Darmstadt. Nos. I—XLVI. October 1854—Mai 1857. *Darmstadt.* 8vo.

Statuten des mit allerhöchster landesherrlicher Genehmigung bestehenden Vereins für Erdkunde und verwandte Wissenschaften zu Darmstadt. Zweiter Abdruck. *Darmstadt,* 1852. 8vo.

Catalog der Bibliothek des Vereins für Erdkunde und verwandte Wissenschaften in Darmstadt. I. Bücher aufgestellt in Dezember 1856. 8vo. pp. 30.

DEIDESHEIM.

Pollichia: Naturwissenschaftlicher Verein der bayerischen Pfalz.

Erster Jahresbericht der Pollichia, eines naturwissenschaftlichen Vereins der bayerischen Pfalz. Herausgegeben von dem Ausschusse des Vereins. *Landau*, 1843. 8vo.

Zweiter Bericht.	*Neustadt* a. d.	*Haardt*,	1844.
Dritter	"	"	"	1845.
Vierter	"	"	"	1846.
Fünfter	"	"	"	1847.
Sechster	"	"	"	1848.
Siebenter	"	"	"	1849.
Achter	"	"	"	1850.
Neunter	"	"	"	1851.
Zehnter	"	"	"	1852.
Elfter	"	*Speyer*,		1853.
Zwölfter	"	*Neustadt* a. d.	*Haardt*,	1854.

Statuten der Pollichia, eines naturwissenschaftlichen Vereins für die Pfalz. Zweite Ausgabe. *Neustadt* a. d. *H.*, 1855. 8vo.

DRESDEN.

Kœnigliche Polytechnische Schule.

Organisationsplan der Königlichen Polytechnischen Schule zu Dresden genehmight durch Ministerial-Verordnung vom 14 März 1855. *Dresden.* 4to.

Correspondenz-Blatt des Gesammtvereines der deutschen Geschichts- und Alterthums-Vereine. Im Auftrage des Directoriums des Gesammtvereines herausgegeben von Professor Dr. M. L. Löwe. Nos. I, II, 1852. *Dresden.* 4to.

Programm zu den am 26 und vom 29 bis 31 Marz 1855 mit den Schülern der Koniglichen Polytechnischen Schule und der Königlichen Baugewerkenschule zu Dresden zu haltenden Prüfungen. *Dresden.* 4to.

Idem, zu den Prüfungen am 10, 11, 12, und 18 März 1856; 30 und 31 März und 1 und 2 April 1857.

DRESDEN.

Koenigliche Blinden-Anstalt zu Dresden.

Jahresbericht über die Königliche Blinden-Austalt zu Dresden auf das Jahr 1856. *Dresden.* 8vo.

Miscellanea.

Hedwigia. Ein Notizblatt für kryptogamische Studien. Nos. 1—9. *Dresden,* 1852—1854. 8vo.

EMDEN.

Naturforschende Gesellschaft.

Jahresbericht über die Verrichtungen und den Zustand der Naturforschenden Gesellschaft in Emden im Jahre 1842—1847. *Emden,* 1843—1848. 8vo.

Jahresbericht über die Wirksamkeit und den Zustand, &c., im Jahre 1848—1852. *Emden,* 1849—1853. 8vo.

Jahresbericht der Naturforschenden Gesellschaft in Emden für 1853—1856. *Emden,* 1854—1857. 8vo.

Verzeichniss der Naturaliensammlung der Naturforschenden Gesellschaft in Emden. Erstes Heft. *Emden,* 1835. 16mo.

Kleine Schriften der Naturforschenden Gesellschaft in Emden. Die Gewitter des Jahres 1855. Ein Beitrag zur Physiologie der Atmosphäre von Dr. M. A. F. Prestel. *Emden,* 1856. 8vo.

Kleine nautische Ephemeriden für das Jahr 1846. Berechnet für den Meridian von Greenwich. Herausgegeben von H. C. Begemann. *Emden.* 8vo.

Idem for 1847, 1848, 1849, 1850, 1851, 1852, 1853, and 1854.

ERFURT.

Miscellanea.

Miscellania Physico-Medico-Mathematica, oder angeheme, curieuse und nützliche Nachrichten von Physical- und Medicinischen auch dahin gehörigen Kunst- und Literatur-Geschichten, welche in den Winter- und Frühlings-Monaten des Jahres 1727 in Deutschland und andern Reichen sich zugetragen haben, oder bekannt worden

ERFURT.

Miscellanea.—*Continued.*

sind, von D. Andreas Elias Büchner. *Erffurt*, 1731. 4to.

Idem, des Jahres 1728, 1729, 1730. *Erffurt*, 1732—1734.

ERLANGEN.

Universitæts-Bibliothek.

Die Universität Erlangen von 1743 bis 1843. Zum Jubiläum der Universität 1843. *Erlangen.* 8vo.

FRANKFURT AM MAIN.

Gartenbaugesellschaft "Flora."

Protokoll-Auszüge und Verhandlungen der Gartenbaugesellschaft Flora zu Frankfurt am Main. Jahrg. I—VIII, 1848–55. *Frankfurt am Main*, 1852–56. 8vo.

Physikalischer Verein zu Frankfurt.

Statuten des Physikalischen Vereins. *Frankfurt am Main*, 1836. 8vo. pp. 16.

Jahresbericht des Physikalischen Vereins zu Frankfurt am Main für das Rechnungsjahr 1846–47—1853–54. 8vo.

Senckenbergische naturforschende Gesellschaft.

Museum Senckenbergianum. Abhandlungen aus dem Gebiete der beschreibenden Naturgeschichte, von *Mitgliedern der Senckenbergischen naturforschenden Gesellschaft* in Frankfurt am Main. I, 1834; II, 1837; III, 1845. *Frankfurt am Main.* 4to.

Abhandlungen, herausgegeben von der *Senckenbergischen Naturforschenden Gesellschaft.* Bde I, II, I. *Frankfurt am Main*, 1854–55, 1856. 4to.

Verein fur Geographie und Statistik.

Mittheilungen über physisch-geographische und statistische Verhältnisse von Frankfurt am Main von dem *geographischen Vereine* daselbst. Hefte II, III. *Frankfurt am Main*, 1840, 1841. 4to.

FRANKFURT AM MAIN.

Verein fur Geographie und Statistik.—*Continued.*

Jahresbericht des Geographischen Vereins zu Frankfurt a. M. 1853–54 und 1854–55. 12mo.

Satzungen des Frankfurter Vereins für Geographie und Statistik 1854. *Frankfurt am Main.* 8vo.

Miscellanea.

Polytechnisches Notizblatt für Gewerbtreibende, Fabrikanten und Künstler. Herausgegeben und redigirt von Prof. Dr. Rud. Böttger in Frankfurt a. M. Jahrg. X, No. 1, 1855. 8vo.

FREIBERG.

Kœniglich-Sæchsische Bergakademie.

Kalender für den Sächsischen Berg- und Hüttenmann auf das Jahr 1827. Herausgegeben von der *Königl. Bergakademie zu Freiberg. Dresden & Freiberg.* 8vo.

Idem, for 1828—1851.

Jahrbuch für den Berg- und Hüttenmann auf das Jahr 1852. Herausgegeben und verlegt von der *Königl. Bergakademie zu Freiberg. Freiberg.* 8vo.

Idem, for 1853—1857.

Magazin für die Oryktographie von Sachsen. Ein Beitrag zur mineralogischen Kenntniss dieses Landes und zur Geschichte seiner Mineralien. In freien Heften herausgegeben von Johann Carl Friesleben. Hefte I—XV, 1828—1848. Extrahefte, I—IV, 1843—1848. *Freiberg.* 8vo.

FREIBURG.

Gesellschaft fur Befœrderung der Naturwissenschaften.

Berichte über die Verhandlungen der Gesellschaft für Beförderung der Naturwissenschaften zu Freiburg i. B. Redigirt vom Sekretär der Gesellschaft Dr. Maier, unter Mitwirkung von Prof. *Ecker* und *Müller.* Heft I. *Freiburg i. B.*, 1855. 8vo.

FREIBURG.

Gesellschaft fur Befœrderung, etc.—*Continued.*

Ueber die Photographie des Spectrums von Dr. L. v. BABO und Dr. J. MÜLLER. *Freiburg im Breisgau.* 4to.

FRIEDBERG.

Blinden-Anstalt.

Vierter Jahres-Bericht der Blinden-Anstalt zu Friedberg im Grossherzogthum Hessen, nebst Rechnungs-Ablage vom 1 Januar 1853 bis zum 31 Dezember 1853. *Friedberg,* 1854. 8vo.

Sechster Jahresbericht 1855. *Friedberg,* 1856.

Siebenter " 1856. " 1857.

GIESSEN.

Oberhessische Gesellschaft fur Natur- und Heilkunde.

Zweiter Bericht der Oberhessischen Gesellschaft für Natur- und Heilkunde. *Giessen,* 1849. 8vo.

Dritter Bericht, &c. *Giessen,* 1853.

Vierter Bericht, &c. " 1854.

Fünfter Bericht, &c. " 1855.

Sechster Bericht, &c. " 1857.

Miscellanea.

Jahresbericht über die Fortschritte der reinen, pharmaceutischen und technischen Chemie, Physik, Mineralogie und Geologie. Unter Mitwirkung von *H. Buff, E. Dieffenbach, C. Ettling, F. Knapp, H. Will, F. Zamminer,* herausgegeben von JUSTUS LIEBIG und HERMANN KOPP. *Giessen,* 1847—1853. 8vo.

(*Purchased.*)

GLOGAU.

Miscellanea.

Uranus, oder tägliche, für Jedermann fassliche Uebersicht aller Himmelserscheinungen im Jahre 1846. Bearbeitet und zusammengestellt von *Ernst Schubert* und *Hugo von Rothkirch,* und herausgegeben von Dr. P. H. L. VON BOGUSLAWSKI. *Glogau,* 1845. 8vo.

Idem, im Jahre 1847. *Glogau,* 1846. 8vo.

GŒRLITZ.

Naturforschende Gesellschaft.

Abhandlungen der Naturforschenden Gesellschaft zu Görlitz. Bde I—VI, VII, I, 1855. *Görlitz*, 1827—1851. 8vo.

Statuten der Naturforschenden Gesellschaft zu Görlitz. *Görlitz*, 1848. 12mo. pp. 16.

Oberlausitzische Gesellschaft der Wissenschaften.

Verzeichniss Oberlausizischer Urkunden. Bd. I. vom Jahre 965 bis 1490; II. vom Jahre 1490 bis 1803. Herausgegeben von *der Oberlausizischen Gesellschaft der Wissenschaften* in Görlitz. *Görlitz*, 1799—1824. 4to.

Geschichte der Oberlausitzischen Gesellschaft der Wissenschaften in den ersten 50 Jahren. Eine Jubelschrift zur dritten Säkularfeier derselben am 16 August 1854, von Dr. C. G. Th. Neumann. *Görlitz*, 1854. 8vo.

Neues Lausitzisches Magazin. Im Auftrage der *Oberlausitzischen Gesellschaft der Wissenschaften* herausgegeben durch deren Secretär, Dr. Ernst Tillich. Bde XXIII—XXXI, XXXIII. *Görlitz*, 1846-56. 8vo.

GŒTTINGEN.

Gœttingischer Verein Bergmænnischer Freunde.

Studien des Göttingischen Vereins Bergmännischer Freunde. Bde III—VI. *Göttingen*, 1833—1854. 8vo.

Kœnigliche Gesellschaft der Wissenschaften.

Abhandlungen der Königlichen Gesellschaft der Wissenschaften zu Göttingen. Bde I—VI, 1838-53. *Göttingen*, 1843-56. 4to.

Erste Säcularfeier der Königlichen Gesellschaft der Wissenschaften zu Göttingen am 29sten November 1851.—I. Zur Erinnerung an Albrecht von Haller und zur Geschichte der Societäten der Wissenschaften. Festrede gehalten von Rudolph Wagner.—II. Ein Blick auf die äussere Geschichte der Königlichen Gesellschaft der Wissenschaften zu Göttingen in ihrem ersten Jahrhundert,

GŒTTINGEN.

Kœnigliche Gesellschaft der Wissenschaften.—*Continued.*

vorgelesen von JOH. FRIEDR. LUDW. HAUSMANN. *Göttingen*, 1852. 4to.

Nachrichten von der G. A. Universität und der Königl. Gesellschaft der Wissenschaften zu Göttingen, January 30, 1854. 16mo. pp. 25—56.

Göttingische Gelehrte Anzeigen. Unter der Aufsicht der *Königl. Gesellschaft der Wissenschaften.* 1841—1851. *Göttingen.* 33 vols. 12mo.

Physikalisch-ökonomische Bibliothek, worinn von den neuesten Büchern, welche die Naturgeschichte, Naturlehre und die Land- und Stadtwirthschaft betreffen, zuverlässige und vollständige Nachrichten ertheilet werden, von JOHANN BECKMANN. Bde I—XX. *Göttingen*, 1770–98. 8vo.

GOTHA.

Geographische Anstalt.

Mittheilungen aus Justus Perthes' Geographischer Anstalt über wichtige neue Erforschungen auf dem Gesammtgebiete der Geographie von Dr. A. PETERMANN. 1855, 1856, 1857. *Gotha.* 4to.

Thuringer Gartenbau-Vereins zu Gotha.

Sechszehnter Jahresbericht des Thüringer Gartenbau-Vereins zu Gotha für das Jahr 1844—1845. *Gotha.* 8vo.

Siebzehnter Jahresbericht. *Gotha*, 1851.
Achtzehnter " " 1852.
Neunzehnter " " 1852.
Zwanzigster " " 1853.

GREIFSWALD.

Baltischer Verein fur Fœrderung der Landwirthschaft.

Verhandlungen des Baltischen Vereines für Förderung der Landwirthschaft. Jahrg. 1849–53. *Greifswald*, 1850—1854. 8vo.

GREIFSWALD.

Gartenbau-Verein fur Neuvorpommern und Rugen.

Erster und zweiter Jahresbericht und Mittheilungen des Gartenbau-Vereins fur Neuvorpommern und Rügen. *Greifswald*, 1847. 8vo.

Dritter Jahresbericht. *Greifswald*, 1848.

Vierter und fünfter Jahresbericht. " 1850.

Sechster und siebenter " " 1852.

Achter und neunter " " 1854.

K. P. Staats- u. landwirthschaftl. Academie Eldena.

Ueber Staats- und landwirthschaftliche Academien und deren Verbinding mit Universitäten, nebst einer kurzen Nachricht über die königlich preussische Staats- und landwirthschaftliche Academie Eldena bei Greifswald, von Dr. E. Baumstark. *Greifswald*, 1839. 8vo.

Jahrbücher der Königlich preussischen Staats- und landwirthschaftlichen Academie Eldena. Bde I—III. *Greifswald*, 1848—1853. 8vo.

Miscellanea.

Archiv für Mathematik und Physik, mit besonderer Rücksicht auf die Bedürfnisse der Lehrer an höheren Unterrichtsanstalten. Herausgegeben von Johann August Grunert. Thle XX—XXII, XXIV—XXIX, XXX, 1. *Greifswald*, 1853—1857. 8vo.
(*From Prof. J. A. Grunert.*)

Archiv skandinavischer Beiträge zur Naturgeschichte. Herausgegeben von Christian Friedrich Hornschuch. I, II. *Greifswald*, 1845, 1850. 8vo.
(*Purchased.*)

HALLE.

Naturforschende Gesellschaft.

Abhandlungen der Naturforschenden Gesellschaft zu Halle. I, 1; II, III, IV, 1. *Halle*, 1853-56. 4to.

HALLE.

Naturwissenschaftlicher Verein in Halle.

Jahresbericht des Naturwissenschaftlichen Vereins in Halle. Zweiter Jahrg. vom Juni 1849—1850. *Berlin*, 1850. 8vo.

Dritter Jahrgang 1850. *Berlin*, 1851.
Vierter " 1851. " 1852.
Fünfter " 1852. " 1853.

(*Jahrg. I, VI, et seq. wanting.*)

Zeitschrift für die gesammten Naturwissenschaften. Herausgegeben von dem Naturwissenschaftlichen Vereine für Sachsen und Thüringen in Halle. Bde I—IX, Jahrg. 1853–57. *Halle.* 8vo.

Auszug aus den Sitzungs-Protokollen des Naturwissenschaftlichen Vereins in Halle. (Erstes Jahr vom Juni 1848—Juni 1849.) *Halle.* 8vo.

Statuten des Naturwissenschaftlichen Vereines in Halle. *Halle*, 1850. 8vo.

Abhandlungen des Naturwissenschaftlichen Vereines für Sachsen und Thüringen in Halle. Herausgegeben von C. Giebel und W. Heintz. Ersten Bandes Erstes Heft. *Berlin*, 1856. 4to.

Thuringisch-sæchsischer Verein.

Neue Mittheilungen aus dem Gebiete historisch-antiquarischer Forschungen. Im Namen des mit der Königl. Universität Halle-Wittenberg verbundenen Thüringisch-sächsischen Vereins für Erforschung des vaterländischen Alterthums und Erhaltung seiner Denkmale herausgegeben von dem Secretair desselben, Dr. R. Ed. Förstemann. Bde I—VII. *Halle*, 1834–46. 8vo.

Miscellanea.

Allgemeine Monatsschrift für Literatur. Herausgegeben von Dr. L. Ross und Dr. G. Schwetschke. 1850, I, II; 1851, II; 1852, I, II; 1853, I, II; 1854. *Halle.* 8vo. (*Purchased.*)

Der Naturforscher. Stück II—XXX. *Halle*, 1774—1804. 8vo.

Linnæa. Ein Journal für die Botanik in ihrem ganzen

HALLE.

Miscellanea.—*Continued.*

Umfange. Herausgegeben von D. F. L. von SCHLECHTENDAL. Bde I—XXVIII, Jahrg. 1835–56. *Berlin* und *Halle.* 8vo.

(*Wanting Vol. IV & XXVI,* VI.)

Botanische Zeitung. Jahrg. XI, Stück 20, 22; XII, 45; XIII, 14, 37. *Halle,* 1843—1845. 4to.

Archiv für die Physiologie, von den Professoren D. JOH. CHRIST. REIL und D. J. H. F. AUTENRIETH. Bde I—XII. *Halle,* 1796—1815. 8vo.

Deutsches Archiv für die Physiologie. In Verbindung mit den Herrn *Albers, Autenrieth, Blumenbach, Döllinger, Dzóndi, Emmert, Ermen, Harles, Horkel,* u. anderen, herausgegeben von J. F. MECKEL. Bde I—VIII. *Halle und Berlin.* 1815–23. 8vo.

Unterhaltungen für Dilettanten und Freunde der Astronomie, Geographie und Meteorologie. Herausgegeben von G. A. JAHN. Jahrg. I—X, XI, 1—38, 42—50. *Leipzig* und *Halle,* 1847–57. 8vo.

(*Wanting IV, Title & No.* 7; *V, Title & Nos.* 22, 36—38; *VII,* 2, 33; *VIII,* 7—11, 27—31, 39; *IX, Title & No.* 44; *X,* 40—42; *XI,* 39—41.)

Jahrbuch der Chemie und Physik, als eine Zeitschrift des Wissenschaftlichen Vereins zur Verbreitung von Naturkenntniss und höherer Wahrheit; herausgegeben von Dr. J. S. C. SCHWEIGGER und Dr. FR. W. SCHWEIGGER-SEIDEL. 1825, I, II, III; 1826, I, II, III; 1827, I, II, III; 1828, I, II, III; 1829, I, II, II; III, III, IV [forming Vols. XXXIII—LVII of the "Journal für Chemie und Physik." See under *Nürnberg*]. *Halle.* 8vo.

(*From Dr. J. S. C. Schweigger.*)

HAMBURG.

Allgemeine Armen-Anstalt.

Nachrichten an Hamburgs wohlthätige Einwohner über den Fortgang der allgemeinen Armen-Anstalt. Nachrichten IV—IX, XXXVII. *Hamburg,* 1791, 1816. 4to.

(*Bound up with the Preetzer Wochenblatt.*)

HAMBURG.

Naturwissenschaftliche Gesellschaft.

Bericht uber die Thätigkeit der Naturwissenschaftlichen Gesellschaft in Hamburg seit ihrer Stiftung bis zu der 200sten Versammlung derselben am 29 November 1854; abgestattet von K. G. ZIMMERMANN, Dr. *Hamburg.* 8vo.

Mittheilungen aus den Verhandlungen der Naturwissenschaftlichen Gesellschaft in Hamburg vom Jahre 1845. *Hamburg,* 1846. 8vo.

Jahresbericht der Hamburgischen Naturwissenschaftlichen Gesellschaft. Abgestattet am 8 Januar 1847 vom Präsidenten derselben. *Hamburg.* 8vo.

Naturwissenschaftlicher Verein.

Abhandlungen aus dem Gebiete der Naturwissenschaften, herausgegeben von dem *Naturwissenschaftlichen Vereine* in Hamburg. I, 1846; II, II, 1852; III, 1856. *Hamburg.* 4to.

Sternwarte.

Meteorological Observations made at the Observatory of Hamburg by M. RÜMKER. 1853—1856. 4to.

Miscellanea.

Allgemeine deutsche Naturhistorische Zeitung. Im Auftrage der Gesellschaft *Isis* in Dresden und unter Mitwirkung der Herren *A. E. Brehm, R. Brehm,* etc., herausgegeben von Dr. ADOLPH DRECHSLER. Neue Folge. I—III. *Hamburg,* 1855—1857. 8vo.

Hamburgisches Magazin, oder gesammelte Schriften, zum Unterricht und Vergnügen, aus der Naturforschung und den angenehmen Wissenschaften überhaupt. Bde I—XXVI. *Hamburg,* 1748-62. 8vo.

Dreyfaches Universalregister und Repertorium über die 26 Bände des Hamburgischen Magazins, oder der gesammleten Schriften aus der Naturforschung, der Œkonomie und den nützlichen Wissenschaften. *Hamburg* und *Leipzig,* 1767. 8vo.

Neues Hamburgisches Magazin, oder Fortsetzung gesammelter Schriften aus der Naturforschung, der allgemeinen

HAMBURG.

Miscellanea.—*Continued.*

Stadt- und Land-Oekonomie und den angenehmen Wissenschaften überhaupt. Bde I—XVIII. *Hamburg* und *Leipzig*, 1767–77. 8vo.

Hamburg und Altona. Eine Zeitschrift zur Geschichte der Zeit, der Sitten und des Geschmacks. 1801–2, I—IV; 1803, I—IV; 1804, I—IV; 1805, I—IV. *Hamburg.* 8vo.

HANNOVER.

Gewerbe-Verein fur das Kœnigreich Hannover.

Mittheilungen des Gewerbe-Vereins für das Königreich Hannover. Neue Folge. Jahrg. 1853—1857. Redaktion: Direktor KARMARSCH.—Amtsassessor VON RUDLOFF. *Hannover.* 4to.

Miscellanea.

Archiv der Pharmacie. Unter Mitwirkung der Herrn *Bredschneider*, *Casper*, *Droste*, &c., herausgegeben von L. BLEY. Zweite Reihe. Bde LXXXI—LXXXIV, LXXXIX—XCII. (Der ganzen Folge Bde CXXXI—CXXXIV, CXXXIX—CXLII.) *Hannover*, 1855, 1857. 8vo.

HEIDELBERG.

Miscellanea.

Heidelberger Jahrbücher der Literatur. Jahrg. XLIII, XLIV, XLV, No. 15. 1850, 1851, 1852. *Heidelberg.* 8vo.

(*Purchased. Wanting Jahrg. XLIV, No.* 60.)

HERMANNSTADT.

Verein fur Siebenburgische Landeskunde.

Jahresbericht des Vereines für Siebenbürgische Landeskunde für das Jahr 1853, vom Vereins-Sekretär. *Hermannstadt*, 1854. 8vo. pp. 17.

INNSBRUCK.

Ferdinandeum.

Neue Zeitschrift des Ferdinandeums für Tirol und Vorarlberg. Herausgegeben von den Kuratoren desselben. Bde I—XII, 1835—1846. 8vo.

Zeitschrift des Ferdinandeums für Tirol und Vorarlberg. Herausgegeben von dem Verwaltungs-Ausschusse desselben. Dritte Folge. Hefte I—III, VI. *Innsbruck*, 1853, 1857. 8vo.

Ferdinandeum. Vierundzwanzigster combinirter Jahresbericht des Verwaltungs-Ausschusses für die Jahre 1847—1850. *Innsbruck*, 1851. 8vo.

Fünfundzwanzigster Jahresbericht 1851–1852. *Innsbruck*, 1853. 8vo.

Sechsundzwanzigster Jahresbericht 1853–1854. *Innsbruck*, 1856. 8vo.

Siebenundzwanzigster Jahresbericht 1855–1856. *Innsbruck*, 1857. 8vo.

Naturhistorisches Landesmuseum von Kærnten.

Jahrbuch des Naturhistorischen Landesmuseums von Kärnten. Herausgegeben von J. L. Canaval. Jahrg. I, II, 1852, 1853. *Klagenfurt*. 8vo.

(*From the University Library.*)

JENA.

Grossherzogl. herzogl. sæchs. Gesammt-Universitæt.

Annales Academiæ Jenensis. I. *Jenæ*, 1823. 4to.

Verein fur Thuringische Geschichte und Alterthumskunde.

Zeitschrift des Vereins für Thüringische Geschichte und Alterthumskunde. Erster Band. *Jena*, 1852—1854. 8vo.

Miscellanea.

Isis oder Encyclopädische Zeitung von Oken. Jahrg. 1817—1848. *Jena*, *Zurich*, and *Leipzig*. 4to.

KARLSRUHE.

Grossherzogliche Hofbibliothek.

Zeitschrift für die Geschichte des Oberrheins. Herausgegeben von dem Landesarchive zu Karlsruhe, durch den Direktor desselben, F. J. MONE. Bde I—VI. *Karlsruhe*, 1850—1855. 8vo.

KIEL.

Landwirthschaftlicher Generalverein des Herzogthums Holstein.

Landwirthschaftliches Wochenblatt für die Herzogthümer Schleswig-Holstein und Lauenburg. Herausgegeben von *dem Landwirthschaftlichen Generalverein des Herzogthums Holstein*, 1854. *Kiel*. 4to.

Universitæt zu Kiel.

Schriften der Universität zu Kiel aus den Jahren 1854-56. Bde I—III. *Kiel*, 1855-57. 4to.

Schleswig-Holstein-Lauenburgische Gesellschaft fur vaterlændische Geschichte.

Archiv für Staats- und Kirchengeschichte der Herzogthümer Schleswig-Holstein, Lauenburg und der angrenzenden Länder und Städte. Namens der *S. H. L. Gesellschaft für vaterländische Geschichte*, redigirt von MICHELSEN und ASMUSSEN. Bde I—V. *Altona*, 1833—43. 8vo.

Nordalbingische Studien. Neues Archiv der Schleswig-Holstein-Lauenburgischen Gesellschaft für vaterländische Geschichte. Bde I—V, VI, I. *Kiel*, 1844-51. 8vo.

Urkundenbuch zur Geschichte des Landes Dithmarschen. Gesammelt und Namens *der Schleswig-Holstein-Lauenburgischen Gesellschaft fur Vaterländische Geschichte* herausgegeben von ANDR. LUDW. JAC. MICHELSEN. *Altona*, 1834. 4to.

Urkundenbuch zur Geschichte des Landes Wirthmarschen. Gesammelt and Namens der *Schleswig-Holstein-Lauenburgischen Gesellschaft für vaterländische Geschichte*

KIEL.

Schleswig-Holstein-Lauenburgische Gesellschaft fur vaterlændische Geschichte.—*Continued.*

herausgegeben von A. L. J. Michelsen. *Altona*, 1834. 4to.

Urkundensammlung der Schleswig-Holstein-Lauenburgischen Gesellschaft für vaterländische Geschichte. Bde I, 1839–49; II, I, 1842, II, 1848. *Kiel.* 4to.

Schleswig-Holstein-Lauenburgische Gesellschaft fur die Sammlung und Erhaltung vaterlændischer Alterthumer.

Erster Bericht der Königl. Schleswig-Holstein-Lauenburgischen Gesellschaft für die Sammlung und Erhaltung vaterländischer Alterthümer. Erstattet von dem Vorstande gedachter Gesellschaft. *Kiel*, 1836. 8vo.

Zweiter Bericht,	1837.	Eilfter Bericht,	1846.
Vierter "	1832.	Zwölfter "	1847.
Fünfter "	1840.	Dreizehnter "	1848.
Sechster "	1841.	Vierzehnter "	1849.
Achter "	1843.	Fünfzehnter "	1850.

Der Silberfund von Farve beschrieben und Namens der *S. H. L. Gesellschaft für Sammlung und Erhaltung vaterländischer Alterthümer* bekannt gemacht von Dr. J. Friedlænder und Prof. K. Mullenhoff. *Kiel*, 1850. 8vo. pp. 68.

Zur Runenlehre. Zwei Abhandlungen von R. v. Liliencron und K. Mullenhoff, Professoren in Kiel. *Halle*, 1852. 8vo. pp. 67.

Miscellanea.

Astronomische Nachrichten, begründet von H. C. Schumacher. Herausgegeben von Professor Dr. C. A. F. Peters. XXXIX—XLIII, XLV. *Altona*, 1855–57. 4to.

KŒNIGSBERG.

Kœnigliche Universitæts-Sternwarte.

Astronomische Beobachtungen auf der Königlichen Universitäts-Sternwarte in Königsberg, von F. W. Bessel. Abthl. I—XXXI, 1813—1852. *Königsberg*, 1815—57. fol.

(*Wanting XXIX.*)

Miscellanea.

Königsberger Naturwissenschaftliche Unterhaltungen. Bde I, 1847; II, i, 1848, ii, 1851, iii, 1852. Neue Folge. I, i, 1854, ii, 1856. *Königsberg.* 8vo.

KREMSMÜNSTER.

Magnetische Observatorium.

Ueber das Magnetische Observatorium in Kremsmünster und die vom Jahre 1839-50 aus den Beobachtungen abgeleiteten Resultate von P. Augustin Reslhuber. *Wien*, 1854-57. 4to.

Idem, in den Jahren 1851, 1852, 1853. *Wien*, 1856.

Idem, im Jahre 1854. *Wien*, 1857.

LEIPZIG.

Deutsche Morgenlændische Gesellschaft.

Zeitschrift der Deutschen Morgenländischen Gesellschaft, herausgegeben von den Geschäftsführern. Bde I—XI. *Leipzig*, 1847—1857. 8vo.

Jahresbericht der Deutschen Morgenländischen Gesellschaft für das Jahr 1845. *Leipzig*, 1846. 8vo.

Abhandlungen für die Kunde des Morgenlandes, herausgegeben von *der Deutschen Morgenländischen Gesellschaft* unter der verantwortlichen Redaction des Prof. Dr. Hermann Brockhaus. Bd. I, ii. *Leipzig*, 1857. 8vo.

Furstlich Jablonowski'sche Gesellschaft.

Jahresbericht der Fürstlich Jablonowski'schen Gesellschaft im März 1854 & April 1856. *Leipzig.* 8vo.

Preisschriften gekrönt und herausgegeben von der Fürst-

LEIPZIG.

Furstlich Jablonowski'sche Gesellschaft.—*Cont'd.*

lich Jablonowski'schen Gesellschaft zu Leipzig.—IV. J. ZECH, Astronomische Untersuchungen über die wichtigeren Finsternisse, welche von den Schriftstellern des classischen Alterthums erwähnt werden. *Leipzig*, 1853. 8vo.

Kœniglich Sæchsische Gesellschaft der Wissenschaften.

Abhandlungen der Königlich Sächsischen Gesellschaft der Wissenschaften. Bde I, II. *Leipzig*, 1846, 1850. 8vo.

Berichte über die Verhandlungen der Königlich Sächsischen Gesellschaft der Wissenschaften zu Leipzig. Bde I, II. Aus den Jahren 1846, 1847—1848. *Leipzig*, 1848, 1849. 8vo.

Idem. Philologisch-historische Classe. Bde I—VII, VIII, I, II. *Leipzig*, 1849—1856. 8vo.

Idem. Mathematisch-physische Classe. Bde I—VIII, IX, I. *Leipzig*, 1849—1857. 8vo.

Bericht über die Schriften welche die Kœniglich Sæchsische Gesellschaft der Wissenschaften in Leipzig seit ihrer Begründung bis jetzt veröffentlicht hat. *Leipzig*, 1853. 8vo. pp. 10.

DROBISCH (M. W.), Nachträge zur Theorie der Musikalischen Tonverhältnisse. *Leipzig*, 1855. 8vo.

DROBISCH (M. W.), Ueber Musikalische Tonbestimmung und Temperatur. *Leipzig*. 8vo.

SEBECK (A.), Ueber die Querschwingungen gespannter und nicht gespannter elasticher Stäbe. *Leipzig*, 1849. 8vo.

MOBIUS (A. F.), Uber die Grundformen der Linien der dritten Ordnung. *Leipzig*, 1849. 8vo.

WEBER (WILH.), Elektro-dynamische Maassbestimmungen, insbesondere Widerstandsmessungen. *Leipzig*, 1850. 8vo.

WEBER (WILH.), Elektro-dynamische Maassbestimmungen, insbesondere über Diamagnetismus. *Leipzig*, 1852. 8vo.

KOHLRAUSCH (R.) und WILHELM WEBER, Elektro-dynamische Maassbestimmungen, insbesondere Zurückführung der Stromintensitäts-Messungen auf mechanisches Maas. *Leipzig*, 1856. 8vo.

LEIPZIG.

Kœniglich Sæchsische Gesellschaft der Wissenschaften.—*Continued.*

Hofmeister (W.), Beiträge zur Kenntniss der Gefässkryptogamen.—I. Die Entwickelungsgeschichte der Isoëtes lacrustis. *Leipzig*, 1852. 8vo.

Hofmeister (W.), Beitrage zur Kenntniss der Gefässkryptogamen.—II. Farrnkräuter. Ophioglosseen. Salvinia. Mit 13 Tafeln. *Leipzig*, 1857. 8vo.

Polemii Silvii Laterculus. Herausgegeben von Theodor Mommsen. *Leipzig*, 1853. 8vo.

Volusii Maeciani Distributio Partium. Herausgegeben von Theodor Mommsen. *Leipzig*, 1853. 8vo.

Schlömilch (O.), Ueber einige allgemeine Reihenentwickelungen und deren Anwendung auf die elliptischen Funktionen. *Leipzig*, 1854. 8vo.

Schlömilch (O.), Ueber die Bestimmung der Massen und der Trägheitsmomente symmetrischer Rotationskörper von ungleichförmiger Dichtigkeit. *Leipzig*, 1854. 8vo.

D'Arrest (H.), Resultate aus Beobachtungen der Nebelflecken und Sternhaufen. Erste Reihe. *Leipzig*, 1856. 8vo.

Hansen (P. A.), Auseinandersetzung einer zweckmässigen Methode zur Berechnung der absoluten Störungen der kleinen Planeten, 1856–7. Zweite Abhandlung. *Leipzig*, 1857. 8vo.

Hankel (W. G.), Elektrische Untersuchungen. Zweite Abhandlung: Ueber die thermoelektrischen Eigenschaften des Boracites. *Leipzig*, 1857. 8vo.

Polytechnische Gesellschaft.

Die Leipziger Polytechnische Gesellschaft. Fünfter Bericht. 1844—1856. *Leipzig*, 1857. 8vo. pp. 70.

University Library.

Die urkundlichen Quellen zur Geschichte der Universität Leipzig in den ersten 150 Jahren ihres Bestehens, von Friedrich Zarncke. *Leipzig*. 8vo.

Leipziger Repertorium der deutschen und ausländischen Literatur. Unter Mitwirkung der *Universität Leipzig*

LEIPZIG.

University Library.—*Continued.*

herausgegeben von Dr. E. G. GERSDORF. Jahrg. VII—XIII. *Leipzig*, 1849—1855. 8vo.

(*Wanting, Jahrg. I—VI; IX*, III, *Heft* 5; *X*, III.)

Miscellanea.

Acta Eruditorum, Annis MDCLXXXII—MDCCXXXI publicata. *Lipsiae.* 4to.

Nova Acta Eruditorum, Annis MDCCXXXII—MDCCXLV publicata. *Lipsiae.* 4to.

Akademische Monatsbericht. Centralorgan für die Gesammtinteressen deutscher Universitäten. Herausgegeben under der Mitwirkung der Herren Professoren Dr. *Bluhme* in Bonn, Dr. *Bülau*, Dr. *Erdmann* in Leipzig, Dr. *Hoffmann* in Würzburg, Hofrath Dr. *Oppolzer* in Wien, Geheimrath Dr. *V. Vangerow* in Heidelberg, und anderer akademischer Lehrer von Dr. J. J. LANG und Dr. H. TH. SCHLETTER. Der "Deutschen Universitäts-*Zeitung*" Jahrg. III, 1851; IV, 1852; V, 1853 (*sign.* 15 and 16 *wanting*); VI, I, II, III, 1854. *Leipzig.* 8vo.

Allgemeine Encyklopädie der Wissenschaften und Künste in alphabetischer Folge von genannten Schriftstellern bearbeitet und herausgegeben von J. S. ERSCH und J. G. GRUBER. Erste Section. Bde I—LXVI. *Leipzig*, 1818—1857. Zweite Section. I—VI, VIII—XVII, XIX—XXXI. *Hamburg* und *Leipzig*, 1827—1855. Dritte Section. I—XIX, XXI—XXV. *Hamburg* und *Leipzig*, 1830—1850. 4to.

(*From F. A. Brockhaus.*)

Allgemeine Encyklopädie der Physik. Bearbeitet von *C. W. Brix* in Berlin, *G. Decher* in Augsburg, *F. C. O. Von Feilitzsch* in Griefswald, *F. Grashof* in Berlin, *F. Harms* in Kiel, *H. Helmholtz* in Bonn, *G. Karsten* in Kiel, *H. Karsten* in Rostock, *C. Kuhn* in München, *J. Lamont* in München, *F. Metz* in Augsburg, *J. Pfeffer* in Augsburg, *E. E. Schmidt* in Jena, *F. Schultz* in Rostock, *L. Siedel* in München, *G. Weyer* in Kiel. Herausgegeben

LEIPZIG.

Miscellanea.—*Continued.*

von Gustav Karsten. Lief. I—III. *Leipzig*, 1856, 1857. 8vo.

Allgemeine Literatur-Zeitung vom Jahre 1849. Erster Band. Januar bis Juni. *Halle* und *Leipzig*. 4to.

Annalen der Physik. Angefangen von D. Friedr. Albr. Carl Gren, fortgesetzt von Ludwig Wilhelm Gilbert. Bde I—LXXVI. *Halle* und *Leipzig*, 1799—1824. 8vo.

Sach- und Namen-Register zu den 76 Bänden der vom Prof. Dr. Ludwig Wilhelm Gilbert vom Jahre 1799 bis 1824 herausgegebenen Annalen der Physik und der physikalischen Chemie. Angefertigt von Heinrich Müller. *Leipzig*, 1826. 8vo.

Annalen der Physik und Chemie. Zweite Reihe. Herausgegeben zu Berlin von J. C. Poggendorff. Bde I—XXVII, 1834—1842. *Leipzig*. 8vo.
(*Vol. XIX wanting.*)

Idem. Dritte Reihe. XIII—XXX, 1848—1853. Ergänzungsbände I, III, IV. Vierte Reihe. I—XI, 1854–57.
(*Wanting Vierte Reihe, II,* iii, iv; *III.*)

Biographisch-literarisches Handwörterbuch zur Geschichte der exacten Wissenschaften, enthaltend Nachweisungen uber Lebensverhältnisse und Leistungen von Mathematikern, Astronomen, Physikern, Chemikern, Mineralogen Geologen usw. aller Völker und Zeiten, gesammelt von J. C. Poggendorff. Erste Lieferung. *Leipzig*, 1858. 8vo.

Anzeiger für Bibliographie und Bibliothekwissenschaft. Herausgegeben von Dr. Julius Petzholdt. *Dresden* und *Leipzig*, 1840—1847. *Halle*, 1848—1854. 8vo.
(*Wanting*, 1853, v, vi; 1854, i—x.)

Zeitung für Zoologie, Zootomie und Palæontologie. Herausgegeben von Dr. E. d'Alton, und Dr. H. Burmeister. Jahrg. 1848, i, ii. *Leipzig*. 4to.

Archiv für Anatomie und Physiologie. In Verbindung mit mehreren Gelehrten herausgegeben von Johann Friedrich Meckel. I—VI, 1826—1832. *Leipzig*. 8vo.

Archiv für den thierischen Magnetismus. In Verbindung mit mehreren Naturforschern herausgegeben von Dr.

LEIPZIG.

Miscellanea.—*Continued.*

C. A. Eschenmayer, Dr. D. G. Kieser, Dr. Fr. Nasse. Bde I—X. *Altenburg* und *Leipzig*, 1817—1821. 8vo.

Conversations-Lexikon der neuesten Zeit und Literatur. In vier Bänden. I—IV. *Leipzig*, 1832—1834. 8vo.

Allgemeine deutsche Real-Encyklopädie für die gebildeten Stände. (Conversations-Lexikon.) I—XII. *Leipzig*, 1833-37. 8vo.

Universal-Register des Conversations-Lexikons. *Leipzig*, 1839.

Illustrirte Zeitung. Wöchentliche Nachrichten über alle Ereignisse, Zustände und Persönlichkeiten der Gegenwart. Bde I—XVIII, 1843—1852. *Leipzig*. fol.

Journal für Praktische Chemie. Herausgegeben von Otto Linne Erdmann und Gustav Werther. Siebzigsten Bandes sechstes Heft. *Leipzig*, 1857. 8vo.

Neue gesellschaftliche Erzählungen für die Liebhaber der Naturlehre, der Haushaltungswissenschaft, der Arztneykunst und der Sitten. I—IV. *Leipzig*, 1758—1762. 8vo.

Rhea. Zeitschrift für die gesammte Ornithologie. Im Vereine mit ornithologischen Freunden herausgegeben von Dr. Friedrich August Ludwig Thienemann. Hefte I, II. *Leipzig*, 1846, 1849. 8vo.

Serapeum. Zeitschrift für Bibliothekwissenschaft, Handschriftenkunde und ältere Litteratur. Im Vereine mit Bibliothekaren und Litteraturfreunden herausgegeben von Dr. Robert Naumann. Jahrg. I—XVI. *Leipzig*, 1840—1855. 8vo.

Wöchentliche Unterhaltungen für Dilettanten und Freunde der Astronomie, Geographie und Witterungskunde. Herausgegeben von Dr. G. A. Jahn. [See under *Halle*, p. 56: Unterhaltungen für Dilletanten und Freunde der Astronomie, &c.]

Zeitschrift für wissenschaftliche Zoologie. Herausgegeben von Carl Theodor v. Siebold und Albert Kölliker. I—VI, VII, i, ii, iii. *Leipzig*, 1849—1855. 8vo.

(*Purchased.*)

LEIPZIG.

Miscellanea.—*Continued.*

Zeitschrift für die Entomologie. Herausgegeben von ERNST FRIEDRICH GERMAR. II, I. *Leipzig*, 1840. 8vo. (*From Prof. Jaeger.*)

LÜNEBURG.

Naturwissenschaftlicher Verein.

Denkschriften des Naturwissenschaftlichen Vereins für das Fürstenthum Lüneburg in Lüneburg. Erster Band. Monographie des Borazites von C. H. OTTO VOLGER. *Hannover*, 1855. 8vo.

Naturwissenschaftlicher Verein des Fürstenthums Lüneburg. *Lüneburg*, 1857. 4to.

LUXEMBOURG.

Societe des Sciences Naturelles du Grand-Duche de Luxembourg.

Société des Sciences Naturelles du Grand-Duché de Luxembourg. Tomes I—III. *Luxembourg*, 1853—1855. 8vo.

MANNHEIM.

Sternwarte.

Die Sternwarte zu Mannheim. Beschrieben von ihrem Curator, dem Staats- und Cabinetstrath Klüber. *Mannheim*, 1811. 4to.

Verein fur Naturkunde.

Jahresberichte des Mannheimer Vereines für Naturkunde. 1839–56. 8vo.

MARBURG.

Gesellschaft zur Befœrderung der gesammten Naturwissenschaften.

Schriften der Gesellschaft zur Beförderung der gesammten Naturwissenschaften zu Marburg. Bde I—VIII. *Marburg*, 1823—1857. 8vo.

MEININGEN.

Verein fur Pomologie und Gartenbau.

Der Verein für Pomologie und Gartenbau in Meiningen. Hefte I—VI. *Meiningen*, 1846–57. 8vo.

MEISSEN.

Isis.

Chronik des Gartenwesens und Feuilleton der Isis. (*Chas. A. Geyer.*) Jahrg. 1851—1853. *Meissen*. 4to.

MERSEBURG.

Central-Direction fur die Provinz Sachsen.

Zeitschrift des landwirthschaftlichen Central-Vereins der Provinz Sachsen. Jahrg. IV—VII, *Zörbig*, 1847–50. 4to. VIII—X, *Bedra* und *Halle*, 1851–53. XI—XIII, *Wallendorf*, 1854–56. 8vo.

MÜNCHEN (MUNICH).

Kœniglich-Bayerische Akademie der Wissenschaften.

Geschichte der baierischen Akademie der Wissenschaften, auf Verlangen derselben verfertigt von LORENZ WESTENRIEDER. Thle I, II, 1759—1800. *München*, 1784, 1807. 8vo.

Abhandlungen der Churfürstlich-baierischen Akademie der Wissenschaften. I—X, 1763—1776. *München*. 4to.
(*From the Königliche Hof- und Staats-Bibliothek.*)

Neue philosophische Abhandlungen der Baierischen Akademie der Wissenschaften. I—VII. *München*, 1780–97. 4to.

Historische Abhandlungen der Koniglich-Baierischen Akademie der Wissenschaften. I—V, 1807—1823. *München*. 4to.
(*From the Königliche Hof- und Staats-Bibliothek.*)

Abhandlungen der Philosophisch-philologischen Classe der Königlich bayerischen Akademie der Wissenschaften.

MÜNCHEN.

Kœniglich Bayerische Akademie der Wissenschaften.—*Continued.*

I—VI, 1835—1852; VII, 1853; VIII, I, 1856; II, 1857. *München.* 4to.

Abhandlungen der Mathematisch-physikalischen Classe der Königlich bayerischen Akademie der Wissenschaften. I—VII, 1832—1855; VIII, I, 1857. *München.* 4to.

Abhandlungen der Historischen Classe der Königlich-bayerischen Akademie der Wissenschaften. I—VI, 1833—1852; VII, 1853; VIII, I, 1856. *München.* 4to.

Bulletin der Königl. Akademie der Wissenschaften. Jahrg. 1847—1853. *München.* 4to.

Almanach der Königlich-bayerischen Akademie der Wissenschaften für die Jahre 1849 & 1855. *München.* 12mo.

Gelehrte Anzeigen. Herausgegeben von Mitgliedern der *K. bayer. Akademie der Wissenschaften.* Bde I—XLIV. *München,* 1835—1857. 4to.

Kœnigliche Hof- und Staats-Bibliothek.

(*See K. Bayer. Akademie der Wissenschaften.*)

Landwirthschaftlicher Verein.

Zeitschrift des landwirthschaftlichen Vereins in Bayern. (Jahrg. XLVI des Centralblattes.) *München,* 1856. 8vo.

Munchener Verein fur Naturkunde.

Namen der Mitglieder des Münchener Vereins für Naturkunde. Uebergeben am Stiftungsfeste im May 1849, von G. TILESIUS. *München.* 8vo. pp. 8.

Statuten des Münchener Vereins für Naturkunde. Uebergeben am Stiftungsfeste, im Mai 1849, von G. TILESIUS. *München,* 1849. 8vo. pp. 8.

Polytechnischer Verein.

Kunst- und Gewerbe-Blatt. Herausgegeben von dem Polytechnischen Verein für das Königreich Bayern. Redigirt durch Dr. KAJ. G. KAISER. Jahrg. XLI, XLII. *München,* 1855, 1856. 4to.

MÜNCHEN.

Kœnigliche Sternwarte.

Ueber das magnetische Observatorium der königl. Sternwarte bei München. Eine öffentliche Vorlesung gehalten in der festlichen Sitzung der königl. Akademie der Wissenschaften am 25 August 1840, von Dr. J. Lamont. *München*, 1841. 4to.

Resultate der magnetischen Beobachtungen in München während der dreijährigen Periode 1840, 1841, 1842. Von J. Lamont. *München*, 1843. 4to.

Annalen der königlichen Sternwarte bei München, auf öffentliche Kosten herausgegeben von Dr. J. Lamont. Bde I—IX (vollst. Samml. XVI—XXIV), 1848—1857. *München*. 8vo.

NEUBRANDEBURG.

Verein der Freunde der Naturgeschichte in Mecklenburg.

Archiv des Vereins der Freunde der Naturgeschichte in Mecklenburg. Hefte I—VIII, X, XI. Herausgegeben von Ernst Boll. *Neubrandeburg*, 1847—1856. 8vo. (*From L. Vortisch.*)

NÜRNBERG.

Germanisches Museum.

Organismus der Germanischen Nationalmuseums zu Nürnberg. *Nürnberg* und *Leipzig*, 1855. 8vo.

Dritter Jahresbericht des Germanischen National Museums zu Nürnberg, von Anfang September 1855 bis 1 October 1856. *Nürnberg*, 1856. 4to.

Denkschriften des Germanischen Nationalmuseums. Bd. I, i, ii. *Nürnberg*, 1856. 8vo.

Anzeiger für Kunde der Deutschen Vorzeit. Organ des Germanischen Museums. Neue Folge. Vierter Band. *Nürnberg*, 1857. 4to.

Naturhistorische Gesellschaft.

Abhandlungen der Naturhistorischen Gesellschaft zu Nürnberg. Heft I. *Nürnberg*, 1852. 8vo.

NÜRNBERG.

Miscellanea.

Archiv für die gesammte Naturlehre, in Verbindung mit *Bischof, Förstemann, C. G. Gmelin, Grischow, F. v. Paula Gruithhuisen, Hallaschka, Pl. Heinrich, A. v. Humboldt, John, Kleefeldt, Lichtenberg, Marx, Olbers, Pleischl, Prechtl, Schmidt, Schön, Späth, Wöllner* und *Zimmermann*, herausgegeben vom Dr. K. W. G. Kastner. Bde I—XXVII. *Nürnberg*, 1824–35. 8vo.

Murr (Christ. Gottl. von), Journal zur Kunstgeschichte und zur allgemeinen Litteratur. I—XVII. *Nürnberg*, 1775–89. 16mo.

Neues Journal für Chemie und Physik, herausgegeben vom Dr. J. S. C. Schweigger. Band IX, i, ii, iii. *Nürnberg*, 1823. 8vo.

PESTH.

A' Magyar Tudos Tarsasag (*The Hungarian Scientific Association.*)

(See under *Buda.*)

PRAG (PRAGUE).

Bœhmisches Museum.

Verhandlungen der Gesellschaft des vaterländischen Museums in Böhmen. 1823, 1824, 1828, 1831—1844, 1846—1853, 1855, 1856. *Prag.* 8vo.

Das vaterländische Museum in Böhmen im Jahre 1842. *Prag.* 8vo.

Nowoceská Bibliothéka, wydáwaná nákladem *Ceskeho Museum.* V.—*Josefa Jungmanna* Slowesnost. XII.—*W. Wladiwoje Tomka* deje University Prazské. XV.—*Ign. Jana Hanuse* Rozbor Filosofie Tomáse ze Stitneho. XVIII.—*W. Wladiwoje Tomka* Dejepis Prahy. *Praze*, 1846, '49, '52, '55. 8vo.

Casopis Ceského Museum 1852, 1854, 1855. Redaktor, Vaclav Nebesky. *Praze.* 8vo.

PRAG.

Kœniglich-Bœhmische Gesellschaft der Wissenschaften.

Abhandlungen der Königlichen böhmischen Gesellschaft der Wissenschaften. Fünfte Folge. Bde I—IX. *Prag*, 1841—1857. 4to.

Uebersicht sämmtlicher in den bisherigen Bänden von Abhandlungen der K. böhmischen Gesellschaft der Wissenschaften vorkommenden Aufsätze. Für die Abhandlungen der K. böhm. Gesellschaft der Wissenschaften. *Prag*, 1823. 8vo.

Systematisch und chronologisch geordnetes Verzeichniss sämmtlicher Werke und Abhandlungen der Königl. böhmischen Gesellschaft der Wissenschaften. Verfasst von IGN. J. HANUS. *Prag*, 1854. 8vo.

Vorträge gehalten in der öffentlichen Sitzung der Königlichen böhmischen Gesellschaft der Wissenschaften bei ihrer ersten Jubelfeier am 14 September, 1836. *Prag*, 1837. 8vo.

Uebersicht der Sitzungen der Königl. Böhm. Gesellschaft der Wissenschaften im Studienjahre 1852-1853. fol. pp. 2.

Neue Statuten der K. böhm. Gesellschaft der Wissenschaften. *Prag*. 4to. pp. 4.

Berichte über die Versammlungen der Königlichen böhmischen Gesellschaft der Wissenschaften in ihren Sections-Versammlungen von 1840 und 1841. *Prag*, 1842. 4to.

Würdigung der alten böhmischen Geschichtschreiber. Eine von der K. böhmischen Gesellschaft der Wissenschaften gekrönte Preisschrift von FRANZ PALACKY. *Prag*, 1830. 8vo.

Magnetische und meteorologische Beobachtungen zu Prag, in Verbindung mit mehreren Mitarbeitern ausgeführt und auf öffentliche Kosten herausgegeben von KARL KREIL und KARL JELINEK. Jahrg. I—VIII, X, 1841—1851. Herausgegeben von Dr. JOS. G. BÖHM und Dr. ADELBERT KUNES. Jahrg. XII, XIV—XVII, 1854-57. *Prag*. 4to.

Magnetische und geographische Ortsbestimmungen in Böh-

PRAG.

Kœniglich-Bœhmische Gesellschaft der Wissenschaften.—*Continued.*

men, ausgeführt in den Jahren 1843—1845, von KARL KREIL. *Prag,* 1846. 4to.

Magnetische und geographische Ortsbestimmungen, im österreichischen Kaiserstaate ausgeführt von KARL KREIL und KARL FRITSCH. Jahrg. I—V, 1846—1851. *Prag.* 4to.

Resultate aus den Magnetischen Beobachtungen zu Prag von KARL KREIL. *Wien,* 1855. 4to.

K. k. patriotisch-œkonomische Gesellschaft.

Neue Schriften der Kais. königl. patriotisch-ökonomischen Gesellschaft im Konigreiche Böhmen. I—X. *Prag,* 1828–46. 8vo.

Verhandlungen und Mittheilungen der K. k. patriotisch-ökonomischen Gesellschaft im Konigreiche Böhmen, und des mit ihr verbundenen Schafzüchter-, so wie des pomologischen Vereins. Bde I, II. *Prag,* 1849, 1850. 8vo.

Centralblatt der Land- und Forstwirthschaft in Böhmen. Herausgegeben von der *K. k. patriotisch-ökonomischen Gesellschaft im Königreiche Böhmen.* (Nebst den unentgeltlich beigegebenen: Verhandlungen und Mittheilungen der K. k. patriotisch ökonomischen Gesellschaft in Böhmen.) Jahrg. I—VII, 1850—1856. *Prag.* 4to.

Wochenblatt der Land-, Forst-, und Hauswirthschaft für den Bürger und Landmann. Herausgegeben von der *K. k. patriotisch ökonomischen Gesellschaft im Königreiche Böhmen.* Jahrg. I—VII, 1850—1856. *Prag.* 4to.

Týdennik, casopis pro polní, lesni a domácí hospodárstwi. Rocn. 1850—1853. *V Praze.* 4to.

Hospodárské Noviny. Rocn. V—VII, 1854—1856. *V Praze.* 4to.

Naturhistorischer Verein "Lotos."

Lotos, Zeitschrift für Naturwissenschaften herausgegeben vom *Naturhistorischen Vereine "Lotos" in Prag.* Jahrg. I—V. *Prag,* 1851—1855. 8vo.

(*Purch'd. Nov'r No. and Title-page for* 1853 *wanting.*)

PRAG.

Schafzuchter-Verein fur Bohmen.

Verhandlungen des Ausschusses des Schaftzüchter-Vereins für Böhmen. Hefte I—XIX. *Prag*, 1830–55. 8vo.

Miscellanea.

Neue Physicalische Belustigungen. Bde I, II. *Prag*, 1770–71. 8vo.

PREETZ.

Miscellanea.

Preetzer Wochenblatt und Handels Anzeiger für den Bürger und Landmann. Nos. XX—XXXVII, 1833. *Preetz*. 4to.

REGENSBURG.

K. bayerische botanische Gesellschaft.

Denkschriften der Königlich-bayerischen botanischen Gesellschaft zu Regensburg. III. *Regensburg*, 1841. 4to.

Flora, oder allgemeine botanische Zeitung; herausgegeben von der *K. bayer. botanischen Gesellschaft zu Regensburg*. Neue Reihe. Jahrg. I—XIII. *Regensburg*, 1843—1855. 8vo.

Zoologisch-mineralogischer Verein.

Abhandlungen des Zoologisch-mineralogischen Vereines in Regensburg. I—VII. *Regensburg*, 1849—1856. 8vo.

Korrespondenz-Blatt des Zoologisch-mineralogischen Vereines in Regensburg. Jahrg. I—XI. *Regensburg*, 1847—1857. 8vo.

ROSTOCK.

Mecklinburgische naturforschende Gesellschaft.

Auszüge aus den Verhandlungen der Mecklinburgischen naturforschenden Gesellschaft. Erstes Heft. *Rostock*, 1837. 8vo.

ROSTOCK.

Naturwissenschaftliches Institut der Universitæt.

Beiträge zur Kenntniss der amerikanischen Manatis. Von HERMANN STANNIUS. Mit 2 lith. Taf. *Rostock*, 1846. 4to.

SCHWERIN.

Verein fur mecklenburgische Geschichte und Alterthumskunde.

Erster Bericht über die dem Grossherzoglich-mecklenburgischen Antiquarium zu Schwerin in dem Zeitraume von 1834 bis 1844 gewordenen Vermehrungen, als Fortsetzung des Friderico-Franciscei, von G. C. F. LISCH. *Schwerin*, 1844. 8vo.

Quartalbericht des Vereins für mecklenburgische Geschichte und Alterthumskunde. VIII—XV; XVI, I, II; XVII, XVIII, I; XIX, I; XXII, XXIII, I. *Schwerin*, 1842—1857. 8vo.

Jahrbücher und Jahresbericht des Vereins für mecklenburgische Geschichte und Alterthumskunde; herausgegeben von LISCH und BARTSCH. Jahrg. III—XXII. *Schwerin*, 1838—1857. 8vo.

(*From L. Vortisch.*)

Register über I—XX. Jahrgang der Jahrbücher und Jahresberichte des Vereins für mecklenburgische Geschichte und Alterthumskunde. Von J. G. C. RITTER. Reg. I—III. *Schwerin*, 1844–56. 8vo.

Miscellanea.

Archiv für Landeskunde in den Grossherzogthümern Mecklenburg und Revüe der Landwirthschaft. 1853, 1854. *Schwerin*. R. 8vo.

SPEYER.

Sternwarte des kœnigl. Lyzeums in Speyer.

Astronomische Beobachtungen angestellt auf der Sternwarte des königl. Lyzeums in Speyer, von F. M. SCHWERD. I. Abth. Beobachtungen des Jahrs 1826. *Speyer*, 1829. 4to.

STETTIN.

Entomologischer Verein.

Entomologische Zeitung. Herausgegeben von dem *Entomologischen Vereine zu Stettin.* Jahrg. I—XVIII. *Stettin,* 1840—1857. 8vo.

Linnaea Entomologica. Zeitschrift herausgegeben von dem *Entomologischen Vereine in Stettin.* Bde I—XII. *Stettin,* 1846—1858. 8vo.

STUTTGART.

Kœnigl. Centralstelle fur Gewerbe und Handel.

Gewerbeblatt aus Württemberg. Herausgegeben von der *K. Centralstelle für Gewerbe und Handel.* Jahrg. 1853, 1854, 1856. *Stuttgart.* 8vo.

Kœnigl. Centralstelle fur die Landwirthschaft.

Wochenblatt für Land- und Forstwirthschaft. Jahrg. VIII. *Stuttgart* und *Augsburg,* 1856. 4to.

Verein fur vaterlændische Naturkunde.

Jahreshefte des Vereins für vaterländische Naturkunde in Württemberg. Jahrg. I—XIII. *Stuttgart,* 1845—1857. 8vo.

Württembergische Jahrbücher für vaterländische Geschichte, Geographie, Statistik und Topographie. Jahrg. 1850—1855. *Stuttgart.* 8vo.

Wurttembergischer Alterthums-Verein.

Jahreshefte des Wirtembergischen Alterthums-Vereines. Hefte II—V, VII. *Stuttgart,* 1825-28. fol.

Erster Rechenschaftsbericht des Württembergischen Alterthums-Vereins für das Jahr 1844. *Stuttgart.* 4to.

Zweiter Rechenschaftsbericht für 1845. *Stuttgart.* 4to.
Dritter " " 1846 und 1847. "
Vierter " " 1848 und 1849. "
Sechster " vom 1 Jan. 1852 bis 30 Juni 1854. "
Siebenter " vom 1 Juli 1854 bis 31 Dec. 1855. "

STUTTGART.

Wurttembergischer Alterthums-Verein.—*Continued.*

Schriften des Württemb. Alterthums-Vereins. Heft I, 1850; III, 1854; IV, 1856. *Stuttgart.* 8vo.

Mitglieder-Verzeichniss des Württembergischen Alterthums-Vereins im August 1853. 8vo.

Wurttembergischer ærztlicher Verein.

Medicinisches Correspondenz-Blatt des Württembergischen ärztlichen Vereins. Herausgegeben von den DD. J. F. BLUMHARDT, G. DUVERNOY, A. SEEGER. Jahrg. I, No. 29, 1832; VII, No. 18, 1837; XIX, No. 25, 1849; XXIII, No. 26, 1853. *Stuttgart.* 4to.

Deutsche Ornithologen-Gesellschaft.

Naumannia. Archiv für die Ornithologie, vorzugsweise Europa's. Organ der deutschen Ornithologen-Gesellschaft. Herausgegeben von EDWARD BALDAMUS. Jahrg. I—IV, VII, I—III. *Stuttgart* und *Leipzig*, 1850–54, 1857. 8vo.

(*Purchased.*)

Miscellanea.

Neue Encyklopädie der Wissenschaften und Künste für die Deutsche Nation. I—VII. *Stuttgart,* 1847–54. 8vo. (*Wanting VI,* III, IV ; *VII,* II.)

Neue illustrirte Zeitschrift. Bde III—X, 1847—1854. *Stuttgart.* fol.

Polytechnisches Journal. Herausgegeben von Dr. JOHANN GOTTFRIED DINGLER. Bde I—CXXXV. Herausgegeben von Dr. EMIL MAXIMILIAN DINGLER. Bde CXXXVI—CXLIV, I—IV. *Stuttgart* und *Augsburg,* 1820–57. 8vo.

Technologische Encyklopädie oder alphabetisches Handbuch der Technologie, der technischen Chemie und des Maschinenwesens. Zum Gebrauch für Kameralisten, Oekonomen, Künstler, Fabrikanten und Gewerbtreibende jeder Art. Herausgegeben von JOH. JOS. PRECHTL. Bde I—XVI, XIX. *Stuttgart,* 1830–53. 8vo.

Miscellanea.—*Continued.*

Idem. Kupfertafeln. Lief. I—XVI, XIX. *Stuttgart.* Oblong fol.

THARAND.

Kœniglich Sæchsische Akademie fur Forst- und Landwirthe.

Forstwirthschaftliches Jahrbuch, herausgegeben von der *Königlich Sächsischen Akademie für Forst- und Landwirthe zu Tharand.* Bde I—VII. *Dresden* und *Leipzig,* 1842—1851. 8vo.

Jahrbuch der Königl. Sächs. Akademie für Forst- und Landewirthe zu Tharand. Herausgegeben von den akademischen Lehrern: Freih. v. Berg, A. Cotta, Dr. H. Krutzsch, Pressler, Dr. Schober, Dr. Stein, und Dr. A. Stöckhardt. (Des Forstwirthschaftlichen Jahrbuches Bde VIII, X—XII.) Neue Folge. Bde I, III—V, *Leipzig,* 1852, 1854—1857. 8vo.

TÜBINGEN.

Universitæts-Bibliothek.

Tübinger Universitäts Schriften aus den Jahren 1846–55. *Tübingen,* 1847—1856. 4to.

WEIMAR.

Miscellanea.

Notizen aus dem Gebiete der Natur- und Heilkunde gesammelt und mitgetheilt von Ludwig Friedrich v. Froriep. Bde I—L. *Erffurt* und *Weimar,* 1822–36. 4to.

Neue Notizen aus dem Gebiete der Natur- und Heilkunde gesammelt und mitgetheilt von Ludwig Friedrich v. Froriep. I—XL. *Weimar,* 1837–46. 4to.

Notizen aus dem Gebiete der Natur- und Heilkunde gesammelt und mitgetheilt von M. A. Schleiden und Dr. Robert Froriep. Dritte Reihe. I—XI. *Weimar,* 1847—1849. 4to.

Tagsberichte über die Fortschritte der Natur- und Heil-

WEIMAR.

Miscellanea.—*Continued.*

kunde, erstattet von Dr. Robert Froriep. *Weimar.* 8vo.

Geographie und Ethnologie. 1852.
Mineralogie und Geologie. 1852.
Physik und Chemie. 1852.
Botanik. 1852.
Anatomie und Physiologie. I, II, 1852.
Zoologie und Palæontologie. I, II, III, 1850 & 1852.
Staatsarzneikunde und medicinische Statistik. 1852.
Psychiatrie, bearbeitet von J. F. H. Albers. 1852.
Hygiene und Pharmakologie, von Dr. C. Ph. Falck. 1852.
Nerven- und Geisteskrankheiten. 1852.
Geburtshülfe und Kinderkrankheiten. 1852.
Medicinische Klinik. I, II, 1851, 1852.
Chirurgische Klinik. I, II, 1851, 1852.
(*Purchased.*)

WETZLAR.

Deutsche Gesellschaft fur Hydrologie.

Balneologische Zeitung. Correspondenzblatt der Deutschen Gesellschaft für Hydrologie. Herausgegeben von Hofrath Dr. Louis Spengler zu Bad Ems. I—IV, V, i—x. *Wetzlar*, 1855–57. 8vo.
(*Wanting II, Nos.* 21, 22; *IV*, i.)

WIEN (VIENNA).

Kaiserliche Akademie der Wissenschaften.

Denkschriften der Kaiserlichen Akademie der Wissenschaften. Philosophisch-historische Classe. II—VIII. *Wien*, 1851—1857. fol. & 4to.
(*Wanting I.*)

Sitzungsberichte der Philosophisch-historischen Classe der Kaiserlichen Akademie der Wissenschaften. VI—XXII, XXIII, i—iv. *Wien*, 1851—1857. 8vo.

WIEN.

Kaiserliche Akademie der Wissenschaften.—*Cont'd.*

Denkschriften der Kaiserlichen Akademie der Wissenschaften. Mathematisch-naturwissenschaftliche Classe. I—IV. fol. V—XIII. 4to. *Wien*, 1850—1857.

Tafeln zu den Denkschriften der Kaiserlichen Akademie der Wissenschaften. Mathematisch-naturwissenschaftliche Classe. Erster Band. Erste Abtheilung: Abhandlungen von Mitgliedern der Akademie. *Wien*, 1850. fol.

Sitzungsberichte der Mathematisch-naturwissenschaftlichen Classe der Kaiserlichen Akademie der Wissenschaften. IV—XXIII, XXIV, I, II. *Wien*, 1850—1857. 8vo.

Almanach der Kaiserlichen Akademie der Wissenschaften. III, V—VII. *Wien*, 1853, 1855–57. 8vo.

Mitglieder der Kaiserlichen Akademie der Wissenschaften (am Schlusse des Jahres 1853). 4to. pp. 6.

Fontes Rerum Austriacarum. Oesterreichische Geschichtsquellen. Erste Abtheilung: Scriptores. I, 1855. Zweite Abtheilung: Diplomataria et Acta. V—XIII, XV, 1852—1857. *Wien*. 8vo.

Archiv für Kunde österreichischer Geschichts-Quellen. Bde VI—XVII. *Wien*, 1851—1857.

(*2d part of Vol. IX wanting.*)

Notizenblatt. Beilage zum Archiv für Kunde österreichischer Geschichtsquellen. Herausgegeben von der *historischen Commission der Kaiserlichen Akademie der Wissenschaften in Wien*. Jahrg. II—VI. *Wien*, 1852—1856. 8vo.

(*Wanting Vol. I, and Nos.* 1 *&* 2 *of Vol. II.*)

Annalen des Wiener Museums der Naturgeschichte. I, II, 1836; II, I, 1839. *Wien*. 4to.

(*Purchased.*)

Jahrbücher der K. K. Central-Anstalt für Meteorologie und Erdmagnetismus von Karl Kreil. Band IV. Jahrg. 1852. Herausgegeben durch *die Kaiserliche Akademie der Wissenschaften*. *Wien*, 1856. 4to.

Monumenta Habsburgica. Sammlung von Actenstücken und Briefen zur Geschichte des Hauses Habsburg in dem

WIEN.

Kaiserliche Akademie der Wissenschaften.—*Cont'd.*

Zeitraume von 1473 bis 1576. Zweite Abtheilung: Kaiser Karl V. und König Philipp II. *Wien*, 1857. 8vo.

Doctoren-Collegium der medicinischen Facultæt.

Oesterreichische Zeitschrift für practische Heilkunde. Herausgegeben vom *Doctoren-Collegium der medicinischen Facultæt in Wien.* Redigirt von JOSEPH JOHANN KNOLZ und GEORG PREYSS. Jahrg. II, III. *Wien*, 1856, 1857. 4to.

(*Jahrg. III wants Title and Contents.*)

K. K. Geologische Reichsanstalt.

Jahrbuch der Kaiserlich-königlichen geologischen Reichsanstalt. Jahrg. I—VII, VIII, I. *Wien*, 1850—1857. royal 8vo.

Allgemeine Uebersicht der Wirksamkeit der K. K. geologischen Reichsanstalt. Jahre 1850—1852. *Wien*. 8vo.

Uebersicht der Resultate mineralogischer Forschungen in den Jahren 1844—1849. Von Dr. G. A. KENNGOTT. *Wien*, 1852. 4to.

Idem, in den Jahren 1850 & 1851. *Wien*, 1853.

" im Jahre 1852. *Wien*, 1854.

Abhandlungen der K. K. Geologischen Reichsanstalt. I, 1852; II, 1855. *Wien*. 4to.

K. K. Hof- und Staats-Druckerei.

Geschichte der K. K. Hof- und Staats-Druckerei in Wien, von einem Typographen dieser Anstalt. *Wien*, 1851. 8vo.

Geschichte der K. K. Hof- und Staats-Druckerei in Wien, von einem Typographen dieser Anstalt. [In German, English, Italian, and French.] *Wien*, 1851. 8vo.

Album der K. K. Hof- und Staats-Druckerei in Wien. I—IV. *Wien*, 1851. fol.

WIEN.

K. K. Geographische Gesellschaft.

Mittheilungen der Kaiserlich-königlichen Geographischen Gesellschaft. Band I. Heft I. Redigirt von FRANZ FOETTERLE. *Wien*, 1857. 8vo.

Geschäfts-Ordnung der Kaiserlich-königlichen Geographischen Gesellschaft. pp. 6. 8vo.

Verzeichniss der Gesammt-Versammlungen der K. K. Geographischen Gesellschaft. *Wien*, 1856. 8vo. pp. 9.

Die Geographische Gesellschaft in Wien. Jan. 5, Feb. 4, März 1, April 5, Mai 6, Sep. 11, Nov. 4, Dec. 2, 16, 30, 1856; Jan. 20, Feb. 17, 1857. fol.

Bericht über die Durchstechung der Landenge von Suez an die K. K. Geographische Gesellschaft, von der hierzu gewählten Commission bestehend aus den Herren V. Freiherrn *v. Andrian*, K. Freiherrn *v. Czörnig*, etc. Berichterstatter FRANZ FOETTERLE. Jahrg. I, II. *Wien*, 1857. 8vo.

K. K. Handels-Ministerium.

Mittheilungen über Handel, Gewerbe und Verkehrsmittel, so wie aus dem Gebiete der Statistik überhaupt, nach Berichten an des K. K. Handels-Ministerium. Herausgegeben von der *Direction der administrativen Statistik*. I, II. *Wien*, 1850, 1851. 8vo.

Mittheilungen aus dem Gebiete der Statistik. Herausgegeben von der *Direction der administrativen Statistik* im K. K. Handels-Ministerium. I, I. *Wien*, 1852. 8vo.

K. K. Landwirthschafts-Gesellschaft.

Verhandlungen der Kais. kön. Landwirthschafts-Gesellschaft in Wien. Dritter Folge. V, I. *Wien*, 1855. 4to.

Allgemeine Land- und Forstwirthschaftliche Zeitung. Herausgegeben von der *K. K. Landwirthschafts-Gesellschaft in Wien*. Redigirt von Prof. Dr. JOSEPH ARENSTEIN. Jahrg. VII, Nos. 4 & 5. *Wien*, 1857. royal 8vo.

K. K. Orientalische Akademie.

Zur ersten Saculär-Feier der K. K. Akademie der orientalischen Sprachen im Jänner, 1854. *Wien*, 1854. 8vo.

WIEN.

K. K. Sternwarte.

Annalen der K. K. Sternwarte in Wien. Nach dem Befehle seiner K. K. apost. Majestät auf öffentliche Kosten herausgegeben von CARL VON LITTROW. Dritter Folge Bde I—VI. *Wien*, 1851—1856. 8vo.

Meteorologische Beobachtungen an der Wiener Sternwarte in den Jahren 1851, 1852, 1853, 1854, 1855. 4to.

Zoologisch-botanischer Verein.

Verhandlungen des Zoologisch-botanischen Vereins in Wien. I—VI. *Wien*, 1851—1856. 8vo.

Separatabdruck naturwissenschaftlicher Abhandlungen aus den Schriften des Zoologisch-botanischen Vereins in Wien. *Wien*, 1856. 8vo.

Bericht uber die österreichische Literatur der Zoologie, Botanik und Palaeontologie, aus den Jahren 1850, 1851, 1852, 1853. *Wien*, 1855. 8vo.

Miscellanea.

Naturwissenschaftliche Abhandlungen, gesammelt und durch Subscription herausgegeben von WILHELM HAIDINGER. Bde I—IV. *Wien*, 1847—1851. 4to.

Berichte über die Mittheilungen von Freunden der Naturwissenschaften in Wien; gesammelt und herausgegeben von WILHELM HAIDINGER. I—VII, 1846—1850. *Wien*, 1847—1851. 8vo.

Wiener entomologische Monatschrift. Bd. I, No. I, Juli 1857. 8vo.

WIESBADEN.

Verein fur Naturkunde.

Jahrbücher des Vereins für Naturkunde im Herzogthum Nassau. Hefte I—XI. *Wiesbaden*, 1844-56. 8vo.

Medicinische Jahrbücher für das Herzogthum Nassau. Hefte I—XIII. *Wiesbaden*, 1843-54. 8vo.

WÜRZBURG.

Physikalisch-medicinische Gesellschaft.

Verhandlungen der Physikalisch-medicinischen Gesellschaft in Würzburg. I—VIII. *Erlangen* und *Würzburg*, 1850 -58. 8vo.

Statuten der Physikalisch-medicinischen Gesellschaft in Würzburg. *Würzburg*, 1852. 8vo. pp. 15.

Berichte von der Königlichen zootomischen Anstalt zu Würzburg. Zweiter Bericht für das Schuljahr 1847-48. *Leipzig*, 1849. 4to.

Polytechnischer Verein.

Gemeinnützige Wochenschrift. Organ für die Interessen der Technik, des Handels, der Landwirthschaft und der Armenpflege. Jahrg. II—VII. *Würzburg*, 1852—1857. 8vo.

Satzungen des Polytechnischen Vereins zu Würtzburg. *Würtzburg*, 1853. 8vo. pp. 27.

Verzeichniss der Kupferstich-Sammlung des Polytechnischen Vereins zu Würzburg. *Würzburg*, 1855. 8vo.

Jahres-Bericht des Polytechnischen Vereins zu Würzburg. Abtheilung für Schulen und wissenschaftliche Technik. Bekannt gemacht bei der öffentlichen Vertheilung der Schulpreise den 24 August 1856. *Würzburg*. 4to.

Der Polytechnische Verein zu Würzburg in den ersten fünfzig Jahren seines Bestehens. Eine Festgabe zur fünfzigjährigen Stiftungs-Feier. Nach den Akten, von M. F. Chemnitz. *Würzburg*, 1856. 4to.

SWITZERLAND.

Allgemeine Schweizerische Gesellschaft fur die gesammten Naturwissenschaften.

Neue Denkschriften der allgemeinen Schweizerischen Gesellschaft für die gesammten Naturwissenschaften. Bde I—XIV. (Nouveaux Mémoires de la Société helvé-

Allgemeine Schweizerische Gesellschaft.—*Cont'd.*

tique des Sciences Naturelles.) *Neuchâtel & Zurich*, 1837—1855. 4to.

Actes de la Société helvétique des Sciences Naturelles. (Verhandlungen der Schweizerischen naturforschenden Gesellschaft.) Sessions XXX—XL, 1845—1855. 8vo.

Die wichtigsten Momente aus der Geschichte der drei ersten Jahrzehende der Schweizerischen naturforschenden Gesellschaft. (Coup d'œil historique sur les 32 premières années d'existence de la Société helvétique des Sciences Naturelles.) *Zürich*, 1848. 8vo.

Verzeichniss der Mitglieder der allgemeinen Schweizerischen Gesellschaft für die gesammten Naturwissenschaften. (Catalogue des Membres de la Société helvétique des Sciences Naturelles.) *Zürich*, 1852. 8vo.

BASEL.

Gesellschaft fur vaterlændische Alterthumer.

Mittheilungen der Gesellschaft für vaterländische Alterthümer in Basel. I, II, V—VII. *Basel*, 1843—1857. 4to.

Antiquarische Mittheilungen aus Basel. Die Grabhügel in der Hardt eröffnet und beschrieben von Prof. W. VISCHER. *Zürich*, 1842. 4to. pp. 16 and 3 plates.

Beiträge zur vaterländischen Geschichte. Herausgegeben von der *Historischen Gesellschaft* zu Basel. Bde III, IV. *Basel*, 1846, 1854. 8vo.

Museum.

Festschrift zur Einweihung des Museums in Basel, am 26 November 1849. *Basel.* 4to.

Naturforschende Gesellschaft.

Bericht über die Verhandlungen der Naturforschenden Gesellschaft in Basel vom August 1834 bis Juni 1848. I—X. *Basel*, 1835—1852. 8vo.

Verhandlungen der Naturforschenden Gesellschaft in Basel. Hefte I—IV. *Basel*, 1854-57. 8vo.

BERN.

Naturforschende Gesellschaft.

Mittheilungen der Naturforschenden Gesellschaft in Bern aus den Jahren 1843—1855. *Bern*, 1843—1855. 8vo.

GENEVE (GENEVA).

Observatoire.

Observations Astronomiques faites à l'Observatoire de Genève dans les Années 1841—1850. Par E. PLANTAMOUR. I—X. *Genève*. 4to.

Résumé des Observations Thermométriques et Barométriques faites à l'Observatoire de Genève et au Grand St.-Bernard pendant les dix années 1841 à 1850, suivi de Tables Hypsométriques calculées d'après la formule de Bessel par E. PLANTAMOUR. *Genève*, 1851. 4to.

Societe de Physique et d'Histoire Naturelle de Geneve.

Mémoires de la Société de Physique et d'Histoire Naturelle de Genève. I—XIV. *Genève & Paris*, 1821—1855. 4to.

Miscellanea.

Supplément à la Bibliothèque Universelle de Genève.—Archives des Sciences Physiques et Naturelles. Tomes I—XXIX. *Genève* et *Paris*, 1846—1855. 8vo.

LAUSANNE.

Societe Vaudoise des Sciences Naturelles.

Bulletin de la Société Vaudoise des Sciences Naturelles. IV; V, Nos. 38—41. *Lausanne*, 1854—1857. 8vo.

NEUCHATEL.

Societe des Sciences Naturelles.

Mémoires de la Société des Sciences Naturelles de Neuchâtel. Tomes I—III. *Neuchâtel*, 1836—1846. 4to.

Bulletin de la Société des Sciences Naturelles de Neuchâtel. I; II; III, pp. 95—182; IV, I. *Neuchâtel*, 1844—1856. 8vo.

ZURICH.

Ecole Polytechnique Federale.

Ecole Polytechnique Suisse. Rapports, &c. 1854–56. 8vo.

Gesellschaft fur vaterlændische Alterthumer in Zurich.

Erster Bericht über die Verrichtungen der Antiquarischen Gesellschaft in Zürich vom 1 Juli 1844 bis 1 Juli 1845. *Zürich.* 4to.

Zweiter Bericht, vom 1 Juli 1845 bis 1 Juli 1846.
Dritter " " 1846 " 1847.
Vierter " " 1847 " 1848.
Fünfter " " 1848 " 1849.
Sechster " " 1849 " 1850.
Siebenter " " 1850 " 1851.
Achter " " 1851 " 1852.
Neunter " " 1852 " 1853.
Zehnter " " 1853 " 1854.
Elfter " " 1854 " 1855.
Zwölfter " " 1855 " 1856.

Katalog der Bibliothek der Antiquarischen Gesellschaft in Zürich. *Zürich,* 1855. 8vo.

Mittheilungen der Antiquarischen Gesellschaft in Zürich. Bde III, v, V—X, XI, i—iv, vi. *Zürich,* 1849—1857. 4to.

Die Stædte- und Landes-Siegel der Schweiz. Ein Beitrag zur Siegelkunde des Mittelalters von E. Schulthes. Fortgesetzt von Dr. Ferdinand Keller. Hefte IV, V. *Zürich,* 1856. 4to.

Naturforschende Gesellschaft.

Abhandlungen der Naturforschenden Gesellschaft in Zürich. I—III. *Zürich,* 1761—1766. 8vo.

Vierteljahrsschrift der Naturforschenden Gesellschaft in Zürich. Redigirt von Dr. Rudolf Wolf. Jahrg. I, II. *Zürich,* 1856, 1857. 8vo.

Meteorologische Beobachtungen angestellt auf Veranstaltung der Naturforschenden Gesellschaft in Zürich. *Zürich,* 1837—1846. 4to.

ZURICH.

Naturforschende Gesellschaft.—*Continued.*

Denkschrift zur Feier des hundertjährigen Stiftungsfestes der Naturforschenden Gesellschaft in Zürich am 30 November, 1846. *Zürich.* 4to.

Mittheilungen der Naturforschenden Gesellschaft in Zürich. I—X. *Zürich*, 1847—1856. 8vo.

BELGIUM.

ANVERS (ANTWERP).

Societe de Pharmacie.

Journal de Pharmacie publié par la *Société de Pharmacie* d'Anvers. Tomes X, XI. *Anvers*, 1854, 1855. 8vo.

BRUXELLES (BRUSSELS).

Academie Royale des Sciences, des Lettres et des Beaux-Arts.

Nouveaux Mémoires de l'Académie royale des Sciences et Belles-Lettres de Bruxelles. Tomes XII—XIX. *Bruxelles*, 1839—1845. 4to.

Mémoires de l'Académie royale des Sciences, des Lettres et des Beaux-Arts de Belgique. XX—XXX. *Bruxelles*, 1847—1857. 4to.

Mémoires couronnés et Mémoires des Savants étrangers, publiés par *l'Académie royale des Sciences et Belles-Lettres de Bruxelles.* Tomes XII—XVIII. *Bruxelles*, 1837—1845. 4to.

Idem, publiés par *l'Académie royale des Sciences, des Lettres et des Beaux-Arts de Belgique.* XIX—XXVIII. *Bruxelles*, 1847—1856. 4to.

Mémoires couronnés et Mémoires des Savants étrangers, publiés par *l'Académie royale des Sciences, des Lettres et des Beaux-Arts de Belgique.* Collection in 8vo. Tomes I—VI. *Bruxelles*, 1840—1855. 8vo.

(*Wanting Vol. III, Part 2; Vol. IV; Vol. V, Part 2, after p.* 96.)

BRUXELLES.

Academie Royale des Sciences, des Lettres et des Beaux-Arts.—*Continued.*

Rapport décennal des Travaux de l'Académie royale des Sciences et Belles-Lettres de Bruxelles depuis 1830; par M. A. QUETELET. (Lu à la séance publique du 16 déc. 1840.) *Bruxelles.* 8vo.

Académie royale des Sciences, des Lettres et des Beaux-Arts de Belgique. Arrêtés royaux concernant sa réorganisation. *Bruxelles,* 1845. 8vo.

Bulletins de l'Académie royale des Sciences, des Lettres et des Beaux-Arts de Belgique. XII—XXIII, 1845—1856. *Bruxelles.* 8vo.

Annexe aux Bulletins de l'Académie royale des Sciences, des Lettres et des Beaux-Arts de Belgique. 1853-54. *Bruxelles,* 1854. 8vo.

Annuaire de l'Académie royale des Sciences et Belles-Lettres de Bruxelles. Années V—VIII, 1839-42; X, 1844; XI, 1845. *Bruxelles.* 24mo.

Annuaire de l'Académie royale des Sciences, des Lettres et des Beaux-Arts de Belgique. Années XIII—XIX, XXI—XXIII. *Bruxelles,* 1847—1857. 8vo.

Observatoire Royal.

Annales de l'Observatoire royal de Bruxelles, publiées aux frais de l'Etat, par le Directeur A. QUETELET. IV—IX, XI. *Bruxelles,* 1845—1857. 4to.

Annuaire de l'Observatoire royal par le Directeur A. QUETELET. 1848, 1854, 1856, 1857. *Bruxelles.* 24mo.

Almanach Séculaire de l'Observatoire royal de Bruxelles par le Directeur A. QUETELET. *Bruxelles,* 1854. 12mo.

Rapport adressé à M. le Ministre de l'Intérieur sur l'état et les Travaux de l'Observatoire Royal, pendant les années 1847, 1848, 1849, 1856; par le Directeur A. QUETELET. *Bruxelles.* 8vo.

Societe des Gens de Lettres Belges.

Société des Gens de Lettres Belges. Deuxième anniversaire de la fondation de la Société. Séance publique du 11

BRUXELLES.

Societe des Gens de Lettres Belges.—*Continued.*

novembre 1849. Compte rendu. *Bruxelles*, 1849. 8vo. (*From Baron Jules de St. Genois.*)

GAND (GHENT).

Universite de Gand.

Annales Academiæ Gandavensis. MDCCCXXVII—MDCCCXXVIII. *Gandavi*, 1831. 4to.

Annales des Universités de Belgiques, ou Recueil contenant les lois, arretés et réglements relatifs à l'enseignement supérieur, les mémoires couronnés aux concours universitaires, et d'autres documents académiques. Année II—IX, 1843—1850. *Bruxelles*, 1844—1852. 8vo.

Kunst- en Letter-blad uitgegeven door F. A. SNELLAERT. Jaerg. I—IV. *Gent*, 1840—1843. 4to.

Miscellanea.

Annales de Littérature médicale étrangère. Rédigées par J. F. KLUYSKENS. I—XVIII, 1805—1814. *Gand.* 8vo.

LIEGE.

Societe Royale des Sciences de Liege.

Mémoires de la Société royale des Sciences de Liège. I—XII. *Liège*, 1843—1857. 8vo. (*Wanting IX.*)

LOUVAIN.

Universite Catholique.

Annales Academiæ Lovaniensis anni noni a die XVIII Octobris MDCCCXXV ad diem II Oct. MDCCCXXVI. Rectore Magnifico FRANCISCO JOSEPHO DUMBECK atque Academiæ Graphiario GERARDO JOANNE MEYER. IX, I, II. *Lovanii*, 1837. 4to.

Annuaire de l'Université Catholique de Louvain. Années IV, VIII—XII, XV, XVI, XVIII. *Louvain*, 1840—1854. 12mo.

LOUVAIN.

Universite Catholique.—*Continued.*

Société Littéraire de l'Université Catholique de Louvain Choix de Mémoires. Tomes I—V. *Louvain,* 1841—1850. 8vo.

MONS.

Societe des Sciences, des Arts et des Lettres du Hainaut.

Mémoires et Publications de la Société des Sciences, des Arts et des Lettres du Hainaut. Tomes III—X, 1842—1852. IIe Série.—Tomes I, 1852—1853; III, 1854–55. *Mons,* 1842—1856. 8vo.

FRANCE.

Congres Scientifique de France.

Congrès Scientifique de France. Cinquième Session, tenue à Metz, en septembre 1837. *Metz,* 1838. 8vo.

Dixième Session, à Strasbourg, 1842. Tomes I & II. *Strasbourg,* 1843.

Documents extraits du Compte-rendu de la dixième Session du Congrès Scientifique. *Strasbourg,* 1844. 8vo.

Congrès des Délégués des Sociétés Savantes des Départements, tenu au Luxembourg, dans l'ancienne Chambre des Pairs. Séance du 15 mars 1850. Présidence de M. Thevenot. *Caen,* 1850. 8vo.

Institut des Provinces de France.

Annuaire de l'Institut des Provinces et des Congrès Scientifiques.—1851. *Paris.* 12mo.

AMIENS.

Societe des Antiquaires de Picardie.

Mémoires de la Société des Antiquaires de Picardie. Documents inédits concernant la province. I, 1845; II, 1853; IV, 1855. *Amiens.* 4to.

AMIENS.

Societe des Antiquaires de Picardie.—*Continued.*

Mémoires de la Société des Antiquaires de Picardie. Deuxième série. Tomes I—III. *Amiens* et *Paris*, 1851—1854. 8vo.

Table générale des matières contenues dans les dix premiers volumes des Mémoires de la Société des Antiquaires de Picardie. *Amiens*, 1850. 8vo.

Bulletin de la Société des Antiquaires de Picardie. 1853, I—IV; 1854, I—IV; 1855, I—III. *Amiens.* 8vo.

Annuaire administratif et historique de la Somme, pour les années 1852 et 1853, publié sous les auspices du conseil général du Départment, par la *Société des Antiquaires de Picardie. Amiens*, 1852. 8vo.

Histoire général de la province de Picardie. Livr. II, 1853. *Amiens.* 4to.

Séance publique du 29 juin 1854, et Inauguration de la Statue de Pierre l'Ermite à Amiens. *Amiens*, 1854. 8vo.

Délibération du 23 décembre 1852, concernant les travaux de la Cathédrale d'Amiens. *Amiens*, 1853. 8vo.

ANGOULEME.

Societe d'Agriculture, Arts et Commerce du Departement de la Charente.

Annales de la Société d'Agriculture, Arts et Commerce du Département de la Charente. XXXIV, I & II, 1852. *Angoulême.* 8vo.

ARCUEIL.

Societe d'Arcueil.

Mémoires de Physique et de Chimie, de la Société d'Arcueil. Tomes I, II. *Paris*, 1807, 1808. 8vo.
(*Purchased.*)

BEZIERS.

Societe Archeologique.

Bulletin de la Société Archéologique de Beziers. Tomes I—VI, XIII. *Beziers*, 1837—1844, 1852. 8vo.

Supplément à la huitième Livraison du Bulletin. Essai sur

BEZIERS.

Societe Archeologique.—*Continued.*

la Formation et sur le Développement du Langage des Hommes. Par M. I. AZAIS. 8vo.

BORDEAUX.

Academie des Sciences, Belles-Lettres et Arts de Bordeaux.

Recueil des Actes de l'Académie des Sciences, Belles-Lettres et Arts de Bordeaux. XIII, 1851; XIV, 1852; XVI, 1854; XVII, III, IV, 1855; XVIII, II, III, IV, 1856. *Bordeaux.* 8vo.

Rapport lu à l'Académie des Sciences, Belles-Lettres et Arts de Bordeaux, dans sa Séance du 26 avril 1855, par M. CH. DES MOULINS. *Bordeaux*, 1855. 8vo.

Societe des Sciences Physiques et Naturelles de Bordeaux.

Mémoires de la Société des Sciences Physiques et Naturelles de Bordeaux. I, I, II. *Paris* et *Bordeaux*, 1854, 1855. 8vo.

Societe Linneenne de Bordeaux.

Bulletin d'Histoire Naturelle de la Société Linnéenne de Bordeaux. Deuxième édition. I (1826), 1830; II, 1845. *Bordeaux.* 8vo.

Actes de la Société Linnéenne de Bordeaux. V—XIX, 1832—1853. *Paris* et *Bordeaux.* 8vo.

Analyse des Travaux de la Société Linnéenne de Bordeaux, pendant les années 1832—1835. Par M. J. L. LAPORTE. *Bordeaux.* 8vo.

Séance publique d'hiver de la Société Linnéenne de Bordeaux (4 novembre 1853). Discours d'ouverture, par M. CH. DES MOULINS, Président. *Bordeaux.* 8vo.
Idem (6 novembre 1855).

Une Visite au Berger des Eaux-Bonnes (Pierre Sacaze-Gaston). Discours prononcé à l'Ouverture de la Séance publique d'hiver de la Société Linnéenne de Bordeaux,

BORDEAUX.

Societe Linneenne de Bordeaux—*Continued.*

le 4 novembre 1852, par. M. CHARLES DES MOULINS. *Bordeaux*, 1852. 8vo.

Le Nouveaux Jardin des Plantes. Discours prononcé dans la Séance publique d'hiver de la Société Linnéenne de Bordeaux, le 4 novembre 1853, par M. DURIEN DE MAISONNEUVE. *Bordeaux*, 1853. 8vo.

CAEN.

Academie Royale des Sciences, Arts et Belles-Lettres.

Mémoires de l'Académie royale des Sciences, Arts et Belles-Lettres de Caen. 1847, 1849, 1851, 1852, 1855, 1856. *Caen.* 8vo.

Bulletin de l'Instruction publique et des Sociétés savantes de l'Académie de Caen. Première année, I & II, 1840-41; Deuxième année, I & II, 1841-42; Troisième année, I & II, 1842-43. *Caen.* 8vo.

Séance publique du 24 novembre 1853. Discours d'ouverture prononcé par M. A. CHARMA. *Paris*, 1853. 8vo.

Societe d'Agriculture et de Commerce de Caen.

Précis des travaux de la Société royale d'Agriculture et de Commerce de Caen. I, 1801—1810; II, 1827; IV, 1836. *Caen.* 8vo.

Société Royale d'Agriculture et de Commerce de Caen. Rapports, &c. 1818-34, 1834—38, 1839-44, 1845-50. *Caen.* 8vo.

Societe des Antiquaires de Normandie.

Mémoires de la Société des Antiquaires de Normandie. IIe Série.—II, 1841; IV, 1844; VI, 1852; VII, 1847; VIII, 1851; IX, 1851; X, 1853. IIIe Série.—I, 1855; II, 1856. *Paris.* 4to.

Discours prononcé par M. GUIZOT à la Séance solennelle de la Société des Antiquaires de Normandie, le lundi 27 août 1838. *Caen.* 8vo.

[Prize Announcement.] *Caen*, 1851. 8vo. pp. 2.

CAEN.

Societe de Medecine.

Séance extraordinaire de la Société de Médecine de Caen, tenue le 10 juin 1853. *Caen.* 8vo.

Societe Linneenne de Normandie.

Mémoires de la Société Linnéenne de Normandie. V—X. *Paris,* 1835—1855. 4to.

Mémoires de la Société Linnéenne du Calvados. 1824 et 1825. *Caen.* 8vo.

CHERBOURG.

Societe Academique.

Mémoires de la Société Académique de Cherbourg. 1852. *Cherbourg.* 8vo.

Societe des Sciences Naturelles.

Mémoires de la Société des Science Naturelles de Cherbourg. I, I, 1852; II, 1854; III, 1855; IV, 1856. *Cherbourg.* 8vo.

CLERMONT-FERRAND.

Academie des Sciences, Belles-Lettres et Arts.

Annales Scientifiques, Littéraires et Industrielles de l'Auvergne. XXVIII, XXIX. *Clermont-Ferrand,* 1855, 1856. 8vo.

DIJON.

Academie des Sciences, Arts et Belles-Lettres.

Mémoires de l'Académie de Dijon. I, 1769; II, 1774. *Dijon.* 8vo.

Analyse des Travaux de l'Académie, pendant le cours de l'an 12. *Dijon,* 1805. 8vo.

Séance publique de l'Académie des Sciences, Arts et Belles-Lettres de Dijon, tenue le 22 août 1810. *Dijon,* 1810. 8vo.

DIJON.

Academie des Sciences, Arts et Belles-Lettres.— *Continued.*

Idem, séance tenue le	4	juillet	1818.
"	"	22	avril	1819.
"	"	24	août	1821.
"	"	23	"	1823.
"	"	20	"	1825.
"	"	17	décembre	1827.
"	"	25	août	1829.
"	"	26	"	1836.
"	"	31	juillet	1841.
"	"	21	août	1843.

Mémoires de l'Académie des Sciences, Arts et Belles-Lettres de Dijon. Années 1830—1850. *Dijon.* 8vo.

Mémoires de l'Académie des Sciences, Arts et Belles-Lettres de Dijon. Deuxième série. Tomes I—V, 1851—1856. *Dijon,* 1852—1857. 8vo.

Description d'un nouveau genre D'Edenté Fossile renfermant plusieurs espèces voisines du Glyptodon. Atlas. Par L. Nodot. *Dijon.* 4to.

EVREUX.

Societe libre d'Agriculture, Sciences, Arts et Belles-Lettres de l'Eure.

Recueil des Travaux de la Société libre d'Agriculture, Sciences, Arts et Belles-Lettres de l'Eure. IIIe série. Tome II, 1852—1853. *Evreux,* 1854. 8vo.

LILLE.

Societe des Sciences, de l'Agriculture et des Arts de Lille.

Mémoires de la Société royale des Sciences, de l'Agriculture et des Arts de Lille. 1847, 1850—1853. *Lille.* 8vo.

Mémoires de la Société Impériale des Sciences, de l'Agriculture et des Arts de Lille. Supplément à l'année 1853 et Table générale de la Ire série. *Lille,* 1856. 8vo.

LYON (LYONS).

Academie des Sciences, Belles-Lettres et Arts de Lyon.

Compte-rendu des Travaux de l'Académie royale des Sciences, Belles-Lettres et Arts de Lyon. 1824—1826, 1835, 1837, 1839, 1841. *Lyon.* 8vo.

Mémoires de l'Académie des Sciences, Belles-Lettres et Arts de Lyon. Classe des Sciences.—II, 1847. Classe des Lettres.—I, II, 1845, 1846. *Lyon.* 8vo.

Mémoires de l'Académie nationale des Sciences, Belles-Lettres et Arts de Lyon. Nouvelle série. Classe des Sciences.—I, 1851. Classe des Lettres.—I, 1851. *Lyon.* 8vo.

Societe d'Agriculture, Histoire Naturelle et Arts utiles de Lyon.

Compte-rendu des Travaux de la Société d'Agriculture, Histoire Naturelle et Arts utiles de Lyon. 1812-1813, 1814, 1814-1815, 1817, 1819-1820, 1821, 1822-1823, 1823-1824. *Lyon*, 1813—1824. 8vo.

Mémoires de la Société d'Agriculture, Histoire Naturelle et Arts utiles de Lyon. 1825-1827, 1828-1831, 1832, 1833-1834, 1835-1836. *Lyon*, 1828—1837. 8vo.

Annales des Sciences Physiques et Naturelles, d'Agriculture et d'Industrie, publiées par la *Société royale d'Agriculture*, &c. de Lyon. I—XI, 1838—1848. Deuxième série. I—III, 1849—1851. *Lyon* et *Paris.* 8vo.

(*Wanting: livr.* 1, 2, 3 *of Vol. II; livr.* 1—5 *of Vol. III; livr.* 1—4 *of Vol. IV; livr.* 2—5 *of Vol. V; and liv.* 1, 3, 4 *of Vol. VI.*)

Notice sur les Travaux de la Société royale d'Agriculture, Histoire Naturelle et Arts utiles de Lyon, pendant le cours de l'année 1832, lu dans la séance publique du 3 septembre même année, par L. F. Grognier. *Lyon*, 1832. 8vo.

Rapport à la Société royale d'Agriculture, Histoire Naturelle et Arts utiles de Lyon, sur l'Essai comparatif des différentes Charrues, fait par ordre de la Chambre royale d'Agriculture de Savoie, par C. Gariot. Imprimé par

LYON.

Societe d'Agriculture, Histoire Naturelle et Arts utiles de Lyon.—*Continued.*

ordre de la *Société d'Agriculture de Lyon.* *Lyon,* 1831. 8vo.

Rapport fait à la Société royale d'Agriculture, Histoire Naturelle et Arts utiles de Lyon, au nom de la commission chargée de proposer des sujets de Prix pour être décernés en 1833 et 1837, lu dans la séance du 5 août 1832. Commissaires: MM. Gensoul, Buisson, Jurie, et Bottex, rapporteur. Imprimé par ordre de la Société. *Lyon,* 1833. 8vo.

Rapport fait à la Société royale d'Agriculture, Histoire Naturelle et Arts utiles de Lyon, sur la Féte agricole du Comice de Meyzieu (Isère), tenue le 27 mai 1834; par Charles Gariot. Imprimé par ordre de la Société. *Lyon,* 1834. 8vo.

Société royale d'Agriculture, Histoire Naturelle et Arts utiles de Lyon. Séance publique, tenue le 23 juillet 1835. *Lyon,* 1835. 8vo.

Societe Linneenne de Lyon.

Société Linnéenne de Lyon. Compte-rendu des Travaux des années 1839—1842, 1844. *Lyon.* 8vo.

Annales de la Société Linnéenne de Lyon. Années 1847-1849, 1850-1852. *Lyon,* 1850, 1852. 8vo.

LE MANS.

Societe d'Agriculture, Sciences et Arts de la Sarthe.

Analyse des Travaux de la Société royale des Arts du Mans, depuis l'époque de son institution, en 1794, jusqu'à la fin de 1819. Première Partie. Sciences Mathématiques et Physiques. Par A. P. Ledru. *Au Mans,* 1820. 8vo.

Bulletin de la Société royale d'Agriculture, Sciences et Arts du Mans. Tomes III, IV, 1838—1841. *Le Mans,* 1840, 1843. 8vo.

Bulletin de la Société d'Agriculture, Sciences et Arts de la Sarthe. V—VIII, 1842—1849. IIe série. I—IV, 1850—1856. *Le Mans,* 1844—1856. 8vo.

LE MANS.

Societe d'Agriculture, Sciences et Arts de la Sarthe.—*Continued.*

Mémoires de la Société d'Agriculture, Sciences et Arts de la Sarthe. I, I, 1855. *Le Mans.* 8vo.

MARSEILLE (MARSEILLES).

Academie des Sciences, Lettres et Arts de Marseille.

Histoire de l'Académie de Marseille, depuis sa fondation en 1726 jusqu' en 1826; par Mr. J. B. Lautard. I—III, *Marseille,* 1826—1843. 8vo.

Lettres archéologiques sur Marseille, par M. J. B. Lautard. Seconde édition. *Marseille,* 1844. 8vo.

MENDE.

Societe d'Agriculture, Industrie, Sciences, et Arts, du Departemente de la Lozere.

Mémoires et Analyse des Travaux de la Société d'Agriculture, Commerce, Sciences et Arts de la ville de Mende, chef-lieu du departement de la Lozère. 1827, 1828, 1829, 1830, 1831, 1832–33, 1833–34, 1834–35, 1835–36, 1837–38, 1839–40, 1841–42, 1843–44, 1845–46, 1847, 1848, 1849. *Mende.* 8vo.

Bulletin de la Société d'Agriculture, Industrie, Sciences et Arts du département de la Lozère. Tomes I—VIII, 1850—1857. *Mende.* 8vo.

(*Wanting IV, from page* 132; *VI, from page* 59.)

METZ.

Academie Imperiale de Metz.

Mémoires de l'Académie Impériale de Metz. (Société des Lettres, Sciences et Arts de Metz.) Années I—XXXV, XXXVII, XXXVIII, 1819—1857. *Metz* et *Paris,* 1821—1856. 8vo.

METZ.

Societe d'Histoire Naturelle du Departement de la Moselle.

Bulletin de la Société d'Histoire Naturelle du département de la Moselle. Cah. I—VIII, 1843—1857. *Metz.* 8vo.

MONTPELLIER.

Academie des Sciences et Lettres.

Académie des Sciences et Lettres de Montpellier. Séance publique de l'année 1847.

Académie des Sciences et Lettres de Montpellier. Mémoires de la section des Lettres: Tomes I, 1847—1854; II, 1855—1857. Mémoires de la section des Sciences: I, 1847—1850; II, 1851-54; III, 1855-57. Mémoires de la section de Médecine: I, 1849—1853; II, 1857. *Montpellier.* 4to.

(*Wanting, Section des Lettres: Tome I, pp.* 119—552.)

Académie des Sciences et Lettres de Montpellier. Rapport lu dans la séance de l'Académie du 25 janvier 1858 au nom de la Section des Lettres, par M. Victor de Bonald, sur un Projet d'Association de l'Institut et des Académies de Province. Présenté à l'Académie de Lyon, par *M. Bouillier. Montpellier*, 1858. 4to. pp. 15.

Societe Archeologique.

Mémoires de la Société Archéologique de Montpellier. I, 1840; II, 1850; III, 1850—1854; IV, pp. 1—144. *Montpellier.* 4to.

Thalamus Parvus. Le Petit Thalamus de Montpellier, publié pour la première fois d'après les manuscrits originaux par la *Société Archéologique* de Montpellier, 1840. *Montpellier.* 4to.

Publications de la Société Archéologique de Montpellier. Documents historiques. No. 6. Les Coutumes de Perpignan. *Montpellier*, 1848. 4to.

NIMES.

Academie du Gard.

Mémoires de l'Académie du Gard. 1835—1857. *Nîmes.* 8vo. (12 vols.)

Compte-rendu des Travaux de l'Académie du Gard, en séance publique du Conseil Général et du Conseil Municipal le 25 août 1854. Par M. NICOT. *Nîmes.* 8vo.

Réglement de l'Académie du Gard. *Nîmes.* 8vo.

ORLEANS.

Societe des Sciences, Belles-Lettres et Arts d'Orleans.

Mémoires de la Société royale des Sciences, Belles-Lettres et Arts d'Orléans. I—IX, 1837—1849. *Orléans.* 8vo.

PARIS.

Academie Nationale Agricole, Manufacturiere et Commerciale.

Journal Mensuel des Travaux de l'Académie nationale Agricole, Manufacturière et Commerciale, fondée en 1830; et de la Société française de Statistique Universelle. Années XXI—XXVII, 1851—1857. *Paris.* 8vo. (*Wanting* 1851, *January—July;* 1852, *November;* 1853, *June;* 1854, *August;* 1855, *May* and *June;* 1857, *August—October.*)

Cercle generale d'Horticulture.

Bulletin des Travaux de la Société, et Journal des Améliorations pratiques en matière de Jardinage. Tomes II. II. III. V. VI, III. II—VI, IV, V. *Paris,* 1844—1847. 8vo. [For continuation, see under *Société d'Horticulture de la Seine,* p. 108.]

Ecole des Chartes.

Bibliothèque de l'Ecole des Chartes. Revue d'érudition consacrée spécialement à l'étude du Moyen Age. Tome III. Quatrième série. *Paris,* 1857. 8vo.

Livret de l'Ecole des Chartes, publié par la Société de l'Ecole des Chartes. *Paris,* 1852. 16mo.

PARIS.

Ecole des Mines.

Annales des Mines, ou recueil de Mémoires sur l'Exploitation des Mines et sur les sciences et les arts qui s'y rapportent; redigées par les Ingénieurs des Mines, et publiées sous l'autorisation du Ministre des Travaux Publics. Quatrième série.—Tomes IX—XX, 1846—1851. Cinquième série. —Mémoires: I—VII, IX, pp. 233—700, X—XII, 1852 —1857. Partie administrative: I—III, IV, pp. 1—186, V, pp. 39—294, VI, 1852—1857. *Paris.* 8vo. (*Wanting: Livr.* 4—6 *of* 1855, *and* 1 *of* 1856.)

Table Alphabétique et Analytique des matières contenues dans la 4e série des Annales des Mines. *Paris,* 1852. 8vo.

Institut de France: Academie des Inscriptions et Belles-Lettres.

Histoire de l'Académie royale des Inscriptions et Belles-Lettres, avec les Mémoires de Litérature tirés des régistres de cette Académie. Tomes I—L, 1666—1793. *Paris,* 1736—1808. 4to.

Tableau général raisonné et méthodique des ouvrages contenus dans le Recueil des Mémoires de l'Académie royale des Inscriptions et Belles-Lettres, depuis sa naissance jusques et compris l'année 1788, servant de Supplément aux Tables de ce Recueil. *Paris,* 1791. 4to.

Institut de France: Academie des Sciences.

Regiæ Scientiarum Academiæ Historia, in qua præter ipsius Academiæ Originem et Progressus, variasque Dissertationes et Observationes per triginta quatuor annos factas, quàm plurima Experimenta et Inventa, cùm Physica tùm Mathematica, in certum ordinem digeruntur. Secunda editio priori longe auctior. Autore JOANNE-BAPTISTA DU HAMEL, ejusdem Academiæ socio. *Parisiis,* 1701. 4to.

Histoire (et Mémoires) de l'Académie royale des Sciences. 1666—1790. *Paris,* 1733—1797. 4to. (107 vols.)

Table alphabétique des Matières contenues dans l'Histoire et les Mémoires de l'Académie royale des Sciences, publiée

PARIS.

Institut de France: Academie des Sciences.—*Cont'd.*

par son ordre, et dressée par M. Godin, de la même Académie. I—IV, 1666—1730. *Paris*, 1729—1734. 4to.

Table générale des Matières, &c. Par M. Demours. V—X, 1731—1790. *Paris*, 1747—1809. 4to.

Nouvelle Table des Articles contenus dans les volumes de l'Académie royale des Sciences de Paris, dans ceux des Arts et Métiers publiés par cette Académie, et dans la Collection Académique. I—IV, 1775—1776. *Paris.* 4to.

Suites des Mémoires de l'Académie royale des Sciences. 1720—1764. *Paris.* 4to. (7 vols.)

Mémoires de l'Institut national des Sciences et Arts, Littérature et Beaux-Arts. I—V, 1798—1804. *Paris.* 4to.

Mémoires de l'Institut national des Sciences et Arts. Sciences mathématiques et physiques. I—VI, 1798—1806. *Paris.* 4to.

Mémoires de la classe des Sciences mathématiques et physiques de l'Institut de France. 1806—1815. *Paris*, 1806—1818. 4to. (8 vols.)

Mémoires de l'Académie royale des Sciences de l'Institut de France. I—XVI, XXI, 1816—1838, 1847. *Paris*, 1818—1838, 1847. 4to.

Mémoires de Mathématique et de Physique, présentés à l'Académie royale des Sciences, par divers Sçavans, et lûs dans ses Assemblées. Tomes I—XI, 1750—1786. *Paris.* 4to.

Mémoires preséntés à l'Institut des Sciences, Lettres et Arts, par divers Savans, et lus dans ses Assemblées. Sciences mathématiques et physiques. I, II, 1806, 1811. *Paris.* 4to.

Mémoires présentés par divers savans à l'Académie royale des Sciences de l'Institut de France et imprimés par son ordre. Sciences mathématiques et physiques. I—VI, XIII, 1827—1835, 1852. *Paris.* 4to.

Machines et Inventions approuvées par l'Académie royale des Sciences. I—VII, 1666—1754. *Paris*, 1735—1777. 4to.

PARIS.

Institut de France: Academie des Sciences.—*Cont'd.*

Recueil des Pièces qui ont remporté les prix de l'Académie royale des Sciences. I—IX, 1720—1772. *Paris*, 1721—1777. 4to.

Jugement de l'Académie royale des Sciences et Belles-Lettres sur une Lettre prétendue de Leibnitz. *Paris.* 4to.

Rapports et discussions de toutes les classes de l'Institut de France, sur les Ouvrages admis au concours pour les Prix décennaux. *Paris*, 1810. 4to.

Rapport historique sur les progrès des Sciences mathématiques depuis 1789—1808 et sur leur état actual. Redigé par M. Delambre. *Paris*, 1810. 4to.

Base du Système Métrique Décimal, ou Mesure de l'Arc du méridien compris entre les parallèles de Dunkerque et Barcelone, exécutée en 1792 et années suivantes, par MM. Mechain et Delambre. Suite des Mémoires de l'Institut. I—III. *Paris*, 1806—1810. 4to.

(*All the preceding obtained by purchase.*)

Comptes-rendus hebdomadaires des séances de l'Académie des Sciences, publiés, conformément à une décision de l'Académie en date du 13 juillet 1835, par MM. les Secrétaires perpétuels. I—XLVI, 1835—1858. *Paris.* 4to.

Institut National de France. Annuaire pour l'année 1851. *Paris*, 1851. 16mo.

Institut de France: Academie des Sciences Morales et Politiques.

Mémoires de l'Institut national des Sciences et Arts. Sciences morales et politiques. I—V. *Paris*, 1798—1804. 4to.

Mémoires de l'Académie royale des Sciences morales et politiques de l'Institut de France. Deuxième série. I—VII, 1837—1850. *Paris.* 4to.

Idem. Savans étrangers. Tomes I, II, 1841, 1847. *Paris.* 4to.

Séances et Travaux de l'Académie des Sciences Morales et Politiques. IIe série. Tome VI (XVIe de la Collec-

PARIS.

Institut de France: Academie des Sciences Morales et Politiques.—*Continued.*

tion), pp. 85—198, 1849. IIIe série. Tome IV (XXIVe de la Collection), pp. 1—216, 1853. *Paris.* 8vo.

Institut Historique.

Journal de l'Institut Historique. I—XII, 1834—1840. *Paris.* 8vo.

L'Investigateur. Journal de l'Institut Historique. IIe série. I—X, 1841—1850. IIIe série. I—VII, 1851—1857. *Paris.* 8vo.

(*Wanting: IIIe série. Livr.* 214, 215, 220, 224, 247, 248.)

Congrès Historique Européen, réuni à Paris au nom de l'Institut Historique. Discours et Compte-rendu des Séances. 1835, I, II, 1837, 1838, 1839, 1843. *Paris,* 1836—1843. 8vo.

Ministere de la Marine.

Annales Hydrographiques. Recueil d'avis, instructions, documents et mémoires relatifs à l'Hydrographie et à la Navigation, publié par le *Dépôt général de la Marine.* I—VI, 1848—1851. *Paris.* 8vo.

Ministere de l'Instruction Publique.

Annuaire des Sociétés savantes de la France et de l'Etranger. Publié sous les auspices du *Ministère de l'Instruction publique.* I, 1846. *Paris.* 8vo.

Museum d'Histoire Naturelle.

Archives du Muséum d'Histoire Naturelle, publiées par les professeurs-administrateurs de cet établissement. Tomes I, 1839; II, 1841; III, 1843; IV, 1844; V, 1852; VI, 1852; VII, 1853—1855; VIII, 1855-6; IX, 1856-57. *Paris.* 4to.

Societe des Antiquaires de France.

Annuaire de la Société (royale, impériale) des Antiquaires de France. 1848—1851, 1853. *Paris.* 12mo.

PARIS.

Societe des Antiquaires de France.—*Continued.*

Mémoires de la Société (royale, impériale) des Antiquaires de France. XVII—XX, 1844—1850. *Paris.* 8vo.

Societe de Biologie.

Comptes-rendus des séances et Mémoires de la Sociéte de Biologie. Deuxième série. I, 1854. *Paris*, 1855. 8vo. (*Purchased.*)

Societe d'Encouragement pour l'Industrie Nationale.

Bulletin de la Société d'Encouragement pour l'Industrie Nationale. Deuxième série. Tome IV, mai et juin 1857. *Paris.* 4to.

Societe Ethnologique.

Mémoires de la Société Ethnologique. Tomes I, II. *Paris*, 1841, 1845. 8vo.

Bulletin de la Société Ethnologique de Paris. Tome I, 1847. *Paris.* 8vo.

Societe Francaise pour la Conservation des Monuments Historiques.

Congrès Archéologique de France. Séances générales tenues à Bourges (Cher), en octobre 1849, par la Société française pour la Conservation des Monuments historiques. *Paris*, 1850. 8vo.

Societe de Geographie.

Bulletin de la Société de Géographie. I, III—XX, 1822, 1825—1833. Deuxième série. I—XX, 1834—1843. Troisième série. I—XIV, 1844—1850. Quatrième série. I—XV, 1851—1858. *Paris.* 8vo.

(*Wanting, Ie série: Tables des Matières of Vol. I; Vol. II. IVe série: June No. of Vol. V; July, August, & September Nos. of Vol. VI.*)

Annuaire du Bureau des Longitudes. 1830—1834, 1837—1849, 1851. *Paris.* 12mo.

PARIS.

Societe de Geographie.—*Continued.*

Quelques Mots sur le Danemark, la Suède et la Norvége à propos des Elémens de Géographie générale de M. Adrien Balbi; par M. De la Roquette. *Paris.* 8vo. pp. 17.

Societe Geologique de France.

Mémoires de la Société Géologique de France. Deuxième série. I, 1844; II, 1846; III, 1848; IV, 1851; V, I, 1854. *Paris.* 4to.

Bulletin de la Société Géologique de France. Deuxième série. I—XIV, 1843—1857. *Paris*, 1844–57. 8vo. (*Wanting XIII, pp.* 1—32.)

Notice Biographique sur Mercier de Boissy, par M. D'Archiac. Lue à la Société Géologique de France, dans la séance du 15 décembre 1856. *Paris.* 8vo.

Notice sur la Vie et les Travaux de Jules Haime, par M. D'Archiac. Lue à la Société Géologique de France, dans la séance du 15 décembre 1856. *Paris.* 8vo.

Societe d'Histoire Naturelle.

Actes de la Société d'Histoire Naturelle de Paris. I, I, 1792. *Paris.* fol.

Societe d'Horticulture de la Seine.

Bulletin des Travaux de la Société ou Journal des Améliorations pratiques en matière de Jardinage. Tomes VI —XII, 1848—1854. *Paris.* 8vo. [For the previous volumes, see under *Cercle générale d'Horticulture*, p. 102.]

Societe Imperiale et Centrale d'Agriculture.

Séance publique tenue le dimanche 12 mai 1850, à deux heures, au Luxembourg. Présidée par *M. Chevreul. Paris*, 1850. 8vo.

Séance publique de rentrée tenue le mercredi 13 novembre 1850, à deux heures, au Luxembourg. Présidée par *M. Dumas. Paris*, 1850. 8vo.

PARIS.

Societe Imperiale et Centrale d'Horticulture.

Annales de la Société d'Horticulture de Paris, et Journal spécial de l'état et des progrès du Jardinage. I—X, XII—XLIV, 1827—1853. *Paris.* 8vo.

Séance publique de la Société Impériale d'Horticulture de Paris et Centrale de France, tenue à la suite de sa 24e Exposition, le dimanche 15 Mai 1853. Présidence de *M. Payen*, Président. *Paris*, 1853. 8vo.

Journal de la Société Impériale et Centrale d'Horticulture. I—III, 1855–57. *Paris.* 8vo.

Liste des Membres de la Société Impériale et Centrale d'Horticulture. 1856, 1857, 1858. *Paris.* 8vo.

Composition du Bureau et des Comités pour l'année 1852. *Paris.* 8vo.

Exposition de Mai 1853. Catalogue. *Paris.* 8vo.

Exposition de Septembre 1853. Catalogue. *Paris.* 8vo.

Commission d'organisation de l'Exposition de 1857. *Paris.*

Exposition des Produits et Objets d'Art et d'Industrie Horticoles. 1857. *Paris.* 8vo.

Societe Imperiale Zoologique d'Acclimatation.

Société Zoologique d'Acclimatation. Réglement constitutif. *Paris.* 8vo.

Bulletin de la Société Zoologique d'Acclimatation. I, 1854; II, 1855; III, i, ii, 1856; IV, 1857. *Paris.* 8vo.

Bulletin Mensuel de la Société impériale Zoologique d'Acclimatation. Allocution de M. Isidore Geoffroy-Saint-Hilaire, Président de la Société Zoologique d'Acclimatation, dans la Réunion préparatoire du 20 janvier 1854. *Paris*, 1855. 8vo.

Societe Meteorologique de France.

Annuaire de la Société Météorologique de France. II, i, feuilles 1—24; ii, 1—22; III, i, 1—5, 17—23, 27—29, 46—50; ii, 1—21; IV, i, 1—3; ii, 1—20; V, ii, 1—11. 1854–57. *Paris.* royal 8vo.

PARIS.

Societe Philomatique de Paris.

Extraits des Procès-verbaux des séances. Pendant les années 1848—1857. *Paris.* 8vo.

Verein deutscher Aerzte in Paris.

Fest-Bericht der zehnjährigen Stiftungsfeier des Vereins deutscher Aerzte in Paris. *Paris*, 1854. 4to.

Denkschrift zur Feier des zehnjæhrigen Stiftungsfestes des Vereins deutscher Aerzte in Paris. *Paris*, 1854. 4to.

Miscellanea.

Annales de Chimie, ou recueil de Mémoires concernant la Chimie et les arts qui en dépendent. Tomes I—XLVI, L—XCVI, 1790—1815. *Paris.* 8vo.

Tables générales raisonnées des Matières contenues dans Vols. I—XXX, XXXI—LX, LXI—XCVI des Annales de Chimie. 3 vols. *Paris*, 1801, 1807, 1821. 8vo.

Annales de Chimie et de Physique. I—LXXV, 1816—1840. Troisième série: I—XIV, XV, pp. 1—28, 385—512, XVI—XXXVI, L, pp. 257—384, LI, pp. 287—384. 1841—1852, 1857. *Paris.* 8vo.

Tables générales raisonnées des Matières contenues dans les Vols. I—XXX, XXXI—LX, LXI—LXXV, des Annales de Chimie et de Physique. 3 vols. *Paris*, 1831, 1840, 1841. 8vo.

Annales des Sciences Naturelles, comprenant la Zoologie, la Botanique, l'Anatomie et la Physiologie comparées des deux règnes, et l'Histoire des Corps organisés fossiles. Troisième série: Zoologie et Botanique. XIII—XX, 1850—1853. Quatrième série: Zoologie et Botanique. I—IV, VII. 1854, 1855, 1857. *Paris.* 8vo. (*Purchased.*)

Annuaire des Deux Mondes. Histoire générale des divers Etats. 1851—1852, 1854—1855, 1856—1857. *Paris.* 8vo.

Annuaire Météorologique de la France pour 1849—1852, par MM. J. Haeghens, Ch. Martins et A. Berigny, avec des Notices Scientifiques, par MM. Abria, G.

PARIS.

Miscellanea.—*Continued.*

Aime, &c., et des Séries Météorologiques, par MM. Abria, &c., 2e—4e Année. *Paris*, 1850—1853. roy. 8vo.

Archives générales de Médecine, Journal complémentaire des Sciences Médicales, publié par le Dr. Raige Delorne. IVe série. Tome XXIX, pp. 1—128. 1852. *Paris.* 8vo.

Archives de Physiologie, de Thérapeutique et d'Hygiène, sous la direction de M. Bouchardat. No. 1, Janvier 1854. Mémoire sur la Digitaline et la Digitale, par E. Homolle et Quevenne. *Paris*, 1854. 8vo.

(*From the Editor.*)

Bulletin général et universel des Annonces et des Nouvelles Scientifiques; dédié aux savants de tous les pays et à la Librairie nationale et étrangère: publié sous la direction de M. le Bon de Ferussac. I—IV, 1823. *Paris.* 8vo.

Bulletin des Sciences naturelles et de Géologie. Deuxième section du Bulletin universel des Sciences et de l'Industrie, publié sous la direction de M. le Bon de Ferussac. I—XXVII, 1824—1831. *Paris.* 8vo.

(*Purchased.*)

Dictionnaire raisonné universel d'Histoire Naturelle; contenant l'Histoire des Animaux, des Végétaux et des Minéraux, et celle des Corps célestes, des Météores, et des autres principaux Phénomènes de la Nature. Avec l'Histoire et la Description des Drogues simples tirées des trois règnes; et le détail de leurs usages dans la Médecine, dans l'Economie domestique et champêtre, et dans les Arts et Métiers. Par M. Valmont de Bomare. I—V. *Paris*, 1764. 8vo.

Dictionnaire des Sciences Naturelles, dans lequel on traite méthodiquement des differens Etres de la Nature, considérés soit en aux-mêmes d'après l'état actuel de nos connoissances, soit rélativement à l'utilité qu'en peuvent retirer la Médecine, l'Agriculture, le Commerce et les Arts. Suivi d'une Biographie des plus célèbres Naturalistes. Par plusieurs Professeurs du Jardin du Roi, et des principales Ecoles de Paris. I—LX. *Strasbourg* et *Paris*, 1816—1830. 8vo.

PARIS.

Miscellanea.—*Continued.*

Dictionnaire des Sciences Naturelles. Planches. *Paris,* 1816—1830. 8vo. (12 vols.)

Nouveau Dictionnaire d'Histoire Naturelle appliquée aux Arts, à l'Agriculture, à l'Economie rurale et domestique, à la Médecine, etc., par une Société de Naturalistes et d'Agriculteurs. Nouvelle Edition presqu' entièrement refondue et considerablement augmentée; avec des figures tirées des trois règnes de la Nature. VII—XXXVI. *Paris,* 1817—1819. 8vo.

Wanting I—VI.)

Dictionnaire Classique d'Histoire Naturelle. Par Messieurs *Audouin, Isid. Bourdou, Ad. Brongniart, De Candolle, Daudebard de Férussac, A. Desmoulins, Drapiez, Edwards, Flourens, Geoffroy de Saint-Hilaire, A. De Jussieu, Kunth, G. De Lafosse, Lamouroux, Latreille, Lucas* fils, *Presle-Duplessis, C. Prévost, A. Richard, Thiébaut de Berneaud,* et *Bory de Saint-Vincent.* Ouvrage dirigé par ce dernier collaborateur, et dans lequel on a ajouté, pour le porter au niveau de la science, un grand nombre de mots qui n'avaient pu faire partie de la plupart des Dictionnaires antérieurs. I—XVII. With Atlas. *Paris,* 1822—1831. 8vo.

Journal d'Agriculture Pratique. Quatrième série. Tome VIII, pp. 1—48. *Paris,* 1857. 8vo.

Journal des Savans. Années 1847, 1848, 1850, 1851. *Paris.* 4to.

(*Wanting:* 1847, *Jan., Feb., March;* 1848, *June, July, Aug., Sept., Oct., Nov., Dec.;* 1850, *Jan., Feb., March, April, May;* 1851, *Sept., Oct., Nov., Dec.*)

L'Année Scientifique et Industrielle, ou Exposé annuel des Travaux scientifiques, des Inventions et des principales applications de la Science à l'Industrie et aux Arts, qui ont attiré l'attention publique en France et à l'Etranger. Par Louis Figuier. Deuxième Année. *Paris,* 1858. 12mo.

L'Institut, Journal universal des Sciences et des Sociétés savantes en France et à l'Etranger. Ire Section. XVII,

PARIS.

Miscellanea.—*Continued.*

—XXII, 1849—1854. IIe Section. XIV—XIX, 1849—1854. *Paris.* 4to.

(*Wanting: Ire Section, Nos.* 990, 992, 999, 1018, 1042, 1044, 1045, 1078, 1079; *IIe Section, Nos.* 200, 201, 209, 210. *Also Titles and Tables of Contents to all but Vol. XII of the Ist Section.*)

Magazin de Zoologie. I—VIII, 1831—1838. *Paris.* 8vo.

Magazin de Zoologie, d'Anatomie comparée et de Paléontologie. Deuxième série. I—VII, 1839—1843. *Paris.* 8vo.

Revue des Deux Mondes. Années XX—XXVII. *Paris,* 1850—1857. 8vo.

(*Wanting Jan.* 1, *June* 15, 1854; *Aug.* 1, *Nov.* 15, *Dec.* 15, 1857.)

Revue Scientifique et Industrielle. Sous la direction du Docteur QUESNEVILLE. I—XVIII. *Paris,* 1840—1844. 8vo.

Revue Zoologique, par la Société Cuviérienne; association universelle pour l'avancement de la Zoologie, de l'Anatomie comparée et de la Paléontologie. Journal mensuel. Publié sous la direction de M. F. E. GUERIN-MENEVILLE. 1838—1848. *Paris.* 8vo. (11 vols.)

Revue et Magazin de Zoologie pure et appliquée. Recueil mensuel destiné à faciliter aux savans de tous les pays les moyens de publier leurs observations de Zoologie pure et appliquée à l'industrie et à l'agriculture, leurs travaux de Paléontologie, d'Anatomie et de Physiologie comparées, et à les tenir au courant des nouvelles découvertes et des progrès de la science. Par Messieurs F. E. GUERIN-MENEVILLE et AD. FOCILLON. 2e série. I—IX, 1849—1857. *Paris.* 8vo.

(*Purchased.*)

Tablettes Européennes. Revue Politique et Littéraire. Tome deuxième. 1re Année. 16e Livraison. *Paris,* 1849. 8vo.

8

ROUEN.

Academie des Sciences, Belles-Lettres et Arts de Rouen.

Précis analytique des Travaux de l'Académie royale des Sciences, Belles-Lettres et Arts de Rouen. 1842—1854. *Rouen*, 1843—1854. 8vo. (12 vols.)

SAINT-LO.

Annuaire du département de la Manche. Années IV—IX, 1832—1837; XI, XII, 1839, 1840; XVI, XVII, 1844, 1845; XXIII—XXV, 1851—1853; XXIX, 1857. *Saint-Lô*. 8vo.

(*From M. Jules Travers, of Caen.*)

SAINT-QUENTIN.

Societe Academique.

Société Académique de Saint-Quentin. Annales Agricoles, Scientifiques et Industrielles du département de l'Aisne. Deuxième série. Tome X, 1852; XI, 1853 et 1854. *Saint-Quentin*, 1853, 1855. 8vo.

STRASBOURG.

Societe des Sciences, Agriculture et Arts de Strasbourg.

Mémoires de la Société des Sciences, Agriculture et Arts de Strasbourg. I, II, 1811, 1823. *Strasbourg*. 8vo.

Nouveaux Mémoires de la Société des Sciences, Agriculture et Arts du département du Bas-Rhin. I—III, 1832—1842. *Strasbourg*. 8vo.

Bulletin agricole de la Société des Sciences, Agriculture et Arts du département du Bas-Rhin. 1843—1849. *Strasbourg*. 8vo.

Séance publique de la Société des Sciences, Agriculture et Arts du Bas-Rhin. 1846—1849. *Strasbourg*. 8vo.

Journal de la Société des Sciences, Agriculture et Arts du département du Bas-Rhin. 1826. Nos. II, III, IV. *Strasbourg*. 8vo.

STRASBOURG.

Societe du Museum d'Histoire Naturelle.

Mémoires de la Société du Muséum d'Histoire Naturelle de Strasbourg. Tomes II, 1835; III, 1840—1846; IV, 1850—1853. *Strasbourg.* 4to.

TOULOUSE.

Academie des Sciences, Inscriptions et Belles-Lettres.

Histoire et Mémoires de l'Académie royale des Sciences, Inscriptions et Belles-Lettres de Toulouse. I, 1782; IV, 1790. *Toulouse.* 4to.

Histoire et Mémoires de l'Académie royale des Sciences, Inscriptions et Belles-Lettres de Toulouse, depuis son établissement en 1807; pour faire suite à l'Histoire et aux Mémoires de l'ancienne Académie. I—VI, 1827—1843. *Toulouse.* 8vo.

Mémoires de l'Académie (royale, nationale) impériale des Sciences, Inscriptions et Belles-Lettres de Toulouse. Troisième série. I—VI, 1844—1850. Quatrième série. I—IV, VI, 1851—1854, 1856. Cinquième série. I, 1857. *Toulouse.* 8vo.

Annuaire de l'Académie (royale, nationale) impériale des Sciences, Inscriptions et Belles-Lettres de Toulouse pour l'année 1846, 1848—1851, 1854. *Toulouse.* 32mo.

Statuts et Règlements de l'Académie (royale) nationale des Sciences, Inscriptions et Belles-Lettres de Toulouse. 1847, 1849. 32mo.

WISSEMBOURG.

Miscellanea.

Archives de la Flore de France et d'Allemagne. Journal Botanique, redigé par F. SCHULTZ. Première partie, 1854—1855. *Wissembourg.* 8vo.

ITALY.

Riunione degli Scienziati Italiani.

Atti della prima Riunione degli Scienziati Italiani tenuta in Pisa nell' Ottobre del 1839. *Pisa*, 1840. 4to.

Idem. Seconda edizione, aumentata dell Orazione dell Prof. ROSINI per l'Inaugurazione della statua del Galileo, e della Biografia del Cav. Pr. Gerbi. *Pisa*, 1840. 4to.

Il Congresso di Pisa, Lettere di GOTTARDO CALVI. *Milano*, 1839. 8vo. pp. 88.

Atti della seconda Riunione, Settembre 1840. *Torino*, 1841. 4to.

Atti della terza Riunione, Settembre 1841. *Firenze*, 1841. 4to.

Atti dei Congressi degli Scienziati Italiani, raccolti ed ordinati dall' Accademia degli Aspiranti Naturalisti; con note e comenti. Editore il socio ordinario Dottor LIONARDO DOROTEA. I—VI. *Napoli*, 1844—1845. 8vo.

Diaro del settimo Congresso degli Scienziati Italiani in Napoli dal 20 di Settembre a' 5 di Ottobre dell' anno 1845. No. 1—20 di Settembre. 4to.

Relazione del settimo Congresso degli Scienziati Italiani in Napoli nel 1845. Del Professore CARLO GEMMELLARO, uno de due Deputati rappresentanti l'Accademia Gioneia al detto Congresso, letta nella seduta ordinaria del 20 Novembre 1845. *Catania*, 1845. 4to. pp. 27.

Ottavo Congresso degli Scienziati Italiani in Genova nel Settembre 1846, rapporto dei Deputati dell' Accademia Fisio-medico-statistica di Milano, Dottore GIUSEPPE FERRARIO e Consigliere nobile FERDINANDO DE HERRA, Scudiere di S. M. I. R. Ap., ecc. Letto nella tornata accademica del giorno 21 Dicembre 1846. *Milano*, 1847. 8vo. pp. 11.

Dei Lavori scientifici dell' VIII Congresso Italiano radunato in Genova nel Settembre del 1846. Relazione del Dottore CARLO LURATI. Vol. I, II. *Lugano*, 1847. 8vo.

Alcune Osservazioni sopra i Congressi scientifici Italiani. Lettera di Tizio a Sempronio e riposta di Sempronio a Tizio. *Milano*, 1847. 8vo. pp. 16.

BOLOGNA.

Accademia delle Scienze dell' Istituto di Bologna.

Novi Commentarii Academiae Scientiarum Instituti Bononiensis. I, 1834; II, 1836; III, 1839; IV, 1840; V, 1842; VI, VII, 1844; VIII, 1846; IX, X, 1849. *Bononiae.* 4to.

Indices Generales in Novos Commentarios Academiae Scientiarum Instituti Bononiensis. *Bononiae*, 1855. 4to.

Rendiconto delle Sessioni ordinarie dell' Accademia delle Scienze dell' Istituto di Bologna. (Estratto dal Bullettino delle Scienze Mediche.) Vol. I. *Bologna*, 1833. 8vo.

Rendiconto delle Sessioni dell' Accademia delle Scienze dell' Istituto di Bologna dal Novembre 1837 al Novembre 1838, 1838–39, 1839–40, 1840–41, 1841–42, 1842–43, 1843–44, 1844–45, 1845–46, 1846–47, 1847–48, 1848–49, 1849–50, 1850–51, 1851–52, 1852–53, 1853–54, 1854–55. *Bologna.* 8vo.

Memorie della Accademia delle Scienze dell' Istituto di Bologna. I, II, 1850; III, 1851; IV, 1853; V, 1854; VI, 1855. *Bologna.* 4to.

Annali di Storia Naturale. I—IV. *Bologna*, 1829—1830. 8vo.

Nuovi Annali delle Scienze Naturali. I—X. *Bologna*, 1838—1843. 8vo.

Nuovi Annali delle Scienze Naturali e Rendiconto delle Sessioni della Società Agraria, e dell' Accademia delle Scienze dell' Istituto di Bologna. Serie II. I—X, 1844—1848. Serie III. I—X, 1850—1854. *Bologna.* 8vo.

Imperial Regio Istituto Geologico.

L'Imperial Regio Istituto Geologico dell' Impero d'Austria e Rivista degli studj di Mineralogia, Geologia e Paleontologia nella Monarchia Austriaca 1850—1853. Di Adolfo Senoner. *Bologna*, 1854. 8vo. pp. 52.

Miscellanea.

Repertorium Italicum complectens Zoologiam, Mineralogiam, Geologiam et Palaeontologiam. Cura J. Josephi Bianconi. Vol. I, II. *Bononiae*, 1853, 1854. 8vo.

BRESCIA.

Ateneo di Brescia.

Commentarj della Accademia di Scienze, Lettere, Agricultura, ed Arti del Dipartimento del Mella per l'anno 1808. *Brescia*, 1808. 8vo.

Idem per l'anno		1809.	*Brescia*,	1814. 8vo.
"	"	1810.	"	1811.
"	"	1811.	"	1812.

Commentarj dell' Ateneo di Brescia per l'anno 1812. *Brescia*, 1814. 8vo.

Idem per l'anno		1813—1815.	*Brescia*,	1818.
"	"	1816, 1817.	"	1818.
"	"	1818, 1819.	"	1820.
"	"	1820.	"	1823.
"	"	1821.	"	1824.
"	"	1822.	"	1824.
"	"	1823.	"	1824.
"	"	1824.	"	1825.
"	"	1825.	"	1826.
"	"	1826.	"	1827.
"	"	1827.	"	1828.
"	"	1828—40.	"	1829—42.
"	"	1842—50.	"	1844—50.

(*Wanting* 1841.)

CATANIA.

Accademia Gioenia di Scienze Naturali.

Atti dell' Accademia Gioenia di Scienze Naturali di Catania. I—XX, 1825—1843. Serie seconda. I—VIII, 1844—1853. *Messina* and *Catania*. 4to.

Relazione Accademica del' anno XXIV dell' Accademia Gioenia, letta nella tornata ordinaria del di 8 Giugno 1848, & XXV 24 Giugno 1849, dal Segretario generale Prof. CARLO GEMMELLARO. *Catania*, 1849. 4to.

FIRENZE (FLORENCE).

Accademia del Cimento.

Saggi di naturali Esperienze fatte nell' Accademia del Cimento. Terza Edizione fiorentina, preceduta da Notizie

FIRENZE.

Accademia del Cimento.—*Continued.*

storiche dell' Accademia stessa, e segnitata da alcune Aggiunte. *Firenze,* 1841. 4to.

Notizie sulla Storia delle Scienze fisiche in Toscana, cavate da un manoscritto inedito di Giovanni Targioni-Tozzetti. *Firenze,* 1852. 4to.

LUCCA.

Reale Accademia Lucchese di Scienze, Lettere ed Arti.

Atti dell' I. e R. Accademia Lucchese di Scienze, Lettere ed Arti. I—XV. *Lucca,* 1821—1855. 8vo.

Memorie e Documenti per servire all' Istoria del Principato Lucchese (della Città e Stato di Lucca). Tomo I, 1813; II, 1814; III, i, 1816; ii, 1817; IV, i, 1818; ii, 1836; V, i, 1844; ii, 1837; iii, 1841; VII, 1834; IX, 1825; X, 1831. *Lucca.* 4to.

(*Wanting VI & VIII.*)

MILANO (MILAN).

Accademia Fisio-medico-statistica di Milano.

Diario ed Atti dell' Accademia Fisio-medico-statistica di Milano. 1846, 1847, 1848, 1854. *Milano.* 4to.

Imperiale Regio Istituto Lombardo di Scienze, Lettere ed Arti.

Giornale dell' I. R. Istituto Lombardo di Scienze, Lettere ed Arti. I, 1841; II, III, 1842; IV, 1843; V, 1844; VI, 1845; VII, 1846; VIII, 1847. *Milano.* 8vo.

Giornale dell' I. R. Istituto Lombardo di Scienze, Lettere ed Arti e Biblioteca Italiana. Nuova serie. I, 1847; II, 1850; III, 1851; IV, 1852; V, 1853; VI, 1854; VII, 1855. *Milano.* 4to.

Memorie dell' I. R. Istituto Lombardo di Scienze, Lettere ed Arti. I, 1843; II, 1845; III, 1852; IV, 1854; V, 1856. *Milano.* 4to.

MILANO.

Osservatorio.

Osservazioni sull' Intensità e sulla Direzione della Forza Magnetica, istituite negli anni 1836, 1837, 1838, all' I. R. Osservatorio di Milano da CARLO KREIL e PIETRO DELLA VEDOVA. *Milano*, 1839. 8vo.

Primo Supplemento alle Effemeridi Astronomiche di Milano. 1838. 8vo.

Effemeridi Astronomiche di Milano. 1841—1855. Con Appendice di Osservazioni e Memorie Astronomiche. *Milano*, 1840–53. 8vo.

Annuale Astronomico di Milano per l'anno 1837, 1838, 1839. *Milano*. 24mo.

Miscellanea.

Rendiconto della Beneficenza dello Spedale Maggiore e Pio Istituto di Santa Corona in Milano per l'anno 1851. Aggiunte alcune Notizie Statistiche ed Economiche per altri pii stabilimenti della Città e Provincia di Milano chi ricoverano ammalati del Dottore ANDREA BUFFINI. *Milano*, 1852. 4to.

Rendiconto della Benefizenza dell' Ospitale Maggiore e del Pio Istituto di Santa Corona in Milano per l'anno 1852, del Dottore ANDREA VERGA, Direttore. Idem, per l'anno 1853. *Milano*, 1853, 1854. 4to.

Lo Spettatore ossia Varietà Istoriche, Letterarie, Critiche, Politiche e Morali del Signor MALTE-BRUN. Recate in Italiano con Note. Tomi I—XI. *Milano*, 1814—1818. 8vo. (Bound in 23 vols.)

Il Raccoglitore ossia Archivj di Viaggi, di Filosofia, d'Istoria, di Poesia, di Eloquenza, di Critica, di Archeologia, di Novelle, di Belle Arti, di Teatri e Feste, di Bibliografia e di Miscellanee; adorni di Rami. Compilato per DAVIDE BERTOLOTTI. Vol. I—XXIV. *Milano*, 1819—1824. 8vo.

Il Nuovo Ricoglitore ossia Archivj di Geografia, di Viaggi, etc. Opera che succede allo Spettatore Italiano e Straniero, ed al Ricoglitore. Anni I, II, III. *Milano* 1825—1827. 8vo. (6 vols.)

MILANO.

Miscellanea.—*Continued.*

Milano e Lombardi nel 1818 di Davide Bertolotti. *Milano*, 1818. 8vo.

Collezione degli Atti delle solenni Distribuzioni de' Premj d'Industria fatte in Milano ed in Venezia dall' anno 1806 in avanti. Vol. I—VIII. *Milano*, 1824—1857. 8vo.

MODENA.

Societa Italiana delle Scienze.

Memorie di Matematica e di Fisica della Società Italiana delle Scienze residente in Modena. XXIV, I, 1848; II, 1850; XXV, I, 1852; II, 1855. *Modena.* 4to.

NAPOLI (NAPLES).

Accademia degli Aspiranti Naturalisti.

Discorso pronunziato nella solenne e pubblica adunanza dell' Accademia degli Aspiranti Naturalisti dal Fondatore e Direttore della medesima, il giorno 10 Gennajo 1841. *Napoli*, 1841. 8vo. pp. 8.

Atti dei Congressi degli Scienziati Italiani raccolti ed ordinati dall' *Accademia degli Aspiranti Naturalisti*; con Note e Comenti. Editore il Socio ordinario Dottor Lionardo Dorotea. [Programme.] 8vo. pp. 4.

[List of Members and Bibliographical Announcements.] *Napoli*, 1849.

Reale Accademia delle Scienze e Belle Lettere.

Atti della Reale Accademia delle Scienze, sezione della Società Reale Borbonica. I, 1819; II, 1825; III, 1832; IV, 1839; V, I, 1843; II, 1844; VI, 1851–52. *Napoli.* 4to.

Rendiconto della Reale Accademia delle Scienze, sezione della Società Reale Borbonica. Nuova Serie. Anno I, I, II, V, VI, 1852; II, 1853; IV, 1855. *Napoli.* 4to.

Avviso a' Cultori delle Scienze Naturali. 8vo. pp. 3.

NAPOLI.

Reale Osservatorio di Napoli.

Annuario del Reale Osservatorio Astronomico di Napoli. 1847, 1855, 1856. *Napoli.* 24mo.

PADOVA (PADUA).

Imperiale Regia Accademia di Scienze, Lettere ed Arti di Padova.

Saggi Scientifici e Letterarj dell' Accademia di Padova. I, 1786; II, 1789; III, I, II, 1794. *Padova.* 4to.

Memorie della Accademia di Scienze, Lettere ed Arti di Padova. V, 1809. *Padova.* 4to.

Nuovi Saggi della Cesareo-Regia Accademia di Scienze, Lettere ed Arti di Padova. I, 1817; II, 1825; III, 1831; IV, 1838; V, 1840; VI, 1847. *Padova.* 4to.

Rivista Periodica dei Lavori della I. R. Accademia di Scienze Lettere ed Arti di Padova. I—III, 1851–55. *Padova.* 8vo.

PALERMO.

Accademia Palermitana di Scienze e Lettere.

Atti della Accademia di Scienze e Lettere di Palermo. Nuova serie. I. *Palermo*, 1845. 4to.

Miscellanea.

Specchio delle Scienze, o Giornale Enciclopedico di Sicilia. Deposito letterario delle moderne Cognizioni, Scoperte, ed Osservazioni sopra le Scienze ed Arti, e particolarmente sopra la Fisica, la Chimica, la Storia naturale, la Botanica, l'Agricoltura, la Medicina, il Commercio, la Legislazione, l'Educazione, &c. Scritto dal Signor C. S. RAFINESQUE. Tomi I, II. *Palermo*, 1814. 8vo.

ROMA (ROME).

Osservatorio Astronomico del Collegio Romano.

Annali dell' Osservatorio Astronomico diretto dai PP. delle Compagnia di Gesù nel Collegio Romano. I. *Roma,* 1843. 4to.

ROMA.

Osservatorio Astronomico del Collegio Romano.— *Continued.*

Memoria intorno ad alcune Osservazioni fatte alla Specola del Collegio Romano nel corrente anno 1838. *Roma.* 4to.

Memoria intorno a parecchie Osservazioni fatte nella Specola dell' Università Gregoriana in Collegio Romano dagli Astronomi della Compagnia di Gesù l'anno 1839. Pubblicato il dì 31 Gennajo 1840. *Roma.* 4to.

Idem. Anni 1840–41. Pubb. Feb. 1842.
" Anno 1842. " Lugl. 1843.

Osservazioni fatte nella Specola dell' Università Gregoriana in Collegio Romano diretto dai PP. della Compagnia di Gesù. Anno 1843. *Roma.* 4to.

Memorie dell' Osservatorio dell' Università Gregoriana in Collegio Romano diretto dai PP. della Compagnia di Gesù. Anno 1850. *Roma*, 1851. 4to.

Descrizione del Nuovo Osservatorio del Collegio Romano D. C. D. G. e Memoria sui lavori eseguite dal 1852 a tutto Aprile 1856. Del P. Angelo Secchi D. M. C. *Roma*, 1856. 4to.

Accademia Pontificia de' Nuovi Lincei.

Statuti per l'Accademia Pontificia de' Nuovi Lincei. *Roma*, 1847. 4to. pp. 19.

Atti dell' Accademia Pontificia de' Nuovi Lincei publicati conforme alla decisione accademica del 22 Dicembro 1850, e compilati dal Segretario. Tomo I, 1847–48; IV, 1850–51; V, i—iv, vi, vii, 1851–52; VI, 1852–53; VII, i, ii, 1853–54; X, i—vi, 1856–57. *Roma*, 1851—1857. 4to.

TORINO (TURIN).

Reale Accademia delle Scienze.

Memorie della Reale Accademia delle Scienze di Torino. Serie II. I, 1839; II, 1840; III, 1841; IV, 1842; V, 1843; VI, 1844; VII, 1845; VIII, 1846; IX, 1848; X, 1849; XI, 1851; XII, 1852; XIII, 1853; XIV, 1854; XV, 1855; XVI, 1857. *Torino.* 4to.

VENEZIA (VENICE).

I. R. Istituto Veneto di Scienze, Lettere ed Arti.

Atti delle Adunanze dell' I. R. Istituto Veneto di Scienze, Lettere ed Arti. Dal Marzo 1840 all' Ottobre 1841. I. *Venezia*, 1841. 8vo.

	II, 1841–43.	*Venezia*, 1843.	8vo.
	III, 1843–44.	" 1844.	
	IV, 1844–45.	" 1845.	
	V, 1845–46.	" 1846.	
	VI, 1846–47.	" 1847.	
	VII, 1847–48.	" 1848.	
Serie secunda.	I, 1850.	" 1850.	
	II, 1850–51.	" 1851.	
	III, 1851–52.	" 1852.	
	IV, 1852–53.	" 1853.	
	V, 1853–54.	" 1854.	
	VI, & App. 1854–55.	" 1855.	
Serie terza.	I, 1855–56.	" 1855–56.	
	II, 1856–57.	" 1856–57.	

Memorie dell' I. R. Instituto Veneto di Scienze, Lettere ed Arti. V, 1855; VI, I, 1856; II, 1857. *Venezia*. 4to.

VERONA.

Accademia d'Agricoltura, Commercio ed Arti di Verona.

Memorie dell' Accademia d'Agricoltura, Commercio ed Arti di Verona. I, II, 1807; III, 1812; IV, 1813; V, VI, VII, 1815; IX, X, 1824; XI, 1829; XII, XIII, 1831; XIV, 1833; XV, 1834; XVI, 1840; XVII, XVIII, XIX, 1841; XX, 1842; XXI, 1846; XXII, 1848; XXIII, 1849; XXIV, 1850; XXV, 1851; XXVI, 1850; XXVII, XXVIII, 1851; XXIX, 1853; XXX, 1854; XXXI, XXXII, 1855. *Verona*. 8vo.

Storia della Accademia di Agricoltura, Commercio ed Arti di Verona pel triennio 1848–49–50. Compilata dal Socio Antonio Manganotti. Letta nella tornata 2 Dicembre 1852. *Verona*, 1853. 8vo. pp. 46.

SPAIN.

BARCELONA.

Real Academia de Buenas-Letras de la Ciudad de Barcelona.

Real Academia de Buenas-Letras de la Ciudad de Barcelona; Origen, Progresos, y su primera Junta general baxo la proteccion de su Magestad, con los Papeles que en ella se acordaron. Tomo primo. Partes I, II. *Barcelona.* 4to.

MADRID.

Real Academia de Ciencias de Madrid.

Memorias de la Real Academia de Ciencias. Tomos I—IV. *Madrid,* 1850–56. 4to.

Tomo I, containing: Estatutos; 3d Serie, Ciencias Naturales. I, 1850—1854.

Tomo II, containing: 1a Serie, Ciencias Exactes. I, I, 1853.

Tomo III, containing: 2a Serie, Ciencias Fisicas. I, I, 1856.

Tomo IV, containing: 3a Serie, Ciencias Naturales. II, I, 1856.

Programmo para la Adjudication de Premios en el año 1856. *Madrid,* 1855. 4to. pp. 3.

Resúmen de las Actas de la Academia Real de Ciencias de Madrid en el año academico de 1849–53. Leido en la sesion del dia 11 de Octubre, por el Segretario perpetuo, Doctor Don Mariano Lorente. *Madrid,* 1850–54. 4to.

Real Academia de la Historia.

Memorias de la Real Academia de la Historia. I, II, 1796; III, 1799; IV, 1805; VI, 1821; VII, 1832; VIII, 1852. *Madrid.* 4to.

Viage Literario á las Iglesias de España. Su autor Don Jaime Villaneuva. XI—XXII, 1850—1852. *Madrid.* 8vo.

MADRID.

Real Academia de la Historia.—*Continued.*

Memorial Histórico Español: Colleccion de Documentos, Opúsculos y Antigüedades, que publica *la Real Academia de la Historia.* I, II, 1851; III, IV, 1852; V, VI, 1853; VII, 1854. *Madrid.* 8vo.

Noticia de las Actas y Tareas de la Real Academia de la Historia, leida en su Junta publica anual de 24 de Abril de 1853, por Don Pedro Sabau. *Madrid,* 1853. 8vo.

Las Siete Partidas del Rey Don Alfonso el Sabio, cotejadas con varios codices antiguos por *la Real Academia de la Historia.* Tomo II. Partida Segunda y Tercera. Tomo III. Partida Quarta, Quinta, Sexta y Septima. *Madrid,* 1807. 4to.

SAN FERNANDO.

Observatorio de Marina de San Fernando.

Almanaque Náutico para el año 1859, calculado de órden de S. M. en el Observatorio de Marina de la Ciudad de S. Fernando. *Cadiz,* 1857. 8vo.

PORTUGAL.

LISBOA (LISBON).

Academia Real da Historia Portugueza.

Collecçam dos Documentos e Memorias da Academia Real da Historia Portugueza, que neste anno de 1722 se compuzeraõ e se imprimiraõ por ordem dos seus Censores, dedicada a Elrey nosso Senhor, seu Augustissimo Protector, e ordenada pelo Marquez de Alegrete Manoel Telles da Sylva. *Lisboa,* 1722. royal 8vo.

Idem. Anno 1725. *Lisboa.* royal 8vo.
" " 1726. " "
" " 1728. " "
" " 1729. " "
" " 1730. " "
" " 1732. " "
" " 1733. " "

LISBOA.

Academia Real das Sciencias.

Memorias de Litteratura Portugueza, publicadas della *Academia Real das Sciencias de Lisboa.* (*Nisi utile est quod facimus, stulta est gloria.*) I, 1792; II, 1792; III, 1792; IV, 1793; V, 1793; VI, 1796; VII, 1806. *Lisboa.* 8vo.

O Mordomo do Rei. Memoria offerecida á Academia R. das Sciencias de Lisboa por JOSE BARBOSA CANAES DE FIGUEIREDO CASTELLO BRANCO. *Lisboa*, 1851. 8vo.

Apontamentos ácerca da Villa de Soure por JOSE BARBOSA CANAES DE FIGUEIREDO CASTELLO BRANCO. *Lisboa*, 1851. roy. 8vo.

Apontamentos sobre as Relações de Portugal com a Syria no Seculo 12o. Lida na secção de 27 de Outubro de 1853 por JOSE BARBOSA CANAES DE FIGUEIREDO CASTELLO BRANCO. *Lisboa*, 1854. roy. 8vo.

Noticia Chronologica dos Condes de Castella, por JOSE BARBOSA CANAES DE FIGUEIREDO CASTELLO BRANCO, Socio effectivo da Academia Real das Sciences. *Lisboa*, 1854. 4to.

Trabalhos do Observatorio Meteorologico do Infante D. LUIZ na Escola Polytechnica. 2o Anno (1855—1856). *Lisboa*, 1857. fol.

GREAT BRITAIN AND IRELAND.

British Association for the Advancement of Science.

Report of the First and Second Meetings of the British Association for the Advancement of Science; at York in 1831, and at Oxford in 1832. 2d edit. *London*, 1835. 8vo.

3d, at Cambridge, in	1833.	*London*,	1834.
4th, at Edinburgh,	1834.	"	1835.
5th, at Dublin,	1835.	"	1836.
6th, at Bristol,	1836.	"	1837.
7th, at Liverpool,	1837.	"	1838.

British Association for the Advancement of Science.—*Continued.*

8th, at Newcastle,	1838.	*London,*	1839.
9th, at Birmingham,	1839.	"	1840.
10th, at Glasgow,	1840.	"	1841.
11th, at Plymouth,	1841.	"	1842.
12th, at Manchester,	1842.	"	1843.
13th, at Cork,	1843.	"	1844.
14th, at York,	1844.	"	1845.
15th, at Cambridge,	1845.	"	1846.
16th, at Southampton,	1846.	"	1847.
19th, at Birmingham,	1849.	"	1850.
20th, at Edinburgh,	1850.	"	1851.
21st, at Ipswich,	1851.	"	1852.
22d, at Belfast,	1852.	"	1853.
23d, at Hull,	1853.	"	1854.
24th, at Liverpool,	1854.	"	1855.
25th, at Glasgow,	1855.	"	1856.
26th, at Cheltenham,	1856.	"	1857.
27th, at Dublin,	1857.	"	1858.

Meeting of the British Association at Newcastle. Report of the Local Secretaries. *Newcastle,* 1839. 8vo.

Archæological Institute of Great Britain and Ireland.

Proceedings at the annual Meeting of the Archæological Institute of Great Britain and Ireland, at Winchester, September, 1845. *London,* 1846. 8vo.

York Meeting, July,	1846.	*London,*	1847.
Norwich "	1847.	"	1851.
Lincoln "	1848.	"	1850.
Salisbury "	1849.	"	1851.

BATH.

Bath and West of England Agricultural Society.

Journal of the Bath and West of England Society for the Encouragement of Agriculture, Arts, Manufactures, and Commerce, established 1777. I—III, 1853—1855; V, 1857. *London.* 8vo.

BATH.

Bath and West of England Agricultural Society.—*Continued.*

A Catalogue of the Beasts, Horses, Sheep, and Pigs, and of the various Agricultural Implements, etc., exhibited at the Society's Show, June 8th, 9th, and 10th, 1853. *Plymouth,* 1853. 8vo.

BELFAST.

Natural History and Philosophical Society.

[Miscellaneous sheets relating to its Meetings.] 8vo.

Miscellanea.

The Ulster Journal of Archæology. Vols. I—IV, 1853—1856. *Belfast.* 4to.

The Annals of Ulster. Translated from the text of O'Connor's Rerum Hibernicarum Scriptores Veteres, for the *Ulster Journal of Archæology. Belfast,* 1853. 4to. pp. 1—40.

Ulster Chemico-Agricultural Society.

The Journal and Transactions of the Chemico-Agricultural Society of Ulster. I, II, 1849—1854. *Belfast.* 4to.

BERWICK-ON-TWEED.

Berwickshire Naturalists' Club.

Proceedings of the Berwickshire Naturalists' Club. Vol. III, I—VII, 1850—1856; IV, I, 1857. 8vo.

CAMBRIDGE.

Cambridge Philosophical Society.

Transactions of the Cambridge Philosophical Society. I—VIII, 1822—1849; IX, I, 1851; III, 1853; IV, 1856. *Cambridge.* 4to. (*Wanting II,* I; *IX,* II.)

Cambridge Observatory.

Astronomical Observations made at the Observatory at Cambridge. I—XVIII, 1828—1851. *Cambridge,* 1829—1857. 4to.

CAMBRIDGE.

Cambridge Observatory.—*Continued.*

Account of the Northumberland Equatorial and Dome, attached to the Cambridge Observatory. By G. B. AIRY, Esq., M. A. *Cambridge*, 1844. 4to. pp. 39 and Plates.

Observatory of St. John's College.

Astronomical Observations made by the Rev. THOMAS CATTON, B. D. Reduced and printed under the superintendence of *George Biddell Airy, Esq.*, Astronomer Royal. *London*, 1853. 4to. pp. 32.

Cambridge University.

Cambridge Essays. Contributed by Members of the University. *London*, 1855. 8vo.

DUBLIN.

Dublin University Philosophical Society.

Transactions of the Dublin (University) Philosophical Society. I—V, 1842—1851. *Dublin*, 1843—1852. 8vo.

Geological Society.

Journal of the Geological Society of Dublin. I—VII, 1833—1857. *Dublin*, 1838—1857. 8vo.

Royal Dublin Society.

The Journal of the Royal Dublin Society. Vol. I, 1856–57. *Dublin*, 1858. 8vo.

Royal Irish Academy.

Proceedings of the Royal Irish Academy. I—V, VI, I—III, 1836–56. *Dublin*, 1841—1856. 8vo.
(*Wanting IV*, II.)

Transactions of the Royal Irish Academy. I—XXII, 1787—1855; XXIII, I, 1856. *Dublin*. 4to.

List of Members of the Royal Irish Academy. 1846, 1848. *Dublin*. 8vo.

DURHAM.

University Observatory.

Results of Astronomical Observations, made at the Observatory of the University, Durham, from October, 1849, to April, 1852. *Durham*, 1855. 8vo.

EDINBURGH.

The Bannatyne Club.

Bannatyne Club. Nos. XXIII—XXVI. Abstract of the Treasurer's accounts, 1852—1855. 4to.

Album of the Bannatyne Club. No. III. 8vo.

Catalogue of the books printed for the Members of the Bannatyne Club since its institution. February, 1854. 8vo.

Thomas Thomson, Esq., Advocate, President of the Bannatyne Club. 4to. pp. 12.

The Bannatyne Miscellany; containing original papers and tracts, chiefly relating to the History and Literature of Scotland. III. *Edinburgh*, 1855. 4to.

Historical Notices of Scottish Affairs, selected from the manuscripts of Sir John Lauder of Fountainhall, Bart., one of the senators of the College of Justice. I—II, 1661—1688. *Edinburgh*, 1848. 4to.

Historical Observes of Memorable Occurrents in Church and State, from October, 1680, to April, 1686. By Sir John Lauder, of Fountainhall. *Edinburgh*, 1840. 4to.

Some Historicall Observes breiflie mentioning some of the Memorable Occurrents happening ather in Church or State throw Europe but more especially in Scotland and England, being a continuation of remarks of this nature in another 8vo. book. *Edinburgh*, 1680—1686. 4to.

The Letters and Journals of Robert Baillie, A. M., Principal of the University of Glasgow. 1737—1772. In three volumes. *Edinburgh*, 1841—1842. 4to.

(*Purchased.*)

Memoir of the Life and Writings of Robert Baillie. 4to.

Horn et Rimenhild. Recueil de ce qui reste des Poëmes relatifs à leurs aventures composés en français, en anglais et en écossais dans les treizième, quatorzième, quinzièm.

EDINBURGH.

The Bannatyne Club.—*Continued.*

et seizième siècles. Publié d'après les manuscrits de Londres, de Cambridge, d'Oxford et d'Edinburgh, par FRANCISQUE MICHEL. *Paris*, 1845. 4to.

Carte Monialium de Northberwic. Prioratus cisterciensis B. Marie de Northberwic munimenta vetusta que supersunt. *Edinburgi*, 1847. 4to.

Vita Sancti Columbæ: auctore Adamnano Monasterii Hiensis Abbate. *Dublinii*, 1847. 4to.

Liber S. Thome de Aberbrothoc. Registrorum Abbacie de Aberbrothoc Pars prior. Registrum vetus munimentaque eidem coetanea complectens. 1178—1329. *Edinburgi*, 1848. 4to.

Liber S. Thome de Aberbrothoc. Pars altera, Registrum Nigrum necnon Libros Cartarum recentiores complectens. 1329—1536. *Edinburgi*, 1856. 4to.

Registrum S. Marie de Neubotle: Abbacie cisterciensis Beate Virginis de Neubotle Chartarium vetus. Accedit appendix Cartarum originalium. 1140—1528. *Edinburgi*, 1849. 4to.

Registrum Honoris de Morton: a series of ancient Charters of the Earldom of Morton, with other original papers, in two volumes. I. Original papers. II. Ancient charters. *Edinburgh*, 1853. 4to.

Registrum Episcopatus Brechinensis, cui accedunt Cartæ quamplurimæ originales. I. Registrum. II. Appendix Cartarum. *Aberdoniæ*, 1856. 4to.

The Darien Papers: being a selection of original Letters and official documents relating to the establishment of a colony at Darien by the Company of Scotland trading to Africa and the Indies. 1695—1700. *Edinburgh*, 1849. 4to.

Descriptive catalogue of Impressions from ancient Scottish Seals, royal, baronial, ecclesiastical, and municipal, embracing a period from A. D. 1094 to the Commonwealth. Taken from original charters and other deeds preserved in public and private archives. By HENRY LAING, Edinburgh. *Edinburgh*, 1850. 4to.

EDINBURGH.

The Bannatyne Club.—*Continued.*

Origines Parochiales Scotiæ. The Antiquities ecclesiastical and territorial of the parishes of Scotland. I, II, I, II. *Edinburgh,* 1850—1855. 4to.

Original Letters relating to the Ecclesiastical Affairs of Scotland, chiefly written by or addressed to his majesty King James the Sixth, after his accession to the English throne. I, II, 1603—1625. *Edinburgh,* 1851. 4to.

Breviarium Aberdonense. I, II. *Londini,* 1854. 4to.

The Black Book of Taymouth, with other papers from the Breadalbane Charter room. *Edinburgh,* 1855. 4to.

A series of Etchings, chiefly of Views in Scotland. By John Clerk, of Eldin, Esq. 1773—1779. With additional Etchings and Fac-similes from his Drawings. *Edinburgh,* 1855. fol.

Botanical Society of Edinburgh.

First Annual Report, Laws, and Proceedings of the Botanical Society of Edinburgh. Instituted 17th March, 1836. Session 1836–37. Third, fourth, fifth, sixth, seventh, and eighth Reports. 1839–44. *Edinburgh,* 8vo.

Laws, By-laws, and Regulations of the Botanical Society of Edinburgh. Corrected to 1st October, 1841. *Edinburgh,* 1841. 8vo.

Transactions of the Botanical Society. I—III, IV. I, II, V. *Edinburgh,* 1844–56. 8vo.

The Highland and Agricultural Society of Scotland.

Prize Essays and Transactions of the Highland and Agricultural Society of Scotland. XI, pp. 1—56, 125—168. *Edinburgh,* 1835. 8vo.

Premiums offered by the Highland and Agricultural Society of Scotland for promoting Agriculture and Internal Improvement in Scotland in 1836. *Edinburgh.* 8vo.

Royal Observatory.

Astronomical Observations made at the Royal Observatory, Edinburgh. I—XI, 1834—1854. *Edinburgh,* 1838—1857. 4to.

EDINBURGH.

Royal Observatory.—*Continued.*

Extracts from the Letter-press of the Astronomical Observations made at the Royal Observatory, Edinburgh, 1842—1847. *Edinburgh*, 1849—1852. 4to.

Report to the principal Secretary of State for the Home Department on the Royal Observatory of Edinburgh. 1846. 4to.

Royal Scottish Society of Arts.

Transactions of the Royal Scottish Society of Arts. Vol. I, Preface, Index, and pp. 71—91; II; III, I, II, III, V; IV. *Edinburgh*, 1841-55. 8vo.

List of Fellows, Honorary Members, and Associates of the Royal Scottish Society of Arts. 1840. 8vo.

Royal Society of Edinburgh.

Transactions of the Royal Society of Edinburgh. IV—XXI, 1793—1856. *Edinburgh*, 1798—1856. 4to.

Proceedings of the Royal Society of Edinburgh. Sessions 1851-2, 1852-3, 1853-4, 1854-5, 1855-6, 1856-7. *Edinburgh.* 8vo.

Scottish Meteorological Society.

Report of the Preliminary Meeting of the Scottish Meteorological Association. 1855. *Edinburgh.* 8vo.

Society of Antiquaries of Scotland.

Proceedings of the Society of Antiquaries of Scotland. Vols. I, II. *Edinburgh*, 1855, 1856. 4to.

Archæologia Scotica: or Transactions of the Society of Antiquaries of Scotland. I—IV, 1792—1823. *Edinburgh.* 4to.

Miscellanea.

The Edinburgh Philosophical Journal, exhibiting a view of the progress of discovery in natural philosophy, chemistry, natural history, practical mechanics, geography, statistics, and the fine and useful arts. Conducted by Dr. BREWSTER and Prof. JAMESON. I—XIV. *Edinburgh*, 1819—1826. 8vo.

EDINBURGH.

Miscellanea.—*Continued.*

The Edinburgh New Philosophical Journal, exhibiting a view of the progressive improvements and discoveries in the sciences and the arts. Conducted by ROBERT JAMESON. I—LVII. *Edinburgh*, 1826—1854. 8vo.

The Edinburgh New Philosophical Journal, exhibiting a view of the progressive discoveries and improvements in the sciences and the arts. Editors: THOMAS ANDERSON, Sir WILLIAM JARDINE, and JOHN HUTTON BALFOUR. For America, HENRY DARWIN ROGERS. I—VII. New series. *Edinburgh*, 1855—1858. 8vo.

The Edinburgh Journal of Science, exhibiting a view of the progress of discovery in natural philosophy, chemistry, mineralogy, geology, botany, zoology, comparative anatomy, practical mechanics, geography, navigation, statistics, antiquities, and the fine and useful arts. Conducted by DAVID BREWSTER. I—X, 1824—1829. New series. I—VI, 1829—1832. *Edinburgh.* 8vo.

Magazine of Zoology and Botany. Conducted by Sir W. JARDINE, Bart., P. S. SELBY, Esq., and Dr. JOHNSTON. I, II. *Edinburgh*, 1837, 1838. 8vo.

The Edinburgh Journal of Natural and Geographical Science. Under the direction of WILLIAM AINSWORTH and HENRY A. CHEEK. I, II. *Edinburgh*, 1830. 8vo.

Chambers's Journal of Popular Literature, Science, and Arts. New Series. Reprint of the Edinburgh edition. II—VII. *New York*, 1855-57. royal 8vo.

(*Wanting I; II, Parts* VII—X; *IV,* XX—XXIV; *V,* XXVI—XXVIII, XXX.)

Blackwood's Edinburgh Magazine. Vols. LXIX—LXXVIII, LXXIX, Feb. *New York*, 1851—1856. 8vo.

(*Wanting LXXI, April; LXXII, July, Sept., Dec.; LXXIII, Jan., March—May; LXXV, February; LXXVI, Aug., Dec.; LXXVIII, Dec.*)

The Edinburgh Review or Critical Journal. I—CII, CV, I, 1802—1855, 1857. *Edinburgh.* 8vo.

General Index to the Edinburgh Review, from its com-

EDINBURGH.

Miscellanea.—*Continued.*

mencement in October, 1802, to the end of the eightieth volume. *Edinburgh* and *London*, 1813, 1832, 1850. 8vo. (3 vols.)

The North British Review. I—XVI, 1844—1851; XX, XL; XXI—XXIII; XXIV, XLVII, 1854, 1855. *Edinburgh.* 8vo.

(*Purchased.*)

FALMOUTH.

Royal Cornwall Polytechnic Society.

The Twenty-second Annual Report of the Royal Cornwall Polytechnic Society. *Falmouth*, 1854. 8vo.

GREENWICH.

Royal Observatory.

Plan of the Buildings and Grounds of the Royal Observatory, Greenwich, with Explanation and History. *London*, 1847. 4to.

Regulations of the Royal Observatory, Greenwich. 1852. 4to.

Description of the Altitude and Azimuth Instrument erected at the Royal Observatory, Greenwich, in the year 1847. 4to.

Explanation of a proposed construction of Zenith Sector. *Greenwich*, 1848. 4to.

Description of the Transit Circle of the Royal Observatory, Greenwich. 1852. 4to.

Description of the Instruments and Process used in the Photographic Self-registration of the Magnetical and Meteorological Instruments at the Royal Observatory, Greenwich. *London*, 1849. 4to.

Astronomical Observations made at the Royal Observatory at Greenwich. I—IV, I, III; V, I, II (1811—1824); 1825—1835. *London*, 1815—1836. fol.

(*Wanting IV*, II; *V*, III?)

Astronomical Observations made at the Royal Observatory, Greenwich. 1836—1855. *London*, 1837—1857. 4to.

GREENWICH.

Royal Observatory.—*Continued.*

Appendix to Greenwich Observations. 1836. Idem, 1837, 1842, 1847. *London.* 4to.

Appendix to the Greenwich Observations, including the results of Magnetical and Meteorological Observations. 1848. Idem, 1849, 1850, 1851, 1852, 1853, 1854 & 1855. 4to.

Determination of the Longitude of Valentia in Ireland, by transmission of Chronometers (forming the Appendix to the Greenwich Astronomical Observations, 1845). 4to.

Reduction of the Observations of Planets, made at the Royal Observatory, Greenwich, from 1750 to 1830. *London*, 1845. 4to.

Reduction of the Observations of the Moon, made at the Royal Observatory, Greenwich, from 1750—1830. I, II. *London*, 1848. 4to.

Magnetical and Meteorological Observations made at the Royal Observatory, Greenwich, in the years 1840 and 1841, 1842, 1843, 1844, 1845, 1846, 1847. *London*, 1842—1849. 4to.

Reports of the Astronomer Royal to the Board of Visitors. 1836—1856. 4to.

Address of the Astronomer Royal to the Individual Members of the Board of Visitors of the Royal Observatory: and Report of the Astronomer Royal, 1853. Idem, 1855. 4to.

Approximate Right Ascension and North Polar Distance of 720 Stars, from observations made at the Royal Observatory at Greenwich. *London.* fol. pp. 10.

A Catalogue of 1112 Stars, reduced from observations made at the Royal Observatory of Greenwich, from the years 1816 to 1833. *London*, 1833. folio.

Tables containing the sum of three Equations of Aberration, solar Nutation, and Precession, for twenty-three principal fixed Stars, for every day in leap year, the first, second, and third years after. *London.* fol. pp. 48.

The sum of three Equations of Aberration, solar Nutation, and Precession, of forty principal Stars, for every day of

GREENWICH.

Royal Observatory.—*Continued.*

the year, in leap year, the first, second, and third years after. *London.* fol. pp. 85.

Rates of Chronometers on trial for purchase by the Board of Admiralty, at the Royal Observatory. *Greenwich,* 1849. 4to.

KILKENNY.

Kilkenny and South-East of Ireland Archæological Society.

Transactions of the Kilkenny Archæological Society. II, 1852–53. *Dublin,* 1855. 8vo.

Proceedings and Transactions of the Kilkenny and South-East of Ireland Archæological Society. III, 1854–55. *Dublin,* 1856. 8vo.

(*Wanting pp.* 369—408 *inclusive.*)

The Journal of the Kilkenny and South-East of Ireland Archæological Society. Vol. I. New series. 1856–57. *Dublin,* 1858. 8vo.

(*Wanting No.* 7.)

LEEDS.

Geological and Polytechnic Society of the West Riding of Yorkshire.

The Geological and Polytechnic Society of the West Riding of Yorkshire. Established December, 1837. 8vo.

Proceedings of the Geological and Polytechnic Society of the West Riding of Yorkshire. I, II, III, pp. 1—296; IV, pp. 337—544. *Leeds,* 1849—1857. 8vo.

(*Wanting Vol. I, Meetings of June* 4*th and October* 5*th,* 1840 ; *also the remainder of Vols. III and IV.*)

Philosophical and Literary Society.

Laws and Regulations of the Leeds Philosophical and Literary Society. (Instituted the 14th of January, 1820.) Revised and corrected to May 7, 1841. *Leeds.* 8vo. pp. 20.

LEEDS.

Philosophical and Literary Society.—*Continued.*

Reports of the Council of the Leeds Philosophical and Literary Society. V—VII, XI—XXXIII, XXXV—XXXVII, 1824–57. *Leeds.* 8vo.

Transactions of the Philosophical and Literary Society of Leeds, consisting of Papers read before the Society. I, I. *London,* 1837. 8vo.

A Guide to the Museum of the Leeds Philosophical and Literary Society. *Leeds,* 1854. 8vo. pp. 34.

LEICESTER.

Leicester Literary and Philosophical Society.

Leicester Literary and Philosophical Society. Instituted June, 1835. Report of the Council presented to the annual general Meeting, assembled, June, 1855; and a selection of Papers read before the Society since its formation. *Leicester,* 1855. 8vo.

LIVERPOOL.

Historic Society of Lancashire and Cheshire.

Historic Society of Lancashire and Cheshire.—Proceedings and Papers. Sessions I—III, 1848–9, 1849–50, 1850–51. *Liverpool,* 1849—1851. 8vo.

Transactions of the Historic Society of Lancashire and Cheshire. VII, 1854–55; IX, 1856–57. *London,* 1855, 1857. 8vo.

Liverpool Royal Institution.

Report of the State of the Liverpool Royal Institution, made to the Meeting of the Proprietors, 14th March, 1820. By B. A. Heywood, Esq. *Liverpool,* 1820. 8vo.

Liverpool Royal Institution. Report of the Committee presented to the annual Meeting, February 10th, 1837. *Liverpool,* 1837. 8vo.

Idem for 1839–40, 1840–41, 1841–42, 1842–43, 1844, 1845, 1846, 1847, 1848, 1849, 1855–56, 1856–57. *Liverpool.* 8vo.

LIVERPOOL.

Liverpool Royal Institution.—*Continued.*

Addresses delivered at the annual Meetings of the Liverpool Royal Institution. 1825, 1829—1832, 1850—1852. *Liverpool.* 8vo.

LONDON.

Allelodidactic Society.

Transactions of the Allelodidactic Society. I, I, II. *London,* 1847, 1848. 8vo.

The Animals' Friend Society.

The Animals' Friend, or the Progress of Humanity. 5 Nos., from 1834 to 1841. *London.* 8vo.

Astronomical Society of London.

(*See Royal Astronomical Society of London.*)

Mr. Bishop's Observatory, Regent's Park, London.

Astronomical Observations taken at the Observatory, South Villa, Inner Circle, Regent's Park, London. During the years 1839—1851. Under the direction of George Bishop, Esq., F. R. S. *London,* 1852. 4to.

Remarks and Notes to Mr. Bishop's Ecliptical Charts. *London.* 4to.

Board of Trade.

First Number of Meteorological Papers published by authority of the Board of Trade. *London,* 1857. 4to.

British Archæological Association.

The Journal of the British Archæological Association, established in 1843, for the encouragement and prosecution of researches into the arts and monuments of the early and middle ages. I—IX, X, XXXVII, XXXVIII. *London,* 1846—1854.

The Archæological Journal. Published under the direction of the Central Committee of the British Archæological Association for the encouragement and prosecution of

LONDON.

British Archæological Association.—*Continued.*

researches into the arts and monuments of the early and middle ages. I—VII. *London*, 1845—1850. 8vo.

Transactions of the British Archæological Association, at its second annual Congress, held at Winchester, August, 1845, consisting of the Papers read at the several meetings, together with an account of the Exhibitions and Excursions made by the Association. *London*, 1846. 8vo.

Idem. Third annual Congress, held at Gloucester, August, 1846. *London*, 1848.

The British Archæological Association [Programme and List of Officers and Members]. *London*, 1847. 8vo. pp. 12. Idem, Worcester Congress, 1848. 8vo. pp. 4.

The British and Foreign Aborigines' Protection Society.

The Colonial Intelligencer or Aborigines' Friend. Comprising the Transactions of the Abor. Prot. Society, interesting intelligence concerning the Aborigines of various Climes, and Articles upon Colonial Affairs; with comments upon the Proceedings of Government and of Colonists towards Native Tribes. I—IV, 1847—1855. *London.* 8vo.

Report of the Parliamentary Select Committee on Aboriginal Tribes (British Settlements). Reprinted with Comments by the Abor. Prot. Soc. 1837, with Annual Reports of the Abor. Prot. Soc. for 1838—1847. Report on the Indians of Upper Canada. Outline of a System of Legislation for securing protection to the Aboriginal Inhabitants of all Countries colonized by Great Britain. Extracts from the Papers and Proceedings of the Abor. Prot. Soc. from June, 1839, to Sept. 1841. New Zealand and its Native Population. Appeal of the British and Foreign Abor. Prot. Soc., and Proceedings at a Public Meeting held the 11th Nov. 1851, at the London Tavern, on the Kaffir War. *London*, 1837—1851. 8vo.

LONDON.

The British and Foreign Aborigines' Protection Society.—*Continued.*

Some account of the Conduct of the religious Society of Friends towards the Indian Tribes in the Settlement of the Colonies of East and West Jersey and Pennsylvania, with a brief narrative of their Labors for the Civilization and Christian Instruction of the Indians, from the time of their settlement in America to the year 1843. *London,* 1844. 8vo.

British Government.

Observations on days of unusual Magnetic Disturbance, made at the British colonial Magnetic Observatories, under the departments of the Ordnance and Admiralty. I, I, 1840—1841; II, 1842—1844. *London,* 1843—1851. 4to.

Observations made at the Magnetical and Meteorological Observatory at St. Helena. I, 1840—1843. *London,* 1847. 4to.

Observations made at the Magnetical and Meteorological Observatory at Toronto, Canada. I, 1840—1845; II, III, 1846-48. *London,* 1845—1857. 4to.

Observations made at the Magnetical and Meteorological Observatory at Hobarton, in Van Diemen Land, and by the Antarctic Naval Expedition. I—III, 1841—1846. *London,* 1850—1853. 4to.

Observations made at the Magnetical and Meteorological Observatory at the Cape of Good Hope. Printed under the superintendence of Lt. Col. *Edward Sabine.* Vol. I.—Magnetical Observations, 1841 to 1846. *London,* 1851. 4to.

Results of Astronomical Observations made during the years 1834, 5, 6, 7, 8, at the Cape of Good Hope; being the completion of a Telescopic Survey of the whole surface of the visible Heavens, commenced in 1825, by Sir JOHN F. W. HERSCHEL. *London,* 1847. 4to.

LONDON.

British and Foreign School Society.

The Educational Record, with the Proceedings at large of the British and Foreign School Society. I, No. 12. 1851. *London.* 8vo.

British Museum.

Report of the Commissioners appointed to inquire into the Constitution and Government of the British Museum, with Minutes of Evidence. 1847—1849, and Index. *London*, 1850. fol.

The Camden Society.

The Political Songs of England, from the reign of John to that of Edward II. Edited and translated by THOMAS WRIGHT, Esq., M. A., F. S. A., &c. *London*, 1839. 4to.

A Chronicle of the first thirteen years of the reign of King Edward the Fourth. By John WARKWORTH, D. D. *London*, 1839. 4to.

Ecclesiastical Documents, viz: I. A brief History of the Bishoprick of Somerset from its foundation to the year 1174. II. Charters from the Library of Dr. Cox Macro. Now first published by the Rev. JOSEPH HUNTER, F. S. A. *London*, 1840. 4to.

Annals of the first four years of the reign of Queen Elizabeth. By Sir JOHN HAYWARD, Knt. D. C. L. Edited from a MS. in the Harleian Collection, by *John Bruce*, Esq., F. S. A. *London*, 1840. 4to.

Speculi Britanniæ Pars: an Historical and Chorographical description of the County of Essex. By JOHN NORDEN. 1594. Edited from the original manuscript in the Marquess of Salisbury's Library at Hatfield, by *Sir Henry Ellis*. *London*, 1840. 4to.

Kemp's Nine Daies Wonder: performed in a dance from London to Norwich, with an Introduction and Notes, by Rev. ALEXANDER DYCE. *London*, 1840. 4to.

Chronica Jocelini de Brakelonda, de rebus gestis Samsonis Abbatis Monasterii Sancti Edmundi. Nunc primum typis mandata curante JOHANNE GAGE ROKEWODE. *Londini*, 1840. 4to.

LONDON.

The Camden Society.—*Continued.*

The Egerton Papers. A Collection of public and private Documents, chiefly illustrative of the times of Elizabeth and James I., from the original Manuscripts, the property of the Right Hon. Lord Francis Egerton, M. P., President of the Camden Society. Edited by J. PAYNE COLLIER, Esq., F. S. A. *London*, 1840. 4to.

The Chronicle of William de Rishanger, of the Barons' Wars. The Miracles of Simon de Montfort. Edited from Manuscripts in the Cottonian Library, by JAMES ORCHARD HALLIWELL, Esq., F. R. S., &c. *London*, 1840. 4to.

Narratives illustrative of the Contests in Ireland in 1641 and 1690. Edited by THOMAS CROFTON CROKER. *London*, 1841. 4to.

The Second Book of the Travels of Nicander Nucius, of Corcyra. Edited from the original Greek MS. in the Bodleian Library, with an English translation, by the Rev. J. A. CRAMER, D. D. *London*, 1841. 4to.

The Latin Poems commonly attributed to Walter Mapes. Collected and edited by THOMAS WRIGHT, Esq., M. A., F. S. A., etc. *London*, 1841. 4to.

The Private Diary of Dr. John Dee, and the Catalogue of his Library of Manuscripts, from the original Manuscripts in the Ashmolean Museum at Oxford, and Trinity College Library, Cambridge. Edited by JAMES ORCHARD HALLIWELL, Esq. *London*, 1842. 4to.

Rutland Papers. Original Documents illustrative of the Courts and Times of Henry VII. and Henry VIII. Selected from the private Archives of his Grace the Duke of Rutland, &c. &c. &c. By WILLIAM JERDAN, F. S. A., etc. *London*, 1842. 4to.

An Apology for Lollard Doctrines, attributed to Wicliffe. Now first printed from a Manuscript in the Library of Trinity College, Dublin. With an Introduction and Notes, by JAMES HENTHORNE TODD, D. D., V. P. R. I. A., etc. *London*, 1842. 4to.

Three Early English Metrical Romances, with an Introduc-

LONDON.

The Camden Society.—*Continued.*

tion and Glossary. Edited from a MS. in the possession of J. J. Blackburne, Esq., M. P. By John Robson, Esq. *London*, 1842. 4to.

The Diary of Dr. Thomas Cartwright, Bishop of Chester; commencing at the time of his elevation to that See, August, 1686; and terminating with the Visitation of St. Mary Magdalene College, Oxford, October, 1687. Now first printed from the original MS. in the possession of Rev. Joseph Hunter, F. S. A. *London*, 1843. 4to.

Promptorium Parvulorum sive Clericorum, Lexicon Anglo-Latinum Princeps. Auctore Fratre Galfrido, Grammatico dicto, e predicatoribus Lenne Episcopi, Northfolciensi, A. D. circa MCCCCXL. Olim e prelis Pynsonianis editum, nunc ab integro, commentariolis subjectis, ad fidem codicum recensuit Albertus Way. Tomus Prior. *Londini*, 1843. 4to.

A Contemporary Narrative of the Proceedings against Dame Alice Kyteler, prosecuted for Sorcery in 1324, by Richard de Ledrede, Bishop of Ossory. Edited by *Thomas Wright*, Esq., M. A., F. S. A., &c. *London*, 1843. 4to.

Three Chapters of Letters relating to the Suppression of Monasteries. Edited from the originals in the British Museum, by Thomas Wright, Esq., M. A., F. S. A., etc. *London*, 1843. 4to.

Original Letters of Eminent Literary Men of the Sixteenth, Seventeenth, and Eighteenth Centuries: with Notes and Illustrations, by Sir Henry Ellis, K. H., F. R. S., etc. *London*, 1843. 4to.

Chroniques de London, depuis l'an 44 Hen. III. jusqu' à l'an 17 Edw. III. Edited from a MS. in the Cottonian Library, by George James Aungier. *London*, 1844. 4to.

The Thornton Romances. The Early English Metrical Romances of Percival, Isumbras, Eglamour, and Degrevant. Selected from Manuscripts at Lincoln and Cam-

LONDON.

The Camden Society.—*Continued.*

bridge. Edited by JAMES ORCHARD HALLIWELL, Esq., F. R. S., etc. *London*, 1844. 4to.

Three Books of Polydore Vergil's English History, comprising the reigns of Henry VI., Edward IV., and Richard III., from an early translation preserved among the MSS. of the old Royal Library in the British Museum. Edited by Sir HENRY ELLIS, K. H. *London*, 1844. 4to.

Correspondence of Robert Dudley, Earl of Leycester, during his Government of the Low Countries in the years 1585 and 1586. Edited by JOHN BRUCE, F. S. A. *London*, 1844. 4to.

Verney Papers. Notes of Proceedings in the Long Parliament, Temp. Charles I. Printed from original pencil Memoranda taken in the House by Sir Ralph Verney, Knight, and now in the possession of Sir Harry Verney, Bart. Edited by JOHN BRUCE, Esq., F. S. A. *London*, 1845. 4to.

The Autobiography of Sir John Bramston, K. B., of Skreens, in the Hundred of Chelmsford. Now first printed from the original MS. in the possession of his lineal descendant, Thomas William Bramston, Esq., one of the Knights of the Shire for South Essex. *London*, 1845. 4to.

Letters from James Earl of Perth, Lord Chancellor of Scotland, etc., to his Sister the Countess of Erroll and other members of his family. Edited by WILLIAM JERDAN, M. R. S. L. *London*, 1845. 4to.

De Antiquis Legibus Liber. Chronica Maiorum et Vicecomitum Londoniarum et quedam, que contingebant temporibus illis ab Anno MCLXXVIII° ad Annum MCCLXXIV^m^; cum Appendice. Nunc primum typis mandata curante THOMA STAPLETON. *Londoniis*, 1846. 4to.

The Chronicle of Calais in the reigns of Henry VII. and Henry VIII. to the year 1540. Edited from MSS. in

LONDON.

The Camden Society.—*Continued.*

the British Museum, by JOHN GOUGH NICHOLS, F. S. A. *London*, 1846. 4to.

Polydore Vergil's English History, from an early translation preserved among the MSS. of the old Royal Library in the British Museum. Vol. I. Containing the first eight Books, comprising the period prior to the Norman Conquest. Edited by Sir HENRY ELLIS, K. H. *London*, 1846. 4to.

A Relation, or rather a true Account, of the Island of England; with sundry particulars of the customs of these People, and of the Royal Revenues under King Henry the Seventh, about the year 1500. Translated from the Italian, with Notes, by CHARLOTTE AUGUSTA SNEYD. *London*, 1847. 4to.

The Camden Miscellany. Volume the First: Containing, Register and Chronicle of the Abbey of Aberconway. Chronicle of the Rebellion in Lincolnshire, in 1470. Bull of Pope Innocent VIII. on the Marriage of Henry VII. with Elizabeth of York. Journal of the Siege of Rouen, in 1591. Letter of George Fleetwood, describing the Battle of Lutzen and death of Gustavus Adolphus. Diary of Dr. Edward Lake, Chaplain and Tutor to the Princesses Mary and Anne, 1677—1678. *London*, 1847. 4to.

Documents relating to the Foundation and Antiquities of the Collegiate Church of Middleham in the County of York; with an Historical Introduction, and Incidental Notices of the Castle, Town, and Neighborhood. By the Rev. WILLIAM ATHILL, Canon and Sub-Dean of Middleham. *London*, 1847. 4to.

Cavendish Society.

Lists of Members, etc. of the Cavendish Society. *London.*

Chemical Society.

Memoirs and Proceedings of the Chemical Society of London. Vols. I—III, 1841—1848. *London*, 1843—1848. 8vo.

LONDON.

Chemical Society.—*Continued.*

The Quarterly Journal of the Chemical Society of London. I—V, 1849—1853; VI, I, III, IV, 1853—1854; VII, I, II, IV, 1854; VIII, I—III, 1855; IX, X, 1857, 1858. *London.* 8vo.

Entomological Society.

Transactions of the Entomological Society of London. Vol. I, Part I. *London*, 1807. 8vo.

The Transactions of the Entomological Society of London. I—V, 1834—1839. *London*, 1836—1849. 8vo.

Address delivered at the Anniversary Meeting of the Entomological Society of London on the 24th January, 1848. By WILLIAM SPENCE, Esq., F. R. S. *London*, 1848. 8vo.

Ethnological Society.

Journal of the Ethnological Society of London. I, 1848; II, 1850; III, 1852; IV, 1856. *London.* 8vo.

A Manual of Ethnological Inquiry; being a series of Questions concerning the Human Race, prepared by a Subcommittee of the British Association for the Advancement of Science, appointed in 1851, and adapted for the use of Travellers and others, in studying the Varieties of Man. *London*, 1852. 8vo. pp. 15.

Remarks on the Nature, Objects, and Evidences of Ethnological Science: an Address read at the Ethnological Society, at a Conversazione, on Wednesday, June 4, 1851. By RICHARD CULL. *London.* 8vo. pp. 11.

Address to the Ethnological Society of London, delivered at the annual Meeting on the 25th of May, 1855, by JOHN CONOLLY, President; and a Sketch of the recent Progress of Ethnology, by RICHARD CULL. *London.* 8vo.

The Regulations of the Ethnological Society of London. 1850 & 1855. *London.* 8vo. pp. 16 & 15.

List of the Ethnological Society of London on the 25th May, 1855. *London*, 1855. 8vo. pp. 7.

List of Officers and Programme. 8vo. pp. 2.

LONDON.

Geological Society.

Transactions of the Geological Society of London. Second series. II—VII, 1826—1856. *London.* 4to.

Proceedings of the Geological Society of London. I—III, 1826—1842. *London*, 1834—1842. 8vo.

The Quarterly Journal of the Geological Society of London. Edited by the Assistant Secretary of the Geological Society. Part I.—Proceedings of the Geological Society. Part II.—Miscellaneous. I—XI, 1843—1855; XII, I, 1856; XIII, I, IV, 1857. *London.* 8vo.

Address delivered at the Anniversary Meeting of the Geological Society of London on the 20th of February, 1857. By Col. J. E. PORTLOCK, R. E., &c., President of the Society. *London*, 1857. 8vo.

Hakluyt Society.

The History of the great and mighty Kingdom of China and the Situation thereof. Compiled by JUAN GONZALEZ DE MENDOZA. Edited by Sir *Geo. T. Staunton*, Bart. *London*, 1853. 8vo.

Horticultural Society.

Transactions of the Horticultural Society of London. I—VII. *London*, 1812—1830. 4to.

Journal of the Horticultural Society of London. I—IX, 1846—1854. *London.* 8vo.

Charters and Bye-laws of the Horticultural Society of London. *London*, 1816. 4to.

Additional Bye-laws of the Horticultural Society of London. *London*, 1817. 4to.

List of the Horticultural Society of London. January, 1818; May, 1818; January, 1819; May, 1819; May, 1820; May, 1821; May, 1822; May, 1823; May, 1824; March, 1825; May, 1825; May, 1826. *London.* 4to.

Horticultural Society of London. Report of the Garden Committee on the Formation and Progress of the Garden. March 31, 1823; March 31, 1824; March 31, 1825. *London*, 1823, 1824, 1825. 4to.

LONDON.

Institute of Actuaries of Great Britain and Ireland.

Constitution and Laws of the Institute of Actuaries of Great Britain and Ireland, and List of Members. 1852, 1853. *London*, 1852. 8vo.

List of Members of the Institute of Actuaries of Great Britain and Ireland. 1853; 1854–55. *London*, 1853, 1854. 8vo.

The Assurance Magazine and Journal of the Institute of Actuaries. III, I; IV, I, II, IV; V—VII, 1852—1858. *London*. 8vo.

Linnean Society.

Transactions of the Linnean Society. I—XXI, XXII, I, II, 1791—1857. *London*. 4to.

Proceedings of the Linnean Society of London. I, II, 1838—1855. *London*, 1849, 1855. 8vo.

Journal of the Proceedings of the Linnean Society. Botany: I, II, I, II. Zoology: I, II, I, II. *London*, 1857. 8vo.

List of the Linnean Society of London. 1844, 1848, 1851. 4to. 1852, 1854, 1855, 1856, 1857. 8vo.

Address of Thomas Bell, Esq., V. P. R. S., etc., the President, together with Obituary Notices of deceased Members. By JOHN J. BENNETT, Esq., F. R. S., the Secretary. Read at the Anniversary Meeting of the Linnean Society on Thursday, May 24, 1854. Idem, read May 24, 1855, and May 25, 1857. *London*, 1854, 1855, 1857. 8vo.

London Electrical Society.

The Transactions and the Proceedings of the London Electrical Society from 1837 to 1840. *London*, 1841. 4to.

Microscopical Society.

The Transactions of the Microscopical Society of London. I, II, III, I, II, 1840—1851. *London*, 1844—1851. 8vo.

LONDON.

Museum of Practical Geology and Geological Survey.

Memoirs of the Geological Survey of Great Britain, and of the Museum of Practical (Economic) Geology in London. I; II, I, II. *London*, 1846—1848. 8vo.

Memoirs of the Geological Survey of the United Kingdom. Figures and Descriptions illustrative of British Organic Remains. Decades I—VII, 1849—1853. *London.* roy. 8vo.

Prospectus of the Metropolitan School of Science applied to Mining and the Arts. 2d Session, 1852-53; 3d Session, 1853-54. *London*, 1852, 1853. 8vo.

Records of the School of Mines and of Science applied to the Arts. I, I—IV. *London*, 1852, 1853. 8vo.

Industrial Instruction on the Continent. (Being the Introductory Lecture of the Session 1852—1853.) By LYON PLAYFAIR. *London*, 1852. 8vo.

On the Value of an extended Knowledge of Mineralogy and the Processes of Mining. (Being the Introductory Lecture to the Course of Mineralogy and Mining.) By WARINGTON W. SMYTH, M. A. *London*, 1852. 8vo.

On the Educational Uses of Museums. (Being the Introductory Lecture of the Session of 1853—1854.) By EDWARD FORBES, F. R. S., etc. *London*, 1853. 8vo.

Numismatic Society.

The Numismatic Chronicle, and Journal of the Numismatic Society. Edited by JOHN YONGE AKERMAN. XL—XLIII, 1848, 1849. *London.* 8vo.

Philological Society.

Proceedings of the Philological Society. Vols. I—V, 1842—1852. *London*, 1844—1854. 8vo.

Photographic Society.

The Journal of the Photographic Society of London. Containing the Transactions of the Society, and a general record of Photographic Art and Science. IV, 1858. *London.* 8vo. (*Wanting No.* 62.)

LONDON.

Ray Society.

Memorials of John Ray, consisting of his Life by Dr. DERHAM; Biographical and Critical Notices by Sir JOHN E. SMITH, and CUVIER and DUPETIT-THOUARS. With his Itineraries, etc. *London*, 1846. 8vo.

The Correspondence of John Ray, consisting of selections from the Philosophical Letters published by Dr. Derham, and Original Letters of John Ray in the collection of the British Museum. *London*, 1848. 8vo.

A Monograph of the British Nudibranchiate Mollusca: with figures of all the species. By JOSHUA ALDER and ALBANY HANCOCK. I—V. *London*, 1844, 1851. 4to.

A Monograph of the British Naked-eyed Medusæ: with figures of all the species. By EDWARD FORBES. *London*, 1848. 4to.

A Monograph on the sub-class Cirripedia, with figures of all the species. By CHARLES DARWIN. The Lepadidæ; or Pedunculated Cirripedes. *London*, 1851. 8vo.

A Monograph on the sub-class Cirripedia, with figures of all the species. By CHARLES DARWIN, F. R. S., F. G. S. The Balanidæ (or Sessile Cirripedes); The Verrucidæ, etc. etc. etc. *London*, 1854. 8vo.

Reports on the Progress of Zoology and Botany. 1841, 1842. London, 1845. 8vo.

Reports on Zoology for 1843, 1844. *London*, 1847. 8vo.

Reports and Papers on Botany. *London*, 1846, 1849. 2 vols. 8vo.

Outlines of the Geography of Plants. By F. J. F. MEYEN. *London*, 1846. 4to.

On the Alternation of Generations; or, the propagation and development of animals through alternate generations: a peculiar form of fostering the young in the lower classes of animals. By J. J. S. STEENSTRUP. Translated by *Geo. Busk*. *London*, 1845. 8vo.

The Organization of Trilobites, deduced from their living affinities; with a systematic review of the species hitherto described. By HERMANN BURMEISTER. *London*, 1846. 4to.

LONDON.

Ray Society.—*Continued.*

Elements of Physiophilosophy. By LORENZ OKEN, M. D. Professor of Natural History at the University of Zurich, etc. etc. From the German by *Alfred Tulk*, Member of the Royal College of Surgeons of England. *London*, 1847. 8vo.

Bibliographia Zoologiæ et Geologiæ: a Catalogue of all books, tracts, and memoirs on zoology and geology. By LOUIS AGASSIZ. I—IV. *London*, 1848—1854. 8vo.

The Natural History of the British Entomostraca. By W. BAIRD. *London*, 1850. 8vo.

The British species of Angiocarpous Lichens, elucidated by their sporidia. By the Rev. W. A. LEIGHTON. *London*, 1851. 8vo.

Botanical and Physiological Memoirs. Consisting of: I.—The Phenomenon of Rejuvenescence in Nature, especially in the life and development of Plants. By Dr. A. BRAUN. Translated by *A. Henfrey*, F. R. S., etc. II.—On the Animal Nature of the Diatomeæ, with an organographical revision of the Genera established by Kützing. By Prof. G. MENEGHINI. Translated by *Christopher Johnson*, M. R. C. S. E. III.—An Abstract of the Natural History of Protocæcus Pluvialis. By Dr. FERDINAND COHN. Translated by *George Busk*, F. R. S., etc. Edited by *Arthur Henfrey*, F. R. S., F. L. S. *London*, 1853. 8vo.

Redhill Observatory.

A Catalogue of 3735 Circumpolar Stars observed at Redhill in the years 1854, 1855, and 1856, and reduced to mean positions for 1855.0, by RICHARD CHRISTOPHER CARRINGTON. *London*, 1857. royal 8vo.

Royal Agricultural Society of England.

The Journal of the Royal Agricultural Society of England. I—XVIII, 1840—1857. *London*. 8vo.

Index to the Journal of the Royal Agricultural Society of England for Vols. I—XVI. *London*, 1855. 8vo.

LONDON.

Royal Asiatic Society.

The Journal of the Royal Asiatic Society of Great Britain and Ireland. I—X, XI. I, XII, XIII, XV. II, 1834—1855. *London.* 8vo.

Royal Asiatic Society of Great Britain and Ireland. The Twenty-sixth, Twenty-ninth, and Thirty-second annual Reports. 1849, 1852, 1855. *London.* 8vo.

Royal Asiatic Society of Great Britain and Ireland. List of Members, Committees, etc. 1849, 1855. *London.* 8vo.

Royal Astronomical Society.

Regulations of the Astronomical Society of London: established February 8, 1820. *London,* 1820. 12mo. pp. xv and 32.

Memoirs of the Astronomical Society of London. I—XXIV, 1822—1855; XXV, I, 1856. *London.* 4to.

Monthly Notices of the Royal Astronomical Society, containing papers, abstracts of papers, and reports of the proceedings of the Society. I—XVII, 1831—1857. *London.* 8vo.

Royal Geographical Society.

The Journal of the Royal Geographical Society of London. 1830—1831, and I—X, 1831—1841. Index. XI, I; XII, I; XIV—XX, 1844—1851. Index. XXI—XXVI, 1851—1856. *London.* 8vo.

Proceedings of the Royal Geographical Society of London. Vols. I, I—IV, VI, VIII, X; II. 1855—1858. *London.* 8vo.

Addresses at the anniversary Meetings of the Royal Geographical Society. 1841; 1844; 1850-56. *London.* 8vo.

Geographical Notice to the Royal Illustrated Atlas. By Dr. NORTON SHAW. *London.* 8vo. pp. 8.

The Origin, Objects, and Progress of the Royal Geographical Society. *London.* 8vo. pp. 7.

Report of the Council. Read at the Anniversary Meeting on the 28th May, 1855. *London.* 8vo. pp. viii.

LONDON.

Royal Geographical Society.—*Continued.*

African Discovery. A Letter addressed to the President and Council of the Royal Geographical Society. By AUGUSTUS PETERMANN. *London,* 1854. 8vo. pp. 16.

List of Members of the Royal Geographical Society, 1849. *London.* 8vo. pp. 12.

Accessions to the Library of the Royal Geographical Society to May, 1853. *London.* 8vo. pp. xxii.

Balloting List, 28th May, 1855.

Royal Institution of Great Britain.

Notices of the Meetings of the Members of the Royal Institution of Great Britain. Vols. I, II, 1851—1858. *London.* 8vo.

The Royal Institution of Great Britain. A List of the Members, Officers, etc., with the Report of the Visitors for the years 1832, 1850—1856. *London.* 8vo.

The Journal of Science and the Arts. Edited at the *Royal Institution of Great Britain.* Published quarterly. I—VI, 1816—1819. The Quarterly Journal of Literature, Science, and the Arts. VII—XXIX, 1819—1830. *London.* 8vo.

(*The latter obtained by purchase.*)

Royal Society.

Philosophical Transactions, giving some account of the present undertakings, studies, and labors, of the ingenious in many considerable parts of the world. I—LXV, 1665—1775. *London.* 4to.

Philosophical Transactions of the Royal Society of London. LXVI—CXLVI, 1776—1856. *London.* 4to.

(*Wanting* 1831; 1843; 1845; 1847, II, III, IV; 1848.)

The Philosophical Transactions and Collections, abridged and disposed under general heads. I—XI, 1732—1756. *London.* 4to.

A General Index to the Philosophical Transactions. From the First to the end of the Seventieth Volume. By PAUL HENRY MATY, M. A., F. R. S. *London,* 1787. 4to.

LONDON.

Royal Society.—*Continued.*

Abstracts of the Papers communicated to the Royal Society of London. Nos. 8—15, 17, 18, 27, 35, 36, 39, 41, 45, 47, 55, 1831—1842; V (wanting pp. 495—802), 1843—1850; VI, 1850—1854. *London.* 8vo.

Proceedings of the Royal Society of London (being a continuation of the series entitled, "Abstracts of the Papers communicated to the Royal Society of London"). Vol. VII, 1854-55; VIII, 1856-57. *London*, 1856, 1857. 8vo. (*Wanting VII, Nos.* 2, 3.)

A Review of the Works of the Royal Society of London; containing animadversions on such of the papers as deserve particular observation. In eight Parts, under the several heads of Arts, Antiquities, Medicine, Miracles, Zoophytes, Animals, Vegetables, Minerals. By JOHN HILL. *London*, 1751. 4to.

Diplomata et Statuta Regalis Societatis Londini, pro Scientiâ Naturali promovendâ. Jussu Præsidis et Concilii edita. *Londini*, 1819. 4to.

The History of the Royal Society of London for the improving of Natural Knowledge. By THOMAS SPRATT, D. D. *London*, 1722. 4to.

History of the Royal Society from its Institution to the end of the Eighteenth Century. By THOMAS THOMSON, M. D., F. R. S. *London*, 1812. 4to.

A History of the Royal Society, with Memoirs of the Presidents. Compiled from authentic documents, by CHARLES RICHARD WELD. In two volumes. *London*, 1848. 8vo.

Addresses read at the anniversary Meetings of the Royal Society. 1837, 1852, 1853, 1854. *London.* 8vo.

Observations on the Address by the President, and on the Statement by the Council to the Fellows of the Royal Society, respecting Mr. Panizzi, read at their general Meeting, Nov. 30, 1837. [By A. PANIZZI.] With Defence of the Resolution for omitting Mr. Panizzi's Bibliographical Notes from the Catalogue of the Royal Society; and other Tracts relating to the Royal Society. *London.* 8vo.

LONDON.

Royal Society.—*Continued.*

Lists of Fellows of the Royal Society. 1853, 1855, 1856. *London.* 4to.

Society of Antiquaries of London.

Proceedings of the Society of Antiquaries of London. Vols. I, XVI, XVII; II; III; IV, XLVI. *London*, 1848—1857. 8vo.

Archæologia: or miscellaneous Tracts relating to Antiquity, published by the *Society of Antiquaries of London.* Vols. XXXIII—XXXVII. *London*, 1849—1857. 4to.

Supplement to the Description of an Astrological Clock, belonging to the Society of Antiquaries. *London*, 1851. 4to.

Lists of the Society of Antiquaries of London. 1853, 1854, 1855, 1856, 1857. *London.* 8vo.

Society for the Encouragement of Arts, Manufactures, and Commerce.

Transactions of the Society, instituted at London, for the Encouragement of Arts, Manufactures, and Commerce; with the premiums offered. Vols. I—LIV, 1806—1843. *London.* 8vo.

(*Wanting IV.*)

Transactions of the Society of Arts for 1846-7; 1847-8, I, II. *London*, 1847, 1849. 4to.

The Journal of the Society of Arts, and of the Institutions in Union. I—VI, 1852—1858. *London*, 1853—1858. royal 8vo.

(*Wanting Nos.* 18, 19, 26, 27, 193—201.)

Rules and Orders of the Society instituted at London for the Encouragement of Arts, Manufactures, and Commerce. *London*, 1812. 8vo. pp. 39.

Report of the Select Committee. 1841. *London.* 8vo.

List of the Officers of the Society and Premiums for the Sessions 1832-1833, 1833-1834; 1836-1837, 1837-1838. *London*, 1832, 1836. 8vo.

Official Catalogue of the Educational Exhibition opened in

LONDON.

Society for the Encouragement of Arts, Manufactures, and Commerce.—*Continued.*

St. Martin's Hall, July 4, 1854. Edited by G. W. TAPP. *London,* 1854. 8vo.

Lectures on the Results of the Great Exhibition, 1851. Lecture I.—The General Bearing of the Great Exhibition on the Progress of Art and Science. By WILLIAM WHEWELL, D. D., F. R. S. II.—Mining, Quarrying, and Metallurgical Processes and Products. By Sir HENRY DE LA BECHE, C. B., F. R. S. III.—On the Raw Materials from the Animal Kingdom. By RICHARD OWEN, F. R. S. IV.—Chemical and Pharmaceutical Processes and Products. By JACOB BELL, Esq., M. P. V.—On the Chemical Principles involved in the Manufactures of the Exhibition, as indicating the necessity of Industrial Instruction. By LYON PLAYFAIR, C. B., F. R. S. VI.—On Substances used as Food, illustrated by the Great Exhibition. By JOHN LINDLEY, Ph. D., F. R. S. *London.* 8vo.

Society for the Illustration and Encouragement of Practical Science.

The Magazine of Popular Science, and Journal of the Useful Arts. No. I, 1836. *London.* 8vo.

Statistical Society.

Journal of the Statistical Society of London. I—XX, 1839–57. *London.* 8vo.—General Index to the first fifteen Volumes. *London,* 1854. 8vo.

(*Wanting XIII & XVI,* I.)

First Report of the Committee on Beneficent Institutions. I.—The Medical Charities of the Metropolis. *London,* 1857. 8vo.

Regulations and List of Fellows of the Statistical Society of London. 1838. *London,* 1838. 8vo.

List of Fellows of the Statistical Society of London. Sessions 1854–55, 1856, 1857–58. *London.* 8vo.

Objects and Regulations of the Statistical Society of London. 1855. 8vo.

LONDON.

Statistical Society.—*Continued.*

Twentieth anniversary Meeting of the Statistical Society. Session 1853–54. 8vo.

Zoological Society.

Proceedings of the Committee of Science and Correspondence of the Zoological Society of London. I, II, 1830—1832. *London.* 8vo.

Proceedings of the Zoological Society of London. Parts I—XXV, 1833—1857. (Parts XVII—XXV with Plates.) *London.* 8vo.

Transactions of the Zoological Society of London. I—III, 1835—1849; IV, i—iv, 1850–57. *London.* 4to.

A List of the Fellows and Honorary, Foreign, and Corresponding Members of the Zoological Society of London, 1842. List of the Animals in the Gardens of the Zoological Society, with notices respecting them, and a plan of the Gardens, 1833. The Charter, By-Laws, and Regulations of Zool. Soc., 1834. Reports of the Council and Auditors of the Zool. Soc., 1831, 1835, 1838, 1839, 1841, 1844, 1845. (In 1 vol.) *London.* 8vo.

Miscellanea.

Annals of Natural History. *See* Magazine of Zoology and Botany.

Annals of Philosophy; or, Magazine of Chemistry, Mineralogy, Mechanics, Natural History, Agriculture, and the Arts. By Thomas Thomson. I—XXVIII, 1813—1826. *London.* 8vo.

Anti-Slavery Monthly Reporter. II, No. 17, 1828. *London.* 8vo.

The Archæologist, and Journal of Antiquarian Science. I, 1841—1842. *London.* 8vo.

The Architectural Magazine, and Journal of improvement in Architecture, Building, and Furnishing, and in the various arts and trades connected therewith. Conducted by J. C. Loudon. I—V. *London,* 1834—1838. 8vo.

LONDON.

Miscellanea.—*Continued.*

The Artizan. A Monthly Journal of the Operative Arts. IX—XIII, 1851—1855. *London.* 4to.
(*Wanting XIII, No.* 149.)

The Art Journal. New series. IX—XV, 1847—1853. *London.* 4to.—And Illustrated Catalogue 1851. 4to.

The Asiatic and Colonial Quarterly Journal. XI, No. 17, 1850. *London.* 8vo.

The Athenæum; Journal of Literature, Science, and the Fine Arts. 1836—1857. *London.* 4to.

The Banker's Magazine, Journal of the Money Market, and Railway Digest. V, No. 25, 1846; XI—XIV, 1851—1854. *London.* 8vo.

The British Quarterly Review. I—XXII, 1845—1855. *London.* 8vo.

The Canadian, British American, and West Indian Magazine. I, IV—VI. *London,* 1839. 8vo.

The Chemical Gazette, or Journal of Practical Chemistry, in all its applications to Pharmacy, Arts, and Manufactures. Conducted by WILLIAM FRANCIS. VIII, IX, 1850, 1851; XII—XV, 1854—1857. *London.* 8vo.
(*Wanting Nos.* 276, 282, 286, 307, 332, 334, 358.)

The Christian Observer. Conducted by Members of the Established Church. New series. No. 183. *London.* 8vo.

The Christian Reformer, or Unitarian Magazine and Review. IV, No. 39, 1837; IX, No. 99, 1842. *London.* 8vo.

The Civil Engineer and Architect's Journal. I—XVIII. *London,* 1837-55. *London.* 4to.
(*Wanting XIII; XV, Jan., Nov., Dec.; XVI, Jan., Feb.; XVII, May, Dec.; XVIII, Title and Index.*)

Colburn's United Service Magazine and Naval and Military Journal. 1851—1854. *London.* 8vo.

The Colonial Magazine and Foreign Miscellany. XVI, Nos. 63, 65, 66; XVII, Nos. 1—4. 1849. *London.* 8vo.

The Critical Review, or Annals of Literature. Series the

LONDON.

Miscellanea.—*Continued.*

Third, IV—XXIV, 1805—1812. Series the Fourth, I—IV, 1812, 1813. *London.* 8vo.

The Dublin Review. I—XLIV, 1836—1858. *London.* 8vo.

(*Wanting Nos.* 78, 79.)

Encyclopædia Britannica, or Dictionary of Arts, Sciences, and General Literature. Eighth edition. With extensive improvements and additions, and numerous engravings. I—XVI. *London,* 1853—1858. 4to.

Encyclopædia Metropolitana; or Universal Dictionary of Knowledge, on an original plan: comprising the twofold advantage of a philosophical and an alphabetical arrangement, with appropriate engravings. I—XXVI. *London,* 1845. 4to.

Encyclopædia Metropolitana. Second Division.—Applied Sciences. Part XXXIV. Meteorology by GEORGE HARVEY, Esq. *London,* 1849. 4to.

The English Cyclopedia. A new Dictionary of Universal Knowledge. Conducted by CHARLES KNIGHT. Geography. I—III. *London,* 1854-5. 4to.

The European Magazine. XXXVII, March, 1800. *London.* 8vo.

The Farmers' Magazine, and Monthly Journal of Proceedings affecting the Agricultural Interest. Old series. XVII, No. 2, 1842. *London.* 8vo.

The Foreign Quarterly Review. I—XXXVII, 1827—1846. *London.* 8vo.

The Foreign Review and Continental Miscellany. I—V. *London,* 1828—1830. 8vo.

Frazer's Magazine for Town and Country. XLIII—XLVI, XLVIII, 1851—1853. *London.* 8vo.

The Gentleman's Magazine. New series. I—XLII, 1834—1854. *London.* 8vo.

(*Wanting XXXVIII.*)

Household Words, a Weekly Journal. Conducted by CHARLES DICKENS. I, II. *London* and *New York,* 1850, 1851. 8vo.

LONDON.

Miscellanea.—*Continued.*

The Illustrated London News. I, 1842; II, 1843; IV, 1844; VI, 1845; XX, XXI, 1852. *London.* fol.

The Journal of Botany, being a second series of the Botanical Miscellany; containing Figures and Descriptions of such Plants as recommend themselves by their novelty, rarity, or history, or by the uses to which they are applied in the Arts, in Medicine, and in Domestic Economy; together with occasional Botanical notices and information. By WILLIAM JACKSON HOOKER. I—IV. *London,* 1834—1842. 8vo.

A Journal of Natural Philosophy, Chemistry, and the Arts. Illustrated with engravings. By WILLIAM NICHOLSON. I—XXXVI, 1802—1813. *London.* 8vo.

The Journal of Psychological Medicine and Mental Pathology, Nos. I, II, III. New series. Edited by FORBES WINSLOW. *London,* 1856. 8vo.

Labourers' Friend Magazine. XI, No. 128, 1841. *London.* 8vo.

The Lancet. A Journal of British and Foreign Medicine, Physiology, Surgery, Chemistry, Criticism, Literature, and News. 1852—1856. *London.* royal 8vo.

The London and Edinburgh Philosophical Magazine and Journal of Science. Conducted by Sir DAVID BREWSTER, RICHARD TAYLOR, and RICHARD PHILLIPS. I—XVI. New and united series of the Philosophical Magazine and Journal of Science. 1832—1840. *London.* 8vo.

The London, Edinburgh, and Dublin Philosophical Magazine and Journal of Science. Conducted by Sir DAVID BREWSTER, RICHARD TAYLOR, RICHARD PHILLIPS, and ROBERT KANE. XVII—XXXVII. New and united series of the Philosophical Magazine, Annals of Philosophy, and Journal of Science. 1840—1850. *London.* 8vo.

The London, Edinburgh, and Dublin Philosophical Magazine and Journal of Science. Conducted by Sir DAVID BREWSTER, RICHARD TAYLOR, RICHARD PHILLIPS, Sir

LONDON.

Miscellanea.—*Continued.*

ROBERT KANE, and WILLIAM FRANCIS. Fourth series. I—XV, 1851—1858. *London.* 8vo.

The London Geological Journal and Record of Discoveries in British and Foreign Palæontology. I—III, 1846–47. *London.* 8vo.

The London Journal of Arts and Sciences; containing reports of all new Patents, with a description of their respective principles and properties: also, original communications on subjects connected with Science and Philosophy; particularly such as embrace the most recent inventions and discoveries in Practical Mechanics. By W. NEWTON. I—XIV, 1820—1827. Second series. I—IX, 1828—1832. *London.* 8vo.

The London Journal of Arts and Sciences, and Repertory of Patent Inventions. Conducted by W. NEWTON. Conjoined series. I—XXXIX, 1832—1851. *London.* 8vo.

The London Polytechnic Magazine and Journal of Science, Literature, and the Fine Arts. January—June, 1844. Edited by THOMAS STONE, M. D. *London*, 1844. 8vo.

The Magazine of Natural History, and Journal of Zoology, Botany, Mineralogy, and Geology. Conducted by J. C. LOUDON. I—IX, 1829—1836. *London.* 8vo.

The Magazine of Natural History. Conducted by EDWARD CHARLESWORTH. I—IV. New series. 1837—1840. *London.* 8vo.

Magazine of Zoology and Botany. Conducted by Sir W. JARDINE, P. J. SELBY, and Dr. JOHNSTON. I, II. *London*, 1837, 1838. 8vo.

The Annals and Magazine of Natural History, including Zoology, Botany, and Geology (being a continuation of the "Magazine of Zoology and Botany," and of Loudon and Charlesworth's Magazine of Natural History). Conducted by Sir W. JARDINE, P. J. SELBY, Dr. JOHNSTON, Sir W. J. HOOKER, and RICHARD TAYLOR. I—XX,

LONDON.

Miscellanea.—*Continued.*

1838—1847. Second series. I—XXII, 1848—1857 *London.* 8vo.

(*Wanting: Second series, XI, Jan. & Feb.*)

The Mechanics' Magazine. Edited by R. A. Brooman. I, Nos. 1—4, 12; V, 399; XVII, 468, 534; XXIII, 633; XXVII, 721—729; LXII—LXVII. *London,* 1855—1857. 8vo.

(*Wanting also Nos.* 1638, 1639, 1640, 1711, 1780, 1837, 1843.)

The Medico-Chirurgical Review and Periscope of Practical Medicine. New series. Fascic. III, No. 18, 1828. *London.* 8vo.

The Mirror of Literature, Amusement, and Instruction. XXII, No. 627, 1833. *London.* 8vo.

The Monthly Magazine. XLIX, IV. *London,* 1820. 8vo.

The Monthly Review, or New Literary Journal. A periodical work, giving an account, with proper abstracts of, and extracts from, the new books, pamphlets, &c., as they come out. By several hands. I—LXXXI, 1749—1789. *London.* 8vo.

A General Index to the Monthly Review, from its commencement to the Seventieth volume. In two volumes. *London,* 1786. 8vo.

A Continuation of the General Index to the Monthly Review; commencing at the Seventy-first, and ending with the Eighty-first volume. *London,* 1796. 8vo.

The Monthly Review, or Literary Journal, enlarged. I—LXXXVIII, 1790—1819. *London.* 8vo.

The Natural History Review: a quarterly journal including the Transactions of the Belfast Natural History and Philosophical Society, Cork; Cuvierian Society, Dublin; Natural History Society, Dublin; University Zoological Association; and the Literary and Scientific Institution of Kilkenny. For the sessions 1853—1856. I, II, III, I, II. *London,* 1854—1856. 4to.

The Nautical Magazine, and Naval Chronicle. I, Nos. 7,

LONDON.

Miscellanea.—*Continued.*

10, 1837; XVI, No. 4, 1847; XXI, Nos. 6, 8, 1852. *London.* 8vo.

Notes and Queries: a medium of inter-communication for literary men, artists, antiquaries, genealogists, &c. I—VIII, X, III—VI, XI, XII, 1849—1855. *London.* 4to.

The Patent Journal and Inventors' Magazine. XII, pp. 105—116. 1851. *London.* 4to.

The Penny Cyclopædia of the Society for the Diffusion of Useful Knowledge. I—XXVII, 1833—1843. Supplement, I, pp. 1—192, 241—384, 433—576. *London.* royal 8vo.

The Penny Magazine of the Society for the Diffusion of Useful Knowledge. I—IX, 1832—1840. *London.* royal 8vo. New series. I—V, 1841—1845. *London.* 8vo.

The Philosophical Magazine, or Annals of Chemistry, Mathematics, Astronomy, Natural History, and General Science. By RICHARD TAYLOR and RICHARD PHILLIPS. I—XI. *London,* 1827—1832. 8vo.

Punch, or the London Charivari. XXIV. *London,* 1853. 4to. (*Wanting Nos.* 610, 624, 644, 649.)

The Quarterly Journal of Education. I, II. *London,* 1831. 8vo.

The Quarterly Journal of Pure and Applied Mathematics. Edited by J. J. SYLVESTER and N. M. FERRERS, assisted by *G. G. Stokes, A. Cayley,* and *M. Hermite,* corresponding Editor in Paris. I, II, Jan. and May. *London,* 1856, 1857. 8vo.

The Quarterly Review. I—XCVII, CXCIII, 1802—1855. *London.* 8vo.

Register of the Arts and Sciences. IV, No. 93. *London,* 1827. 8vo.

The Register of Arts and Journal of Patent Inventions; being an improved series and a continuation of "The Register of the Arts and Sciences." IV, No. 81. *London,* 1830. 8vo.

The Repertory of Arts, Manufactures, and Agriculture. XXVIII, No. 165. Second series. 1816. *London.* 8vo.

LONDON.

Miscellanea.—*Continued.*

The Repertory of Patent Inventions, and other discoveries and improvements in Arts, Manufactures, and Agriculture. XI, pp. 17—120. *London,* 1831. 8vo.

Reports of the British and Foreign Bible Society, with extracts and correspondence, &c. I—XII, 1805—1839. *London.* 8vo.
(*Purchased.*)

The Retrospective Review. I—XIV, 1820—1826. The Retrospective Review, and Historical and Antiquarian Magazine. Second series. I, II, 1827, 1828. *London.* 8vo.

Robert Owen's Journal, explanatory of the means to well-place, well-employ, and well-educate the Population of the World. Parts I—V, X, XII, XVII, XXII, 1850—1852. *London.* 8vo.

Robert Owen's Millennial Gazette. Nos. X, XI, 1857. *London.* 8vo.

Scientific Memoirs, selected from the Transactions of Foreign Academies of Science and Learned Societies, and from Foreign Journals. Edited by RICHARD TAYLOR. I. *London,* 1837. 8vo.

Sharpe's London Magazine: a Journal of Entertainment and Instruction for general reading. 1845—1847. Sharpe's London Magazine. Conducted by Mrs. S. C. HALL. New series. II. *London.* 8vo.

Simmonds's Colonial Magazine and Foreign Miscellany. Edited by P. L. SIMMONDS, Esq. XIII, No. 50. *London,* 1848. 8vo.

The Spectator. A weekly Journal of News, Politics, Literature, and Science. XXIV, 1851; No. 1517, 1857. *London.* fol.

Vivarium Naturæ, or the Naturalist's Miscellany: or Coloured Figures of Natural Objects drawn and described immediately from Nature. By G. SHAW, M. D., F. R. S.; the Figures by F. P. NODDER. I—IV. *London.* 8vo.

The West Indian Reporter. I—XII, 1827; XXIV, 1829. *London.* 8vo.

LONDON.

Miscellanea.—*Continued.*

The Westminster Review. I—XL, 1824—1842. *London,* 1825—1843. 8vo.

The Westminster and Foreign Quarterly Review. XLVI —XLIX, 1846—1849. *London.* 8vo.

The Westminster Review. New series. I—IV, 1852, 1853.

The Zoological Journal. I—V, 1824—1834. *London,* 1825—1835. 8vo.

The Zoological Miscellany; being Descriptions of new or interesting Animals, by WILLIAM ELFORD LEACH, M. D., F. R. S., & W. S. Illustrated with Coloured Figures, drawn from Nature, by R. P. NODDER. I—III, & I vol. Plates. *London,* 1814—1817. 8vo.

The Zoologist: a popular Miscellany of Natural History. Conducted by EDWARD NEWMAN. IX—XVI. *London,* 1851—1858. 8vo.

(*Wanting X, April, May, Nov., Dec.; XI, Jan. and Feb.; XV, August.*)

MANCHESTER.

Literary and Philosophical Society.

Memoirs of the Literary and Philosophical Society of Manchester. I—V, 1785—1798. Second series. I—XIII, 1805—1856. *London.* 8vo.

MARKREE.

Catalogue of Stars near the Ecliptic, observed at Markree during the years 1848—1856, and whose places are supposed to be hitherto unpublished. I—IV. *Dublin,* 1851—1856. royal 8vo.

NEWCASTLE-UPON-TYNE.

Natural History Society of Northumberland, Durham, and Newcastle-upon-Tyne.

Transactions of the Natural History Society of Northumberland, Durham, and Newcastle-upon-Tyne. I, II. *Newcastle,* 1831, 1838. 4to.

OXFORD.

Ashmolean Society.

Abstracts of the Proceedings of the Ashmolean Society. I, II, III, XXXI—XXXIV, 1832—1856. *Oxford*, 1844, 1854. 8vo.

(*Wanting Nos.* XXII, XXX.)

Transactions of the Ashmolean Society. I, II. *Oxford*, 1838, 1853. 8vo.

(*Wanting I, Nos.* I, VIII; *II*, VI.)

On the Land and Fresh Water Mollusca inhabiting the neighborhood of Oxford. By J. F. WHITEAVES. *Oxford*, 1857.

On the Flowering Plants and Ferns of Oxfordshire and the contiguous Counties. By MAXWELL T. MASTERS. *Oxford*, 1857.

Report on the Mortality and Public Health of Oxford during the years 1849, 1850. *Oxford*, 1854. 8vo.

Radcliffe Observatory.

Astronomical Observations made at the Radcliffe Observatory, Oxford, 1840—1855. I—XVI. *Oxford*, 1842—1856. 8vo.

List of Institutions and Persons to whom copies of the Radcliffe Observations are presented by the Radcliffe Trustees. *Oxford*. 8vo. pp. 7.

PENZANCE.

Royal Geological Society of Cornwall.

Transactions of the Royal Geological Society of Cornwall. Instituted February 11, 1814. I—VI, 1818—1846. *Penzance*. 8vo.

Royal Geological Society of Cornwall. Thirty-fourth annual Report of the Council, with the President's Address, and papers and notices read to the Society. Also, thirty-fifth, thirty-sixth, thirty-seventh, thirty-eighth, and thirty-ninth Reports. *Penzance*, 1847—1851. 8vo.

WALES.

Cambrian Archæological Association.

Cambrian Archæological Association. [List of Officers and Members, etc. etc.] *London.* 8vo. pp. 8.

YORK.

Yorkshire Philosophical Society.

Proceedings of the Yorkshire Philosophical Society. I, I. *London* and *York*, 1849. 8vo.

GREECE.

ATHENS.

Le Spectateur de l'Orient. Nos. 81, 83—86. *Athènes*, 1857. fol.

AFRICA.

ALEXANDRIA.

Societe Egyptienne.

Mémoire sur le Lac Moeris. Presenté et lu à la Société Egyptienne le 5 juillet 1842. Par LINANT DE BELLEFONDS. *Alexandrie*, 1843. 4to.

ASIA.

MAURITIUS.

Societe d'Histoire Naturelle de l'Isle Maurice.

Procès-Verbaux de la Société d'Histoire Naturelle de l'Isle Maurice du 6 octobre 1842 au 28 août 1845. L. BOUTON, Secrétaire. *Maurice*, 1846. 4to.

BATAVIA.

Bataviaasch Genootschap van Kunsten en Wetenschappen.

Verhandelingen van het Bataviaasch Genootschap van Kunsten en Wetenschappen. XX, 1844; XXI, 1846–47. 8vo. XXII, 1849; XXIII, 1850; XXIV, 1852; XXV, 1853; XXVI, 1854–57. *Batavia.* 4to.

Overzigt der Geschiedenis van het Bataviaasch Genootschap van Kunsten en Wetenschappen. Van 1778—1853. Door Dr. P. BLEEKER. *Batavia,* 1853. 4to. pp. 24.

Tijdschrift voor Indische Taal-, Land-, en Volkenkunde. Uitgegeven door *het Bataviaasch Genootschap van Kunsten en Wetenschappen.* I—III. *Batavia,* 1853—1855. 8vo.

Verslag der Werkzaamheden van het Bataviaasch Genootschap van Kunsten en Wetenschappen van September 1850 tot April 1852. Namens het Bestuur des Genootschaps voorgelezen in de Algemeene Vergadering op den 27sten April 1852. Door Dr. P. BLEEKER. *Batavia,* 1852. 4to. pp. 32.

Natuurkundige Vereeniging in Nederlandsch Indië.

Natuur- en Geneeskundig Archief voor Neêrland's-Indië. I—IV, 1844–47. *Batavia.* 8vo.

Natuurkundig Tijdschrift voor Nederlandsch Indië. Uitgegeven door *de Natuurkundige Vereeniging in Nederlandsch Indië.* Jaarg. II—V, 1851–53; VII, v, vi, 1854; IX, i, ii, 1855; XII, i—iii, 1856. *Batavia.* 8vo.

(*Wanting Title and Contents to II, IV, V.*)

BOMBAY.

Bombay Geographical Society.

Transactions of the Bombay Geographical Society. I—X, 1836—1852. *Bombay,* 1844—1852. 8vo.

BOMBAY.

Bombay Government.

Selections from the Records of the Bombay Government:

No. I. Report by Captain Wingate, Revenue Survey Commissioner, on the Plan of Survey and Assessment most suitable to the Province of Khandesh, and also the Instructions issued on the subject of Government. *Bombay*, 1852. fol.

II. Report by Captain Wingate, Superintendent of Revenue Survey and Assessment, Southern Mahratta Country (now Revenue Survey Commissioner), on the subject of introducing a Survey and Revision of Assessment in the Rutnagherry Collectorate: also a Letter from the Revenue Commissioner, S. D., submitting the above Report, and the Instructions issued by Government. *Bombay*, 1852. fol.

III. Memoir on the Zilla of Baroche; being the result of a Revenue, Statistical and Topographical Survey of that Collectorate; executed by order of the Bombay Government, under the Superintendence of Lieut.-Col. MONIER WILLIAMS, late Surveyor-General, Bombay Presidency. *Bombay*, 1855. fol.

IV. Report on the Village Communities of the Deccan, with especial reference to the claims of the Village Officers in the Ahmednuggur Collectorate to "Purbhava Huks," or remuneration from their Villages, independent of what they receive from Government. By Mr. R. N. GOODDINE. *Bombay*, 1852. fol.

V. Report explanatory of the Revised Assessment introduced into the Talookas of Badamee and Bagulkote, in the Belgaum Collectorate. By Captain WINGATE, Revenue Survey Commissioner: also, Papers relative to the suggestions made by Captain Wingate for constructing, for purposes of Irrigation, Masonry Dams across the Krishna, Gutpurba, and Mulpurba Rivers; and the instructions issued on the above subjects by Government. *Bombay*, 1853. fol.

VI. Report on the Experimental Revenue Settlement of certain villages in the broken and hilly country forming

BOMBAY.

Bombay Government.—*Continued.*

the Kownaee Talooka of the Nassick Sub-Collectorate, by C. E. FRASER TYTLER, Esq., acting 3d Assistant Collector of Ahmednuggur; and Letters on the subject from H. E. GOLDSMID, Esq. (late Superintendent of Survey in Nassick Districts), and J. VIBART, Esq., Revenue Commissioner; also, the Instructions of Government thereon. *Bombay*, 1853. fol.

VII. Report on the Management of Canals and Forests in Scinde, by Lieut.-Col. WALTER SCOTT, of the Bombay Engineers. *Bombay*, 1853. fol.

VIII. Report on the District of Sahitee, lately resumed from his Highness Ali Morad. By Lieut. J. T. JAMESON, Deputy Collector of Hydrabad in Sindh. *Bombay*, 1853. fol.

IX. Inam Commissioner's Report on the claim of Mahadajee Oorf Nago Punt Sadasew Baput to the Village of Modugay, in the Padshapoor Talooka of the Belgaum Collectorate, and the Instructions issued thereon by Government. *Bombay*, 1853. fol.

X. Reports on the Purgunnas of Puranteej, Hursol, Morassa, Bayur, and Veerumgam of the Ahmedabad Collectorate, by Lieutenant (now Lieut.-Col.) P. M. MELVILL, employed on the survey of that Collectorate. Also Reports on the portions of the Duskroee Purgunna situated in the Ahmedabad and Kaira Collectorates, by Capt. J. CRUIKSHANK, Revenue Surveyor, Guzerat. *Bombay*, 1853. fol.

XI. Reports on the portions of the Dholka Purgunna situated in the Ahmedabad and Kaira Collectorates; also on the Mehemoodabad and Nureead Purgunnas, and on the Oomret and Bhaluj Tuppas, in the Kaira Collectorate; and on the Pitlad Purgunna and Nepar Tuppa, in the same Collectorate. By Capt. J. CRUIKSHANK, Revenue Surveyor, Guzerat. *Bombay*, 1853. fol.

XII. Reports on the Revenue Survey Settlements of the Hoobullee, Nuwulgoond, Kode, and Dharwar Talookas of the Dharwar Collectorate, by Capt. G. WINGATE,

BOMBAY.

Bombay Government.—*Continued.*

Superintendent of Revenue Survey and Assessment in the Southern Mahratta Country (now Revenue Survey Commissioner). Also an extract from a Report on the History, &c., of the District of Chikodee, in the Belgaum Collectorate, by C. J. MANSON, Esq., Assistant Inam Commissioner (now Inam Commissioner.) *Bombay*, 1853. fol.

XIII. Reports on the Districts lately resumed from Meer Alli Moorad, in Sindh. By Lieutenants WEBSTER, LESTER, and DICKSON, Deputy Collectors in the Shikarpore Collectorate. *Bombay*, 1853. fol.

XIV. Report on proposed Canal and Railway in Scinde, by Lieut. CHAPMAN; with accompanying Letters, by Major H. B. TURNER and H. B. E. FRERE, Esq. *Bombay*, 1854. fol.

XV. Proceedings relative to the Resumption of Certain Villages and Lands held by the late Anajee Nursew; and claimed as hereditary Inams by his Son, Konher Row Anajee. *Bombay*, 1855. fol.

Selections from the Records of the Bombay Government. New series:

No. I. On the Supply of Water to Bombay. *Bombay*, 1854. royal 8vo.

II. Report on the Southern Districts of the Surat Collectorate. By A. F. BELLASIS, Esq., First Assistant Collector. *Bombay*, 1854. royal 8vo.

III. Papers connected with the settlement, under Act No. VI of 1851, of the Foras Lands in Bombay. *Bombay*, 1854. royal 8vo.

IV. Report on the Collectorate of Sholahpore; by Messrs. J. D. INVERARITY and J. S. INVERARITY. Statistical Report by Mr. A. SUMMERS. *Bombay*, 1854. royal 8vo.

V. Report on the Collectorate of Ahmedabad, by E. G. FAWCETT, Esq. A short account of the Chootas, a Tribe inhabiting portions of the valley of the Hubb, and of the country adjacent to the Western Frontier of

BOMBAY.

Bombay Government.—*Continued.*

Scinde. By Lieut. C. J. STEUART, Deputy Collector, Kurrachee. *Bombay*, 1854. royal 8vo.

VII. Statistical Report of the Colaba Agency. By W. M. HEARN, Clerk, Agent's Office, Alibagh. *Bombay*, 1854. royal 8vo.

IX. Bombay, Baroda and Central India Railway. *Bombay*, 1855. royal 8vo.

XI. Report on the Sanitary State and Sanitary Requirements of Bombay. (With Appendices.) By H. CONYBEARE, Esq. *Bombay*, 1855. royal 8vo.

XVI. Tours for Scientific and Economical Research, made in Guzerat, Kattiawar, and the Conkuns, in 1787–88, by Dr. HOVE. Published from the MS. in the Banksian Library, British Museum, under the care of ALEXANDER GIBSON, F. L. S. *Bombay*, 1855. royal 8vo.

XIX. Surveys by the Great Indian Peninsula Railway Company of the North Eastern Extension from Munmar to Mirzapore. *Bombay*, 1855. royal 8vo.

XX. Memorandum on the Water of Nullas in Jungle Districts, as productive of disease; and the necessity of providing Wells as the indispensable preliminary to the material improvement of such Districts. By A. BETTINGTON, C. S. With the opinions of the Medical Board, the Conservator of Forests, the two Revenue Commissioners, and the several Collectors; and the resolution of Government passed thereon. *Bombay*, 1855. royal 8vo.

XXI. Official Correspondence relative to the Assessment of the Omercote and Narra Districts in Sind; and Statistical returns of the Province of Sind, for the year 1853–54. *Bombay*, 1855. royal 8vo.

XXII. Second Report, with Appendices on the Supply of Water to Bombay, by H. CONYBEARE. Also, Observations on Mr. Conybeare's second Water Report, by Major J. H. G. CRAWFORD. *Bombay*, 1855. royal 8vo.

XXVII. Memorandum on Municipal Conservancy in the Districts of the Bombay Presidency, Sind, and Sattara.

BOMBAY.

Bombay Government.—*Continued.*

By E. PRATT, Assistant Secretary to the Government, General Department. *Bombay*, 1856. royal 8vo.

XXVIII. Correspondence illustrative of the practice of the Peshwa's Government regarding Adoptions, and the circumstances under which Adopted Sons could succeed to Property held from the State. *Bombay*, 1856. royal 8vo.

XXIX. Correspondence regarding the Concealment by the Hereditary Officers and others of the Revenue Records of the former Government, and the remedial measures in progress. *Bombay*, 1856. royal 8vo.

XXX. I.—Correspondence exhibiting the nature and use of the Poona Duftur, and the measures adopted for its preservation and arrangement since the introduction of British Rule. II.—A Selection of Papers explanatory of the origin of the Inam Commission, and of its progress, from its experimental organization in A. D. 1843 in one District of the Dharwar Collectorate, until extended to the whole of the Southern Muratha Country, the Deccan, and Khandeish, and constituted a Judicial Tribunal by Act XI of 1852. Comprising also Correspondence relating to alienated Land Revenue generally throughout the Bombay Presidency. *Bombay*, 1856. royal 8vo.

XXXII. Correspondence relating to the Canal Clearances in the Hydrabad Collectorate in 1854–55. *Bombay*, 1856. royal 8vo.

XXXIII. Papers relative to a project for Wet and Dry Docks in the Harbor of Bombay. *Bombay*, 1856. royal 8vo.

XXXIV. Official Correspondence on the Abolition of Statute or forced Labor in Sind. *Bombay*, 1856. royal 8vo.

XXXV. Report by the Collector of Kurrachee on the Hilly Region forming the Western part of that Collectorate: also a Letter from the Acting Commissioner in Sind, submitting the above Report; and the Instructions

BOMBAY.

Bombay Government.—*Continued.*

issued by Government on the subject. *Bombay*, 1856 royal 8vo.

XXXVI. Official Correspondence regarding the Ford Wah, in the Shikarpoor Collectorate, Sind. 1855–56. *Bombay*, 1856. royal 8vo.

XXXVIII. Correspondence relating to the tenure of the Possessions in the Deccan held by his Highness Jyajee Rao Sindia under the Treaty of Surje Anjungaum. *Bombay*, 1856. royal 8vo.

XL. Papers regarding the Revenue Settlement effected in the Districts of Omerkote and Thurr; and on the condition and system of management of the Thurr and Parkur Districts. *Bombay*, 1856. royal 8vo.

XLII. Report of Captain W. L. Merewether, Acting Political Superintendent, Frontier of Upper Sind, with other Papers relating to the Enlargement of the Bigaree Canal, in Upper Sind. *Bombay*, 1857. royal 8vo.

XLIV. Report of the Examination of the Mineral Districts of the Nerbudda Valley. By J. H. Blackwell, Esq., Mineral Viewer for Bombay. *Bombay*, 1857. royal 8vo.

De Lisle, A. Report on the question of Weighing or Measuring Salt, together with a sheet of Diagrams, and a sketch of a Weighing-Machine. *Bombay*, 1851. 8vo. pp. 31.

Index to Books and Papers on the Physical Geography, Antiquities, and Statistics of India. By George Buist, LL.D. *Bombay*, 1852. 8vo.

Rules for the Guidance of the Native Establishments of the Southern Mahratta Country Revenue Survey Department. By Capt. G. Wingate, Superintendent of the Survey. Translated by Mr. *W. S. Price*, Assistant Superintendent. *Bombay*, 1853. fol.

A Statement and Remarks relating to the Expenses of Irrigation from Wells in the Deccan, Khandesh, &c. By Capt. Meadows Taylor, Deputy Commissioner, Raichore Dovab. *Bombay*, 1856. 8vo. pp. 15.

BOMBAY.

Bombay Government.—*Continued.*

Atlas to Geological Papers on Western India, including Cutch, Sinde, and the S. E. Coast of Arabia; to which is appended a Summary of the Geology of India. Edited for the Government by H. J. CARTER, Assistant Surgeon, H. C. S. Bombay. *Bombay*, 1857. oblong fol.

The following were received while this Catalogue was in press:

VIII. Statistical Report on the Principality of Kolhapoor. Compiled by Major D. C. GRAHAM. *Bombay*, 1854. 8vo.

X. Memoir on the Sawunt Waree State. By Mr. W. COURTNEY and Major J. W. AULD. With brief Notes relative to the State by the latter officer. To which are appended a Census of the Sawunt Waree District for the year 1851; prepared by Mr. H. L. ANDERSON. A Paper containing information relative to the Sawunt Waree State; prepared in the year 1818, by Captain GIDEON HUTCHINSON. Copies of Treaties, Agreements, &c., concluded by the Hon. East India Company with the Sawunt Waree State, between the year 1730 and 1843. Observations on Ancient Copper Tablets, excavated in the Sawunt Waree Districts, accompanied by fac-similes and translations of the inscriptions thereon; by Major G. LE GRAND JACOB. Statistical Report on the Portuguese Settlements in India. Extracted, in the year 1850, from official documents, by Captain KOOL. To which are added copies of Treaties, &c., concluded between Great Britain and Portugal, between the years 1661 and 1850. *Bombay*, 1855. 8vo.

XII. Memoir of the Mahee Kanta; prepared in May 1845, by Captain J. R. KEILY, with subsequent additions. To which are appended a Statement of the several Talookas under that Agency; showing the amount of Grandsdana and Jumabundee paid by each to his Highness the Gaekwar, &c. &c.; by Captain W. LANG. Statistical Information; by Major C. R. WHITELOCK. Memoir on the Edur State, by Major W. MILES. Minute by the Hon-

BOMBAY.

Bombay Government.—*Continued.*

ourable Mr. J. P. Willoughby, and Extracts from the Proceedings of the Government thereon, relative to the question of Succession to the Chiefship of Ahmednuggur, in the Mahee Kanta, consequent on the election of its chief, Tukht Sing, to the Throne of Jodhpoor. Copies of Engagements, &c., between the Peshwa and Gaekwar; and between the Honourable East India Company and the Gaekwar and the chiefs in the Mahee Kanta. *Bombay*, 1855. 8vo.

XIII. A History of Sind, embracing the period from A. D. 710 to A. D. 1590; written in Persian, at the close of the sixteenth century, by Mahomed Masoom; and translated into English in the year 1846, by Captain George Grenville Malet. *Bombay*, 1855. 8vo.

XIV. Memoir on the Physical Character of the Nesbudda River and Valley; with Remarks on the practicability of the river being rendered a navigable stream. Also a descriptive detail of the Mineral Resources of the Nesbudda Valley; and an Analysis of the past Correspondence of Government on the subject of the Coal Beds in its vicinity, by Surgeon E. Impey. To which are appended, a Selection from the Records of the Bombay Government, 1838—1851, relating to the Nesbudda River and the Mineral Districts of the Valley; and Extracts from Reports, by J. J. Berkley and Lieut. Col. J. P. Kennedy. With Accompaniments to the latter Report. *Bombay*, 1855. 8vo.

XV. Memoir and brief Notes relative to the Kutch State; by Lieut. S. N. Raikes. Historical Sketch of Kutch, by Captain Charles Walter. Statements containing Names of the towns and villages in the Kutch Territory, their estimated annual Revenue, &c.; by Mr. Arthur Malet. Observations by Mr. J. G. Lumsden, on a Map prepared by him, showing the possessions of his Highness the Rao, and the dependent Chiefs, &c., in Kutch, furnished to Mr. Ogilvy by his Highness the Rao. Memoir on the Trade, &c., of the Port of Mandvee in Kutch;

BOMBAY.

Bombay Government.—*Continued.*

by the late Lieut. R. LEECH. Medical Topography of Bhooj, by Surgeon JAMES BURNES. Routes between Bhooj and Ahmedabad, by Lieut. Col. J. HOLLAND. To which are added, Copies of Treaties, Engagements, &c., entered into by the Honourable East India Company with the Kutch State, between 1809 and 1851. *Bombay*, 1855. 8vo.

XVII. Memoirs on Shikarpoor; the Synds of Rau and Bukhur; the Khyrpoor State; the States and Tribes on the Frontier of Upper Sind; the Bay, Harbour, Town, and Trade of Kurachee; the Province of Lees; the City of Tatta, and its environs. Journal of Captain L. BROWN, while at Kahun in A. D. 1840. Routes leading from Kurachee to Jerruck, &c. Reports on the Country between Kurachee, Tatta, and Sehwan. Narratives of Visits to Beyla, and the port of Sonmeeanee. Report on the Munchur Lake, and Arul and Nara Rivers. Memorandum relative to the Trade in Indigo, in countries bordering on the Indus. Memoirs on the River Indus. Remarks on the Plants, and Articles of Cultivation in Sind; Notes relative to the Population, the Chiefs, &c., in that Province; the Pearl Fishery, Sea Fishery, and Salt Beds of Sind. Report on the Purguna of Chandookah, in Upper Sind, Routes from Kurachee, &c., to Bhooj, Tatta, Jeruk, Sukkur, &c. Parts I, II. *Bombay*, 1855. 8vo.

XXIII. Sketches of Native States under the Political Agency in the Rewa Kauta. Prepared by Major R. WALLACE. The Rewa Kauta Tributaries, and the Fortified Places in that Province. Report on the Hill Fort of Powagur; List of the Towns and Villages in the Rewa Kauta; their estimated Revenues, &c. Geological and Statistical Notes on portions of the Rewa Kauta Districts, and Description of the Iron Ores of that Province, by the late Major G. FULLJAMES. Historical Sketch, &c., of the petty State of Baria, by J. P. WILLOUGHBY. Settlement of the Naikra Country, effected in the year

BOMBAY.

Bombay Government.—*Continued.*

1838, by A. MALET. Claim of the Babee of Balasuior to exercise Sovereignty over the Satoomba Talooka. Memoir on the Rajpeepla State, by J. P. WILLOUGHBY. Routes in, and Reports, &c., on the Rajpeepla and adjoining Districts, surveyed during the years 1852 to 1855. Investigation into the disputed Succession to the Gadee of Rajpeepla, by J. P. WILLOUGHBY. Reports by Mr. J. P. WILLOUGHBY on the Resources, &c., of Rajpeepla, and various proceedings connected with that State. Settlements based on a system of conciliation, effected by Mr. J. P. Willoughby, during the years 1822 to 1826, for the reclamation, &c., of the turbulent Bheels, Naikras, and Mahwasees residing in the Rajpeepla and other Districts. Extracts from Reports by Major WALLACE on the Punchmahal Districts. Parts I, II. *Bombay*, 1856. 8vo.

XXIV. Historical and other Information, connected with the Province of Oman, Muskat, Buhrein, and other places in the Persian Gulf. Reports on the Island of Kenn; on Bassadore; the Harbour of Grane; and the Island of Pheleechi. The Rise and Progress of, and Past Policy of the British Government towards, the Arab Tribes of the Persian Gulf; their Resources, Localities, &c. Chronological Tables of Events, from 1716 to 1843, connected with the Government of Muskat, and the Arab Tribes of the Persian Gulf. Rise and Progress of the Government of Muskat; and miscellaneous Information connected with that Government, from 1694 to 1853. Treaties, Engagements, &c., with the Imaum of Muskat, &c. Notes of a Visit to Zanzibar in the year 1834. Information connected with the Possessions, Revenues, Families, &c., of the Imaum of Muskat; the Ruler of Bahrein; and the chiefs of the Maritime Arab States in the Persian Gulf. Historical Sketches of the Joasmee, Uttoobee, Wahabee, Beniyas, Boo Felasa, Ejman, and Amulgavine Tribes of Arabs, from the year 1716 to the year 1853. Memoir descriptive of the Navigation of the Gulf of Persia;

BOMBAY.

Bombay Government.—*Continued.*

accompanied by brief Notices of the manners, customs, religion, commerce, and resources of the people inhabiting its shores. Measures adopted by the British Government for the Suppression of the Slave Trade in the Persian Gulf. *Bombay*, 1856. 8vo.

XXV. Historical Sketches of, and brief Notes relative to, the native States of Pahlunpoor, Radhunpoor, Warye, Terwara, Thurad and Morwara, Wao, Sooegaum, Deodur, Santulpoor and Charchut, Bhabhur, and Kanruj; comprised within the charge of the Political Superintendent of Pahlunpoor. List of the Districts, Talookas, Purgunas, and villages subject to the jurisdiction of the Political Superintendent at Pahlunpoor; the names of the Chiefs, their Capitals, Revenues, &c. Information relative to the fortified places in the Pahlunpoor Districts. Measures adopted by the Government of Bombay for the Prevention of Suttee and Infanticide, in the Pahlunpoor Districts. *Bombay*, 1856. 8vo.

XXVI. Rough Notes containing historical, statistical, and other Information connected with the petty States of Junjeera, and Jowar, in the Fanna Collectorate; Sucheen, Dhurumpoor, and Bansda, in the Surat Collectorate; Cambay, in the Kaira Collectorate; Penth, in the Nasik Sub-Collectorate; and the petty Native States under the control of the Collector of Khandesh. Historical narrative of the City of Cambay, from Sanskrit and Persian Books, and oral traditions; comprising, also, a brief sketch of the Province of Guzerat at various periods. Observations on the "Bore," or rushing tide in the Northern Parts of the Gulf of Cambay, and the entrances of the Mahee and Saburmutee Rivers. Proceedings connected with the question of Succession to the Penth Estate, in consequence of the death, in the year 1857, without male issue, of Dulput Rao, Raja of that petty Principality. Historical Sketch of the Bheel Tribes inhabiting the Province of Khandesh; accompanied by an Outline, down to the close of the year 1855, of the prin-

BOMBAY.

Bombay Government.—*Continued.*

ciples of the conciliatory line of policy which, from the year 1825, has been observed towards these rude tribes by the Bombay Government. *Bombay*, 1856. 8vo.

XXXI. Correspondence exhibiting the results of the scrutiny by the Inam Commission of the Lists of Deccan Surinjams prepared in 1844 by the Agent for Sirdars, Mr. Warden, and revised under orders from Government in 1847 by his successor, Mr. Brown; containing, also, the Proceedings which have taken place regarding these Holdings from the introduction of British Rule to the present period, and the Rules by which their continuance is now regulated. *Bombay*, 1856. 8vo.

XXXVII. Historical, Geographical, and Statistical Memoirs on the Province of Kattywar; and on the Districts of Babriawar and Okhamundal; also a Report on the Iron of Kattywar, by Captain G. Le Grand Jacob. Miscellaneous Notes connected with the native States in Kattywar; and Information relative to the wandering tribes in the Province; by Captain J. T. Barr. Statistical and other Information connected with the Districts of Jhalawar, Kattywar, Muchoo Kanta, Hallar, Soruth, Burda, Gohelwar, Oond, Surweya, and Babriawar; prepared by Mr. D. A. Blane. Memoir on the Province of Kattywar, with Remarks on the Runn of Kutch and the District of Okhamundul; by the late Captain J. Macmurdo. Lists of Fortified Places in the Province of Kattywar. Report relative to the first Introduction of Vaccination into Kattywar in the year 1808. Treaties connected with Kattywar. Names, Titles, &c., of the principal chiefs of Kattywar. *Bombay*, 1856. 8vo. Map of the Province of Kattywar.

XXXIX. Part I. Reports on the Resources, &c., of the Districts of Neriad, Matur, Mondeh, Beejapoor, Dholka, Dundooka, and Gogo, the Tuppa of Napar, and the Kusba of Ranpoor, in Guzerat; accompanied by brief Notes relative to the Condition of that Province previous to the close of the last century. With Memoirs on the

BOMBAY.

Bombay Government.—*Continued.*

Districts of Jhalawar, Kattywar Proper, Muchoo Kanta, Nowanuggur, Gohelwar, Poorbunder, Soruth, and Hallar, in Kattywar; accompanied by Miscellaneous Information connected with that Province. By the late Colonel ALEXANDER WALKER. Part II. Measures adopted for the Suppression of Female Infanticide in the Province of Kattywar, &c. By the late Colonel ALEXANDER WALKER, and by Mr. J. P. WILLOUGHBY, and his successors in office. *Bombay*, 1856. 8vo.

XLI. Memoir on the Satara Territory. Early History, &c., of the Bhonslays of Satara. Brief Notes relative to the Satara Jageerdars. Notes on the Climate and Diseases of Satara. Census taken in September, 1848, of the Satara Districts. Reports on the Revenues, Resources, &c., of the lapsed Satara Territory. Reports on the old Public Buildings of Mahomedan Architecture at Beejapoor, in the Satara Districts, &c. &c. *Bombay*, 1857. 8vo.

XLIII. Memoirs by Commander JAMES FELIX JONES. Steam-Trip to the North of Baghdad, in April 1846; with Notes on various objects of interest en route. Journey for the purpose of determining the Tract of the ancient Nahrwan Canal, undertaken in April 1848; with a glance at the past History of the Territory of the Nahrwan. Journey to the frontier of Turkey and Persia, through a part of Kurdestan. Researches in the vicinity of the Median Wall of Xenophon, and along the old course of the River Tigris; and discovery of the site of ancient Opis. Memoirs on the Province of Baghdad. Notes on the Topography of Nineveh, and the other cities of Assyria; and on the general Geography of the Country between the Tigris and the Upper Zab; founded upon a Trigonometrical Survey made in the year 1852. *Bombay*, 1857. 8vo.

XLVI. Annual Progress Reports of the Executive Engineers in the Southern, Central, and Northern Provinces

BOMBAY.

Bombay Government.—*Continued.*

of the Bombay Presidency in 1856–57. *Bombay*, 1857. 8vo.

XLVII. Report on a Project for the supply of Water to the Poona Cantonment. By Captain PHILIP LEWIS HART. With Plans and Sections (in a separate case). *Bombay*, 1858. 8vo.

XLVIII. A short Review of Mr. Plowdon's Report on the Salt Excise of the Bombay Presidency. By N. A. DALZELL. *Bombay*, 1858. 8vo. pp. 21.

Royal Asiatic Society.

The Journal of the Bombay Branch of the Royal Asiatic Society. I; II; III, XII, XIV; IV; V; 1841—1857. *Bombay*, 1844—1854. 8vo.

CALCUTTA.

Asiatic Society of Bengal.

Journal of the Asiatic Society of Bengal. New series. Vol. XXII, VII; XXIII, II—VII, 1853, 1854. *Calcutta.* 8vo.

HONG KONG.

Asiatic Society of China.

Transactions of the China Branch of the Royal Asiatic Society. Parts III, IV, 1851–52, 1853–54. *Hong Kong*, 1853, 1855. 8vo.

A Letter on the Population of China. By Sir JOHN BOWRING. Read to the Society 8th August, 1855. [Extract from the Transactions.]

Miscellanea.

The China Mail. I—VIII, 1845—1852. *Hong Kong.* fol.

MADRAS.

East India Company's Observatory at Madras.

Astronomical Observations made at the Honorable the East India Company's Observatory at Madras in the years 1843—1847, 1848—1852. *Madras*, 1848, 1854. 4to.

Literary Society & Auxiliary of the Royal Asiatic Society.

The Journal of Literature and Science. Published under the Auspices of the Madras Literary Society, and Auxiliary of the Royal Asiatic Society. I—XVI, XVII, pp. 1—159, 1833—1851. *Madras*, 1834—1853. New series. I, II, 1856, 1857. *Madras*. 8vo.

BRITISH AMERICA.

CANADA EAST.

MONTREAL.

Departement de l'Instruction Publique.

Journal de l'Instruction Publique. Redigé par l'Honorable PIERRE J. O. CHAUVEAU, Redacteur en chef, et par M. JOSEPH LENOIR, Assistant Redacteur. Vol. I. *Montréal*, 1857. 4to.

Natural History Society.

Twenty-fifth, twenty-sixth, and twenty-seventh Annual Reports of the Natural History Society of Montreal. 1853, 1854, 1855. *Montreal*. 8vo.

The Canadian Naturalist and Geologist, and Proceedings of the Natural History Society of Montreal. I, I, II, III, VI; II, I, III—VI, 1856, 1857. *Montreal*. 8vo.

Societe d'Agriculture du Bas-Canada.

Journal d'Agriculture, et Transactions de la Société d'Agriculture du Bas-Canada. II, 1849; IV, 1851; VI, I, II, 1853. *Montreal*. 8vo.

MONTREAL.

Societe d'Agriculture du Bas-Canada.—*Continued.*

Prize List of the Agricultural Association of Lower Canada for 1853. *Montreal.* 16mo. Idem for 1856. *Montreal.* 4to.

The Farmers' Journal and Transactions of the Lower Canada Board of Agriculture. V, I—III, 1857. *Montreal.* 8vo.

Miscellanea.

The British American Journal of Medical and Physical Science. Edited by ARCHIBALD HALL, M. D., and ROBERT L. MACDONNELL, M. D. I—III, V. *Montreal,* 1845—1850. 4to.

Journal of Education. Vol. I. *Montreal,* 1857. 4to.

QUEBEC.

Literary and Historical Society.

Transactions of the Literary and Historical Society of Quebec. IV, III, 1853. *Quebec,* 1855. 8vo.

CANADA WEST.

TORONTO.

Canadian Institute.

The Canadian Journal: a Repertory of Industry, Science, and Art, and a Record of the Proceedings of the Canadian Institute. I—III, 1852—1855. 4to. New series. I, II, 1856—1857. *Toronto.* 8vo.

Supplement to the Canadian Journal. Reports on the Improvement and Preservation of Toronto Harbor. *Toronto,* 1854. 4to.

University College.

[List of Officers and Programme.] 8vo. pp. 14.

Miscellanea.

Journal of Education. X, I—III, V, VII, VIII, XII. *Toronto,* 1857. 4to.

JAMAICA.

KINGSTON.

Jamaica Society of Arts.

The Transactions of the Jamaica Society of Arts. I, II, 1854—1856. *Kingston.* 4to.

NEW BRUNSWICK.

FREDERICTON.

New Brunswick Society for the Encouragement of Agriculture, Home Manufactures, and Commerce.

Journal of the New Brunswick Society. Instituted at Fredericton, N. B., August 30, 1849. *Fredericton*, 1850. 8vo.

PRINCE EDWARD ISLAND.

Royal Agricultural Society.

Report of the Royal Agricultural Society of Prince Edward Island for 1855 and 1857. *Charlotte Town*, 1855, 1857. 12mo.

Hints to the Farmers of Prince Edward Island, by JUDGE PETERS. *Charlotte Town*, 1851. 12mo.

SPANISH AMERICA.

CUBA.

HABANA (HAVANA).

Real Acuerdo de la Audiencia Pretorial de la Habana.

Colleccion de las Disposiciones Gubernativas, Administrativas, Económicas, &c., mandadas poner en observancia en esta Isla de Cuba. Tomo II, pp. 5—36. *Habana*, 1849. 8vo.

HABANA.

Real Sociedad Economica de Amigos del Pais.

Acta de las Juntas Generales que celebro la Real Sociedad Económica de Amigos del Pais de la Habana. 1829—1833, 1855. *Habana*, 1830—1834, 1856. 8vo.

Memorias de la Sociedad Económica de la Habana. Nos. IV, VII, VIII, IX, XII, 1817; XIV, XVI, XVII, XIX, XXIII, XXIV, 1818; XLIX, LI—LIII, 1824. Segunda edicion. I, I, 1835; XV, I, II, 1842; XVII, V, VI; XVIII, II—VI; XIX, I, II, IV, V, VI, 1854—1855; XX, 1855. Segunda serie. I, III—V; II, I—III, V, VI; III; IV; V, II—VI; VI; VII, I—III, 1846-49. *Habana*. 8vo.

Anales de las Reales Junta de Fomento y Sociedad Económica de la Habana. I, III—VI; II; III, II, III, V. *Habana*, 1849, 1850. 8vo.

Annales y Memorias de la Real Junta de Fomento y de la Real Sociedad Económica de la Habana. I—III, I—VI, 1853-56. *Habana*, 1854-57. 8vo.

Estatutos de la Real Sociedad Económica de la Habana. *Habana*, 1846. 8vo. pp. 39.

Relacion Historica de los Beneficios hechos á la Real Sociedad Economica, Casa de Beneficencia y demas Dependencias de aquel cuerpo por el Escmo. Señor Don Francisco Dionisio Vives. *Habana*, 1832. sm. fol. pp. 36.

Exposiciones Publicas de Industria, Ganado, Objetos agricoles y Belles Artes. *Habana*, 1854. 8vo. pp. 10.

Documentos relativos a la Instalacion de la Real Sociedad Economica. *Habana*, 1856. 8vo. pp. 24. Idem. *Habana*, 1856. 16mo. pp. 48.

Real Sociedad Patriotica de la Habana.

Memorias de la Real Sociedad Patriotica de la Habana. I—XIV, 1836—1842. *Habana*. 8vo.
(*Wanting Nos.* 1, 27, 38, 39, 42—44, 47, 48.)

Tareas de la Real Sociedad Patriotica de la Habana en el año de 1815. *Habana*, 1816. 8vo.

Seidell, F. [Letter advocating the formation by the Society of a Geógraphico-Historical Dictionary of the Island of Cuba.] *Habana*, 1812. 8vo. pp. 3.

HABANA.

Miscellanea.

La Cartera Cubana. Director VICENTE ANTONIO DE CASTRO. I—V, 1838–40. *Habana.* 8vo.

MEXICO.

MEXICO.

Sociedad Mexicana de Geografia y Estadistica.

Boletin de Geografia y Estadística de la Republica Mexicana, presentado al Supremo Gobierno por la Comision de Estadistica Militar. Nos. 2, 3, 4, 6, 7. *México,* 1849. 8vo.

Boletin de la Sociedad Mexicana de Geografia y Estadistica. Tomo I, Nos. 1, 8—11; II. *México,* 1850. 8vo.

Ley de 28 Abril de 1851, legalizando la ecsistencia de la Sociedad Mexicana de Geografía y Estadística, y el reglamento que ella ha acordado para su gubierno interior. *Mèxico,* 1851. 8vo. pp. 30.

SOUTH AMERICA.

CHILE.

SANTIAGO.

Universidad de Chile.

Anales de la Universidad de Chile. 1843—1854 (11 vols.); Jan.—March, 1855. *Santiago,* 1846—1855. 8vo.

Anales de la Universidad de Chile. 1843—1851. *Santiago,* 1846—1852. 4to.

Miscellanea.

Monitor de las Escuelas Primarias. I—III, I—VIII, 1852—1855. *Santiago de Chile.* 4to.

POLYNESIA.

SANDWICH ISLANDS.

HONOLULU.

Royal Hawaiian Agricultural Society.

Transactions of the Royal Hawaiian Agricultural Society. II, I, II, 1854, 1855. *Honolulu*, 1854, 1855. 8vo.

SUPPLEMENT.

DENMARK.

KJÖBENHAVN.

Kongelige Nordisk Oldskrift-Selskab.

Société Royale des Antiquaires du Nord [Report of Annual Meeting of 1858. List of new Members, etc.] 8vo. pp. 4.

Société Royale des Antiquaires du Nord le premier Janvier 1858. [List of Members, Books published, etc.] 8vo. pp. 12.

Grönlands Historiske Mindesmaerker, udgivne af *det Kongelige Nordiske Oldskrift-Selskab.* Bde I—III. *Kjöbenhavn,* 1838–45. 8vo.

Islendinga Sögur, udgivne efter gamle Haandskrifter af *det Kongelige Nordiske Oldskrift-Selskab.* Bde I, II. *Kjöbenhavn,* 1843, 1847. 8vo.

Færeyinga Saga eller Færoboernes Historie i den Islandske Grundtext med Færoisk og Dansk oversættelse. Udgiven af Carl Christian Rafn. *Kjöbenhavn,* 1832. 8vo.

Antiquitates Americanæ. Edidit *Societas Regia Antiquariorum Septentrionalium.* Studio et opera Caróli Christiani Rafn. *Hafniae,* 1845. fol.

Inscription Runique du Pirée. Interprétée par C. C. Rafn et publié par *la Société Royale des Antiquaires du Nord. Copenhague,* 1856. 8vo.

Antiquités de l'Orient, Monuments Runographiques interprétés par C. C. Rafn, et publiés par *la Société Royale des Antiquaires du Nord. Copenhague,* 1856. 8vo. pp. 48.

Sur la Construction des Salles dites des Géants par S. M.

KJÖBENHAVN.

Kongelige Nordisk Oldskrift-Selskab.—*Continued.*

le Roi FREDERIC VII de Danemark. *Copenhague*, 1857. 8vo. pp. 19.

Atlas de l'Archéologie du Nord, représentant des Echantillons de l'Age de Bronze et de l'Age de Fer. Publié par la *Société Royale des Antiquaires du Nord. Copenhague*, 1857. fol.

A Map of Vinland from accounts contained in Old Northern MSS. By CHAS. C. RAFN. Published by *the Royal Society of Northern Antiquaries. Copenhagen*, 1837.

General Chart exhibiting the discoveries of the Northmen in the Arctic Regions and America during the 10th, 11th, 12th, 13th, and 14th Centuries, from accounts contained in Old Northern Manuscripts. By CHAS. C. RAFN. Published by *the Royal Society of Northern Antiquaries. Copenhagen*, 1837.

Antiquités Russes d'après les Monuments Historiques des Islandais et des Anciens Scandinaves. Editées par *la Société Royale des Antiquaires du Nord.* Tomes I, II. *Copenhague*, 1850, 1852. fol.

En Vandring gjennem Jægerspriis's Have og Lund. Aftrykt af Annaler for Nordisk Oldkyndighed og Historie for Aaret MDCCCLVI. *Kjöbenhavn*, 1858. 8vo. pp. 40.

Cabinet d'Antiquités Américaines à Copenhague. Rapport Ethnographique. *Copenhague*, 1858. 8vo.

Lexicon Poeticum antiquae Linguae Septentrionalis. Conscripsit SVEINBJÖRN EGILSSON. Edidit *Societas Regia Antiquariorum Septentrionalium.* Fasc. IV. *Hafniae*, 1859. 8vo.

Miscellanea.

Naturhistorisk Tijdsskrift. Udgivet af HENRIK KROYER. III, IV. Second series. I, II. *Kjöbenhavn*, 1840–49. 8vo.

RUSSIA.

HELSINGFORS.

Societas Scientiarum Fennica.

Ofversigt af Finska Vetenskaps-Societetens Forhandlingar. IV, 1856—1857. *Helsingfors*, 1857. 4to.

Bidrag till Finlands Naturkännedom, Etnografi och Statistik, utgifna af *Finska Vetenskapssocieteten.* Hfte I, II, IV. *Helsingfors*, 1857-58. 8vo.

ST. PETERSBURG.

Imper. Russkoe Geographitsheskoe Obshtshestvo.

Société Impériale Géographique de Russie. Procès-verbal de l'Assemblée générale du 5 Novembre 1858. 8vo. pp. 3.

Kaiserlich œffentliche Bibliothek.

Auszug aus dem Jahresberichte der St. Petersburger Kaiserlich öffentlichen Bibliothek für 1857. *St. Petersburg*, 1858. 8vo. pp. 20.

HOLLAND.

AMSTERDAM.

Koninklijke Akademie van Wetenschappen.

Jaarboek van de Koninklijk Akademie van Wetenschappen. April 1857—April 1858. *Amsterdam.* 8vo. pp. 80.

Catalogus van de Boekerij der Koninklijke Akademie van Wetenschappen. Deel I, Stuk 1. *Amsterdam*, 1858. 8vo.

Stad Bibliotheek.

Catalogus van de Bibliotheek der Stad Amsterdam. Gedeelte III, IV. *Amsterdam*, 1858. 8vo.

AMSTERDAM.

Vereeniging voor Volksvlijt.

De Volksvlijt. Tijdschrift voor Nijverheid, Landbouw, Handel en Scheepvaart. Uitgegeven door *de Vereeniging voor Volksvlijt, te Amsterdam.* Onder redactie van de Directeuren Prof. S. BLEEKRODE, Mr. C. A. VAN EIJK, Dr. S. SARPHATI, Dr. W. C. H. STARING, 1858. *Amsterdam.* 8vo.

ARNHEM.

Openbare Bibliotheek.

Catalogus van de Openbare Bibliotheek te Arnhem. *Arnhem,* 1858. 8vo.

HERTOGENBOSCH.

Provinciaal Genootschap van Kunsten en Wetenschappen in Noordbrabant.

Handelingen van het Provinciaal Genootschap van Kunsten en Wetenschappen in Noordbrabant. 1837—1857. *Hertogenbosch,* 1837—1858. 8vo.

Reglement van het Provinciaal Genootschap van Kunsten en Wetenschappen in Noordbrabant. *Hertogenbosch,* 1850. 8vo. pp. 19.

Catalogus der Bibliotheek van het Provinciaal Genootschap van Kunsten en Wetenschappen in Noordbrabant. *Hertogenbosch,* 1853. 8vo.

GEUS (A. de). Geschiedkundige Beschrijving der Overlaten in de Provincie Noord-Braband. Uitgegeven door *het Provinciaal Genootschap van Kunsten en Wetenschappen in Noord-Braband.* Met vijf Bijlagen en drie Platen. *Breda,* 1844. 4to.

Verzameling van Kronyken betrekkelijk de Stad en Meijerij van 's Hertogenbosch. Uitgegeven door *het Provinciaal Genootschap van Kunsten en Wetenschappen in Noord-Braband.* Stuk I—III. *Hertogenbosch,* 1846–48. 8vo.

HERMANS (Dr. C. R.). Analytische Opgave der gedrukte Charters, Diploma's, Handvesten, Plakaten, Keuren, Ordonnantien, Reglementen en andere Staatsstukken, betrekkelijk de Provincie Noord-Braband, van het Jaar

HERTOGENBOSCH.

Provinciaal Genootschap, etc.—*Continued.*

704 tot en met het Jaar 1648. Uitgegeven door *het Provinciaal Genootschap van Kunsten en Wetenschappen in Noord-Braband. Hertogenbosch*, 1844. 8vo.

HERMANS (Dr. C. R.). Verzameling van Charters en Geschiedkundige Bescheiden, betrekkelijk het Land van Ravestein. Uitgegeven door *het Provinciaal Genootschap van Kunsten en Wetenschappen in Noord-Braband.* Deel I, II. *Hertogenbosch*, 1848—1850. 8vo.

(*Wanting Preface and Index to Deel II.*)

——— Verzameling van zeldzame Oorkonden betrekkelijk het Beleg van 's Hertogenbosch in den Jare 1629. Uitgegeven door *het Provinciaal Genootschap van Kunsten en Wetenschappen in Noord-Braband.* Eerste Stuk. *Hertogenbosch*, 1850. 8vo.

——— Vlugtig Overzigt der Verzamelingen van het Provinciaal Genootschap van Kunsten en Wetenschappen in Noord-Brabant, ten dienste der Leden van het Xde Landhuishoudkundig Congres, te houden den 19–23 Junij 1855, te 's Hertogenbosch. *Hertogenbosch*, 1855. 8vo. pp. 30.

FIJNJE (H. F.). Vervolg op de Geschiedkundige Beschrijving der Overlaten in de Provincie Noord-Brabant. Uitgegeven door *het Provinciaal Genootschap van Kunsten en Wetenschappen in Noord-Brabant.* Met vijf Bijlagen en eene Kart. *Hertogenbosch*, 1853. 4to.

LEIDEN (LEYDEN).

Maatschappij der Nederlandsche Letterkunde.

Nieuwe Reeks van Werken van de Maatschappij der Nederlandsche Letterkunde te Leiden. Deel X. *Leiden*, 1857. 8vo.

Nederlandsche Entomologische Vereeniging.

Tijdschrift voor Entomologie. Uitgegeven door *de Nederlandsche Entomologische Vereeniging*, onder redactie van Prof. J. VAN DER HOEVEN, Dr. M. C. VERLOREN en Mr. S. C. SNELLEN VAN VOLLENHOVEN. Deel II, Afl. 1, 2. *Leiden*, 1858. 8vo.

ZWOLLE.

Overijsselsche Vereeniging tot Ontwikkeling van Provinciale Welvaart.

Verslag van de Ontwerpen voor eene Vaste Brug over den Ijssel bij het Katerveer. 1852—1856. *Zwolle.* 1856. 8vo. pp. 32.

Catalogus van de Boekerij der Overijsselsche Vereeniging tot Ontwikkeling van Provinciale Welvaart geplaatst op het Museum benevens het Reglement voor het Lezen der Boeken. *Kampen,* 1857. 8vo. pp. 78.

GERMANY.

AGRAM.

K. K. Gymnasium.

Programm des k. k. Gymnasiums zu Agram am Schlusse des Schuljahres 1857. *Agram,* 1857. 4to. pp. 32.

Handels- und Gewerbekammer fur Kroatien.

Bericht der Handels- und Gewerbekammer für Kroatien an das hohe Kais. königl. Ministerium für Handel, Gewerbe und öffentliche Bauten über den Zustand der Urproduktion, der Gewerbe, des Handels und der Verkehrsmittel ihres Bezirkes während des Jahres 1852. Idem, 1853—1856. *Agram,* 1853—1858. 8vo.

Kroatisch-Slavonische Landwirthschafts-Gesellschaft.

Monatsblatt der Kroatisch-slavonischen Landwirthschafts-Gesellschaft. Jahrg. IX. *Agram,* 1850. 8vo.

Verhandlungen der Forst-Section der Landwirthschafts-Gesellschaft für Croatien und Slavonien im Jahre 1852. Redigirt vom Vorstande der Forst-Section. *Agram.* 4vo.

ALTENBURG.

Geschichts- und Alterthumsforschende Gesellschaft des Osterlandes.

Mittheilungen der Geschichts- und Alterthumsforschenden Gesellschaft des Osterlandes. Bde I, Heft 4. II—IV, V, I. *Altenburg*, 1844–59. 8vo.

Erster und Zweiter Bericht über das Bestehen und Wirken der Geschichts- und Alterthumsforschenden Gesellschaft des Osterlandes. 1838–40. *Altenburg.* 8vo.

Dritter Bericht. 1841–42. *Altenburg.* 8vo.

Statuten der Geschichts- und Alterthumsforschenden Gesellschaft des Osterlandes. *Altenburg*, 1854. 8vo. pp. 8.

AUGSBURG.

Naturhistorischer Verein.

VIII. Bericht des Naturhistorischen Vereins in Augsburg. 1855. 8vo.

IX. Bericht. 1856.
X. " 1857.
XI. " 1858.

BERLIN.

Entomologischer Verein.

Berliner Entomologische Zeitschrift. Herausgegeben von *dem Entomologischen Vereine in Berlin.* Jahrg. I, II. *Berlin*, 1857–58. 8vo.

(*From Baron d'Osten-Sacken.*)

Kœniglich Preussische Akademie der Wissenschaften.

Berliner Astronomisches Jahrbuch für 1836, 1837, 1838. *Berlin*, 1834–36. 8vo.

Verein fur Eisenbahnkunde.

Verhandlungen des Vereins für Eisenbahnkunde in Berlin. 1856—1857. *Berlin.* 8vo.

BERLIN.

Miscellanea.

Allgemeine deutsche Bibliothek. Bde I—LXIII. *Berlin* und *Stettin*, 1766–85. 8vo.

Anhang zu dem Ersten bis Zweyundfünfzigsten Bande der Allgemeinen deutschen Bibliothek. 1771–80. *Berlin* und *Stettin*. 8vo.

Wochenschrift für Gärtnerei und Pflanzenkunde. Herausgegeben von Prof. Dr. Karl Koch und G. A. Fintelmann. 1858; 1859, Nos. 1—14. *Berlin*. fol.

BRÜNN.

K. K. Mæhrisch-Schlesische Gesellschaft zur Befœrderung des Akerbaus, der Natur- und Landeskunde.

Mittheilungen der Kaiserl. königl. Mährisch-Schlesische Gesellschaft zur Beförderung des Ackerbaus, der Natur- und Landeskunde in Brünn, 1852–58. *Brünn*. 4to.

Verhandlungen der Forst-Section für Mähren und Schlesien 1850, pp. 411—477; 1851, Heft 1—3; 1853, 4; 1854–57; 1858, 1—3. *Brünn*. 8vo.

Werner-Verein zur geolog. Durchforschung von Mæhren und Schlesien.

Erster Jahresbericht der Direktion des Werner-Vereins zur geologischen Durchforschung von Mähren und Schlesien für das Verwaltungsjahr 1851–52. *Wien*, 1852. 8vo. pp. 82.

Zweiter Jahresbericht	1852.	*Wien*,	1853.
Dritter "	1853.	"	1854.
Fünfter "	1856.	*Brünn*,	1856.
Sechster "	1856.	"	1857.
Siebenter "	1857.	"	1858.

CRACAU.

Uniwersytet Krakowski.

Rocznik Towarzystwa Naukowego z Uniwersytetem Krakowskim polaczonego. Tom I—XV. *w Krakowie*, 1817—1833. 8vo.

CRACAU.

Uniwersytet Krakowski.—*Continued.*

Rocznik Towarzystwa Naukowego Krakowskiego z Uniwersytetem Jagiellonskim polaczonego (zlaczonego). Roczet Nowy. Tom II—VIII. *w Krakowie*, 1843—1252. 8vo.

Rocznik Ces. Król. Towarzystwa Naukowego Krakowskiego. Roczet Trzeci. Tom I. *w Krakowie*, 1858. 8vo.

CZERNOWITZ.

Verein fur Landeskultur und Landeskunde im Herzogthume Bukowina.

Mittheilungen des Vereins für Landeskultur und Landeskunde im Herzogthume Bukowina. Neue Folge. Band I, Hfte 1—3. *Czernowitz*, 1857–58. 8vo.

DARMSTADT.

Gartenbau-Verein.

Zeitschrift des Gartenbau-Vereins zu Darmstadt. Jahrg. VI, 1857. *Darmstadt.* 8vo. pp. 35.

DRESDEN.

Das Kœnigliche Mineralogische Museum.

Das Königliche Mineralogische Museum in Dresden, geschildert auf Hohe Veranlassung von Hanns Bruno Geinitz. *Dresden*, 1858. 8vo. pp. 110.

Verein fur Huhnerzucht.

Statuten des Vereins für Hühnerzucht zu Dresden. *Dresden*, 1855. 8vo. pp. 2.

Mitglieder-Verzeichniss und Jahresbericht des Vereins für Hühnerzucht zu Dresden, 1856. *Dresden*, 8vo. pp. 15.

GRÆTZ.

Historischer Verein fur Innerœsterreich.

Schriften des Historischen Vereines für Innerösterreich. In zwanglosen Heften. Heft I. *Grätz*, 1848. 8vo.

GRÆTZ.

Das Steiermarkisch-stændische Joanneum.

Vierunddreissigster Jahresbericht des Steiermarkisch-ständischen Joanneums zu Grätz für das Schuljahr 1845. Herausgegeben von den Curatoren dieses Institutes. *Grätz*, 1846. 4to. pp. 46.

Vierzigster Jahresbericht 1851. *Grätz*, 1852. 4to. pp. 30.

Historischer Verein fur Steiermark.

Mittheilungen des Historischen Vereines für Steiermark. Herausgegeben von dessen Ausschusse. Hfte IV. *Grätz*, 1850–55. 8vo.

Die Steiermarkischen Schützen-Freiwilligen-Bataillone und ihre Leistungen in den Jahren 1848 und 1849. Herausgegeben von dem Ausschusse des *Historischen Vereines für Steiermark*. *Grätz*, 1857. 8vo. pp. 47.

Steiermarkischer Industrie- und Gewerbe-Verein.

Bericht des Steiermärkischen Industrie- und Gewerbe-Vereins der Zehnten Versammlung in Grätz am 22 April 1852. *Grätz*, 1852. 4to. pp. 6.

XI. Versammlung 1853. 4to.
XII. " 1854. 4to.
XIII. " 1855. 4to.
XVI. " 1858. fol.

Industrie-Verein. Steiermarkische Abtheilung. Rechnungs-Ausweis für das Jahr 1850. Idem für das Jahr 1851. *Grätz*, 1851, 1852. 4to. broadside.

Industrie- und Gewerbe-Blatt. Herausgegeben vom *Steiermarkischen Industrie- und Gewerbe-Verein*. Jahrg. I, II, III, Nos. 1—47. *Grätz*, 1856–58. 4to.

Verein zur Befœrderung und Unterstutzung der Industrie und der Gewerbe in Innerœsterreich.

Protokoll der fünften allgemeinen Versammlung des Vereines zur Beförderung und Unterstützung der Industrie und der Gewerbe in Innerösterreich, dem Lande ob der Enns und Salzburg, abgehalten am 30 März 1843 *Grätz*. 4to.

GRÆTZ.

Verein zur Befœrderung und Unterstutzung der Industrie und Gewerbe in Innerœsterrich.—*Cont'd.*

der Sechsten	Versammlung	17 October	1844.
" Siebenten	"	3 April	1846.
" Achten	"	21 Juni	1847.
" Neunten	"	5 Decem.	1850.
" Zehnten	"	22 April	1852.
" Eilften	"	7 "	1853.
" Zwölften	"	17 Februar	1854.
" Dreizehnten	"	18 März	1855.
" Vierzehnten	"	2 "	1856.
" Fünfzehnten	"	19 "	1857.
" Sechzehnten	"	21 "	1858.

Berichte der Direction des Vereines zur Beförderung und Unterstützung der Industrie und der Gewerbe in Innerösterreich, dem Lande ob der Enns und Salzburg, über ihre Wirksammkeit seit der am 21 Juli 1847 in Grätz abgehaltenen achten allgemeinen Versammlung, nebst der zweiten Ergänzung zur II Auflage des Bücherkatalogs der Directions-Bibliothek. *Grätz*, 1849. 16mo. pp. 16.

Bericht der Direction des Vereines zur Beförderung und Unterstützung der Industrie und der Gewerbe in Innerösterreich, dem Lande ob der Enns und Salzburg. Erstattet der neunten in Grätz am 5 December 1850 abgehaltenen allgemeinen Versammlung der Vereinsmitglieder. *Grætz*, 1850. 4to. pp. 8.

Bericht über sämmtliche Erzeugnisse, welche für die erste zu Klagenfurt im Jahre 1838 veranstaltete, und bei Gelegenheit der Anwesenheit Sr. Majestät des Kaisers eröffnete Industrie-Ausstellung des Vereines zur Beförderung und Unterstützung der Industrie und der Gewerbe in Innerösterreich. *Grätz*, 1839. 8vo.

Zweite Ausstellung zu Grätz 1841. *Grätz*, 1843.

Dritte " zu Laibach 1844. " 1845.

Verzeichniss der zur dritten, bei Gelegenheit der hochbeglückenden Anwesenheit Allerhöchst ihrer Majestatën des Kaisers und der Kaiserin in Laibach, am 4 September

GRÆTZ.

Verein zur Befœrderung und Unerstutzung der Industrie und Gewerbe in Innerœsterreich.—*Cont'd.*

1844 eröffneten, von der Direction des Vereins zur Beförderung und Unterstützung der Industrie und Gewerbe in Innerösterreich. *Laibach.* 8vo. pp. 30.

Verzeichniss der zu der von Seite des Vereins zur Beförderung und Unterstützung der Industrie und Gewerbe in Innerösterreich, dem Lande ob der Enns und Salzburg veranstalteten vierten Gewerbe-Production-Ausstellung zu Linz im September 1847 eingesendeten Ausstellungs-Gegenstände, nebst Namen der Aussteller und Bezeichnung der verkäuflichen Artikel. *Linz,* 1847. 8vo. pp. 42.

HERMANNSTADT.

K. K. Katholisches Staats-Gymnasium.

Programm und Jahresbericht des K. k. katholischen Staats-Gymnasiums in Hermannstadt für das Schuljahr 1856. *Hermannstadt,* 1856. 4to. pp. 46.

Programm des Gymnasiums A. C. zu Hermannstadt für das Schuljahr 1852–3. *Hermannstadt,* 1853. 4to. pp. 51.

Siebenburgischer Verein fur Naturwissenschaften.

Verhandlungen und Mittheilungen des Siebenbürgischen Vereins für Naturwissenschaften zu Hermannstadt. Jahrg. I—VII; IX, 1—6. *Hermannstadt,* 1850–58. 8vo.

Statuten des Siebenbürgischen Vereins für Naturwissenschaften zu Hermannstadt. *Hermannstadt,* 1855. 8vo. pp. 7.

INNSBRUCK.

Ferdinandeum.

Fresken-Cyclus des Schlosses Runglstein bei Bozen. Nach original Gemälden gezeichnet u. lithografirt von Ignaz Seelos. Herausgegeben von *dem Ferdinandeum* in Innsbruck. Oblong. pp. 10.

KARLSBAD.

Montanischer Verein im Erzgebirge.

Zeitschrift des Montanischen Vereines im Erzgebirge. 1856, Nos. 1—12. *Karlsbad.* 4to.

KLAGENFURT.

K. K. kærntnerische Landwirthschaft-Gesellschaft.

Mittheilungen über Gegenstände der Landwirthschaft und Industrie Kärntens. Herausgegeben von *der k. k. Landwirthschaft Gesellschaft* und *dem Gewerbe- und Industrie-Vereine* in Kärnten. Jahrg. I—XIV; XV, 1—9. *Klagenfurt*, 1844–58. 4to.

Naturhistorisches Landesmuseum von Kærnten.

Jahrbuch des Naturhistorischen Landesmuseums von Kärnten. Herausgegeben von J. L. Canaval. Jahrg. I—III. *Klagenfurt*, 1852–54. 8vo.

LEIPZIG.

Deutsche Morgenlændische Gesellschaft.

Indische Studien. Beiträge für die Kunde des indischen Alterthums. Im Vereine mit mehreren Gelehrten herausgegeben von Dr. Albrecht Weber. Mit Unterstützung *der Deutschen Morgenländischen Gesellschaft.* Bde I—IV. *Berlin*, 1850–58. 8vo.

(*Wanting III*, 1.)

Kœniglich Sæchsische Gesellschaft der Wissenschaften.

Hansen (P. A.). Theorie der Sonnenfinsternisse und verwandten Erscheinungen. *Leipzig*, 1858. 8vo.

Hankel (W. G.). Elektrische Untersuchungen. Dritte Abhandlung: Ueber Elektricitätserregung zwischen Metallen und erhitzten Salzen. *Leipzig*, 1858. 8vo.

Statistisches Central-Archiv.

Berichte des Statistischen Central-Archives von Dr. Otto Hübner zu Berlin. Nos. 1, 2. Grossbrittannien und Irland. *Leipzig*, 1858. fol.

LEIPZIG.

Miscellanea.

Illustrirter Kalender für 1852, 1856, 1858, 1859. *Leipzig.* royal 8vo.

LEUTSCHAU.

Evangelisches Gymnasium zu Resmark.

Programm des evang. Gymnasiums A. C. zu Resmark für das Schuljahr 1855–56. *Leutschau.* 4to. pp. 20.

LINZ.

Handels- und Gewerbekammer Oberœsterreichs.

Jahres-Bericht der Handels- und Gewerbekammer für das Erzherzogthum ob der Enns über Industrie, Handel und Verkehr für die Jahre 1854, 1858 und 1856. *Linz,* 1857. 8vo.

Auszug aus dem Statistischen Berichte der Handels- und Gewerbekammer Oberösterreichs für das Jahr 1856. *Linz,* 1857. 8vo.

Museum Francisco-Carolinum.

Fünfter Bericht über das Museum Francisco-Carolinum. *Linz,* 1841. 8vo.

Eilfter Bericht. *Linz,* 1850.
Dreizehnter " " 1853.
Vierzehnter " " 1854.
Fünfzehnter " " 1855.
Sechszehnter " " 1856.
Siebenzehnter " " 1857.

Beiträge zur Landeskunde für Oesterreich ob der Enns und Salzburg. Lief. 1—5, 8—12. *Linz,* 1840—1846, 1853—1857. 8vo. [Combined with the preceding "Berichte."]

Verzeichniss der im Museum Franzisko-Carolinum vorhandenen Druckschriften. *Linz,* 1845. 8vo.

LÜNEBURG.

Naturwissenschaftlicher Verein.

Siebenter Jahresbericht über die Thätigkeit des Naturwissenschaftlichen Vereins für das Fürstenthum Lüneburg. *Lüneburg*, 1858. 4to. pp. 4.

MARBURG.

Gesellschaft zur Befœrderung der gesammten Naturwissenschaften.

Der Wetterauer Gesellschaft für Naturkunde zur Feier ihres fünfzigjährigen Bestehens am 11 August 1858 im Namen der Gesellschaft zur Beförderung der gesammten Naturwissenschaften zu Marburg. *Marburg.* 4to. pp. 25.

MELK.

K. K. Obergymnasium.

Sechster Jahres-Bericht des Kaiserlich königlichen Obergymnasiums zu Melk. *Wien*, 1856. 4to. pp. 28.

MÜNCHEN.

Kœniglich-Bayerische Akademie der Wissenschaften.

Neue historische Abhandlungen der Churfürstlichen baierischen Akademie der Wissenschaften. Bde I—V. *München*, 1779–98. 4to.

Neue historische Abhandlungen der baierischen Akademie der Wissenschaften. Bde I, II. *München*, 1804. 8vo.

Abhandlungen der Baierischen Akademie über Gegenstände der schönen Wissenschaften. Band I. *München*, 1781. 8vo.

Physikalische Abhandlungen der Königlich-baierischen Akademie der Wissenschaften. Abth. I, II. *München*, 1803, 1806. 8vo.

Denkschriften der Königlichen Akademie der Wissenschaften zu München für die Jahre 1808—1812. *München*, 1809—1812. 4to.

MÜNCHEN.

Polytechnischer Verein fur das Kœnigreich Bayern.

Gesammelte Schriften des Johann Nep. v. Fuchs. Zum ehrenden Andenken herausgegeben von dem Central-Verwaltungs-Ausschusse *des Polytechnischen Vereins für das Königreich Bayern. München*, 1856. 4to.

Kœnigliche Sternwarte.

Jahres-Bericht der Königlichen Sternwarte bei München für 1852 & 1854. *München*, 1852, 1854. 8vo.

Jahrbuch der Königlichen Sternwarte bei München, für 1838, 1839, 1840, 1841. Verfasst und herausgegeben von Dr. J. LAMONT. Jahrg. I—IV. *München*. 12mo.

Astronomische Beobachtungen, angestellt auf der Königl. Sternwarte zu Bogenhausen von dem ordentlichen Mitgliede der Akademie der Wissenschaften J. SOLDER. Theile I—IV. *München*, 1834–38. 4to.

Astronomischer Kalender für das Königreich Bayern auf das gemeine Jahr 1850 verfasst und herausgegeben an der königl. Sternwarte bei München von Dr. J. LAMONT. Idem 1851—1853. *München*, 1849–52. 8vo.

Annalen fur Meteorologie, Erdmagnetismus und verwandte Gegenstände. Herausgegeben von Dr. J. LAMONT. Jahrg. 1842—1844. Hfte I—XII. *München*, 1842—1844. 8vo.

Beobachtungen des Meteorologischen Observatoriums auf dem Hohen Peissenberg von 1792—1850, auf öffentliche Kosten herausgegeben von Dr. J. LAMONT. I. Supplementband zu den Annalen der Münchener Sternwarte. *München*, 1851. 8vo.

Meteorologische Beobachtungen aufgerzeichnet an der Königl. Sternwarte bei München in den Jahren 1825—1837. II. Supplementband zu den Annalen der Münchener Sternwarte. *München*, 1857. 8vo.

Bestimmung der Horizontal-Intensitæt des Erdmagnetismus nach absolutem Mass. Von Dr. J. LAMONT. *München*, 1842. 4to. pp. 53.

Resultate des magnetischen Observatoriums in München während der dreijährigen Periode 1843—1844—1845. Beigefügt sind: Magnetische Messungen auf einer Reise

MÜNCHEN.

Kœnigliche Sternwarte.—*Continued.*

nach Deutschland und Frankreich im Jahre 1844 von Dr. J. A. AANGSTROM. *München*, 1846. 4to.

Resultate aus den an der königl. Sternwarte veranstalteten meteorologischen Untersuchungen, nebst Andeutungen über den Einfluss des Clima von München auf die Gesundheits-Verhältnisse der Bewohner. Von Dr. J. LAMONT. *München*, 1857. 4to. pp. 59.

Beschreibung der an der Münchener Sternwarte zu den Beobachtungen verwendeten neuen Instrumente und Apparate. Von Dr. LAMONT. Mit 8 Tafeln. *München*, 1851. 4to. pp. 101.

OLMÜTZ.

K. K. Gymnasium.

Jahres-Bericht über das Kaiserl. königl. Gymnasium zu Olmütz während des Schuljahres 1856. *Olmütz*, 1856. 4to. pp. 43.

PASSAU.

Praktische Gartenbau Gesellschaft in Bayern.

Vereinigte Frauendorfer Blätter. Herausgegeben von *der Praktischen Gartenbau-Gesellschaft in Bayern.* Redigirt von EUGEN FUERST. Jahrg. 1857, 1858. *Passau.* 4to.

PESTH.

Geologische Gesellschaft fur Ungarn.

Erster Bericht der geologischen Gesellschaft für Ungarn. Herausgegeben von JULIUS V. KOVATS. *Pest*, 1852. 8vo. pp. 39.

Kiralyi Magyar Termeszettudomanyi Tarsulat.

A' Magyar Természettudományi Társulat évi Jelentése Tagjairól es Müködesiröl (Annual Reports of Members and Proceedings of the Hungarian Society of Natural Science), 1851–56. *Pesten*, 1857. 8vo. pp. 41.

A' Magyar Természettudományi Társulat Evkönyvei. I—III, 1841–56. *Pesten*, 1851–57. 8vo.

PESTH.

Pesther Obergymnasium.

Programm des Pester Obergymnasiums für das Schuljahr 1856–7. *Pesten*, 1857. 4to. pp. 35.

PRAG.

Bœhmischer Gewerbverein.

Denkschrift des böhmischen Gewerbvereins über den Ausschluss Oesterreichs au den teutschen Zollverein. *Prag*, 1848. 8vo. pp. 46.

PRESBURG.

Verein fur Naturkunde.

Verhandlungen des Vereins für Naturkunde zu Presburg. *Presburg*, 1856, 1857. 8vo.

REICHENBERG.

Œffentliche sechsklassige Ober-Realschule.

Fünfter Jahres Bericht der öffentlichen Sechsklassigen Ober-Realschule zu Reichenberg. 1856. *Reichenberg*. 8vo. pp. 36.

SALZBURG.

K. K. Landwirthschaft Gesellschaft.

Wochenblatt der k. k. Landwirthschaft Gesellschaft in Salzburg. Jahrg. VIII, Nos. 1—6, 8—10, 1858. 8vo.

STETTIN.

Entomologischer Verein.

Catalogus Coleopterorum Europæ. Herausgegeben vom *Entomologischen Vereine* in Stettin. Siebente Auflage. *Stettin*, 1858. 8vo.

STUTTGART.

Das heilgymnastische Institut.

Dritter Bericht über das heilgymnastische Institut vor dem Esslinger Thor Nro. 1 in Stuttgart von seinem Gründer

STUTTGART.

Das heilgymnastische Institut.——*Continued.*

und Leiter HERMAN STEUDEL und dem Arzt der Anstalt Dr. OTTO GÆRTNER. *Stuttgart*, 1858. 4to. pp. 30.

Das Kœnigliche Staatsarchiv.

Wirtembergisches Urkundenbuch. Herausgegeben von *dem Königlichen Staatsarchiv* in Stuttgart. Band II. *Stuttgart*, 1858. 4to.

Verein zur Fursorge fur entlassene Strafgefangene.

Zehnter Rechenschaftsbericht des Vereins zur Fürsorge für entlassene Strafgefangene im Königreich Württemberg erstattet den 3 Februar 1856, in der allgemeinen Versammlung dieses Vereines von dem Centralausschuss desselben. *Stuttgart*, 1856. 8vo. pp. 79.

Eilfter Rechenschaftsbericht 30 November 1857.

Miscellanea.

Neues Jahrbuch für Mineralogie, Geognosie, Geologie und Petrefakten-Kunde. Herausgegeben von Dr. K. C. VON LEONHARD und Dr. H. G. BRONN. Jahrg. 1842. *Stuttgart*, 1842. 8vo.

TRIEST.

Civico Museo Ferdinando Massimiliano.

Civico Museo Ferdinando Massimiliano in Trieste. Alto Protettorato, Cenni Storici, e Statuto. 1846—1856. *Trieste*, 1856. 4to. pp. 61.

K. K. Marine-Sternwarte.

Magnetische Beobachtungen, im östlichen Theile des Mittelmeeres auf Befehl Seiner k. k. Hoheit des durchlauchtigsten Herrn Erzherzogs Ferdinand Max, Obercommandanten der Kaiserl. Königl. Marine, ausgeführt im Jahre 1857 von Dr. F. SCHAUB. *Triest*, 1858. 4to. pp. 37.

TÜBINGEN.

Die Heilanstalt Mariaberg.

Neunter Jahresbericht über die Heilanstalt Mariaberg für schwachsinnige Kinder vom 1sten Juli 1855 bis 1sten Juli 1856. *Tübingen*, 1856. 8vo.

Zehnter Jahresbericht vom Juli 1856 bis Juli 1857.
Elfter " " 1857 " 1858.

WEILBURG.

Verein Nassau'scher Aerzte.

Correspondenzblatt des Vereins Nassau'scher Aerzte für das Jahr 1857. Redigirt von Dr. Peter Menges. *Weilburg*. 8vo.

WIEN.

Doctoren-Collegium der medicinischen Facultæt.

Jahres-Bericht (Zweiter) über die wissenschaftlichen Leistungen des Doctoren-Collegiums der medicinischen Fakultät zu Wien, unter dem Dekanate der Dr. Jos. Schneller im Jahre 1850–51. *Wien*, 1852. 8vo. pp. 24.

Dritter Jahres-Bericht 1852–53. *Wien*, 1853.
Vierter " 1853–54. " 1854.
Fünfter " 1854–55. " 1855.
Sechster " 1855–56. " 1856.

Preyss (Dr. G.). Rede zum Andenken Georg Josef Beer's, gehalten bei Gelegenheit der siebenten Jahresfeier der wissenschaftlichen Thätigkeit des Doctoren-Collegiums der Wiener medicinischen Facultät am 18 April 1857. *Wien*, 1857. 4to. pp. 8.

International Congress fur Statistik.

Rechenschafts-Bericht über die dritte Versammlung des Internationalen Congresses für Statistik, abgehalten zu Wien vom 31. August bis 5. September 1857. *Wien*, 1858. 4to.

Bericht der kais. kön. Sections-Chefs und Directors der administrativen Statistik, Freiherrn von Czœrnig, an die Vorbereitungs-Commission der dritten Versammlung des

WIEN.

International Congress fur Statistik.—*Continued.*

Internationalen statistischen Congresses über den Entwurf eines Programmes für die Verhandlungen dieser Versammlung. *Wien*, 1857. 8vo.

K. K. Gartenbau Gesellschaft.

Verhandlungen der k. k. Gartenbau-Gesellschaft in Wien im Jahre 1858. Heft 1. 8vo.

K. K. Geographische Gesellschaft.

Ansprache gehalten in der zweiten Jahresversammlung der Kaiserlich-königlichen Geographischen Gesellschaft in Wien am 9 November 1858. *Wien*, 1859. 8vo. pp. 12.

K. K. Geologische Reichsanstalt.

Geologische Uebersicht der Bergbaue der Oesterreichischen Monarchie. Im Auftrage der Kaiserlich-königlichen Geologischen Reichsanstalt zusammengestellt von Franz Ritter von Hauer und Franz Foetterle, mit einem Vorworte von *Wilhelm Haidinger*. *Wien*, 1855. 8vo.

Geologische Uebersicht der Bergbaue der Oesterreichischen Monarchie. Im Auftrage der *K. K. Geologischen Reichsanstalt* zusammengestellt von Franz Ritter von Hauer und Franz Fœtterle, mit einem Vorworte von *Wilhelm Haidinger*. *Wien*, 1855. 8vo.

Katalog der Bibliothek des K. K. Hof-Mineralien-Cabinetes in Wien. Zusammengestellt von Paul Bartsch. Herausgegeben von *der Kais. Kön. Geologischen Reichsanstalt*. *Wien*, 1851. 8vo.

K. K. Landwirthschafts-Gesellschaft.

Amtlicher Bericht über die im Mai 1857 abgehaltene fünfzigjährige Jubelfeier der k. k. Landwirthschafts-Gesellschaft in Wien. *Wien*, 1858. 8vo.

Katalog der land- und forstwirthschaftlichen Ausstellung veranstaltet von der k. k. Landwirthschafts-Gesellschaft in Wien. *Wien*, 1857. 8vo.

WIEN.

K. K. Landwirthschafts-Gesellschaft.—*Continued.*

Katalog der mit der land- und forstwirthschaftlichen Ausstellung vereinigten Ausstellung der Gegenstände des Haushaltes des Land und Forstwirthes. *Wien*, 1857. 8vo. pp. 47.

K. K. Ober-Gymnasium zu den Schotten.

Jahresbericht des Kais. kön. Ober-Gymnasiums zu den Schotten in Wien am Schlusse des Schuljahres, 1856, 1857. *Wien.* 4to.

SWITZERLAND.

Versammlung Schweizerischer Naturforscher.

Eröffnungsrede der 43sten Versammlung Schweizerischer Naturforscher in Bern durch den Präsidenten Prof. Dr. B. STUDER den 2 August 1858. 8vo. pp. 28.

BASEL.

Gesellschaft zur Befœrderung des Guten und Gemeinnutzigen.

Geschichte der Gesellschaft zur Beförderung des Guten und Gemeinnützigen in Basel. Einundachtzigstes Jahr 1857. *Basel*, 1858. 8vo.

LAUSANNE.

Asile des Aveugles de Lausanne.

Rapports présentés au Conseil général de l'Asile des Aveugles de Lausanne par le Comité, le Médecin et le Directeur de cet établissement pour les Années 1850, 1851 et 1852. *Lausanne*, 1853. 8vo.

Bibliotheque Cantonale Vaudoise.

Catalogue de la Bibliothèque Cantonale Vaudoise. I. Généralites. II. Histoire. *Lausanne*, 1854. 8vo.

LAUSANNE.

College Cantonal de Lausanne.

Règlement pour le College Cantonal. *Lausanne*, 1847. 8vo. pp. 58.

Ecole Speciale de Lausanne.

Programme des Connaissances exigées pour l'admission à l'Ecole Spéciale de Lausanne. *Lausanne*, 1854. 8vo. pp. 14.

Institution Heuchoz a Chateau d'Oex.

Règlement pour l'Institution Heuchoz à Chateau d'Oex. *Lausanne*, 1850. 8vo. pp. 29.

Institut des Sourds-Muets a Yverdon.

Institut des Sourds-Muets à Yverdon. Projet de Décret, etc. *Lausanne*, 1841. 12mo. pp. 33.

Règlement sur l'Institut des Sourds-Muets. 8vo. pp. 7.

Societe Industrielle d'Horlogerie.

Règlement pour la Société Industrielle d'Horlogerie de Lausanne. *Lausanne*, 1851. 16mo. pp. 12.

Miscellanea.

Règlement pour les Ecoles Publiques Primaires du Canton de Vaud. *Lausanne*, 1847. 8vo. pp. 51.

ZURICH.

Das Schweizerische Polytechnicum.

Verzeichniss der Bibliothek des Schweizerischen Polytechnicums. Dritte Auflage. *Zürich*, 1859. 8vo.

Ecole Polytechnique Federale Suisse.

Programme de l'Ecole Polytechnique Fédérale Suisse pour l'Année Scolaire 1856–57. Idem 1857–58, 1858–59. *Zürich*, 1856—1858. 4to.

WINTERTHÜR.

Miscellanea.

Schweizerische Polytechnische Zeitschrift. Herausgegeben von Dr. P. Bolley und J. K. Kronauer, Bde I, II. *Winterthür*, 1856, 1857. 4to.

BELGIUM.

BRUXELLES.

Societe Royale Linneenne de Bruxelles.

Société Royale Linnéenne de Bruxelles. Exposition extraordinaire de Produits d'Agriculture et d'Horticulture, céreales, légumes, fruits, plantes, fleurs, instruments d'agriculture et de jardinage, qui aura lieu avec le concours du Gouvernement les 23, 24, 25 et 26 septembre, 1859. *Bruxelles.* 8vo. pp. 19.

Miscellanea.

Dictionnaire des Sciences Médicales. Tomes I—XIII. *Bruxelles*, 1828—1830. 8vo.

FRANCE.

BORDEAUX.

Academie de Bordeaux.

Académie de Bordeaux. Le 16 novembre 1857 Rentrée solennelle des Facultés et de l'Ecole Préparatoire de Médecine et de Pharmacie. Compte-Rendus des Travaux de l'Année Scolaire 1856-1857, 1857-1858. *Bordeaux*, 1857, 1858. 8vo.

Chambre de Commerce de Bordeaux.

Extraits des Procès-Verbaux, Lettres et Mémoires de la Chambre de Commerce de Bordeaux. Seconde série. Vol. I—VIII. *Bordeaux*, 1851—1857. 8vo.

BORDEAUX.

Chambre de Commerce de Bordeaux.—*Continued.*

Catalogue des Livres composant la Bibliothèque de la Chambre de Commerce de Bordeaux. Avec Supplément. *Bordeaux*, 1852. 8vo.

Societe Philomathique de Bordeaux.

Bulletin de la Société Philomathique de Bordeaux. 2me série. Année I, 1, 2; II, 1—4; III, 2. *Bordeaux*, 1856—1858. 8vo.

CAEN.

Societe Linneenne de Normandie.

Bulletin de la Société Linnéenne de Normandie. Vol. I. Année 1855-56. *Caen*, 1856. 8vo.

DIJON.

Miscellanea.

La Bourgogne. Revue Œnologique et Viticole par C. Ladrey. Livr. I, 1859. *Dijon.* 8vo.

MACON.

Academie de Macon.

Annales de l'Académie de Maçon. Société des Arts, Sciences, Belles-Lettres et d'Agriculture. Rédigées et mises en ordre par Leonce Lenormand. Tomes I—III. *Macon*, 1851—1855. 8vo.

MULHOUSE.

Societe Industrielle de Mulhouse.

Bulletin de la Société Industrielle de Mulhouse. Nos. 145, 146. *Mulhouse*, 1858, 1859. 8vo.

Règlement de la Société Industrielle de Mulhouse. *Mulhouse*, 1856. 8vo. pp. 30.

Programme des Prix proposés par la Société Industrielle de Mulhouse, dans son Assemblée Générale du 26 mai 1858, pour être décernés dans l'Assemblée Générale de mai 1859. *Mulhouse*, 1858. 8vo. pp. 48.

NANCY.

Academie de Stanislas.

Mémoires de l'Académie de Stanislas, 1857. *Nancy*, 1858. 8vo.

ORLEANS.

Societe Archeologique de l'Orleanais.

Mémoires de la Société Archéologique de l'Orléanais. Tomes II, III, IV. *Orléans* et *Paris*, 1853—1858. 8vo.

Idem. Atlas. Tomes II, IV. fol.

PARIS.

Bibliotheque Imperiale.

Bibliothèque Impériale—Département des Imprimés. Catalogue de l'Histoire de France. Publié par ordre de l'Empéreur. Tomes I—V. *Paris*, 1855—1858. 4to.

Bibliothèque Impériale—Département des Imprimés. Catalogue des Sciences Médicales. Publié par ordre de l'Empéreur. Tome I, Livr. 1. *Paris*, 1857. 4to.

Depot des Cartes et Plans de la Marine.

Annales Hydrographiques, Recueil d'Avis, Instructions, Documents et Mémoires relatifs à l'Hydrographie et à la Navigation, publié au Dépôt des Cartes et Plans de la Marine. Tomes VII—XV. *Paris*, 1852—1858. 8vo.

Kerhallet (C. P. de). Manuel de la Navigation à la Côte Occidentale d'Afrique. Tomes I—III. *Paris*, 1857—1858. 8vo.

Ecole Polytechnique.

Jamin (M. J.). Cours de Physique de l'Ecole Polytechnique. Vol. I. *Paris*, 1858. 8vo.

Institut de France.

Histoire de l'Académie Française par Pellison et D'Olivet. Avec une Introduction, des Eclaircissements et Notes par *M. Ch. L. Livet.* Tomes I, II. *Paris*, 1858. 8vo.

PARIS.

Institut de France: Academie des Inscriptions et Belles-Lettres.

Mémoires de l'Institut Impérial de France, Académie des Inscriptions et Belles-Lettres. Tomes XIV—XIX; XX, 2; XXI; XXIII, 2. *Paris*, 1845—1858. 4to.

Mémoires présentés par divers Savants à l'Académie des Inscriptions et Belles-Lettres de l'Institut Impérial de France. Première série.—Sujets divers d'Erudition. Tomes I—V. Deuxième série.—Antiquités de la France. Tomes I—III. *Paris*, 1844—1858. 4to.

Notices et Extraits des Manuscrits de la Bibliothèque Impériale et autres Bibliothèques, publié par l'Institut Impérial de France, faisant suite aux Notices et Extraits lus au Comité établi dans l'Académie des Inscriptions et Belles-Lettres. Tomes XI—XIV, XVI, XVII, XVIII, 1; XIX, 2. *Paris*, 1827—1858. 4to.

Institut de France: Academie des Sciences.

Mémoires de l'Académie des Sciences de l'Institut Impérial de France. Tomes XXIV, XXVII, 1. *Paris*, 1854, 1856. 4to.

Mémoires présentés par divers Savants à l'Académie des Sciences de l'Institut Impérial de France et imprimés par son ordre. Sciences Mathématiques et Physiques. Tomes XII, XIV, XV. *Paris*, 1854—1858. 4to.

Institut de France: Academie des Sciences Morales et Politiques.

Mémoires de l'Académie des Sciences Morales et Politiques de l'Institut de France. Tomes VIII, IX. *Paris*, 1852, 1855. 4to.

Societe de Secours des Amis des Sciences.

Société de Secours des Amis des Sciences. Fondée le 5 mars 1857 par L. J. Thénard. Compte-Rendu de la première Séance Publique Annuelle, tenue le 15 avril 1858 dans le local de la Société d'Encouragement. *Paris*, 1858. 8vo.

PARIS.

Societe Geologique de France.

Bulletin de la Société Géologique de France. Tomes I—VI. *Paris*, 1830—1835. 8vo.

Societe Imperiale et Centrale d'Horticulture.

Société Impériale et Centrale d'Horticulture. Rapport fait au nom de la Commission de Comptabilité sur les comptes de l'Exercice 1858. *Paris*, 1859. 4to. pp. 12.

Societe Linneenne de Paris.

Mémoires de la Société Linnéenne de Paris, précédés de son Histoire pendant les Années 1823—1827. Tomes III—VI. *Paris*, 1825—1828. 8vo.

Societe Medicale Allemande de Paris.

Recueil de Travaux lus à la Société Médicale Allemande de Paris. Publié par MM. H. Meding et A. Martin. Première Année. *Paris*, 1858. 8vo.

Societe Orientale de France.

Revue de l'Orient de l'Algérie et des Colonies, Bulletin de la Société Orientale de France. Recueil consacré à l'étude de la Géographie, de l'Histoire, des Voyages, de la Littérature, des Sciences, de la Colonisation, de l'Agriculture, du Commerce, des Religions, des Moeurs et Coutumes des Peuples, des diverses Contrées de l'Orient, etc. Rédigé avec le concours de la Société Orientale et avec la collaboration de Membres de l'Institut, d'Orientalistes, de Consuls et de Voyageurs. Nouvelle série. Tomes I—VI. *Paris*, 1855—1857. 8vo.

Miscellanea.

Annales des Sciences Naturelles. Tomes I—XXX. Seconde série. Tomes I—V. *Paris*, 1824—1836. 8vo.

Idem. Atlas des Tomes I—XII. Années 1824—1827. *Paris*. 4to.

Annuaire de Médecine et de Chirurgie pratiques, pour 1855, '56, '57, '58. *Paris*. 32mo.

PARIS.

Miscellanea.—*Continued.*

Catalogue Annuel de la Librairie Française pour 1858. Publié par CH. REINWALD. *Paris.* 8vo.

Dictionnaire des Sciences et des Arts. Tomes I—III. Par M. LUNIEN. *Paris*, 1806. 8vo.

Encyclopédie Méthodique. Tomes III, VI. *Paris*, 1777, 1789. 4to.

Tableau Encyclopédique et Méthodique des Trois Règnes de la Nature. Ichthyologie. Par M. l'Abbé BONNATERRE. *Paris*, 1788. 4to.

TOULOUSE.

Societe Imperiale de Medecine, Chirurgie et Pharmacie.

Société Impériale de Médecine, Chirurgie et Pharmacie de Toulouse. Compte-Rendu des Travaux. Depuis le 10 mai 1857 jusqu'au 9 mai 1858. *Toulouse*, 1858. 8vo.

ITALY.

BOLOGNA.

Scuola Anatomica di Bologna.

MEDICI (M.). Compendio Storico della Scuola Anatomica di Bologna dal Rinascimento delle Scienze e delle Lettere a tutto il Secolo XVIII. Con un Paragone fra la sua Antichità e quella delle Scuole di Salerno e di Padova. *Bologna*, 1857. royal 8vo.

MILANO.

Accademia Fisio-medico-statistica di Milano.

Atti dell' Accademia Fisio-medico-statistica di Milano. Anno Accademico 1857–58. Nuova serie. Vol. III, Disp. 1—3. *Milano*, 1858. 8vo.

MILANO.

Museo Civico di Milano.

Collectiones Rerum Naturalium Musaei Mediolanensis. Mollusca Terrestria et Fluviatilia, 1846. royal 8vo. pp. 35.

Cenni sul Museo Civico di Milano ed Indice Sistematico dei Rettili ed Anfibi esposti nel medesimo. *Milano,* 1857. 8vo. pp. 61.

Museo dei Fratelli Villa.

Dispositio Systematica Conchyliarum Terrestrium et Fluviatilium quae adservantur in Collectione Fratrum Ant. et Jo. Bapt. Villa. *Mediolani,* 1841. 8vo. pp. 62.

VILLA (A.). Note su alcuni Insetti osservati nel periodo dell' Ecclisse dell' 8 Luglio, 1842. *Milano,* 1842. 8vo. pp. 4.

——— Osservazioni Entomologiche durante l'Eclisse del 9 Ottobre 1847. *Milano.* 8vo. pp. 8.

——— Sulla Monografia del Bombice del Gelso del Dottor Emilio Cornalia. *Milano,* 1857. 8vo. pp. 11.

——— Intorno agli Studj Geologici e Paleontologici sulla Lombardia del Sacerdote Professore Antonio Stappani. *Milano,* 1858. 8vo. pp. 12.

——— Intorno tre opere di Malacologia del Sig Drouet di Troyes. *Milano,* 1856. 8vo. pp. 19.

VILLA (G. B.). Osservazioni Geognostiche e Geologiche fatte in una gita sopra alcuni Colli del Bresciano e del Bergamasco. *Milano,* 1857. 8vo. pp. 8.

——— Catalogo dei Coleopteri della Lombardia. *Milano,* 1844. 8vo. pp. 77.

——— Catalogo dei Molluschi della Lombardia. *Milano,* 1844. pp. 10.

VILLA (A. e G. B.). Sulla Constituzione Geologica e Geognostica della Brianza e segnatamente sul Terreno Cretaceo. *Milano,* 1844. 8vo. pp. 46.

——— Ulteriori Osservazioni Geognostiche sulla Brianza. *Milano,* 1857. 8vo. pp. 8.

——— Utilità dei Boschi Montani nella Lombardia specialmente a riparo del Disastri Meteorici, modo di

MILANO.

Museo dei Fratelli Villa.—*Continued.*

Rimetterli, Conservarli, e Diffenderli dai Guasti massime degli Insetti. *Milano*, 1847. 8vo. pp. 88.

VILLA (A. e G. B.). Notizie intorno al genere Melania. Memoria Malacologica dei Fratelli Villa. *Milano*, 1855. 8vo. pp. 10.

Societa d'Incoraggiamento Arti e Mestieri.

Relazione Annuale sulle Operazioni della Società d'Incoraggiamento Arti e Mestieri. Adunanza Generale dei Socj 24 agosto 1856. *Milano*, 1856. 8vo. pp. 64.

Societa d'Incoraggiamento di Scienze, Lettere ed Arti.

Discorso letto dal Signor FRANCESCO PELUSO nelle sale della Società d'Incoraggiamento di Scienze, Lettere ed Arti, in occasione della Solenne Distribuzione dei Premj d'Orticoltura, il giorno 8 di settembre 1856. *Milano*, 1856. 8vo. pp. 10.

NAPOLI.

Reale Accademia delle Scienze e Belle Lettere.

Memorie della Reale Accademia delle Scienze del 1852 in avanti ripartite nelle tri Classi di Matematichi, Scienze Naturali, e Scienze Morali. Vol. I, Fasc. 3; II, 1854—1857. *Napoli*, 1857. 4to.

Regale Accademia Ercolanese di Archeologia.

Memorie della Regale Accademia Ercolanese di Archeologia. Vols. I—VIII. *Napoli*, 1822—1856. 4to.
(*From his Majesty, the King of Naples.*)

R. Orto Botanico di Napoli.

Catalogo delle Piante che si coltivano nel R. Orto Botanico di Napoli. Corredato della Piante del medesimo, e di Annotazioni. *Napoli*, 1845. 4to.

NAPOLI.

Miscellanea.

Hercvlanensivm Volvminvm qvae svpersvnt. Tomi I—VI, VIII—XI. *Neapoli*, 1793—1855. fol.
(*From his Majesty, the King of Naples.*)

GREAT BRITAIN AND IRELAND.

EDINBURGH.

Bannatyne Club.

Origines Parochiales Scotiæ. The Antiquities Ecclesiastical and Territorial of the Parishes of Scotland. Vols. I, II. *Edinburgh*, 1851—1855. 4to.

Registrum Cartarum Ecclesie Sancti Egidii de Edinburgh. A Series of Charters and Original Documents connected with the Church of St. Giles, Edinburgh, 1344—1567. *Edinburgh*, 1859. 4to.

Original Letters of Mr. JOHN COLVILLE, 1582—1603. To which is added his Palinode, 1600. With a Memoir of the Author. *Edinburgh*, 1858. 4to.

A Catalogue of the Graduates in the Faculties of Arts, Divinity, and Law, of the University of Edinburgh, since its foundation. *Edinburgh*, 1858. 8vo.

GREENWICH.

Royal Observatory.

Description of the Galvanic Chronographic Apparatus of the Royal Observatory, Greenwich. *London*, 1857. 4to.

LIVERPOOL.

Historic Society of Lancashire and Cheshire.

Transactions of the Historic Society of Lancashire and Cheshire. Vols. VIII, X. *London*, 1856, 1858. 8vo.

LONDON.

British Museum.

Catalogue of the Tortoises, Crocodiles, and Amphisbænians in the Collection of the British Museum. *London*, 1844. 12mo. pp. 80.

Catalogue of the Specimens of Snakes in the Collection of the British Museum. *London*, 1849. 12mo.

Catalogue of Marine Polyzoa in the Collection of the British Museum. Parts I, II. Cheilostomata. *London*, 1852, 1854. 12mo.

Catalogue of the Specimens of Lizards in the Collection of the British Museum. *London*, 1845. 12mo.

Catalogue of the Mollusca in the Collection of the British Museum. Part I.—Cephalopoda Antepedia. II.—Pteropoda. IV.—Brachiopoda Ancylopoda, or Lamp-Shells. *London*, 1849—1853. 12mo.

Catalogue of Phaneropneumona, or Terrestrial Operculated Mollusca, in the Collection of the British Museum. *London*, 1852. 12mo.

Catalogue of the Specimens of Mammalia in the Collection of the British Museum. Part I. Cretacea. II. Seals. III. Ungulata Furcipeda. *London*, 1850—1852. 12mo.

Catalogue of the Genera and Sub-genera of Birds contained in the British Museum. *London*, 1855. 12mo.

List of the Specimens of British Animals in the Collection of the British Museum. Part XVII. Nomenclator of Anoplura, Euplexoptera, and Orthoptera. *London*, 1855. 12mo.

Nomenclature of Coleopterous Insects in the Collection of the British Museum. Part I.—Cetoniadæ. II.—Hydrocanthari. III.—Buprestidæ. IV.—Cleridæ. VI.—Passalidæ. *London*, 1847—1852. 12mo.

Bell (T.). Catalogue of Crustacea in the Collection of the British Museum. Part I.—Leucosiadæ. *London*, 1855. 12mo.

Boheman (C. H.). Catalogue of Coleopterous Insects in the Collection of the British Museum. Part VII.—Longicornia I. Part VIII.—Longicornia II. Part IX.—Cassididae. *London*, 1856. 12mo.

LONDON.

British Museum.—*Continued.*

Carpenter (P. P.). Catalogue of the Collection of Mazatlan Shells, in the British Museum. *London*, 1857. 12mo.

Deshayes. Catalogue of the Conchifera or Bivalve Shells in the Collection of the British Museum. Part I. Veneridæ, Cyprinidæ, and Glauconomidæ. II. Petricoladæ (concluded); Corbiculadæ. *London*, 1853, 1854. 12mo.

Gray (G. R.). List of the Specimens of Birds in the Collection of the British Museum. Part I. Accipitres. II. Section I—Fissirostres. III. Section I—Ramphastidæ. IV.—Columbæ. *London*, 1848—1856. 12mo.

Gray (J. E.). Guide to the Systematic Distribution of Mollusca in the British Museum. Part I. *London*, 1857. 8vo.

——— List of the Mollusca in the Collection of the British Museum. Part I. Volutidæ. *London*, 1855. 12mo.

Gunther (Dr. A.). Catalogue of Colubrine Snakes in the Collection of the British Museum. *London*, 1858. 8vo.

——— Catalogue of the Batrachia Salientia in the Collection of the British Museum. *London*, 1858. 8vo.

Hagen (Dr. H.). Catalogue of the Specimens of Neuropterous Insects in the Collection of the British Museum. Part I. *London*, 1858. 12mo. pp. 34.

Pfeiffer (Dr. L.). Catalogue of Auriculidæ, Proserpinidæ, and Truncatellidæ in the Collection of the British Museum. *London*, 1857. 12mo.

Smith (F.). Catalogue of Hymenopterous Insects in the Collection of the British Museum. Parts V, VI. *London*, 1857, 1858. 12mo.

Vernon Wollaston (T.). Catalogue of the Coleopterous Insects of Madeira in the Collection of the British Museum. *London*, 1857. 8vo.

Walker (F.). List of the Specimens of Lepidopterous Insects in the Collection of the British Museum. Parts XI—XVI. *London*, 1857—1858. 12mo.

LONDON.

British Museum.—*Continued.*

WALKER (F.). List of the Specimens of Homopterous Insects in the Collection of the British Museum. Supplement. *London*, 1858. 12mo.

WALTON (J.). List of British Curculionidæ, with Synonyma. *London*, 1856. 12mo. pp. 46.

WHITE (A.). Catalogue of Coleopterous Insects in the Collection of the British Museum. Part VIII. Longicornia II. *London*, 1855. 12mo.

List of the Specimens of British Animals in the Collection of the British Museum. Part V.—Lepidoptera. [First edition.] *London*, 1850. 12mo.

List of the Specimens of British Animals in the Collection of the British Museum. Part I.—Centroniæ or Radiated Animals. II.—Sponges. III.—Birds. IV.—Crustacea. V.—Lepidoptera. VI.—Hymenoptera. VII.—Mollusca, Acephala, and Brachiopoda. VIII.—Fish. IX.—Eggs of British Birds. X.—Lepidoptera. XI.—Anoplura, or Parasitic Insects. XII.—Lepidoptera. XIII.—Nomenclature of Hymenoptera. XIV.—Nomenclature of Neuroptera. XV.—Nomenclature of Diptera, I. XVI.—Lepidoptera (completed). XVII.—Nomenclature of Anoplura, Euplexoptera, and Orthoptera. *London*, 1848—1855. 12mo.

List of the Osteological Specimens in the Collection of the British Museum. *London*, 1847. 12mo.

List of the Specimens of Mammalia in the Collection of the British Museum. *London*, 1843. 12mo.

Catalogue of the Specimens and Drawings of Mammalia and Birds of Nepal and Thibet presented by B. H. Hodgson, Esq., to the British Museum. *London*, 1846. 12mo.

List of the Specimens of Fish in the Collection of the British Museum. Part I.—Chondropterygii. *London*, 1851. 12mo.

KAUP (J. J.). Catalogue of Lophobranchiate Fish in the Collection of the British Museum. *London*, 1856. 12mo.

LONDON.

British Museum.—*Continued.*

KAUP (Dr.). Catalogue of Apodal Fish in the Collection of the British Museum. *London*, 1856. 8vo.

GRONOW (L. T.). Catalogue of Fish collected and described by Laurence Theodore Gronow, now in the British Museum. *London*, 1854. 12mo.

Catalogue of Pulmonata or Air-Breathing Mollusca in the Collection of the British Museum. Part I. *London*, 1855. 12mo.

Catalogue of the Bivalve Mollusca in the Collection of the British Museum. Part I.—Placentadæ and Anomiadæ. *London*, 1850. 12mo. pp. 22.

Catalogue of the Recent Echinida, or Sea Eggs, in the Collection of the British Museum. Part I.—Echinida Irregularia. *London*, 1855. 12mo.

Catalogue of the Species of Entozoa, or Intestinal Worms, contained in the Collection of the British Museum. *London*, 1853. 12mo.

Nomenclature of Molluscous Animals and Shells in the Collection of the British Museum. Part I.—Cyclophoridæ. *London*, 1850. 12mo.

List of the Specimens of Myriapoda in the Collection of the British Museum. *London*, 1844. 12mo. pp. 15.

NEWPORT (G.). Catalogue of the Myriapoda in the Collection of the British Museum. Part I.—Chilopoda. *London*, 1856. 12mo.

List of the Specimens of Crustacea in the Collection of the British Museum. *London*, 1847. 12mo.

Catalogue of the Specimens of Amphibia in the Collection of the British Museum. Part II.—Batrachia Gradientia, etc. *London*, 1850. 12mo.

GRAY (J. E.). Catalogue of Shield Reptiles in the Collection of the British Museum. Part I.—Testudinata (Tortoises). *London*, 1855. 4to. pp. 79.

D'ORBIGNY (Prof. A.). List of the Shells of the Canaries in the Collection of the British Museum. Collected by MM. Webb and Berthelot. *London*, 1856. 12mo. pp. 32.

LONDON.

British Museum.—*Continued.*

D'Orbigny (Prof. A.). List of the Shells of South America in the Collection of the British Museum. *London*, 1854. 12mo. pp. 89.

——— List of the Shells of Cuba in the Collection of the British Museum. Collected by M. Ramon de la Sagra. *London*, 1854. 12mo. pp. 48.

Eydoux and Souleyet. List of Mollusca and Shells in the Collection of the British Museum. *London*, 1855. 12mo. pp. 27.

List of the Coleopterous Insects in the Collection of the British Museum. Part I.—Cucujidæ. *London*, 1851. 12mo. pp. 25.

List of the Specimens of Hymenopterous Insects in the Collection of the British Museum. Parts I, II.—Chalcidites. *London*, 1846, 1848. 12mo.

Smith (F.). Catalogue of Hymenopterous Insects in the Collection of the British Museum. Part I.—Andrenidæ and Apidæ. II.—Apidæ. III.—Mutillidæ and Pompilidæ. IV.—Sphegidæ, Larridæ, and Crabronidæ. *London*, 1853—1856. 12mo.

——— Catalogue of British Hymenoptera in the Collection of the British Museum. Part I.—Apidæ (Bees). *London*, 1855. 12mo.

Desvignes (T.). Catalogue of British Ichneumonidæ in the Collection of the British Museum. *London*, 1856. 12mo.

Catalogue of the Specimens of Neuropterous Insects in the Collection of the British Museum. Part I.—Phryganides—Perlides. II.—Sialidæ—Nemopterides. III.—Termitidæ—Ephemeridæ. IV.—Odonata. *London*, 1852, 1853. 12mo.

Catalogue of Lepidopterous Insects in the Collection of the British Museum. Part I.—Papilionidæ. *London*, 1852. 4to. pp. 84.

List of the Specimens of Dipterous Insects in the Collection of the British Museum. Parts I—VII. (Suppl. I—III.) *London*, 1848—1855. 12mo.

List of the Specimens of Homopterous Insects in the Col-

LONDON.

British Museum.—*Continued.*

lection of the British Museum. Parts I, II. *London,* 1850, 1851. 12mo.

List of the Specimens of Hemipterous Insects in the Collection of the British Museum. Parts I, II. *London,* 1851, 1852. 12mo.

Synopsis of the Contents of the British Museum. Forty-ninth edition. *London,* 1846. 12mo.

Idem. Fifty-seventh edition. *London,* 1851. 12mo.

The British Museum Historical and Descriptive, with numerous Wood-Engravings. *Edinburgh,* 1850. 8vo.

Hon. East India Company.

HORSFIELD (T.) & F. MOORE. A Catalogue of the Birds in the Museum of the Hon. East India Company. Vols. I, II. *London,* 1854—1858. 8vo.

——— A Catalogue of the Lepidopterous Insects in the Museum of the Hon. East India Company. Vol. I. *London,* 1857. 8vo.

Museum of Practical Geology and Geological Survey.

Second and Third Reports on the Coals suited to the Steam Navy. By Sir HENRY DE LA BECHE and Dr. LYON PLAYFAIR. *London,* 1849, 1851. fol.

Palæontographical Society.

List of the Council, Secretaries, and Members of the Palæontographical Society. 1848, 1851, 1853, 1856. *London.* 4to.

A Monograph of the Crag Mollusca, or Descriptions of Shells from the Middle and Upper Tertiaries of the East of England. By SEARLES V. WOOD. Vol. I.—Univalves. Vol. II.—Bivalves. *London,* 1848, 1850–56. 4to.

A Monograph of the Entomostraca of the Cretaceous Formation of England. By T. RUPERT JONES. *London,* 1849. 4to.

A Monograph of the Permian Fossils of England. By WILLIAM KING. *London,* 1850. 4to.

LONDON.

Palæontographical Society.—*Continued.*

A Monograph of the British Fossil Corals. By H. MILNE EDWARDS and JULES HAIME. Part I.—Introduction; Corals from the Tertiary and Cretaceous Formations. II.—Corals from the Oolitic Formations. III.—Corals from the Permian Formation and the Mountain Limestone. IV.—Corals from the Devonian Formation. V.—Corals from the Silurian Formation. *London*, 1850, 1854. 4to.

Monograph on the Fossil Reptilia of the London Clay. Part I.—Chelonia. By Prof. OWEN and Prof. BELL. Part II.—Crocodilia, Ophidia. By Prof. OWEN. *London*, 1849, 1850. 4to.

A Monograph of the Fossil Chelonian Reptiles of the Wealden Clays and Purbeck Limestones. By RICHARD OWEN. *London*, 1853. 4to.

Monograph on the Fossil Reptilia of the Wealden Formations. By Professor OWEN. Part II.—Dinosauria. III.—Megalosaurus Bucklandi. *London*, 1854, 1856. 4to.

Monograph on the Fossil Reptilia of the Cretaceous Formations. By Prof. OWEN. *London*, 1851. 4to.

A Monograph of the Eocene Mollusca, or Descriptions of Shells from the Older Tertiaries of England. By FREDERIC E. EDWARDS. Part I.—Cephalopoda. II.—Pulmonata. III.—Prosobranchiata. *London*, 1849—1856. 4to.

A Monograph of the Mollusca from the Great Oolite, chiefly from Minchinhampton and the Coast of Yorkshire. By J. MORRIS and JOHN LYCETT. Part I.—Univalves. II, III.—Bivalves. *London*, 1850—1854. 4to.

Monograph of the Echinodermata of the British Tertiaries. By Professor EDWARD FORBES. *London*, 1852. 4to.

A Monograph of British Tertiary Brachiopoda. By THOMAS DAVIDSON. Part I. *London*, 1852. 4to.

A Monograph of British Cretaceous Brachiopoda. By THOMAS DAVIDSON. Part II. *London*, 1852, 1854. 4to.

LONDON.

Palæontographical Society.—*Continued.*

A Monograph of British Oolitic and Liasic Brachiopoda. By THOMAS DAVIDSON. Part III. *London*, 1851, 1852. 4to.

British Fossil Brachiopoda. By THOMAS DAVIDSON. Part IV. With a General Introduction. *London*, 1853. 4to.

Description of the Fossil Remains of Mollusca found in the Chalk of England. By DANIEL SHARPE. Parts I, II, III.—Cephalopoda. *London*, 1853—1856. 4to.

A Monograph on the Fossil Lepadidæ, or Pedunculated Cirripedes of Great Britain. By CHARLES DARWIN. *London*, 1851. 4to.

A Monograph on the Fossil Balanidæ and Verrucidæ of Great Britain. By CHARLES DARWIN. *London*, 1854. 4to.

A Monograph of the Tertiary Entomostraca of England. By RUPERT JONES. *London*, 1856. 4to.

A Monograph on the British Fossil Echinodermata of the Oolitic Formations. By THOMAS WRIGHT. Part I.—Cidaridæ, Hemicidaridæ, and Diademidæ. *London*, 1855. 4to.

Philological Society.

Transactions of the Philological Society. 1856. *London*, 8vo.

Royal College of Surgeons of England.

Synopsis of the Arrangement of the Preparations in the Museum of the Royal College of Surgeons of England. *London*, 1850. 8vo. pp. 104.

Royal Society.

Six Discourses delivered before the Royal Society at their Anniversary Meetings, on the award of the Royal and Copley Medals; preceded by an Address to the Society, on the Progress and Prospects of Science. By Sir HUMPHREY DAVY. *London*, 1827. 4to.

Report on the adjudication of the Copley, Rumford, and Royal Medals; and appointment of the Bakerian,

LONDON.

Royal Society.—*Continued.*

Croonian and Fairchild Lectures. Compiled from the original documents in the Archives of the Royal Society. By JAMES HUDSON. *London*, 1834. 4to.

Royal Society of Literature.

Transactions of the Royal Society of Literature of the United Kingdom. Vols. I, 1, 2; II, 1, 2; III, 1. *London*, 1827—1837. 4to.

Miscellanea.

The Atlantis: a Register of Literature and Science. Conducted by Members of the Catholic University. Nos. II, III. *London*, 1858, 1859. 8vo.

The British Cyclopædia of Natural History. Arranged and edited by CHARLES F. PARTINGTON. Vols. I—III. *London*, 1835—1837. 8vo.

The British and Foreign Medico-Chirurgical Review; or Quarterly Journal of Practical Medicine and Surgery (Reprint). No. 10, 1850; No. 37, 1857. *New York.* 8vo.

The Ibis, a Magazine of General Ornithology. Edited by PHILIP LUTLEY SCLATER, M. A. Vol. I, 1, 2, 3. *London*, 1858, 1859. 8vo.

The London Encyclopædia. Vols. I—XXII. *London*, 1829. 8vo.

The Polytechnic Review and Magazine of Science, Literature, and the Fine Arts. New series. Vol. I, 1—5. *London*, 1844. 8vo.

The Publishers' Circular and General Record of British and Foreign Literature; containing a Complete Alphabetical List of all New Works published in Great Britain and every Work of interest published abroad. Vols. I—XI, XXI. *London*, 1837—1848, 1858. 8vo.

The Year-Book of Facts in Science and Art: exhibiting the most important discoveries and improvements of the past Year; in Mechanics and the Useful Arts; Natural Philosophy; Electricity; Chemistry; Zoology and Bo-

LONDON.

Miscellanea.—*Continued.*

tany; Geology and Mineralogy; Meteorology and Astronomy. By JOHN TIMBS. *London*, 1849—1856, 1858. 8vo.

SALFORD.

Salford Borough Royal Museum and Library.

Borough of Salford. Sixth Annual Report of the Museum and Library Committee to the Council. 1854. *Salford.* 8vo. pp. 12.

SOUTHAMPTON.

Ordnance Trigonometrical Survey.

Ordnance Trigonometrical Survey of Great Britain and Ireland. Account of the Observations and Calculations of the principal Triangulation; and of the Figure, Dimensions, and Mean Specific Gravity of the Earth as derived therefrom. Drawn up by Captain ALEXANDER ROSS CLARKE, under the direction of Lt. Colonel *H. James. London*, 1858. 4to. And 4to. vol. of Plates.

ASIA.

BOMBAY.

Bombay Mechanics' Institution.

BERKLEY (J. J.). An Address delivered at the Annual Meeting of the Bombay Mechanics' Institution, on Saturday, April 11, 1857, by the President. *Bombay*, 1857. 8vo. pp. 28.

——— Paper on the Bhore Ghaut Railway Incline: read at the Bombay Mechanics' Institution, on Monday, December 21, 1857. *Bombay*, 1858. 8vo. pp. 36.

DEMPSEY (G. D.). A Sketch for a Map of Knowledge: read at the Bombay Mechanics' Institution, on Monday, January 18, 1858. With a Map. *Bombay*, 1858. 8vo. pp. 16.

BOMBAY.

Bombay Mechanics' Institution.—*Continued.*

SINCLAIR (R. S.). Lecture on the Laws of Motion: delivered at the Bombay Mechanics' Institution, on Thursday, January 21, 1858. *Bombay*, 1858. 8vo. pp. 42.

GIRAUD (H.). A Lecture on Combustion; and the Sun the source of all Terrestrial Force. Delivered to the Mechanics' Institution of Bombay on the 5th February, 1858. *Bombay*, 1858. 8vo. pp. 12.

CALCUTTA.

Agricultural and Horticultural Society of India.

Transactions of the Agricultural and Horticultural Society of India. Vols. I—VIII. *Calcutta*, 1838—1841. 8vo.

Journal of the Agricultural and Horticultural Society of India. Vols. IX, X, 1, 1854—1857. *Calcutta*, 1857, 1858. 8vo.

Geological Survey of India.

Memoirs of the Geological Survey of India. Vol. I, Part 2. *Calcutta*, 1858. 8vo.

MADRAS.

Hon. East India Company's Observatory.

Result of Astronomical Observations made at the Honorable the East India Company's Observatory at Madras. By T. G. TAYLOR. Vol. II. *Madras*, 1835. 4to.

BRITISH AMERICA.

CANADA EAST.

MONTREAL.

Societe Historique de Montreal.

Mémoires et Documents relatifs à l'Histoire du Canada. Publiés par *la Société Historique de Montréal. Montréal*, 1859. 8vo. pp. 63.

SPANISH AMERICA.

CUBA.

HABANA.

La Colonizadora.

Estatutos de la Sociedad Anónima titulada: La Colonizadora. *Habana*, 1857. 8vo. pp. 15.

Sociedad del Credito Moviliario y Fomento Cubano.

Estatutos y Reglamento de la Sociedad General del Crédito Moviliario y Fomento Cubano. *Habana*, 1857. 8vo. pp. 24.

Sociedad General del Credito Territorial Cubano.

Estatutos y Reglamento de la Sociedad General del Crédito Territorial Cubano. *Habana*, 1857. 8vo. pp. 16.

POLYNESIA.

SANDWICH ISLANDS.

HONULULU.

Royal Hawaiian Agricultural Society.

Transactions of the Royal Hawaiian Agricultural Society. Vol. I, 3, 1852. *Honululu*, 1852. 8vo.

INDEX TO LEARNED SOCIETIES.

Total of Institutions and Societies, publications of which are in the Library of the Smithsonian Institution—501.

INDEX TO MISCELLANEOUS PUBLICATIONS.

Total of Miscellaneous Publications—254.

INDEX TO NAMES OF PLACES.

CPSIA information can be obtained
at www.ICGtesting.com
Printed in the USA
LVHW111508230223
740229LV00002B/62

9 783382 307752